PARNO'S PERIL

The Black Sheep of Soulan: Book 4

I0592741

Creative Texts Publishers products are available at special discounts for bulk purchase for sale promotions, premiums, fund-raising, and educational needs. For details, write Creative Texts Publishers, PO Box 50, Barto, PA 19504, or visit www.creativetexts.com

PARNO'S PERIL
The Black Sheep of Soulan: Book 4
by N.C. REED
Published by Creative Texts Publishers
PO Box 50
Barto, PA 19504
www.creativetexts.com

The following is a work of fiction. Any resemblance to actual names, persons, businesses, and incidents is strictly coincidental. Locations are used only in the general sense and do not represent the real place in actuality.

ISBN: 978-0-692-18014-3

PARNO'S PERIL

N.C. Reed

For the Ranger, the Clerk, and the Chef.
I hope you can see me, and you're proud.
We carry on as best we can without your presence.
We love you still. We always will.

For my wonderful wife and nephew, who are my reason.
They are my sounding board and my helpers when I am stumped.
They keep me going when I'd rather quit.
I love them beyond reason.

TABLE OF CONTENTS

THE CAST

-

Colonel Robert Moore – Commander of King's Own, personal regiment of King Memmnon

Gideon Philo – Minister of Agriculture, Kingdom of Soulan

Roda Finn – inventor, staff of Prince Parno (his patron)

Whip Hubel – perhaps the best archer in Soulan, former instructor to Prince's Own, father of Winnie Hubel and now in charge of 'watching' the eccentric Roda Finn

The Tinker – thought to be a gypsy or descendant of one, once a traveler and repairer of trinkets, served as a spy for Parno and now operates a tavern and 'brothel' within the rear of Soulan army camp in an effort to spy out rogue elements loyal to Parno's brother, the former Lord Marshal. Tinker is a mysterious figure even to those who know and work for him.

Rosala – 'Rosa', oversees the 'brothel' part of the operation, her girls see and cater only to high ranking officers and others of importance. Courtesans rather than prostitutes. She knows more about Tinker than any other, but never speaks of it.

Ezekiel Watts – owner of the Hogshead Inn, which he rents to Tinker. He works as a barman and lives on premises.

Briel- Niece of Rosa's and bar maid

Jaelle – serving girl and seamstress for those at the inn

Aaron Bell – members of Prince's Own, Black Sheep, working at the inn as added protection for Tinker's 'spy ring'.

NORLAND

General Gerald Wilson – commander, 1st Imperial Field Army

Brigadier Britton Sterling – Wilson's Chief of Staff

General Peter Venable – Commander 1st Imperial Infantry Corps

General Joel Vanhoose – Commander 2nd Imperial Infantry Corps

General Darrell Thomas – Commander 3rd Imperial Infantry Corps

General Calisto Jurgen – Commander 4th Imperial Infantry Corps

General Abraham Springfield – Commander 5th Imperial Infantry Corps

General Eric Metz – Commander 6th Imperial Infantry Corps

General Brent Stone – Commander 1st Imperial Cavalry Corps

Brigadier Jerome Baxter – Commander 3rd Imperial Cavalry Division

Colonel 'Smith' – Imperial Secret Police

PROLOGUE

-

The old tree had seen a great many seasons come and go on this mountain.

It had seen snow too deep to be tread, wind so high that many of its kin had fallen to it and then rotted where they lay, and it had seen days hot enough to kill the leaves that helped provide it nourishment. It had lived through four rampaging fires that had swept the mountain over the span of its life, had been home to numerous birds and squirrels and other inhabitants, and had left its mark around it with smaller trees now stretching for the light of the sun, hidden in years past by the greater canopy thrown out by the leaves of the great older tree.

But that great tree was dying. In truth it was all but dead, hanging to life by a mere thread anymore, and still standing merely because it had not yet fallen rather than because it was able to endure against the elements. After a long and full life its time was drawing near.

-

It was called the rule of three, and it was as old perhaps as the world itself and certainly as old as the kingdom. A very simple policy, it meant that if you had to send one, you sent three to make sure one made it.

The Royal Courier Regiment practiced this rule as a policy of their own. Dispatches carried by Royal Courier were typically from a member of the Royal Family, or barring that then someone very highly placed in the Royal Government. Army Corps generals, admirals, provincial governors, and Royal Constables were among the select members of the Soulan Government that were allowed to use riders of the Royal Couriers. No one else was allowed access to their services.

So, it was a typical practice that saw three such couriers dispatched to the Coastal Province Coalition with news that Tammon McLeod had been murdered by his daughter, who was even now in the act of treason and uprising against the rightful heir, Memmnon McLeod, whom she had likewise attempted to murder. Conspiring with her twin brother to seize the throne of Soulan, Sherron McLeod was now a criminal and enemy of the state. Rendering assistance to her or her twin Therron, the former Lord Marshal of the Soulan Army, would be considered an attempt to interfere with the Dynasty of Soulan and would be considered an unfriendly act. Any contact with the twins should be relayed at once to the Royal City, to the attention of Sebastian Grey, Commander of His Majesty's Royal Constabulary.

Three couriers carrying identical messages, mounted on the best horseflesh that a kingdom renowned for its horses could provide. Surely one of them would be able to deliver that message.

Surely.

-

The rider cursed again as his horse reared slightly, nervous from the height as well as the unstable trail they had to follow.

The Royal Courier had cursed a lot today. This area was wickedly dangerous for travel and the trail was only sparsely used because of it. He hadn't wanted to use it but each rider had to take a different route. The luck of the draw has seen him take the short straw, meaning the roughest route was his. The other two routes had seen frequent bandit activity since the war had curtailed patrols so the couriers using them did not have the greatest chance of success. This trail, treacherous as it was, saw no such activity and was considered a safer bet. Assuming one didn't die using it, of course.

Inside his courier bag, sealed with the Royal Seal, was a letter addressed to the governor of the Coastal Provinces. It had to be delivered as soon as possible, he'd been told. Very urgent. Can't delay. He snorted at that. Of course, it was urgent. Why use a Royal Courier if it wasn't urgent?

The horse skittered again as rocks fell beneath them, crumbling from the trail and falling far into the gorge below. The rider reined the horse in and decided to walk the animal for a while. This area was tricky enough without having to stay mounted on a skittish animal. In truth he couldn't blame the horse, though, since he didn't much care for the height either.

"Easy boy," he patted the gelding's big neck and the horse nickered softly. Grabbing the pommel of his saddle, the rider pulled his leg over and started to step down.

Disaster struck from nowhere.

Somewhere behind them a tree fell. In the part of his mind not occupied with his predicament, the rider decided it must have been a very large tree due to the incredible noise it made in crashing to the forest floor.

The gelding, already spooked by his proximity to the edge of a steep and narrow trail, instantly bolted forward, startled by the sudden crash. The rider, caught by surprise with one leg out of the stirrup and in the process of dismounting, tried to regain control of the animal but lost his grip, falling from the horse though his left foot was caught in the stirrup.

Horses chosen for Royal Courier duty were well trained. If their rider was lost they were trained to stop at once in the event of just such an emergency as this. To stop and wait for their rider to remount. They would wait until thirst or hunger drove them to move on, the assumption being that if a rider hadn't remounted by that time he wasn't going to.

But this horse was frightened. His training was no good against that fear and thus when his rider was lost he didn't even realize it, continuing to gallop along the dangerous trail as the rider bumped along behind him, unconscious after having hit his head on a large rock in the trail as he was dragged along.

Scared and confused, the horse didn't note the change in the trail. Didn't see the sharp turn it made. Waiting for his master to tell him to turn, the frightened horse plunged over the side of the mountain, screaming in fear as he drug his rider along with him.

Three thousand feet below the two would lie together, forgotten, having died in service to the kingdom of Soulan. Never to be found, their message forever undelivered.

-

One of the messengers had never left Nasil, or at least never left sight of the city. As he topped a hill just outside the Royal City, he was struck by a single arrow that penetrated his heart and knocked him from his horse. Trained to stop at the loss of his rider the horse had agreeably slowed and turned to look behind him. It would not be necessary to chase him down.

The assailant was grateful for that as he would need the horse later. Just as he would need something else the courier had.

But first, he needed to get the body out of sight.

-

The last courier had simply ran afoul of Mother Nature. Attempting to cross a creek, he had misjudged the speed and depth of the water rushing over the small ford. As a result, both he and his horse were swept away, drowning in the heavy current before they were able to make either shore. It could have happened to anyone, but in this case, it had happened to the worst possible person, as he had been the last survivor.

It was just a freak accident, a culmination of perfect timing as heavy rain on the mountain nearby had filled the creek at just the wrong time. An hour earlier and the courier would have passed without trouble. A day later would have also been fine. But that exact time was not, and the last of the Rule of Three died, pulled beneath the swirling waters and unable to escape, his dispatch case lost in the rushing waters and likely for all time.

For lack of a message, there would be no warning. Warning that might have saved many people a great deal of trouble.

CHAPTER ONE

-

Stephanie Corsin looked out the window of Lady Cumberland's coach as it bumped along the route toward the front. When she had first learned of the Duchess' deceit in tricking her into this trip she had fumed in silence for hours. When they had stopped at an inn the night before to rest, she had gone immediately to her room, refusing to speak to the older woman that she felt had betrayed her.

With the light of a new day shining on her, the young physician's thoughts turned from said betrayal to fear. Not the quaking fear that the two-day invasion of Nasil had left her and many others feeling, but rather a gut-wrenching nervousness that threatened to overwhelm her, leaving butterflies dancing in her stomach.

Edema had told her she had the two or three days it would take to reach the army to figure out what she, Stephanie, would say to Parno McLeod.

As if it were that easy, she snorted delicately to herself, her gaze not really seeing the landscape they were passing through. What could she say to him? She had thoroughly poisoned that well with careless words, spoken in anger and with terrible timing. How was she supposed to undo that? What magic formula could she use to erase those horrible words she had spoken to him on the eve of his rejoining the army?

Parno McLeod was not an overly forgiving man, and she had hurt him. He would likely die under torture without admitting it, but she knew she had. She sat back in her seat, slumping a bit as a cloud of self-inflicted depression settled on her. If she had been able to wrap the cushioned seat around her, she would have.

"Don't slouch, dear," Edema told her casually, not looking up from her novel. "It's bad for your posture and bumping along like we are could even hurt your back."

"I know that," Stephanie shot back at once though without any heat in her tone. "I am a doctor, you know."

"Yes dear, I know," Edema replied as she turned to a new page, never looking up. "Have you thought about what you might say when we arrive?" she asked.

"I've thought about little else, but thinking about it won't make it any easier," the younger woman retorted, though she had straightened in her seat even as she spoke. "There's nothing I can think of that would help."

"I'm sure it will come to you," Edema told her without a hint of concern in her voice.

"I'm glad you're so certain things will work out fine," Stephanie allowed her irritation to creep into her voice this time. "Since this is all your doing after all," she added. "He's going to be furious when we show up against his wishes, Edema. That will only make it so much more difficult for me to talk to him. Assuming he will see me at all."

"He will see you, dear," Edema finally looked at her across the top of the open novel. "And while he may be angry at our presence, he will get over it. You shouldn't dwell on all that and instead be worrying about what you're going to say when you get there."

Stephanie sighed is resignation as she returned to her observation of the country side through the window. It was easier than talking to someone who refused to entertain any opinion other than her own.

-

Unaware that his surrogate mother and former betrothed were on their way to see him, Parno McLeod was nestled very comfortably in bed, his face relaxed in a way it hadn't been since before the war. A hand gently stroked his hair as he slept, eliciting a sound somewhat like a purr from the young prince.

Jaelle still could not help but wonder at her brashness the night before on seeing the handsome Prince of Soulan in the tavern below. She had not realized anyone was inside, let alone the Prince and two of his entourage. She had intended to get something to eat and then turn in for the evening. Instead her night had become a great deal more interesting in just a few minutes.

Cradling the prince slightly as he slept, she could not help but notice how much more peaceful he seemed this morning. Last night he had seemed to be bordering on morose, as if a great weight had been pressing down upon his shoulders. A weight that he alone had to bear, despite being surrounded by others. His handsome features had been creased with a premature aging that made him look far beyond his few years. This morning he looked much more like the very young man he still was.

She shook her head ever so slightly at the crazy situation she found herself in. A serving girl and seamstress in a roadside inn sharing her bed with the Crown Prince of the Kingdom of Soulan. To say it was insane was understatement indeed.

She was not one of 'Rosa's Girls', who entertained a certain class of clientele by way of the rear stairwell. She didn't sell her body in such a way, though she did not look down on those who did. And neither apparently did the sleeping young man she held in her arms. He had smiled at her in an open and friendly way, something few men she met ever did. Most looked down upon her and the others though careful not to say so outright for fear of being ostracized from their company. To them she was no different from the women who plied their trade upstairs rather than on the tavern floor. Theirs was a race of people that had been persecuted since time immemorial, tolerated only because they provided services that others sought. Men who would promise and proposition her whilst drinking beer that she served them would ignore her any other time at best, and at worst...

The Crown Prince, of all people, had not. Rather he had spoken to her just as he would have anyone else, even flirting with her slightly as he had leaned against the wall. He had a roguish, even boyish charm that she imagined few women he had turned it upon had managed to resist. She certainly hadn't, though in honesty she hadn't really tried.

And now he was sleeping in her arms. While some would have wondered how many times the Prince had found himself in this position, and with how many women, Jaelle did not. Instead she simply tried to make him comfortable.

She was unaware of how long she lay there with him, listening to the sounds of the tavern beginning to waken beneath them. At some point however, the Prince began to stir. It took him a few minutes to come around but suddenly she looked at him and realized he was looking back at her.

"Morning," he said softly, then frowned slightly. "It is morning, right?" he asked, and she laughed lightly, her hand still stroking his hair.

"Yes, milord, it is morning," she assured him. "Still somewhat early for us but I suspect not so much for you. Are you hungry?" she asked him.

"I am, actually," Parno nodded, sitting up a bit.

"Then why don't you go ahead and take care of your business while I go and have something prepared for you, eh?" she slid effortlessly from beneath him and stood. Parno drank in her naked form with frank admiration, getting a better look than he had the night before. Well, at least one that he remembered better than the night before.

She smiled lightly as she gathered her robe and towel.

"Two doors down, to the right, is a bath, milord," she told him. "When you are ready, you may make use of it to prepare yourself for the day. I will shower and then either have food prepared for you or else do it myself. Come down when you are ready," she smiled again.

"Thank you, Jaelle," Parno said softly. "I appreciate it."

"You are quite welcome, milord," she assured him, then turned for the door. If she didn't get out of here soon, she wouldn't be leaving for some time. His smile and kindness coupled with that same boyish charm that had enthralled her the previous night threatened to do so again. She exited the room and closed the door, leaning upon it for a moment before she headed for the bath, a soft smile on her face.

-

Parno took his time getting ready. Cold water in the bath woke him in a hurry, forcing away the remaining dregs of sleep. His uniform looked as if it would stand another day, or at least the start of one, and he donned it without much thought. He was surprisingly clear headed as he made his way downstairs considering he had drank a number of Tinker's rather strong tavern brews the night before.

A lone figure was waiting at the foot of the stairs and Parno slowed as Cho Feng turned to look at him.

"Cho, have you been here all night?" Parno asked in surprise.

"I have," the sword master nodded. "Your escort has traded off during the night so someone was always on guard. How was your evening?" he asked solicitously.

"My evening was fine," Parno admitted. "I was more concerned that your night wasn't if you spent it here watching me."

"It is of no concern," Cho Feng assured him. "As I told Brigadier Willard, a warlord must once in a while relieve the tension of command."

"Is that what I am, Cho?" Parno asked softly. "A warlord?"

"Semantics," Feng waved it away. "I believe someone is waiting for you, however," he pointed toward the bar and Parno followed the motion to see Jaelle standing there with a plate.

"Have you eaten?" Parno asked Cho.

"Earlier," Feng nodded. "I believe that particular plate is meant for you alone, my prince," he added with mirth in his voice. "I believe you have gained an admirer."

Parno looked at him with a raised eyebrow then made his way across to where Jaelle waited.

"Fried potatoes and scrambled eggs all right, milord?" Jaelle asked almost shyly. "There is also bread, but it is left from yesterday. They are not baking yet this morning."

"Jaelle, I normally eat a bowl of oatmeal for breakfast," Parno smiled at her. "If I'm lucky there might be a few apple chips or a bit of sugar mixed with it. Yes, potatoes and eggs with day old bread is more than fine."

"Good," she smiled at him, her demeanor relaxing as she set the plate before him with a cup of water.

"You don't have to be so tense around me you know," he told her. "Aren't you eating?" he asked.

"I... I did not wish to presume, milord," she stammered slightly at his unexpected question.

"Don't be silly," Parno told her. "Sit and eat. I'd appreciate the company to be honest."

A bright smile was his reward as she hurried to fix her own breakfast and take a seat next to him. She noticed a tear on the sleeve of his jacket and touched it lightly, running her hand along the breach.

"This looks like it was cut, milord," she said quietly. He looked to where her hand rested and nodded.

"Likely it was. I hadn't noticed it to be honest. I'll have to get it repaired."

It hadn't dawned upon her until this moment that the Prince himself would actually be in combat. She had assumed that he would command from the rear as others of his station did. Clearly this Prince differed from others of his line in more ways than one.

"You may leave it with me if you wish," Jaelle told him, examining the damage more closely. "I take care of sewing and mending for everyone here. I can repair this and return it to you. Likely by tomorrow," she added with a smile.

"There are plenty of people in camp who get paid for that kind of thing, Jaelle," Parno demurred. "One of them can earn their crowns by sewing it up," he chuckled.

"I'm quite sure I can do a better job than any Army tailor, milord," Jaelle persisted. "And it... I would... it would be my privilege to aid you in whatever way I can." She was looking more at the floor than at him, her eyes hooded. Despite that Parno knew she was watching him closely.

"Okay," he smiled ever so slightly. "I appreciate it," he told her as he shrugged out of the jacket and handed it to her. "But please, don't go to any trouble, okay?"

"It will be no trouble, milord," she assured him as she set the jacket aside, laying it on the bar. "Now eat," she motioned to his plate. "You need to maintain your strength," she added, a slight rise to one eyebrow and the faintest ghost of a smirk on her beautiful face.

"So, I do." Parno laughed at her antics.

Behind them Cho Feng watched. He had not expected this but in hindsight he should have. Parno was much more comfortable with what nobles called 'commoners' than he was with said nobles. Where most would never have considered taking a meal with someone like Jaelle, Parno would not hesitate or consider himself too good to do so. It was one of the things that made him such a good leader.

Still, this could be problematic.

As Parno ate his breakfast, Memmnon had finished his and was in his first meeting of the day. Sitting at the conference table facing him were Howard Govan, Gideon Philo, Sebastian Grey, and the King's fiancée Winifred.

"The refugees are preparing to depart, milord," Philo reported. "The first group is scheduled to leave the day after tomorrow. They will have an escort of twenty men from the King's Own and have about a one-week trip ahead of them."

"How many groups total are we looking at?" Memmnon asked.

"Five rather large groups and six somewhat smaller ones, Your Majesty," the Agriculture Minister replied. "The larger groups average around eight thousand while the smaller average about twenty-five hundred."

"So many," Memmnon sighed. "And this isn't all of them, I wager."

"No, milord," Govan took over. "There is another, similar group in Shelby. My assistant and Minister Philo's have already begun organizing the same kind of program there and some are finding their own ways, exchanging labor on some of the larger Delta farms for room and board. Our people are quite hardy," he added with no small satisfaction.

"So they are," Memmnon nodded. "The time has come for us to implement the conscription protocols I believe, gentlemen," he said without fanfare. "I am loathe to do so, but I see no realistic alternative. Those of you who deal with the refugees on a daily basis will speak to those who are trustworthy and weed from their ranks any who are suspicious or troublemakers. We will make use of them defending our Kingdom or kill them if necessary. We are at a point where conscription is all we have left. And as bad as I hate to say it, we will need to include a limited number of women as well."

"My Lord!" Grey erupted at once. "Sire, we cannot cons-"

"Yes, we can, Sebastian, and we will," Memmnon cut him off. "Not for combat roles or even pure military roles for that matter, but women can serve as we have seen right here at home. Parno informed me that he has women serving in observation posts and in some cases, he is even commanding them. So, we will be using women in a greater capacity."

"What we have to do is decide how to go about this," he told them. "Women strong enough to draw a bow will be taught archery and formed into a semi-organized militia. They will not serve in front line units, but they can and will defend their own towns. Rather than force them to cower in hiding and hope the few men left in their village can defend them, we will give them the tools and training to defend themselves. To do otherwise is not acceptable. And, I will say this once, so listen carefully; this is not open for debate. I will not welcome alternatives, discussion or dissension in this matter. I trust I have made myself clear?" his gaze moved from one man to the next. No one objected.

"Good," he nodded. "Please ensure that everyone else knows that. Now, Lady Winifred will depart in four days time with her escort headed to Jason and then to Shelby, and from there wherever she can best accomplish her task of organizing and training women to assist in defending their homes. Some of her Ladies Auxiliary will be accompanying her to assist and to serve as encouragement. Their role in defending the city from the enemy cavalry raid will be retold to show how they aided in our defense, proving to the others that they can indeed do so themselves."

"I would much prefer that this information be restricted to those here at this table and to those whose assistance is needed to carry out that plan. Her movements need to be kept secret as much as possible to ensure her safety. Make sure that happens," his voice took on a warning timber that no one missed.

"Women working for Roda Finn in the Foundry will be exempt from any other kind of service," Memmnon moved on to the next item. "They may volunteer to move, of course, but they will not be conscripted into service of any kind by anyone. The work they are doing there is far too important and they are all volunteers. Make sure that all relevant parties are apprised of this."

"The problem with Therron is officially off the docket for now," he ordered next. "There is no profit to be had in continually worrying over his actions or movements. Admiral Semmes has ordered one of his best men to sea with the few ships he has that are seaworthy in order to interdict Therron and the Halifax. Failing that, Parno has positioned one of his best units at Cove Canton to ensure that no problems are forthcoming from the CPC. I don't expect any, but I won't make the mistake of assuming we won't have them. But for now, do not waste a single minute worrying about what Therron is doing or where he's going. We have far too much to do here and little enough to do it with." Heads around the table nodded in agreement at that.

"Make sure any recommendations for exemptions to the conscription law are submitted promptly. The first one that came to my mind was actually the men of our fishing fleets. We can't afford not to have them working since we need their catch to help feed our people, moreso with the loss we suffered in the raid. Make your choices with care and with a mind toward ensuring that our food production in particular has the manpower we need to get things done. We can't afford losses at harvest time."

"Does anyone have anything else that we need to discuss?" he asked. No one spoke.

"Very well then, we are adjourned." All of them rose as Memmnon exited along with Winifred.

"I hate to leave you," Winnie said softly as the two returned to his rooms.

"I hate for you to be gone," Memmnon sighed. "But you wanted to serve. And no one can do this as well as you can, never mind doing it better. You have the ladies you want to take with you picked out?"

"Yes," Winnie nodded. "All single and all very good shots. They should do fine." She paused a minute before continuing.

"This will take a good while to do," Winnie warned.

"I'm sure it will," Memmnon fought the urge to sigh yet again. "It still needs to be done. If they can raid here, they can raid anywhere. We can't leave the women behind and not teach them how to defend themselves. Simple as that."

"Simple as that," Winnie echoed with a nod. "But not easy."

"No," Memmnon agreed. "Nothing is easy anymore."

-

"So, what's going on?" Parno asked as he strode into his command tent. "Anything happening out of the ordinary?"

"Not as yet, milord," Enri Willard replied. "All is quiet."

"I don't like it," Parno frowned, looking at a map that hadn't changed in days. "This makes no sense. They have every advantage and still they do nothing. I don't understand."

"Nor do I," Davies agreed. "I'm torn between being thankful for the time and wondering what we're missing," he admitted.

"I... I don't know what we could be missing," Parno shook his head hesitantly. "I want to believe that we've covered things pretty well, but as soon as I say it something we overlooked will bite us on the ass for sure."

"Almost certainly," Davies nodded. "Still, if we have overlooked anything, I'm at a loss to identify it. I believe they have adopted your theory from earlier. That they are killing us by simply occupying so much of our territory and are content to wait. But we have no way to confirm that."

"Our scouts are out as usual?" Parno verified.

"Yes sir," Enri nodded. "Patrols are constantly in and out, and we have men working behind their lines as well. I would not go so far as to say they can't move without us knowing, but it's very close to it. Pierce and his men should be back on station by now and we've strengthened the garrison at Nasil with an infantry brigade. Well, it's actually two regiments and an independent battalion, but close enough. We have patrols covering the area all around and observation posts looking at every major road and observing every city of any size."

"The River Guard is set up on the Cumberland and has a regiment of infantry plus an artillery unit in support while we are keeping our own posts on the Tinsee and have a company of archers and a company of crossbowmen in position to fire on any boats attempting to move up river."

"That's all we can do then," Parno nodded as the report ended. "Good work."

"Thank you, milord," several voices replied.

"Enri, call whatever part of my escort got some sleep last night and let's ride the lines."

"Right away, milord."

"You going like that?" Karls asked, having been so quiet that Parno hadn't noticed him.

"Like what?" Parno asked.

"You're out of uniform," was the smirking reply. "Where's your jacket?"

"Ah, I forgot that," Parno nodded. "It had a cut in the sleeve from somewhere. It's being repaired. Harrel," he said softly. Sprigs appeared before the sound of his name faded.

"Milord."

"Would you get me another jacket, please?" Parno asked. "I would appreciate it."

"Of course, milord," Sprigs bowed and went to fetch said jacket.

"Is she pretty?" Karls asked, eyes dancing with merriment.

"Is who pretty?" Parno asked.

"Why, whoever is repairing your jacket, of course," Karls jibed.

"Oh. Yes, actually, she is very pretty," Parno smiled.

"Always a good thing," Karls nodded in mock seriousness. "A seamstress that's pretty."

"I thought that myself," Parno chuckled as he made his way out of the tent. "Let's go and see what we can see."

-

"I th... think I ma... may die."

Buford Beaumont stood with his legs shoulder length apart, doubled over with his hands on his knees, gasping for air. Horace Whipple stood beside him, short of breath but in much better shape than his friend. In fact, he was in better shape than most of the men in either command.

"It's not so bad," Whipple tried not to laugh.

"Ho..how are y... you not gas... gasping for air li... like the rest of us?" Beaumont managed to wheeze out.

"Superior genes, probably," Whipple shot back. "Clean living."

"My a... ass," Beaumont stood, fighting to get his breathing under control. "You've done this before!" he accused with a shaking finger pointed at his friend.

"I have indeed," Whipple nodded. "Early to rise and work out as the sun comes up," he said. "Keeps me in good shape for shooting from horseback."

"Could have told the rest of us about that," Beaumont was still heaving a bit but was at least able to talk normally. Mostly.

"Could have," Whipple was really struggling not to laugh now.

"Bastard," Beaumont growled under his breath.

"That is the rumor," Whipple did laugh then. "At least we don't have it as bad as they do," he nodded to where the men of 2nd Corps were basically laying on the ground after their morning run. Few of them had finished where all of Beaumont and Whipple's men had. Barely perhaps, but they had finished.

"As hard as they had it when the war started, I can't say anything bad about them," Beaumont replied. "We hadn't been on patrol when the Imps hit the bridges, might be us over there with them."

"That is true," Whipple mused. "I was just making the comparison. There's no doubt they have fought hard and against huge odds. They've done well. I hope they can get back to muster soon."

"You know as well as I do that they won't be more than a shadow of the Army Corps that managed to slow the Nor advance," Beaumont shook his head slowly. "Too many veteran soldiers lost for good. Those kids they have training up to replace them just won't be as good."

"They will in time," Whipple noted.

"They ain't got that kind of time," Beaumont reminded him. "None of us do."

There was no answer for that.

Commodore Anthony David stood on the command deck of his cruiser Ocoee as it cut through the seas. To his port was the frigate Turner, and beyond that sailed the cruiser Warrior, which had escaped serious damage due to inadvertently ramming a Soulanie frigate in the last-minute maneuvering Admiral Semmes had ordered during the battle. The frigates Simmons and McCoy sailed on the port and starboard of his small line respectively. A line that represented virtually every seaworthy ship left in the Eastern Fleet.

"Report Mister Riddell," David said to his flag secretary.

"All ships reporting seas are clear, sir," Riddell informed him. "We're maintaining a one mile spread between ships as ordered, with lookouts doubled, sir. We're at the limit where we can see signals."

"Very good then," David nodded. "Carry on."

"Aye, sir," Riddell departed, already forming his next log entry in his mind.

David looked out across the rampaging ocean waters around him and contemplated his mission. It really was rather simple, but far, far from easy. A renegade Navy captain had seized the former Lord Marshal from captivity in exile and was now apparently taking him to Norfok, the major seaport of the Coastal Province Coalition. It was likely that the traitorous Therron McLeod would try and secure assistance from the CPC in returning to his 'rightful place' atop the throne of Soulan.

David felt like retching every time he considered that. It was like some kind of sick joke. Therron McLeod's twin sister had killed her own father, the King of Soulan, and then attempted to murder her own brother the Crown Prince in an attempt to place her twin on the throne and the Imperial invasion be damned.

And now this idiot, Chastain, had played right into Therron's hand and taken him by force from the Royal compound on the Keyhorn, taking him right back into the fray that his exile had removed him from. David's already churning stomach stilled at the idea that this witless fop was running with the former Marshal after all the navy had done to secure the shores of the Kingdom against the Imperial Navy.

He would find him and return him to Savannah in irons, his ships crewed by his own men and marines. Likely the men of Chastain's ships didn't know what was happening but David would take no chances of that sort. And if Chastain refused to surrender? Well...

It would be easier to return just his head to Savannah, anyway.

-

"Any word from our scouts further west?" Parno asked, even though he knew that if there had been he would have already been informed.

"No, milord," Enri replied. "Wherever those Imperial troops went, they are not between us and the Great River. So large a body of horsemen could not hide in the open country for this long."

"True enough," Parno mused. Where had they gone? Or had they gone anywhere?

"For now, we'll work on the assumption this is a ruse," he said finally. "That they were moving troops around out of sight so that we'd go looking for them. For all we know it was just a couple of brigades moving. Even a whole division, strung out for miles, and then when the road disappears, they turn back, out of sight of our scouts. I think they want us to weaken our forces here to go in pursuit of a phantom cavalry force."

"That is possible," Enri Willard agreed. "It would be a good way to try and get us to weaken our front here. Or even to weaken Shelby so they could make a run at the bridge. But I think it more likely that this is a prelude to a renewed assault on our position here."

"Is our scout network solid enough between here and the Great River to ensure they can't get around us, assuming they do cross the river and try to move south?"

"Yes sir," Enri nodded. "We have scouting posts no more than five miles apart and they are riding circuits in both directions at least twice each day. It takes a heavy toll on both men and horses, but it does work. There's not much of a chance at all that a force that size could get by them. There's just too many of them to hide or sneak by."

"Make sure we send couriers to let them know such a move could be coming their way," Parno ordered. "Just so they're aware of it. There may well be Tribal horsemen among them as well, so add that to the warning," he told Harrel Sprigs. "We may be assuming this is a ruse but let's make sure our scouts know that it may be for real so they don't let their guard down."

"Yes sir," Sprigs scribbled a note in his ever-present note book.

"Things look pretty good along the line," Parno noted. "4th and 5th Corps seem to be settled in well. And they look ready."

"They are," Enri nodded. "They've seen no action thus far so they're rested and ready and their kit is in good shape. With both Corps on line now we're mustering just over eighty thousand troops either directly on the line or in immediate support."

"Seems like a lot, doesn't it," Parno sighed. "Trouble is that the Imperial

Army is sitting over there with more than twice that number. Not to mention an army across the river from Shelby."

"That is true sir," Enri nodded. "But if we can buy the time for 1st and 2nd Corps to refit and train up, then we will have a formidable force to oppose them with. We would still be outnumbered, but the odds would be much closer. Close enough not to matter when our troops are so much better quality than theirs."

"It's dangerous to make that assumption," Cho Feng spoke for the first time. "As you have seen, their troops are better quality than you have faced in the past. Do not assume that your edge is sufficient to easily offset their advantage in numbers."

"No, I don't," Enri assured him. "I just believe that quality tops quantity so long as the numbers are close enough. And while the Imperial troops are better than we've ever seen, I think our men have proven they are superior, sir. We've held back numbers far greater than our own so far."

"That is true," Parno nodded. "But holding them back isn't the same as pushing them back. And I am all out of tricks to surprise them with, too. While we have an excellent supply of Roda Finn's weaponry, it's no longer a surprise to them. They will have developed at least some kind of counter for it. It may not work, but we won't know until we see it. And that's dangerous. We will have to adjust on the fly when the enemy has the advantage of numbers and picking the timing of the attack. And I doubt they will be content to wait until we have 1st and 2nd Corps back and ready to fight, either."

"Not likely, that is true," Enri sighed. "But we do at least have 1st Corps nearby, and their losses were not so severe. That is a strong reserve if it's needed. And we now have several cavalry units on hand and in good shape. Well fed and rested horses and veteran troopers."

"All true," Parno nodded again. "They are in fine fettle. It's good to see them here facing off against the Imperials and allowing our exhausted troopers a chance to rest and refit. And perhaps you'll get your wish and they won't hit us until we get at least 1st Corps back. I just can't depend on that. Their Emperor has to be goading them to move. They are an impatient people. Always have been."

-

"Some of the generals are losing patience."

General Gerald Wilson, commander of the 1st Imperial Army turned to look at the man who spoke. Tall, slender, a hawkish nose and jet-black hair, the young brigadier might seem out of place serving as Chief of Staff to someone like Wilson. But the truth was that Britton Sterling was a fighting soldier, well trained and well educated. He could and would help Wilson keep track of what was happening, just as he was doing now.

"Again?" Wilson asked, eyebrows raised. "Are they in that much of a hurry to die?"

"Some appear to be, yes sir," Sterling nodded. "Sir, if I could make a suggestion?"

"Of course," Wilson motioned him to continue.

"The chief complainers and agitators are the infantry division commanders. Their men are restless behind fortifications and that makes the generals restless as well. Have them assemble their men and make a forced march. Twenty miles or so due west. Not only does that burn off their excess energy, it will also give the Soulan Marshal something else to think and worry about."

"Hm," Wilson looked at the wall map. "Can't send them all at once," he murmured, looking at possible marching routes.

"Order one division on a three-day forced march to a point about... twenty-five miles distant. Have them go there and make camp, holding until relieved. On the third day, give that same order to a second division, ordering them to relieve the first, carrying orders for the first to return here within three days. Then the third, and so on," Sterling carefully outlined his plan.

"Given this some thought, have you?" Wilson raised an eyebrow.

"Yes sir," Sterling admitted. "It's my job to anticipate problems you may have and come up with workable solutions."

"So, it is," Wilson nodded his agreement. "Anyone in particular who needs to get this exercise?"

"I'd have to suggest starting with General Taylor's 16th Infantry," Sterling indicated the area where Taylor's division was camped. "He is one of the most vocal and uses his participation in 'repulsing' the Soulan cavalry attack as a reason to listen to him." The younger man then traced a route west.

"They can follow this minor trade route here," he tapped a small map symbol indicating a medium sized village. "Unity."

"Unity," Wilson repeated. "Not a bad place to choose considering our issue," he nodded. "Very well. Have this go through the Corps Commanders as a training exercise, but I want you to detail who goes on these marches and in what order. If any of them object make sure they know these are my orders. If they object after that, let me know." He turned to face his young chief of staff.

"It's time I reminded them who commands this army."

CHAPTER TWO

-

Parno spent a large part of the day riding the lines, reviewing dispositions and checking on the welfare of his troops. With two new Corps in the line it was important for them to realize the same things that 1st and 2nd Corps had learned; the new Marshal cared about the wellbeing of his men.

Having the Marshal stop suddenly in random places and ask soldiers how they were faring caught them by surprise, just as it had their predecessors. How was their trip north? Were they getting enough to eat? Did they lack anything? Did they have ample supplies? Was their equipment up to standards? Their opinion of the Lord Marshal had undergone a massive shift by time the sun began sinking in the west.

Word passed quickly among them that not only was the Marshal personally checking on the wellbeing of his men, but at lunch time he had dropped from his horse and joined a random group of line infantry to take his meal with them, eating the same thing they were served and griping about it just as they did, laughing, joking and talking to them as equals. It was as if he were just another soldier and not as if he were the Crown Prince and Lord Marshal. It was an eye-opening event for soldiers who still only knew of Parno McLeod as the brawling, womanizing 'Playboy Prince'.

Parno and his retinue returned by early evening, the sun not yet fully behind the horizon. Meetings were held with officers voicing concerns over everything from enemy dispositions to food allocations to supply issues and even where they should place latrines. Finally, Enri Willard had enough.

"That's it!" he declared, slamming a fist onto the table and startling several of the assembled officers. "How dare you waste the Marshal's time with such inane drivel as where to place the frigging toilets!" his anger boiled forth. "Did you learn nothing at all in training? Have all of you not been to Royal Officer's School? I wager some few of you have even been to the Royal War College and even one or two of you to the bloody Royal School of Engineering! And despite all of that you sit here with the gall to ask His Highness where to put the Army's latrines!"

"God have mercy on us if this is the quality of officers we have in this Army," his tone was scathing. "Get out," his voice was now low and had taken a new edge. "Get out and never dare set foot in here again with such mundane questions and complaints. Get out!" The last two words were all but a scream of rage as the staff officers were not moving fast enough to suit him.

They got out, scrambling to collect notebooks, forms, papers, maps and all the other trivia they had brought with them. Fifteen seconds after Enri Willard's tantrum ended the tent was effectively empty.

"Are you alright, Enri?" Parno asked after a few seconds of quiet.

"Of all the ridiculous, stupid, idiotic..." Enri seemed to run out of adjectives and trailed off.

"Well, you got rid of them, anyway," Parno patted the older man on the shoulder. "I appreciate it. Wouldn't do for me to start yelling and throwing people about. Ruin my image."

"Indeed," Enri snorted in rye amusement, recognizing that Parno was trying to get him to loosen up. "Indeed, it would. We can't have that."

"Is there anything that actually needs my attention?" Parno turned to more serious matters.

"Not at this time, sir," Enri assured him.

"All right then," Parno slapped him lightly on the back. "In that case I think I will get me something to eat!"

"Thinking of returning to the Hogshead, then?" Enri asked, grinning.

"No, I don't know that I can take another round of that beer tonight," Parno shook his head. "And if I keep staying out all night people will start to talk. Say I'm unfit to be a Prince. A disgrace to the uniform and the Kingdom."

"They already say that," Karls Willard laughed as he walked into the open tent entrance. "Behind your back, of course," he added. "I have come to inform you both that there is a good meal waiting at your tent, milord," Karls bowed theatrically and stood aside to allow Parno precede him through the door.

"Well that is just excellent timing, then," Parno nodded. "Let's go eat."

-

"We're here, ma'am," Captain Winters reported as the carriage jerked to a halt. Both women were relieved to be outside and standing.

"We'll overnight here, My Ladies," he told the two of them. "Horses are winded a bit and more than a little skittish. Seems to be some weather in the air," he looked at the sky. "This inn is comfortable and has good food. They also have a bunkhouse that most of the Company will sleep in and shelter enough for the horses. We'll have a watch set inside the Inn and outside as well, so you can rest easy."

"Thank you," Stephanie smiled up at him. "We appreciate it."

"Yes ma'am," Winters nodded and began to give orders.

"Well, let's see just how comfortable this place is, shall we?" Edema asked brightly, starting for the door. Stephanie followed her, much less enthused.

The place was surprisingly clean for a roadside inn. Clean, well-lit and comfortably furnished to boot. There was a large dining room, a smaller tavern and even a comfortable sitting room with lamps and a fireplace.

"This is almost like someone's home," Stephanie murmured. "Beautiful."

"Thank you," a voice startled the two women and they turned to see a dark-haired man of average height and build walking toward them. "I'm Milton, the proprietor. Welcome. Will you be needing rooms?"

"Yes," Edema nodded. "I require a suite with a bath if you have it for my companion and I, as well as two other rooms, preferably on either side of ours." As she finished four tall troopers in McLeod colors walked inside and stood waiting for orders. Milton frowned for a second, then realization dawned as he turned back to Edema.

"Of course, dear lady," he smiled. "I have something along those lines. However," he frowned ever so slightly in concentration. "I have a suite for you and you companion with a room next door, but... I can only offer you the second room across the hall and down one door. Will that be acceptable?"

"Completely," Edema nodded. "Thank you."

"Not at all," Milton assured her. "Now, I guess I need to warn my kitchen that we'll have extra to feed this evening. How many are in your escort, milady?"

"Sixty," Stephanie said when Edema turned to look at her. "Most will be staying in your bunkhouse if that is alright. Some of them will occupy the two extra rooms and a few will undoubtedly spend the evening here," she motioned around her.

"That will be fine of course," Milton frowned again. "I must see to it that we can provide for so many this late, Milady. Agatha!" he called and almost immediately a young woman in serving maid attire appeared.

"Please show the ladies to their rooms," Milton gave her the keys. "I shall be in the kitchen."

"Yes sir," the woman smiled. "If you please, ladies?"

The troopers followed with their luggage as Edema and Stephanie climbed the stairs and followed Agatha to their door. A real door, Stephanie realized, and not just slabs thrown together.

"Your suite, milady," Agatha gave a slight curtsy as she opened the door and provided Edema with the key. "Your other rooms are there," she pointed next door, "and there," she pointed further down the hallway in the opposite direction, across the hallway.

"Thank you," Edema smiled and took the keys.

"Will there be anything else?" Agatha asked.

"Please let us know when dinner is served?" Edema asked.

"Of course, milady," Agatha nodded. "There is a bell in your room that will ring when meals are ready."

"Wonderful," Edema smiled again. "Thank you so much." She and Stephanie entered, followed by two troopers who carried their bags. They stopped inside the door, waiting.

"There is fine, thank you," Stephanie assured them.

"Milady," the senior man nodded. They set the bags down and withdrew, closing the door behind them. Stephanie knew if she opened the door, they would still be standing there.

"Well, I am going to bathe before we eat," Edema announced.

Bordering on miserable, Stephanie began to undress, preparing for her own bath. She looked forward to washing the dust away.

-

"Looks like the weather is about to make a change," Karls noted, nodding to where very distant lightning was visible in the western night sky.

"Looks that way," Parno agreed. "It is that time of year I guess."

"So, it is, but being in the field like this during a thunderstorm... lots of problems can happen."

"Also, true," Parno nodded. "But there are plans for that and there's no way to supervise the entire army so I have to depend on the commanders to make sure their units are squared away."

"You don't think the Nor will take try to take advantage of this do you?" Karls asked.

"Weather will be just as hard on them as it is on us," Parno shook his head. "There's no profit in daring it. If they're smart, they'll stay where they are."

-

"Is this on the level?" General Brandon Taylor demanded, looking again at the orders clutched in his hands. Taylor commanded the 16th Imperial Infantry Division.

"It does have General Wilson's name on it," his aide nodded.

"Prepare for march? In this weather?" he rummaged around his desk until he found a map. "Where the hell is this... Unity, anyway." His aide looked at the map and finally placed a finger down.

"Here, sir."

"What?" Taylor almost yelled. "Way the hell out there? What's out there?"

"Nothing I can see, sir," his aide replied.

"That's exactly right," Taylor nodded. "Nothing. This says," he shook the written order, "we're to march there, arriving in no more than three days' time, then make camp until relieved. To be on the lookout for any enemy activity whatsoever. There's no enemy activity out there!"

"Doubtful, sir," the aide agreed.

"Assemble brigade and regimental commanders," Taylor sighed heavily. "Thirty minutes. My tent."

"Yes sir," the aide nodded and hurried to pass the orders along. A rumble of thunder could be heard in the distance.

"Of course," Taylor muttered. "Right on schedule."

-

As Parno watched the storm grow closer, he realized it would be a miserable night for all. He reminded his aide to make sure their tenting was secure and then did the same for those on duty in the tents where the army's command structure was laid out. Staff officers began to gather important documents and maps and store them in trunks for safe keeping until the bad weather had passed.

With those arrangements made, Parno decided on a whim that he wasn't going to spend the night in a tent with the wind and rain lashing at him. Summoning Lieutenant Berry, he told his escort commander his plans and suggested that the men of the escort would spend a better night in a certain barn than they would here. Berry agreed though his agreement was a proforma one since he was being issued an order, polite though it might have been. Parno made the same suggestion to Harrel Sprigs, who agreed that a hard bench in a tavern might still be better than a sleepless night in a tent.

From out of nowhere Cho Feng appeared, a raised eyebrow his only comment. When Parno explained, Cho merely nodded as if he had expected such. It took a few minutes to notify Enri Willard and the rest of the staff where he would be, and then a small column of men started for the Hogshead Inn.

-

"Good evening milord," Tinker greeted him as Parno, Cho, Sprigs, Berry and two more troopers entered the tavern. "A rough night to be out, or soon will be," he smiled.

"It is, and to tell the truth I don't want to spend it in a leaky tent," Parno nodded. "Is there room in your barn loft for my escort to spread their bedrolls? And a room for Cho and Harrel?"

"But of course," Tinker nodded at once. "There should be plenty of room for your men in the barn, and the roof is solid. There is hay there to soften your beds, as well. And I have three rooms empty at the moment, so accommodating your staff will not be a problem at all!"

Parno was about to reply when Jaelle came from the kitchen carrying a tray of food. She stuttered a step when she saw him, then smiled brightly as she carried on, delivering the tray to a table in back of the tavern.

"I thought... I mean I assumed..." Parno trailed off, looking from Jaelle to the Tinker and then back.

"No, milord," Tinker answered the unasked question. "She is not one of Rosa's girls. She serves tables and helps in the kitchen and does laundry and mending for the tavern."

"I... I owe her an apology," was all Parno could manage to say.

"I don't believe she will see it that way, my Prince," Tinker grinned at him. "Perhaps you should speak with her? She will be off work in the next half-hour."

"Okay," was all Parno could get out. "I would like to speak to her."

-

"You wanted to see me, milord?"

Parno looked up from his one beer to see Jaelle standing before him, clearly nervous but unafraid. She was still dressed in her serving uniform but even so her beauty was undeniable. He motioned to the chair next to him.

"Please sit with me," he asked rather than ordered. She did so after only a brief hesitation.

"Jaelle, I want to apologize to you," Parno said softly, looking her directly in the eyes. "Last night... Jaelle I... I mean I had no right to assume..."

"You thought I was one of Rosala's girls?" she asked with slight smile. "Please don't be concerned, milord. That happens regularly. But as a rule, none of her ladies are ever seen down here. They have their own lounge and their own entrance to the building. But I promise you aren't the first to make such an assumption and will almost certainly not be the last. It is of no concern."

"It concerns me! Why didn't you tell me, Jaelle?" Parno agonized. "I mean I was drunk… ish… but I wasn't that far gone. I wouldn't have been angry if you... I mean you had every right to... what's so funny?" he demanded, seeing her trying to hide a giggle.

"Milord, here you are the Crown Prince of Soulan and Commander of the Royal Army, yet you are the one man who has ever entered this place who would think of apologizing to a serving girl for assuming she was one of the women who do their work upstairs," she replied, a genuine smile plastered across her face. "You truly are one of a kind, my Prince."

"I knew last night that you had no idea who I was or why I was here," she suddenly found the courage to reach out and take his hand, squeezing it softly in hers. "But... you looked at me not like I was some cheap woman for you to spend your lusts on, but rather like I was beautiful. As if I were special."

"You are beautiful," Parno placed his other hand atop hers. "You're breathtaking. And you are definitely special. More so than I could possibly have realized last night. I am truly sorry that I..."

"But I am not," she interrupted softly, placing a finger gently on his lips. "I am in no way sorry, nor am I sorry to see you this evening. I assume you are here to escape the storm?"

"Well, yes," he replied.

"Then may I be so bold as to offer you the warmth and comfort of my bedchamber once more?" she all but whispered her voice was so low. "Where I can prove to you that I am in no way sorry that you approached me so last evening? That I can prove to you how much your kindness meant to me?"

"I..." Parno started to reply but was interrupted by a small ruckus breaking out in the far corner of the tavern as one rather large man lurched to his feet and began staggering in their direction.

"Here you!" the man bellowed. "When I asked you to sit wit' us and have a drink you refused, said it was ag'in the rules and what not. But you're good to sit wit' him? Soldier boy gets special treatment or something? That it? Or is he paying you more? Maybe that-" he cut off as two rather large troopers moved to stand in his way.

"Mind your tongue," one warned. "You're drunk and haven't the slightest idea who you're talking to."

"You don't give me orders, soldier boy!" the drunk bellowed and took a massive swing at the trooper. The movement was so telegraphed that the soldier waited until the last second before catching the man's arm and using his own leverage to simply flip him over, the drunk landing heavily on his back.

"Here now!" his two friends came up from their table only to be met with a pair of drawn swords. Harrel Sprigs walked calmly to the two and spoke softly to them.

"The man your friend just accosted is the Lord Marshal of the Armies of Soulan and Crown Prince of this Kingdom," his statement was short and to the point. "In view of his drunkenness I will allow it to go unpunished this once, but I would suggest you take your friend and go. And warn him when he wakes, just as I warn you now; reprisals against that young woman or anyone else here at this tavern will result in a visit by the Prince's Own. Perhaps you've heard of them? They're known as the Black Sheep."

The two had been on the verge of challenging the statement until they heard the words 'Black Sheep' and found out that they weren't that drunk, after all.

"Sorry for the misun'erstandin'," one muttered as the two bent to retrieve their friend. "We'll take him and git."

"A wise plan," Harrel nodded. "Please have a safe journey to your destination."

"Thanks," the man nodded as he maneuvered toward the door. Harrel turned toward his Prince and nodded once before resuming his place at a table where he was finishing his paperwork for the day.

"Who is he?" Jaelle asked softly.

"He's my aide," Parno smiled. "He looks after me. It's a tough job," he added seriously.

"Then perhaps he will allow me to do so for tonight?" she suggested, wondering again where she got the courage. Who was she to be speaking so to the Crown Prince?

"I'm sure he'd welcome the rest," Parno laughed softly. "And any unmarried man would be a fool to turn down such a priceless treasure as a night in your arms."

Her face burning at such flattery, Jaelle stood and pulled Parno up with her. She led him to the stairs and then up without a word, the two troopers taking station by the stairwell. Sprigs watched them go and then returned to his work. All three were silently thinking it was surely a great thing to be a prince.

-

"I do apologize for the plain fare, my ladies," Milton said once again as he finished setting the table for them. "We are not accustomed to visitors of such high station."

"It smells delicious," Edema smiled at him. "And you worry too much, Milton. We of such 'high station' as you put it rarely eat so differently from you. I'm willing to bet this will be wonderful."

"High praise indeed, My Lady, and I thank you," Milton bowed. "We are serving your escort in the bunkhouse as well. Please, enjoy."

"Captain, you and the other officers may join us if you like," she told Winters.

"I doubt such a rough bunch as we are would be suitable company ma'am," Winters declined gracefully. "Better we take our own table where we can hide our lack of manners," he smiled.

"Very well," she sighed. She waited until he was out of earshot before telling Stephanie, "He's quite handsome, isn't he? And very well mannered." Edema began dishing up food onto her plate.

"What?" Stephanie looked scandalized by the comment.

"Oh, come now dear," Edema waved a hand. "I'm married and happily so but that doesn't make me blind."

"Good grief," Stephanie shook her head slightly as she fixed her own plate.

"Stop that nonsense," Edema scolded. "There's no law against looking. Or complimenting. So, have you decided how you will approach Parno when we get there?" she asked, changing the subject so quickly that Stephanie was caught by surprise.

"I've actually decided to let you do it," she finally said, an evil smirk appearing as she thought of it. "This was your idea, after all. Better for you to explain it all than for me to try."

"So, you want me to be an intermediary for you then?" Edema took the statement in stride, nodding. "I can do that, of course. I have served in such a capacity before, many times. We need to decide what it is you want to say to him, however. I need time to work out just how to present your argument."

"I was joking, Edema," Stephanie rolled her eyes.

"Yes, I assumed as much," Edema's own smirk blossomed on her face. "I take it you still feel there's no reason to do this? To face him and try to make amends?"

"I don't think it will do any good," Stephanie admitted. "I wish I did. No, if I had a wish, I'd simply wish it away. It never happened and I didn't let my mouth get away from me. That I acted like an adult," she finished miserably.

"I understand," Edema was sympathetic. "But reality says that you have to do this yourself. Since you can't make it not have happened, that means you have to make amends for it."

"You know, it's not as if he will still want to marry me," Stephanie sighed. "Assuming he ever did," she added in a near murmur.

"He did or he'd not have said it," Edema said at once. "No one can talk Parno into anything. Nor can he be bullied. If he said it, he meant it."

"While that is wonderful to know in the abstract, it still leaves me where I am now," Stephanie fought to keep the sarcasm from her voice. "I still was cruel to him, and while he may not can be bullied, he can still be hurt by people close to him. To say he has trust issues is the height of understatement, and I had worked very hard to get him to trust me, so what I did had to have hurt." She looked down at her plate, her appetite suddenly gone. "This won't work."

"We shall see," Edema replied. As if in defiance of that statement, the room was brighter for a second as a flash of lightning illuminated everything for miles. The accompanying clap of thunder shook the building. Milton and others began scrambling to go outside and close the shutters that protected the glass in the windows and pull down anything the wind might damage or blow away.

"We appear to be in for a rough night," Edema said calmly. "Eat up dear. No use in being hungry. This beef is actually quite delicious."

Fighting not to scream, the younger woman pulled her plate back in place and began to pick at her food, wishing she was back in the palace, even with all its intrigue and shenanigans.

-

"A major storm coming, looks like," Memmnon said as he stood on the small balcony outside his office.

"I used to enjoy this," Winnie said from his side. "I used to stand on the point near our cabin and watch the lightning stretch across the sky for hours as storms moved our way." Her voice was distant, almost dreamlike as she remembered her time as a girl. "It made me want to be a lightning bolt so I could flash across the sky like that," she laughed, laying her head on his shoulder as she hugged his arm to her.

"I am glad you are not a lightning bolt, Winifred," Memmnon said as he rubbed her hand with his. "I would sorely miss you, seeing you merely once in a blue storm," he smiled.

"I would storm on you every day," she laughed lightly.

"You do anyway," he laughed with her. "I suspect you will have to delay your departure for a day or so after this," he turned serious. "The roads themselves should be okay, but everything else will be a mess. It will make it difficult for horses and wagons alike, not to mention walking."

"It will just ensure we have an extra day, or even two, to prepare," she shrugged. "One day more or less will make no difference in this."

"I suppose not," Memmnon agreed. This small talk wasn't what he wanted between them, but until they were properly married he was severely limited in how he could interact with her. Propriety demanded that he-

"So, are you going to kiss me or what?" Winnie broke into his thoughts abruptly and he looked down at her.

"What?" he almost stammered. Rather than answer, Winnie raised herself onto her tip-toes and kissed his lips, leaving just a hint of strawberries when she finished. Her eyes were shining with mischief as she pulled slightly back.

"Your turn," she seemed to be daring him. "Stop being such a stick in the mud. We're already engaged to be married. A little kiss here and there won't hurt anything, right?"

Unable to find an argument for that, Memmnon leaned down and captured her lips with his own, just as a particularly bright flash of lightning lit up the palace and everything around it.

"Still wish you were flashing across the sky?" he asked her softly.

"Already am," she replied and kissed him again.

-

While not the storm of the century, the line of thunderstorms that rolled across the valley that night were fierce nonetheless. Heavy rain driven by strong winds and accompanied by dangerous lightning battered both armies in their camps. Tents torn from their lashings went flying, exposing their occupants to the elements. Flying debris created great tears in canvas sidings of tents that managed to stay in place, and most everyone lay miserably under leaking canvas tops no matter how large or comfortable a tent might have been.

Trees were uprooted, roofs were damaged or even blown off, lighting strikes split trees and destroyed buildings. Numerous cattle were killed in a pair of lightning strikes in the Soulan Army Quartermaster's herd and the same thing happened to the Imperial herd minutes later. Flash flooding became a problem as hard rain turned small creeks and streams into raging torrents of water in a matter of minutes. Pleasant campsites became deadly in minutes and many soldiers lost all of their belongings and no few lost their lives trying to save what they could. Soulan's Royal Army was familiar with the ground and with the possibility of such troubles and their actions mitigated such suffering but there were still losses, though the Imperials clearly suffered worse.

For many, it seemed as if the storm would never pass as they huddled inside their tents, trying to stay at least some semblance of dry. It was truly a miserable night for most of the nearly half-million men camped along both sides of the line.

Parno McLeod's escort spent the evening under a roof of tin and wood, lulled to sleep by the rain hitting the roof as they bedded down in comfortable piles of clean hay. Their only downside was switching out for guard duty every two hours, but even that was a break of sorts as they were able to cluster around the fire inside the tavern and warm up and dry out.

Harrel Sprigs and Cho Feng shared a room upstairs not far from Jaelle's room, where Parno was spending the evening. Lightning flashes filled the windows even with the shutters closed and latched, but both men slept soundly with the rain battering the roof to help them drift off to sleep.

Parno himself bathed while Jaelle did the same, he removing the dust and grime and smell of being on horseback most of the day and her removing the scents of smoke, beer and food. Parno was looking out the window at the storm when he felt warm arms encircle him. He turned to see his hostess standing behind him, hair wet from her shower and dressed in a sheer gown that left almost nothing to the imagination. He had seen it before, but the sight of her took his breath away as he drank in her beauty.

"Come away from the window, milord," she told him softly, opening it enough to close and latch the shutters. "It is unlikely that it would be struck, but if you were injured then Tinker would be cross with me."

"Nah, he'd just assume I did something stupid," Parno grinned. "Like standing in the window during a storm," he added. Jaelle laughed at that, a light sound that Parno found almost mesmerizing. He allowed her to pull him toward her bed and the comfort that awaited him there.

"Let us weather the storm together, milord," she whispered in the dim light of a single oil lamp and a number of scented candles.

That sounded fine to him.

-

"Well this is certainly some storm," Edema commented as she watched the window of their suite. Even with the shutters securely fastened the wind driven rain battered at the window as well as the roof above them, the din forcing each woman to speak louder to be heard.

"Perhaps the worst I've seen in some time," Stephanie admitted. "I doubt we will be able to proceed tomorrow, Edema. Not after this."

As if her statement were prophecy there was just then a slight knock on their door. Stephanie answered it to find Captain Winters standing there, hat in hand.

"My ladies, I wanted to tell you that we will not be traveling tomorrow," he sounded apologetic. "Movement will be difficult for the horses and all but impossible for the carriage. Assuming any kind of good weather tomorrow, we should be able to resume our journey by the day after. And the extra day of rest will do the horses good as they are extremely skittish tonight due to the storm."

"Very well, Captain," Stephanie nodded. "Thank you."

"Evening milady," Winters nodded and departed as Stephanie closed their door.

"Well, it could be worse," Edema said philosophically. "This is a comfortable inn with good food and service, and with enough room for all of us. We should be able to spend a day here without too much strain. Not to mention this will give you an extra day to decide what to do about Parno when you arrive at his camp," she added slyly.

"Lucky me," was the acidic reply.

CHAPTER THREE

-

The morning broke with gray cloud cover hovering over most of the valley along with cooler temperatures and mud everywhere. Cursing and thrashing by man and beast alike was the order of the day as movement was severely impeded by the mud left from the heavy downpours that had ended not long before dawn.

Nowhere was that cursing and bellowing more prevalent than the camp of the 16th Imperial Infantry. Given orders to move out with the light of day, officers and men alike had worked through the stormy night to prepare for the move. A rare bright spot in their preparations was the fact that they were to establish the start of a permanent camp in the village of Unity, or at least as permanent as the Imperial lines would be. As a result, wagons already loaded with tents and camp ware were presented to the divisional quartermaster, along with a small herd of cattle for slaughter and several wagons of grains and legumes suitable for both man and beast.

"What a cluster fuck," General Brandon Taylor shook his head again as his boot sank up past his ankle in mud. "We'll never make it there in three days in this mire," he told his senior brigade commander, Harlan Matthews.

"Unlikely," Matthews nodded grimly. "Still, it's not a bad exercise," he added. Taylor's look of incredulity didn't surprise him.

"You're kidding, right?" Taylor demanded.

"No sir," Matthews shook his head. "Sudden orders, move out at dawn, regardless of conditions, forced march of some twenty-five miles in a three-day period. All of this is designed to get the best out of us and our men. And I'm willing to bet that another division gets the same orders before we've been gone a week. Their orders will come at the same time ours did and have them marching to relieve us, and our orders will be to return to camp."

"Ten sovereigns says you're wrong," Taylor said at once.

"Done," Matthews shook his commander's hand. "And with that, I better get over and make sure my lads are getting in line. Thank the Emperor we don't have to break camp here before getting on the road."

"Yeah," Taylor sighed. "Thank the Emperor."

-

Despite the horrid weather the night before, the men of Doak Parsons' Scout Company were still out, screening the Royal Army from any flanking maneuvers or sudden enemy movements. On this particular morning a young archer known as Dagger Earl was sitting in the upper reaches of an abandoned corn crib, his horse resting comfortable down below and making breakfast from the grain left behind. Earl and his horse had weathered the storm together in the protection offered by the small but sturdy building and Earl was even now considering remaining there another day to allow at least some of the mud to dry up rather than force his steed through that kind of mire.

Slowly eating his own breakfast of smoked beef and hardtack, Earl began to hear the faint, distant sounds that could only indicate men on the move. It began with the sound of metal occasionally striking metal. Then came the indistinct sound of men talking, the distance too great to understand what was being said but the sound unmistakable nevertheless. Finally, came the sound of wagons creaking and their drivers cursing as they urged their draft animals on through the muck and the mire left by the rain.

His breakfast forgotten, Earl grabbed his glass and scrambled out of sight of the doorway he had been sitting in. There he got to his feet and cautiously ran his glass out the door, surveying the area in front of him. It took more than a minute for the movement to catch his eye, concealed as it was by the fog. At first, he thought it was a simple patrol or maybe a foraging party, a waste of effort this time of year he thought idly. But the movement continued and the soldiers kept coming, his subconscious automatically keeping count.

He had already seen a full brigade of pennants when the wagons appeared. Counting the wagons, he realized after hitting thirty that this was a major movement of the Imperial Army. This was the kind of thing he was out here for! The urge to jump on his horse and race for his own lines was almost overpowering. Several deep breaths had his thinking clearly once more as he continued to observe, taking the small notebook that all scouts we issued and using it to keep a tally of what he was seeing.

For nearly an hour, Earl watched as marching men struggled to get through the mud. While the minor trade route they were following had some gravel coating to help with dust and mud, the previous night's rain had washed much of it away, leaving ruts full of water and areas where there was nothing but mud.

Still the Imperials kept going, walking on even as they cursed everyone from General someone or other on down. A knot of mounted men came into view mixed in with the wagons and Earl decided based on how they were dressed they must be officers. Probably the commander of this group and his subordinates, Earl decided. Based on everything he had seen so far, Earl was satisfied that this was a full division of Imperial infantry, on the move west for some unknown reason. And it must be some reason indeed to be moving in this muck.

As the last brigade began moving past his position, Earl faced a dilemma. As far as he knew there wasn't another scout out as far as he was at that moment, which meant it was possible he was the only one who knew of this movement. So, did he follow and try to see what the Nor were up to? Or did he race back to the Army's Headquarters and report in what he had seen?

He had until the final Nor soldiers in line were gone from sight to decide.

-

For the second morning in a row, Parno McLeod awoke in the arms of a beautiful woman. But this morning he woke first and she was wrapped in his embrace, a somewhat reversal of the previous morning. He looked at her for a long time, sleeping comfortably with her hair slightly askew, a peaceful look on her face that he immediately hoped he was responsible for.

What am I thinking? he asked himself suddenly. What can I offer her? Nothing but sorrow, he sighed to himself as realization came to him. No matter how attracted he was to her, no matter what might be able to develop between them, he could never be more to her than he was right now. And she deserved far better than to be known as a camp follower or a mistress. Even to the Lord Marshal.

I'm going to make sure she's taken care of, though, he promised himself. I don't know how just yet, but she deserves something better than any of that. I'll figure it out.

He realized with a start that Jaelle was awake and looking at him. She laughed ever so softly at his surprise.

"What are you thinking, my Prince?" she asked quietly, lifting her head to kiss him lightly. "You seem deep in reflection this morning."

"I was thinking of you," Parno admitted. "How I wanted you to be taken care of. What I could do to make that happen. Make life better for you."

"My life is fine the way it is, milord," she sat up next to him. "I do well here and Tinker takes good care of us all. We are safe and have all the necessities of life. Compared to others we are very well off. We are a family of sorts, and we treat each other that way."

"See, for me, being treated like family would not be a good thing," Parno snorted. "My family spends most of their time killing each other or trying to get others to do it for them. I'm glad to hear that you are well cared for," he added.

"I would worry about you otherwise."

The look on her face was one of mingled surprise and suspicion, and he wasn't sure which was more important or was more dominant.

"My Prince," she said finally after a very long minute of silence. "My Prince, what are you thinking about Jaelle?" she spoke of herself in third person.

"I'm thinking you deserve better than something like this," he sighed, sinking back down onto the mattress. "Something better than a man sneaking over to see you whenever he can find the time."

"You are a sweet man, my Prince," Jaelle smiled softly. "But I have need of nothing, I assure you. And do not think that you somehow 'owe' me, for what has passed between us. Do not sully that with the taint of money or other favors. Let it remain what it is; an act of love and nothing more."

She was right, he realized. What was he thinking about a woman he'd known literally for two nights? What the hell was wrong with him? Since when did he start acting like this?

"What is wrong, my Prince?" Jaelle's voice broke him from his own recrimination.

"Just thinking that you're a lot smarter than I am," he told her. "I'm sorry. I don't know what came over me, thinking you needed me to somehow save you from a life you already enjoy."

"The fact that you would if I needed it is more than enough," she promised with a smile and a kiss. "Let me make you breakfast once again and then you must say goodbye, no? You are much too busy to spend so much time here with me."

"Time spent with you is time well spent, but I suppose I do need to get back," he nodded. "It's already lights out, and there's no telling what damage the storm did."

"Then I will go and prepare your meal while you shower and dress," she stood and threw on a dressing gown. "I will see you downstairs."

-

"Are you growing too attached to that young woman, my Prince?"

Cho Feng's words almost didn't penetrate the fog of Parno's mind. It took several seconds before it registered.

"What?" he turned to look at his adviser. "What did you say?"

"I asked if you were becoming too attached to this Jaelle," Cho repeated. "Is she becoming a distraction?"

"Any woman who looks like her is definitely a distraction," Parno snorted. "But if you're asking is she addling my thoughts, then the answer is no. I had a nasty surprise last night when I realized she wasn't one of Rosa's girls as I had thought before, but otherwise she is still just a girl I met in a tavern."

"Lying to me in this instance is acceptable, my Lord," Cho said easily. "Lying to her is less so, but not unforgivable. Lying to yourself, however, is dangerous.

Remember that."

Parno nodded absently at Cho's warning, acknowledging the truth of them without admitting he had done any such thing. He had been on the cusp of trying to make room in his life for Jaelle somehow, rather than simply leaving things between them as they already were. Why would he have thought of that, even for an instant? He chewed that over mentally as he rode toward his own collection of tents that made up not only living quarters but also his command structure.

Damage from the storm was evident everywhere as they rode. Early reports made to him through Harrel indicated that no loss of life had been reported, though the Army had lost several animals due to lightning strikes. There was no way to figure the cost in Crowns as of yet, but Parno was sure it would be high. He shrugged mentally at that, knowing of no way to change it. Even had the damage not been caused by the storms it could just as easily been caused by enemy action. Losses of that nature had to be expected, that was all.

He arrived to find that his own tent had survived and that troopers from the Black Sheep were busy pulling the canvas back tight to eliminate water being held by drooping and water-saturated tent roofs. He found staff members already returning things to normal as maps were set back up and desks covered with reports.

There was one other thing waiting as well.

"Milord," Doak Parsons saluted. "Something you may should hear," he added, motioning the young man behind him forward.

"Dag, put it on the map for the Prince," Parsons ordered.

"Yes sir," Earl nodded. "Milord, I spent the night- me and Rolf- that's my horse, sir," he explained. "Anyway, we weathered that storm last night in an abandoned corn crib about... here, sir," his finger traced along the map until he pinpointed a spot near a minor trade route. "Weather turned the way to mud in most places, milord, and while I was decidin' what I'd do, I heard 'em." He ran his pointing finger back up to that small trade route.

"At least a full division of Nor infantry, sir, moving down the road, west. They wasn't happy being out in that soup, either, milord, nor was they trying to be quiet. Made more noise than... well, they was loud, sir. Wagons full of baggage in the middle of the column, too, sir. Officers mounted, some of them anyways, but no scouts, flankers or pickets around 'em I could see."

"How long ago was this?" Parno asked, examining the map.

"Not more'n two, two-and-a-half hours, sir," the young man promised. "I... I couldn't decide whether to follow or to report, sir," he explained. "I decided to report in case no one else had seen 'em, sir. Trouble is there was no one further out than me, which means by doin' so I lost 'em."

"That's fine," Parno assured him. "You should try and get some rest. I'm sure Mister Parsons can make sure you and Rolf get a good meal and a dry place to bunk down, assuming there is one. Well done, Mister..."

"Earl, sir," the young man snapped to a salute. "Dagger Earl, sir."

"Well done, then, Dagger Earl," Parno patted the man on the shoulder. "Well done, indeed." He turned to Harrel Sprigs.

"Find General Allen."

-

"Well, that was quite the storm, wasn't it?" Edema said over breakfast. Milton the proprietor nodded vigorously.

"Worst we have had in some time, my lady," he agreed. "We've had word of trees blown down, blocking the trail north. Locals are already out clearing the way, but you were wise to delay your travel, it seems. All should be cleared by tomorrow, and if this wind continues it will help dry the ground as well."

"It will be worth the delay not to be caught up in such a mess," Edema agreed. "How did your place of business fare in last night's tempest?"

"A few leaks sprung and one window pane cracked, alas," Milton sighed. "It will be difficult to replace with the war on, but on the whole the damage could have been much worse."

"What about our horses and carriage?" Edema turned to Captain Winters, who had agreed to join them for breakfast.

"Milton has a large barn that we rolled the carriage into, my lady," Winters reported. "And while there wasn't room enough in the barn for so many horses, there is a covered hay barn which is empty this time of year so we made a rope corral inside it to keep the horses under as much cover as possible. It required a guard watch to stand during the night, but none of our horses were injured and your carriage is in fine shape this morning."

"Wonderful," Edema beamed at them. "I am grateful to you Captain for seeing after my own things as well as your horses. And to you, Milton, for allowing us the use of your stables."

"It was my pleasure, of course, my lady," Milton bowed deeply. "Now I must return to work but should you require anything at all, just call out." He made his way toward the kitchen, humming lightly.

"We will rest here for the day, then," Edema told Captain Winters. Even though Winters was in fact the commander of Stephanie's escort, Winters recognized the authoritative tone when he heard it. "It was wise of you to suggest it, and no doubt your men can use the rest after last night. We will resume our travels tomorrow if that meets with your approval."

"That should be fine, my lady," Winters nodded.

"Good. Then I think I will take my own advice and rest for today."

Stephanie hid a sigh as she decided that she had little choice but to try and do the same. She obviously wasn't going anywhere today.

-

"You called for me, sir?" General Gerald Allen reported to Parno's tent within the hour.

"Yes, General. Take a look at this," he handed over a rapidly printed copy of Dagger Earl's report. Allen read the few words and moved to the wall map to trace the movement of the reported division.

"There's nothing there," he said finally, following the projected path of the Imperial column. "It's not bad country, especially for farming, but... it's empty, milord. There's nothing there of any military import. What are they after?"

"That's what I want you to find out," Parno replied. "I suspect this is one of two things, General. The first is that it's a simple exercise and they feel secure enough to send out an infantry group without even the most basic of screens. The second is that they're planning to establish a new camp somewhere to the west. Normally that wouldn't concern me, but we recently had a report of Imperial cavalry leaving the army across the river and heading north," he traced the route those horsemen had taken.

"We lost sight of them here and didn't regain it. As a result, I have all but decided that the whole thing was a feint and that the men we were following, once the road took them out of sight, simply returned to their camp, leaving us chasing ghosts. With this new development, I have to wonder if I was wrong about that."

"Why would that many cavalry need an infantry unit?" Allen asked.

"This infantry unit has an unusually large wagon train, apparently," Parno pointed out. "It's possible that they are going to establish a camp somewhere along here for those cavalry men. It's also possible that they're just following an exercise and this has nothing to do with that cavalry at all. Whichever it is, I want you to find out. Find them and keep them under observation."

"For how long?" Allen asked.

"Determine what they are doing and try to figure how long they intend to do it," Parno ordered. "See if they are joined by anyone else. If they decide to return after a few days, catch them on the road and ambush them. Kill them all."

"Yes sir," Allen stiffened and snapped off a salute.

"Good luck, General."

-

"Make sure those bows are covered well," Winnie ordered as the wagons for her upcoming expedition were packed. "I don't want them damaged or getting wet if we see another rain like this on the trail."

"Yes ma'am," the man sketched a salute as he worked to make sure his load was secure.

There were twelve wagons bearing supplies and equipment, including one blacksmith's wagon and one Royal Engineer wagon with equipment. There was an ambulance with a medical crew, including a physician, three nurses and four orderlies. There was a wagon bearing as many bows and ready-made arrows as could be gathered in the time allowed considering there was a war on.

"We've loaded supplies for an extended trip so we shouldn't be a burden on any town we visit," Senior Captain Andrew Case, her escort commander, informed her. "And we've managed to acquire a good supply of arrows as well. Plus, I scrounged through local armories and found a few dozen swords. They're not the best made weapons or they'd not have been where they were, but they will be a start on arming and training those who want to learn."

"Thank you, Captain," Winnie smiled. "I appreciate it. Do we have sufficient instructors lined up for that?"

"Enough to get them started, anyway," Case assured her. "But as to splitting our group off... the way it's planned now is unacceptable, ma'am."

"In what way?" she demanded.

"You're spreading my command too thin," he told her bluntly. "We can protect you and this train, barely, with the manpower we have available. But dividing the train means dividing the escort, and that is something I'm not prepared to do. It will leave us weak and vulnerable to attack by bandits, or Tribals, which is even worse. We've already had one major raid into our territory as you know. There's nothing to say we won't see another. We will have to keep the train together and cover the ground you want to cover more slowly."

His unit was designed to provide security for one very important woman. With three companies totaling three hundred men, his force was, on paper, a short battalion with his rank set as Senior Captain. Captain Able Conway was Case's second in command, a good and experienced command officer, but the three companies under his command were actually commanded by senior Lieutenants rather than Captains. Lieutenant Andrew Fain commanded First Company, Lieutenant Gerry Rucker Second Company and Lieutenant Joseph Garrett Third Company.

Those Lieutenants would do fine at their assigned roles of protecting their primary, but they were not experienced enough to lead independent commands in the open field escorting wagons in areas where enemy patrols might be encountered, another reason Case had refused to split the escort. And three hundred men were more than enough to protect one woman, but barely enough to protect a wagon train as valuable as the one they had along with that one very important woman.

"I don't want to do that," Winnie shook her head. "It will take too long to get done."

"It won't get done at all if we're dead, ma'am," Case held his ground. "This is the way it has to be."

"I want it done my way," Winnie insisted.

"That isn't going to happen, ma'am," Case replied simply. "It's dangerous. Too much so. I realize you have a lot on your agenda, but we can't risk separating like this in the face of possible enemy opposition. My men are not expendable, and I doubt His Majesty will view you that way either."

Winnie was caught by surprise as Case played the very trump card she had intended to play; Memmnon. She knew that as soon as Case mentioned the added danger to her, that would be the end of it. Memmnon would side with Case and that would be that. Finally, she nodded, reluctant though it was.

"Very well then," she told him. "We'll need to adjust our travel plans accordingly. We'll visit Jason first, then Dyerville, and then-"

"Not Dyerville," Case was shaking his head again. "It's too close to the line and there have been reports of large groups of Imperial cavalry working just over the Great River from there, not to mention that it's only a few dozen miles from the main encampment of the Imperial Army. We aren't going to risk that, my lady. Jason is risk enough, but still far enough south of the lines and with our own army between us and the enemy. I would suggest a compromise where we send runners to the smaller towns further north informing them what you have planned and to meet us in Shelby or in Jason. Once there, we can establish a camp and teach them everything you want them to know while the representatives from the Royal Engineers can educate them on preparing their town defenses. Doing it this way will also make up for the extra time we incur by keeping the train together."

It was a skillful compromise as well as an olive branch and Winnie recognized it as such. She pretended to consider it for a few moments before nodding her head.

"I like it," she admitted to him. "Very well. I will leave it to you to send the runners ahead. Emphasize that this could mean the difference between life or death in the event of a raid. I want to be sure that everyone who wants to be part of this can attend, even if we need to provide wagons for them to ride in."

"I'll see what can be done on that front," Case promised. "If you will pardon me, I'll see to the runners."

Winnie ran over her mission once more in her head, recalculating things to include these new changes. In some ways this would actually improve her position and make it easier to train and equip as many as possible. The down side would be that it would be impossible to see to the defensive structure of each town on an individual level, but... anything would be an improvement.

It would have to be enough because it was all there was.

"We leave tomorrow, assuming there are no further issues," she told the civilian leader of the wagon train. "If there are any problems refer them to Captain Case. Anything he can't see to he will bring to me. Please see to it that we are properly provisioned all around since we don't want anything we need to be a burden on the towns we visit."

"We've made sure, ma'am," he promised. "Even got a smith along for repairs. If anything, we may can help those we come across, at least so long as our supplies last."

"Good. Thank you. I have duties to attend to so I will leave this to your capable hands," she smiled.

"We'll take care of it, ma'am," he promised.

-

"Timing is everything in this mission, do you understand?"

"Yes sir," his listeners replied in unison.

"If you succeed, then make your escape by any means available to you and report back. If you fail, don't bother. I have no use for failures. Clear?"

"Clear, sir."

"You have three days."

CHAPTER FOUR

-

The man known as the Tinker sat on a stool at the bar of the Hogshead tavern and watched a certain employee of his go about her duties. Jaelle had worn a smile all morning long and had even been heard humming softly as she carried out her chores. Tinker had fought to keep a smile from his face at how happy she looked.

He had been more than a touch concerned when Jaelle had taken the Prince to her bed that first night. While he trusted the girl without question, the Prince had been at least slightly inebriated and Jaelle was not a working girl, as such women were often called for some reason lost to time. It had become apparent last evening that the Prince was unaware of that. His shock at finding Jaelle hard at work in the tavern serving tables could have never been feigned, and at any rate the Prince wasn't one to put on an act. He had been genuinely surprised.

And he had been just as embarrassed as he was surprised, Tinker remembered. Parno had clearly not minded sharing the bed of a woman who made her living providing comfort to men but had balked at the idea that he had treated a woman who did not make such a living as if she did. There was embarrassment and no small amount of shame on the young Prince's face as he had spoken first to Tinker and then to Jaelle herself.

Tinker had no idea what had passed between them last evening... well, all right, he had some idea of at least part of what had passed between them, but whatever else had transpired had left Jaelle in a an even better than normal mood today. She was rarely in anything but a good mood to be sure, but today was even brighter than normal. And the only think Tinker could think of that would be responsible for that was a certain Prince.

But what had he told her? Or not told her? Or insinuated perhaps. Tinker was firmly convinced that Parno McLeod could be trusted, but he wouldn't be the first man to lie to a beautiful woman. Finally, Tinker could stand it no longer and called Jaelle to him.

"Yes, Tinker?" she asked.

"How much do you lack being finished?" he asked.

"Not long. Perhaps an hour or a bit more. Is there something else you need me to do?" she asked. Always willing to help.

"No. Allow Mercina to finish your work with the laundry and walk with me," he ordered, standing. "I wish to speak with you in private."

"Very well," a suddenly subdued Jaelle nodded.

"Relax," he told her. "It's not like that. I merely want to talk to you away from prying ears."

A relieved Jaelle followed him outside and the two walked a short way up the road, avoiding the mud by using the rocky way.

"Jaelle, your business is your own, as is your free time," Tinker said. "That being said, I consider it one of my responsibilities to watch after all of you. I trust Parno McLeod and I believe in him… believe him to a be a good man… but... men are fallible, and that is especially true where beautiful women are concerned." He paused for a moment, looking for the proper words.

"He has promised me nothing, Tinker, if that is what you are asking," Jaelle volunteered. "He spoke of something similar last night, but I hushed him. I am not interested. He wanted to insure I have a good life, but I already have one that I like, and told him so. I have people who are family to me and all my needs are met. He is a good man and I think... I think for a few moments he entertained an idea that there could be more between us. You and I know the reality of that, however. There can be no more between the Prince and I than what we have already shared. He cannot do it."

Tinker was surprised by the admission. Both by the Prince thinking along those lines and by Jaelle's refusal. But there was something that must be said.

"Jaelle, do not compare him to others," Tinker warned. "If Prince Parno decided he wanted you by his side, do not think for a moment that any sort of propriety would stop him. He cares nothing for those things. Nor does he draw his power from them. They mean nothing to him whatsoever."

"I do not understand," her face was puzzled.

"Parno McLeod is the Crown Prince, that is true, but he has ascended to those heights from far beneath them and until recently was little better thought of by the Royal Family than we would have been. And, he does not care. He didn't then and he doesn't now. His power does not come from his standing within the Royal Family, but from his standing within the Army. Whereas his brother Therron ruled the Army and dominated it, Parno leads the Army. And always lurking behind him are the Black Sheep. They are few in number, but they are strong. They are utterly merciless and they answer only to him."

"So, if he offered you something, don't think it was an offer idly made. He not only meant it, he can and will do it."

"I... see," Jaelle didn't seem to know how to respond to that.

"I am not saying he has offered you anything, or that he will," Tinker added. "That is between you and he. If he does not, then it may be that he seeks to spare you the eternal enmity that seems to surround him. It is not his fault, but it is his to bear for what reasons God Himself only seems to know. It is difficult to see one so young burdened with so much."

"But regardless, I merely wanted to ensure your wellbeing," he promised with a kindly pat to her shoulder.

"Thank you, Tinker," she smiled brightly at him. "As I told the Prince, you treat us well and watch over us. For that we are all in your debt."

"Ridiculous," Tinker scoffed in jest. "What man would not want to surround himself with beautiful women?"

Her laughter peeled across the distance as they returned to the inn.

-

"All right," General Allen said as his fellow Generals, Thaddeus Coe and Wilton Vaughan gathered around him along with their brigade commanders.

"We're going to spread out a bit, but carefully," he told them. "Each brigade will select scouts to screen our movements, but most importantly to find this column of infantry. We have to swing wide around them or risk them hearing us, so that's what we'll do. We'll approach with only a few men and recon until we locate them. After that we'll stay with them observe for a while and see what happens."

"If they camp for a bit and head back, then we'll destroy them," he added with a near growl. "If we play it right, we can hit them far enough from their own lines that they just disappear."

"That would be a good trick," Coe chuckled "Their high command would bust one for sure looking for an entire division that went AWOL."

"We have to find them first, and then see what they're doing. Be cautious and don't be seen. Get that order out to selected scouts and let's get moving. I'd ideally like to catch up with them by lunch tomorrow at the latest."

-

"I th... think I'm getting better at th... this," Buford Beaumont gasped slightly as he fought to catch his breath.

"I'm pretty sure you are," Horace Whipple wasn't even winded. Damn him.

"Our men are doing well," Whipple continued. "My archers have improved more than I had thought possible to be honest. Their aim while moving has improved by some forty percent."

"Lancers are doing better too," Beaumont agreed. "I admit I thought this was a waste of time, but I don't think that anymore."

"Don't forget our main reason for being here," Whipple reminded him. "This retraining is fine and all, but our primary role here is to prevent Therron from bringing any help from the Coastal Provinces into Soulan. Secondary to that is to be a backstop to Pierce in the central highlands. We should make sure our regimental commanders keep that in mind as well."

"We'll call an officers meeting tonight after evening mess," Beaumont nodded. "We need to do that anyway."

"Have you given any more thought to my proposal?" Whipple asked.

"I have," Beaumont nodded again. "I suggest we discuss it with our regimental commanders this evening as well. And I have an idea I want to run by you on that accord. We shall have to be in agreement on it, and then send a message to the Prince asking his permission and input."

"What is it?"

"Well..."

-

"We've made good time despite the wind not being friendly to us," Captain Anthony Chastain noted as he and Therron McLeod sat on the command deck of the cruiser RSN Halifax. The frigates Seadragon and Seasnake sat to the port and starboard respectfully, in escort positions.

"We need to make better time than this, however," Therron complained. "I need to be in Norfok sooner than later."

"I agree, sir, but this is the best we can do with the wind not cooperating. We're using the oars as well when we tack up but doing so exhausts our men quickly. And it takes them away from other duties. While I have relaxed certain standards that we often let slip in time of war, there are some duties that we cannot shirk since they affect the efficiency of the ship. Still, I estimate we will be in Norfok within the week. We will actually be in Coastal Territorial Waters in the next five days or less, so long as conditions don't worsen."

"I could make better time by land," Therron mused, though his voice was contemplative rather than complaining. "Do you think there is somewhere we can put ashore and I can acquire sufficient horses for myself and a small escort? A squad of your Royal Marines perhaps?"

"I honestly don't know, sir," Chastain admitted. "Let's examine the map and see what we can find." The two looked at the map table and Chastain ran a finger along the coast.

"Port Charles is the last major port in our Kingdom, and we could be there in a little over a day, barring a change in conditions. Port Winton is the last port of call along our own seaboard before we enter Coastal Waters. I admit I've never made port there, so I don't know what the conditions are. You would need at least a dozen horses along with saddlery and tack, plus additional animals for packing.

You would also need to lay in supplies for the trip. We can provide food stuffs but have no gear like tenting or camp ware to speak of."

"Poll your officers and men and see of any of them have first had knowledge of this Port Winton," Therron ordered. "Port Charles is out of the question. My brother's rot runs deep, I'm afraid, so trying to make port there is too risky."

"Very well, sir."

-

"Are you sure this is the route you wish to take, sir?"

In truth Chastain was thrilled at the idea of getting Therron McLeod off his ship, but it would never do to say so.

"No, but I do think it for the best," the prince replied. "I need to reach the Coastal Province Governor as soon as possible, and as you said, the wind doesn't favor us. This will have to do. Thank you for your help, Captain. I won't forget."

"Godspeed, sir," Chastain settled for saying. "Boat away!" he called. The long boat carrying Therron McLeod began to lower to the sea. Soon, that boat and three more were on their way inland. Horses were already waiting for him and his ten-man Royal Marine escort. Chastain had almost been forced to place Major Guilford in irons due to his protests of sending his marines on such a mission when the evidence was clear that Therron McLeod was in fact a traitor to the Crown. But Chastain was perfectly willing to sacrifice ten Marines in an attempt to save his own skin.

And now he had done so.

"I want us underway the minute the boats return," he told Commander Jerome Hart, executive officer of the Halifax. "We're going back where we belong at best speed."

"Aye, sir," Hart nodded.

"I'll be in my cabin."

-

"No movement to speak of milord, other than what Dagger reported this morning," Doak Parsons reported to his Prince. "I've got men prowling all around their position and they are stirring a bit here and there, but the most activity we've seen other than that one division on the move has been unit training in camp. Most like just keeping the rust knocked off, same as we are."

"Sounds likely," Parno nodded, looking at the map. "I don't like this, Mister Parsons. Their army is twice our size and yet they just sit there. Why?"

"They're winning just where they are, sir," Parsons offered a rare opinion. "I'd imagine they know it, too."

"Why do you say that?" Parno asked, interested in what Parsons would say.

"They're occupying a big chunk of our bread basket, milord, and an equally large piece of grazing land. We'll be hurting before winter is over without the food that land would produce, and without the hay and grass that would normally be feeding horses or beef. If that Nor general is smart enough to play the long game, then they're winning just by sitting there. They know we can't throw 'em out, and they can keep us from growing a crop there. Meanwhile, they aren't throwing their men away battering our defenses."

"Exactly," Parno nodded. Parsons' explanation agreed with his own. "What can we do about it?"

"Nothing, sir," Parsons replied. "We can harass, we can interdict supplies like we have been, we can irritate them, but... it would be like a wasp trying to stop a bull. The bull would know the wasp stung him, but he'd just keep moving."

Parno nodded again, hating to have to agree but knowing it was true. There simply wasn't anything to be done at the moment other than hold the line and try to make the lives of the Norland soldiers as miserable as possible.

"Keep me informed, Mister Parsons," he said finally. "I depend on you and your men above all others to be my eyes and ears. Please make sure I see and hear what's happening."

"We'll do so, milord."

-

"This has turned into a pleasant evening," Edema said as she joined Stephanie on the inn's covered portico. "After last night's storm and this morning's fog I wasn't sure what the day would be like. This breeze is welcome," she sat down.

"It is very nice," he younger companion agreed. "Captain Winters informed me a few minutes ago there's no reason we can't continue on tomorrow."

"Wonderful!" Edema exclaimed. "Another two days, three at most, and we will be there. It will be good to see Parno once more. I've not seen him since Tammon's funeral."

"He's not going to be pleased to see us," Stephanie warned yet again. "The best thing to do is turn around and go back. We are asking for trouble if we do this."

"Pish," Edema waved her complaint away. "He may be put out but he won't be angry. Well," she amended, "he may well be angry but he'll get over it."

"If you say so," Stephanie sighed. She had fought this battle many times in the last few days. There was no point in fighting it yet again.

"I know you think this is useless, and it may well be," Edema surprised her. "But you have to know. So, does he. This is too hard on both of you to leave it unresolved. And what if something were to happen to one of you? The other would be left with a bag full of 'what if' and 'if only' that you could never get rid of. Even if the two of you cannot mend your relationship, each of you deserve some kind of closure. If nothing else, Parno doesn't need such a distraction hanging over him. And neither do you."

It was the first time that Edema had actually acknowledged that this might not work. At the same time, Stephanie was forced to admit that Edema made sense. They did need closure, she supposed. She at least needed the opportunity to say she was sorry.

"We'll see, I suppose," she settled for saying into the silence.

-

"Going to the Hogshead this evening?" Karls asked as he entered Parno's tent and sat down uninvited. He was one of perhaps five people in the entire camp that could do so without fear of reprimand. Karls was dirty and sweat-stained, showing signs of his having been working with the training of 1st Corps.

"I hadn't planned on it," Parno replied as he signed yet another form and placed in a pile for Harrel to have delivered. "And please, take a seat. Relax and be comfortable."

"Thanks," Karls smiled. "I brought you something," he offered up a bottle of the Germanian home brew beer that was so popular. Parno took it thankfully.

"Your sins are forgiven," he promised Karls as he removed the cork. "I don't know what they do to this, but damn, it's good," he said after a long pull. "It's on par with Tinker's brew, and that's saying something."

"I need to get over there and give that beer a try," Karls nodded. "I hear the food is good, too."

"Wait for the brisket," Parno nodded. "They serve smoked brisket usually once a week at least, along with roasted potatoes and fresh bread. I promise you'll like it."

"I'll do that," Karls nodded. "1st Corps is coming along pretty well," he grew serious. "I don't think it will take six months to get them up to muster, either. Graham is seriously motivated, and he is passing that on to his men."

"Don't let him get out here in this heat and have a stroke or anything," Parno replied. "I'm still not sure I like him personally, but I have decided that he's probably not an enemy. And he apparently *is* an able commander if nothing else."

"Seems so, and he has his men's respect," Karls nodded. "After we went through culling out Therron's plants he called all of his officers together and they had a nice long chat about loyalty. I think some of his men were surprised and the rest were glad to see something being done about it. It was a win all around as far as I can see. And, like I said, I don't think it will take so long with them. They were in pretty good physical shape to start with."

Before he could say more the sound of several horses arriving outside reached them. A minute later Bret Chad and Preston Wilbanks entered, both removing their hats and saluting.

"Well, you two are a sight for sore eyes," Parno smiled, shaking Chad's hand and then Wilbanks. "I got your reports from the action in the Royal City but I'd love to hear your first-hand stories. Are you too tired to sit and have a beer and maybe something to eat and tell us about it?"

"Give us a few minutes to wash some of the dust off, sir?" Chad asked.

"Let's say a half-hour?" Parno offered. "Supper should be close to done by then and that will give Karls time to go and get the beer he volunteered to get."

"I did?"

"Half-hour then, sir," Wilbanks nodded.

"When did I volunteer for anything, ever?" Karls asked.

-

"... and in the dark, I just didn't want to risk trying to get down the mountain," Wilbanks' voice was still bitter. "Had we been a little faster off the mark, we could have made it."

"Not your fault," Parno shook his head. "And I've been thinking about that since your report. I've got an idea about that problem and I'm going to run it by one of the Royal Engineers but first I want your opinion. What I want to do is widen the trail and pack it down, then establish a line of lamps or torches along the entire path. Establish a small post at about the half-way mark with a couple of men who aren't able to serve on the line but can still ride. As dark approaches, they make the ride up and down and light the lamps."

"With a more secure footing and adequate illumination, movement up and down that trail should be possible even at night, don't you think?"

"I do, actually," Wilbanks replied and Chad was nodding his own agreement. "If the horses can be sure of their footing, they won't be so skittish, and the lamps will give us a corridor to stay inside of if nothing else. The trail really isn't a bad one, it's just that making it up and down in the dark is dangerous."

"It would be a good project for the Engineering school," Karls pointed out.

"I hadn't even thought of that," Parno admitted. "I think I will forward the idea to Professor Pearl and let him run with it. He should be able to get something done on it."

"Now that that's done," he changed subjects, "tell me about Nasil. How bad is the damage, or at least how bad was it when you left? And what other news is there that you picked up on while you were there?

-

"My advisers and I have decided that the first day of autumn would be the ideal time for my coronation as King," Memmnon said over the dinner table he shared with Winnie. Tonight, it was just them, since she would depart in the morning as soon as it was light.

"Autumn," Winnie repeated. "That's still some time away."

"There is a great deal to be done," he admitted. "Honestly, it's all wasted and useless frippery in my opinion but... it is tradition and the people expect it. And I suppose there is something to be said for maintaining some semblance of normalcy in the times we're going through."

"I guess that's a good point," she nodded. "So, I recko-, I assume, that means I need to plan to be back a few days before then?" she corrected herself, about to slip into her old style of speaking.

"It's not required that you be here, or course," Memmnon replied. "But it would mean a great deal to me if you were."

"Then I'll be here," she promised. "Long as the Good Lord's willing, I'll be here."

"At some point after that we will need to begin planning for our wedding," he added, delighting in the blush that attacked her face. "I was going to suggest that you take at least one assistant with you who can take notes as you think of them. You may find certain styles or colors along your trip that you wish to have recorded for future reference."

"That ai-, that's not a bad idea," Winnie agreed. "I was gonna… I was going to take a secretary along anyway, so she can double as that I'm sure."

"I believe that is a sound plan," Memmnon smiled. "I shall miss these evenings with you, Winifred," he said softly. "I shall miss you."

"Me too," she smiled. It was weak, but it was a smile. "But I'm gonna work as hard and as fast as I can to get my job done so I can get back here. I promise."

"I will hold you to that, my dear," he raised a small wine goblet in her direction. "I will hold you to it."

-

"We split up here. From here on, we don't have any friends. We keep moving, and we make sure we arrive at the right time. Anything else is a failure."

The speaker's comrades nodded.

"Then get moving. Keep to the schedule. For the Emperor."

"For the Emperor!" the others chorused. After that, they split apart, each with his own trail and own mission.

CHAPTER FIVE

-

The new day was cooler, but clear. No fog hung over the valley as people began stirring.

Captain Winters watched as his troopers saddled their mounts while the carriage driver and his helper accepted assistance from the inn's hand to prepare the carriage. A brief breakfast had already been served and soon the ladies exited the inn, their baggage already stored on the carriage.

"A pleasure to have had you all here, my ladies," Milton followed them out.

"A delightful place to spend the evening, Milton dear," Edema smiled. "When next we pass this way, we will make use of your business again."

"Thank you, my lady," Milton beamed at that. "That is very kind of you. I wish you a safe and comfortable journey."

"I wish to make as good a time as possible today," Edema informed her driver before entering the carriage. "I want to be in camp before dark tomorrow if at all possible."

"We'll do our best, milady," the man promised.

The carriage was moving as soon as the two has settled in, and Stephanie couldn't fight off a sigh of near depression as the small inn fell from sight.

"It will be alright, dear," Edema promised.

"No, it won't."

-

It was a good weather day, suitable for travel. Rather by horseback or in a carriage, travel was made easier by the previous day of sun and wind which had helped to dry the mud left by heavy rains.

The 16th Imperial Infantry was still struggling miserably despite the better conditions. They had not been able to take advantage of any time to rest, marching through the mud and pushing or pulling wagons that became mired in the ruts left by wagons ahead of them. Shoes and socks soaked with water and coated with mud, pants weighted by mud caked along the cuffs and lower legs and rain-soaked gear made heavy by the water it carried all combined to leave the men exhausted and miserable. A cold camp had not raised anyone's spirits since fires would have helped them dry off and warm food would have helped them warm up alongside a nice fire.

Now with the break of day they were on the road again after a cold, miserable night and an equally cold breakfast of field rations. The road that still lay ahead of them would perhaps be in better shape, so there was at least that. But there was no mistaking that the men of the 16th were miserable. And angry. None more so than their General, Brandon Taylor.

Why the hell were they having to do such a forced march in such weather? There was no enemy out here! There was nothing out here of interest to a division of Imperial infantry. Fields that would not be planted this year, grass that no animals would graze, and trees that he couldn't allow his men to cut and build fires that would warm them up and dry them out. His orders demanded a cold camp and forced march all the way.

And all for nothing as far as he could see.

His men were veterans, elite members of the Imperial Army who had withstood an attack that had crushed two other divisions in a matter of minutes. His troops should be beyond meaningless marches like this. They should be in camp while lesser divisions were out here doing trivial work like this. Looking for what? Ghosts? He would bet the stars of his rank insignia that there wasn't a single Soulan trooper closer to his position than the established lines they had left yesterday.

However, there were Soulan troopers much closer to General Taylor's 'elite' troops than he imagined. The scouts sent out by General Allen and his fellow division commanders had easily found the trail of such a large body of men. It had taken only until late afternoon to catch up to the floundering mass of soldiers and wagons and from that point on they were under constant observation. Word had been sent back to General Allen and he had moved his entire command parallel to the Norland force, keeping abreast of them but roughly five miles distant. He didn't want to alarm them after all.

He wanted to see where they were going and what they were going to do when they arrived.

-

"We're ready to get under way, ma'am," Captain Case reported. "On your say so."

"Alright," Winnie's voice was rather soft. "Go ahead and let the wagons move and let the train shake down. We have a long trip ahead of us."

"Yes ma'am," Case nodded. He departed and Winnie turned to where Memmnon was waiting, almost in the shadows of the morning sun.

"I guess this is it," she said, trying to smile.

"I fear that it is," his cultured voice was in stark contrast to hers. "I wish you safe journey and a swift return," he gave her a traditional farewell. "Please be safe. That is all I ask. Please keep yourself from harm."

Winnie was already regretting her demand to be allowed to serve in some capacity, not because she didn't think she could but simply because leaving was turning out to be much harder than she had expected. But she couldn't back out now. And the work she would be doing was important.

"I promise," she settled for saying. There was so much more she wanted to say, but she settled for that. She embraced him tightly and they exchanged the briefest of kisses before she turned and made her way to the horse that was waiting for her. She had a carriage as well but would ride at least part of the way.

She refused to look back as she rode away. She knew Memmnon would be watching and she doubted she could take it. So, she sat stiffly in the saddle, looking straight ahead, thinking about the trip, about the work she would be engaged in, anything other than the man she was leaving behind.

If anyone saw a tear or two fall from her face, they didn't mention it.

-

Camp life didn't exactly change every day. Individual duties changed for men on work details, but the details themselves remained the same. This day was no different. The weather was better, the conditions somewhat dryer, but the duties were the same as the day before. And the day following.

It was a simple fact that not every day of any war was filled with combat. There were many days that were filled with mind numbing boredom as the same duties were fulfilled day after day. Those days would, on occasion, be filled with equally mind-numbing terror when in combat, so soldiers learned to treasure days of quiet, no matter how boring they might seem.

There was always tomorrow, though. Tomorrow would come soon enough.

-

"We've made good time," Winters told them as they stopped again for the evening. "I expected travel conditions to be much worse. We should arrive tomorrow, barring misfortune."

"Splendid," Edema was pleased to hear.

"I'm tired," Stephanie sighed. "I just want to lie down."

"Aren't you hungry?" Edema asked, concerned.

"No, I'm not," Stephanie was just shy of being short. The closer they got to where Parno was the worse she felt. She was on the verge of trying to hire her own carriage to carry her back. Winters was the commander of her escort after all. If she demanded to go back, he had to take her, didn't he?

"Well, let's get a room then," Edema replied. "You can rest tonight. I'm sure you'll feel better after a good night of rest."

"Oh, of course," Stephanie muttered.

"What?"

"Nothing."

-

"We did good today," Case informed Winnie as she dismounted near her carriage. Case had ordered it parked inside the ring of wagons and a fire prepared for her. She would sleep inside while his troopers maintained a guard around it at night.

"I can tell," she rubbed her butt as she stretched. A trooper took her horse without comment and carried it to be cared for. She didn't notice at first, but then turned to look for it.

"It's fine," Case told her. "She'll get a good rub down and then be fed."

"I can do that," she protested.

"You're the leader of this wagon train," he told her, shaking his head. "There are other duties you have to see to."

"Such as?"

"Speaking to the others for instance, and seeing how they fared during the trip," Case reminded her. "Seeing if anyone has problems you need to have seen to. That sort of thing. Shouldn't be too hard today, since we're just one day out."

"You make it sound like it will be worse later on," she semi-complained.

"Good," Case nodded. "That's how I meant it to sound. We're at least two weeks from Jason and that's if nothing goes wrong at all. And we'll have to cross the river to get there, which will take at least a day with all these wagons. So yeah, you can expect it to get worse. Enjoy it while you can."

-

"Going to the Hogshead ton-"

"Why do you keep asking me that?" Parno looked up as Karls entered his 'office' tent.

"Just curious," Karls shrugged. "Have to keep up with where you are after all."

"Aren't you supposed to be training 1st Corps?" irritation crept into Parno's voice.

"They're being worked to the bone every day by the Sheep, who are enjoying it immensely," Karls snickered. "I had no idea there were so many sadistic people in our regiment."

"Well, they were trained by the best," Parno snorted in amusement. "And no, I'm not going to the Hogshead. Why do you want to know? And don't give me that bullshit about keeping tabs on me. That's what you have Berry for."

"What?" Karls looked stunned for a second before he could recover. "How-

"

"I really am not stupid, Karls," Parno went back to the paperwork before him. "As much as you, Cho, Enri and whoever else likes to pretend that I may be. I know that Berry reports to you on a daily basis."

"And just waited until now to say something?" Karls asked.

"It gave you the illusion of being in control," Parno shrugged. "Same as it did Darvo. It doesn't hurt me any. But your questions are becoming annoying."

"It's no secret you have your eye on a girl over there," Karls stopped pretending. "With things between you and the Doctor ending the way they did-"

"Karls, you are perhaps the best friend I have ever had in the entire world," Parno didn't look up. "I love you like I should have been able to love my brothers. But," he paused here and did look up, "I have told you for the final time to leave that alone. What happened between Stephanie and I is just that; between her and I. Please, don't make me say it again."

"I wasn't going to comment about what's between you two, or not," Karls ignored the cold tone Parno directed at him. "You're my best friend too, you know. And if you've found another woman, I am honor bound to do two things. One is to make sure she's good for you, and to you."

"And the other?" Parno raised an eyebrow.

"To give you sheer hell about it until it gets so old I get tired of it," Karls said with a straight face. Parno tried to keep the stern look on his face but failed miserably, finally bursting out laughing.

"Touché," he finally said. "I did that to you with Dolly, didn't I?"

"So, you did," Karls nodded. "Look, whatever happened with you and Stephanie, that's yours. Or yours and hers. Whatever. I'm just trying to look after you now. That's all."

"I appreciate it," Parno nodded. "But there's nothing there to know. I met a pretty girl, but that's all she is. A pretty girl. More to it, that's all she can be."

"Why?" Karls frowned. "Oh," he added as his brain caught up with him.

"Yes," Parno nodded abruptly. "As much as I like her, and I do like her I'm forced to admit, being by my side would simply make her a target. For wagging tongues, for assassins, for any number of things. So, all she can ever be is a pretty girl."

"I see," Karls nodded, and he really did. "I'm sorry. I won't tease you anymore."

"That would be much appreciated."

-

"I need to go to the camp, Tinker," Jaelle said, a bundle in her arms.

"Whatever for?" Tinker asked, a slight smile gracing his features.

"I have repaired the Prince's jacket and need to return it to him," she presented the bundle.

"I can see to that," Tinker promised.

"I know, but... I would prefer to do it myself," Jaelle managed to smile.

"Jaelle..." Tinker began, but she raised a hand to silence him.

"I know," she said again. "I told you before, Tinker. There is nothing to protect me from. He knows it as well as I do. As well as you do. But... he has so much on him, and he is so weary and alone... it is little enough I can do. Allow me to do it."

"Very well," Tinker smiled sadly. "Have Aaron carry you over there. It is dangerous for you to go alone, and in his care, you will be safe."

"Bell?" Jaelle looked puzzled. "It's not that I do not like him, but..."

"Aaron is much more than he appears, Jaelle," Tinker promised. No one but Rosa knew Bell's real identity.

"I'm sure he's very capable, but-"

"He is one of the Prince's Black Sheep, Jaelle," Tinker dropped the secret on her quietly. "He can insure you are able to get in to see the Prince without difficulty. And no man will challenge you in his presence."

"What?" Jaelle couldn't have been more surprised.

"He was lent to us as protection when the Prince gave us this assignment," Tinker smiled again. "I am sure he chafes at not being in action with his fellows. Or would were it not for Briel's presence, anyway," he added with a dry chuckle.

"I... I see," she almost managed not to stammer. "Then I... I will get him and we will go."

"You do that, Jaelle. Have a pleasant evening."

-

"Halt!" a voice challenged from the dark, and Aaron Bell's hand swept out to still Jaelle's horse.

"State your name and your business!" the challenger stated.

"Sergeant Aaron Bell, Prince's Own," Bell replied calmly. "On my way to the Prince's Headquarters with one civilian."

-

Jaelle had not wanted to doubt Tinker's word, but it was not until Bell appeared in uniform that she had realized the truth of Tinker's words. When she had approached him about carrying her to the camp, he had merely nodded and excused himself, asking her to wait for him at the rear entrance of the Inn.

Fifteen minutes later Bell had appeared, mounted and leading a horse with a sidesaddle. Moreover, he was now adorned in the livery of Prince Parno's Own Regiment, including the badge of the bloody fanged black sheep on his arm above three stripes. The change in him was palpable as he helped her mount and then swung effortlessly back into his own saddle.

"Where is it you need to go, ma'am?" he asked easily.

"Uh... I mean, I need to return the Prince's jacket," the spell of stunned silence was finally broken. "I repaired a cut on the shoulder," she added needlessly.

"Very well," he nodded. "Take a few minutes and we'll be challenged more than once. Just be at ease. We won't have any trouble."

"Hell, you say!" the challenge brought Jaelle back to the present.

"I do say," Bell's voice was cold in reply. "Would you like a taste to see for sure?"

"He's wearing the Prince's livery," another voice said. "And that is definitely a civilian with him," you could almost hear the leer in his voice.

"Mister, you better choose your next words carefully," Bell's voice was even colder if that were possible. "If I have to get off this horse you won't see the sun again this side of hell."

"He's definitely one of 'em," someone muttered. "Pass through. Expect another challenge between here and there."

"Ma'am," Bell didn't bother to reply to the mouthy troopers on watch. Instead he spurred his huge war mount forward, forcing the guard to step aside or be trampled.

"You bastards best learn some manners before I bring her back through here," he almost whispered to the Sergeant in charge of the post. "If you don't, then I'll be back without her. Understand?" Implied was that he would be accompanied by other members of the Black Sheep.

"I'll see to it," the sergeant promised. Bell smiled as he heard the sergeant bellowing a name into the dark as he and Jaelle passed out of earshot.

"Was that for me?" Jaelle asked hesitantly.

"Don't know what you mean, ma'am," Bell's voice was suddenly as warm as ever. "Just exchanging pleasantries with the guards on watch."

She let the lie go, suddenly aware that she didn't really know Bell nearly as well as she had thought.

The rest of the ride in was quiet.

"You have a visitor, milord," Harrel Sprigs said quietly.

"Show him in," Parno barely looked up. It took him a minute to realize that Sprigs was still standing there.

"Harrel?" he looked up. "Show whoever it is in."

"Sir," Sprigs hesitated, but then nodded and held the flap of the tent open.

"Please come in," he said.

Parno could not have been more surprised to see Jaelle walk into his tent if she had been naked. Sprigs took the opportunity to duck out of the tent and allow the flap to close behind him.

"Milord," Jaelle actually curtsied.

"J...Jaelle," Parno stammered slightly. "How in the world did you get here? It's not safe for you to be out-"

"Bell brought me," she replied quietly, still not sure how to take the transformation she had seen the young soldier go through.

"Ah," Parno nodded. "Well, you're certainly safe with him," he nodded. "But what would bring you out here like this at night?" he asked. *Or at all* was unspoken but there nonetheless.

"I have repaired your jacket, milord," she smiled brightly, holding the parcel out to him. Parno couldn't help but smile, shaking his head in mild amusement as he walked over to her and accepted the jacket.

"You didn't have to ride all the away out here for that, Jaelle."

"I know," she said simply. "But I wanted to. Try it on," she urged, holding it open for him to shrug into. He did so more to humor her than for any need to see how it looked. Once it was on, he looked to the shoulder and was surprised to see a barely noticeable seam where the sword cut had been repaired. As he looked at it she was buttoning his jacket for him, an intimate gesture that he appreciated more than he could find words to describe. She finished by straightening the collar for him and then stepping back to look him over.

"Very handsome," she smiled. "If I didn't already know your reputation as a heart breaker was well deserved, this would definitely do it," she gave a short nod as her smile turned mischievous.

"How would you know my reputation anyway?" Parno asked with a raised eyebrow.

"People do talk, my Prince," her smile grew brighter. "I must admit you do present a very dashing figure in uniform," she almost sighed.

"I'm flattered you think so," Parno replied honestly. "And I really appreciate you taking care of this for me."

"You know," she drew the second word out slowly as her head dipped slightly, "I could make sure none of your other clothes need mending while I'm here." Her voice was a medley of teasing innuendo and earnest suggestion. "I am a good seamstress."

"You are," Parno nodded. "But I think my other clothes are okay save for a few missing buttons here and there."

"The Crown Prince? Missing buttons?" Jaelle feigned shock. "We simply can't have that. Think of the scandal!"

Parno couldn't help but laugh. This girl made him laugh, made him feel his real age, made him feel light, as if the heavy load he was bearing had just been lifted away. It was something he could get used to in a hurry if he allowed it. Which he couldn't.

"I do appreciate it," he began but stopped when her finger crossed his lips to silence him.

"I know this cannot be," she whispered. "I know there are limits to anything. But let me do for you what I can. It is not a burden, my Prince," she suddenly moved her hand to caress his face, pushing his hair away from his eyes. The look in her eyes was enough to rob him of air.

"Jaelle, you would never be-"

"I know," she hushed him again. "I do not care. It is alright. As Tinker would say, it is what it is. And it is enough. You may send me away if you wish and I will go, you know that. But if you will let me, even if only for tonight, I will stay with you. You know that I am not... that I..." she struggled, trying to find the right words.

"I know," he nodded, saving her the search. "I know you aren't, and if you were I would never hold it against you nor think less of you for it."

"I know," she caressed his head again in a soothing manner. "And I think that is one of the things I love most about you. You, who have been so misjudged, judge no one. Look down on no one. You have no real idea how rare that is, my Prince. And for that, more than anything, I am so sorry," she leaned forward and kissed him lightly. "You deserve so much more, yet all Jaelle can give you is herself."

"All?" Parno took her hand in his, incredulity in his voice. "That's all? It would seem that I am not the only one who doesn't know how rare they are, Jaelle."

He delighted to see her dusky face blush even in the lantern light. Leaving her standing where she was, Parno went to the entrance to the tent and opened it.

"Harrel?"

"Milord?" the young man appeared as if by magic.

"Please escort Miss Jaelle to my quarters and see to it she has everything she needs."

"At once milord," Harrel almost managed to hide his pleased look.

Almost.

"My lady, if you would?" he held open the tent flap and bowed slightly, his arm pointing more or less toward Parno's private quarters.

"Harrel will show you where I live," Parno told her quietly. "I have work to finish, and then I will join you."

"Very well," she curtsied again. "Oh," she stopped after only one step. "I forgot about Mister Bell!"

"I can see to that," Parno promised.

CHAPTER SIX

-

Parno was awake long before the sun peeked over the horizon, as was his custom. He had already bathed and dressed before Jaelle had even awakened. She raised from her slumber, hair tousled around her like a halo as she smiled at him like a sleepy cat.

My God, she is beautiful, he thought to himself, looking at her.

"Good morning," he said, walking over to where she was pulling her legs beneath her to sit up, pulling the light blanket that covered her around her in a sarong. He kissed her lightly as he sat down beside her.

"Good morning, my Prince," she replied, her voice still drowsy.

"How did you sleep?" he asked. His bed was a bit better than a camp cot or blanket roll, though it was still a bed found in a war camp. Still, being Lord Marshal had some perks.

"I slept wonderfully," she gave him another sleepy smile as she lay her head over on his shoulder. "Once I slept," she added mischievously. He couldn't help but laugh.

"What must you do today?" she asked.

"I must do pretty much what I do every day," he admitted. "Sign useless forms and requests, approve useless orders and ridiculous expenditures of Crown monies, and just basically be a bureaucrat for most of the day. The rest of it I'll spend worrying about what our enemies are doing."

"You sound as if you do not like it," she noted.

"Good, because I don't," he said at once and she giggled. Straightening, she caressed his hair softly.

"My poor Prince," she almost cooed. "Trapped in a position he doesn't want, kept there by a duty he cannot and will not shirk."

"That's me," Parno nodded. "Jaelle, we really need to talk," he turned serious. She tried to place a finger to his lips again but he grabbed her hand before she could, shaking his head.

"No, no more shushing," he told her firmly. "I really like you. A lot. More than I probably should considering the position I find myself in. More than I can allow myself to," he sounded sad.

"I know that people would never accept you having a woman such as I," she told him, smiling faintly. "I told you, it is enough."

"That... you think that's what I'm worried about?" his shock was clearly evident. "That I'm worried about what people think? You obviously don't know my reputation nearly as well as you think you do, Jaelle. I couldn't care less what people think of me or who I spend my time with."

Jaelle hid her own surprise as she heard the very thing Tinker had said to her coming from the Prince himself. She sat up straighter suddenly, realizing that this was not what she had expected it to be.

"No," Parno shook his head. "I don't spend a single second of my day worried about what people think of me, and doubt I ever will. And anyone who had a problem with you would soon find they had a problem with me as well. Don't let such a thing worry you another minute. Understand?"

She nodded, not trusting herself to speak.

"No, the problem is something else entirely," Parno continued. "While what people would say wouldn't bother me, it would certainly bother you in all likelihood, but even that isn't the real problem. The problem is simple; people close to me die. I am a target of the Nor, of subversive elements of our own Kingdom, even of my own brother. If you were with me... if someone realized how close I was becoming to you... there is no way I could keep you safe, Jaelle. You would become a target too. That life you have that you like so much? With Tinker and the others? There would be no going back to it, and even they might be targeted simply because they are important to you. That's why Aaron was with you at the Inn," he added. "Just in case. Not just for you, but for all of you in case someone found out that Tinker works for me."

"I... I see," she managed to stammer, even though she clearly didn't completely see. She had never imagined...

"You are beautiful," he told her, his hand cupping her face tenderly. "You are beautiful but also kind, generous, with a kind and warm and caring heart and I... in another place or time... a time when I wasn't a danger to everyone around me... I think I could even..."

This time she did shush him, softly and gently yet still firmly, her eyes filled with resolve.

"My Prince," she said softly. "Always thinking of anyone other than yourself. Such a rare, rare man." She kissed him with her finger still between their lips. "I understand. I really do, now. Your worry for me warms my heart and my soul. What must be must be. Go and do the things you must do and leave me to... to finish," she settled for saying. "Thank you," she whispered, kissing him one last time.

Parno didn't know what else to say and wasn't sure it would matter, so he got to his feet and pulled on the jacket she had so thoughtfully repaired and returned to him. With a final look at her he picked up his sword and left.

-

"We are making better time than I had anticipated, milady," Winters spoke through the window of the carriage. "We should make the camp by lunch or thereabouts, should nothing change."

"Thank you, Captain," Stephanie smiled weakly. He tipped his hat and road ahead. Stephanie sat back, brooding slightly, but also worried.

"It will be alright, whatever happens," Edema told her confidently. "Remember that you are doing this because you need some type of-"

"For God's sake, I know!" Stephanie finally snapped, and for once Edema didn't snap back, caught by surprise. "My God, whatever would I do without so many people to manage my life for me! All I wanted was a child!" she almost screamed, but caught herself just in time, lest her escort hear her.

"Stephanie," Edema started, but Stephanie was shaking her head violently now.

"No, you've done enough, thank you. Tricking me into this and then practically forcing me to follow through with it. Now here I am, a nervous bloody wreck and about to have to face the man I..." She stopped suddenly, her poise returning as she schooled her features and dried her tears. She pulled a small mirror from her bag and checked her face, removing any trace of tears as best she could.

Edema decided that remaining silent in this case would be best.

-

It was immediately obvious to Harrel Sprigs that Parno was in a dark mood. It was as if there was a cloud following the Prince around, and everyone who could do so was careful to stay outside of that cloud. Harrel was nearly certain he knew what was wrong, or at least the cause, but in his position, there was nothing he could do about it.

He gave Jaelle an hour to bathe and dress before he returned to Parno's tent, where he found her sitting on a freshly made bed, mending clothes. She looked up at him when he entered but didn't offer to get up.

"I can have that taken care of if you'd like," he offered, even though he knew the answer.

"No," she smiled brightly. "No, I would prefer to do it myself this time. I shall not have the chance to do so again. It is little enough that I can do for him."

"I understand," Harrel nodded, and he did. Finally. "If you need anything, you have but to call."

"Thank you."

-

Parno's day wasn't going to get any better.

"Courier from General Allen, sir," Harrel interrupted his daily battle with paperwork. Parno welcomed the break and motioned for Harrel to admit the courier. The message he carried was at least partially good news.

"They were... here, this morning," the traced a place on the map and Harrel made a pencil notation there. "Still moving west. Not making the best time in this muck, but still moving nevertheless."

"Where are they going?" the prince asked.

"I have no clue, sir," Enri Willard admitted. He and General Davies had been summoned when the contents of the courier message had been discovered. "There's just nothing out there, milord."

"It has to be an exercise," Davies offered. "It has to be something they've laid on to keep their men busy. To burn energy and keep the rust knocked off while they sit in camp. This is just the first unit we'll see moving," he predicted.

"Possible," Enri agreed, as he had before. "If it's not then I just don't understand. There's no way that an infantry unit could flank us, and if they were trying to end around the army and hit Shelby, they would send more men than that and do it more quietly."

"Send a runner back to Allen to continue his observations and remind him to keep a close eye on that road. If they're going to send another unit, they should so in another day or so. If the first one returns, then we'll know it's just an exercise. If it doesn't, then it either means they're establishing a permanent presence whereever they stop, or else they are planning to go around us. Either way, we should know for sure in a few days. Until then, we continue as before."

"Yes sir," voices chorused and men filed out, leaving Parno alone once more save for Harrel Sprigs.

"Do I smell food?" he asked Sprigs suddenly.

"It's nearing lunch, sir," the young man nodded.

"Seriously?" Parno was shocked. Where had his day gone.

"Yes sir," Sprigs grinned. "Want me to serve you here?"

"That would be fine," he nodded absently. "I need to get caught up on all this," he indicated the mounting paper on his desk, "while we're stuck here in the mud. Thank you."

"Of course, milord."

-

Word travels quickly through an army camp, but sometimes not nearly quick enough. The arrival of a carriage being escorted by a short company of the

Prince's Own would never go unnoticed, let alone should it happen at mid-day. Despite the stir such an arrival created, word did not reach Harrel Sprigs before the carriage did. Thus, he was just on his was to get lunch for his Prince when the carriage and escort rolled to a stop at the assembly of tents and small buildings that served as the headquarters area for the Soulan Army.

That alone was enough to shock him. Such a carriage with such an escort could only spell trouble ahead. And when he spotted Captain Winters opening the carriage door, he knew immediately who would be exiting. He almost made his escape to warn the Prince but had taken only three steps when he heard his named called.

"Harrel!" Edema Willows called. "Harrel Sprigs!"

Sighing, the young man turned to confront the Lady Duchess Cumberland.

"Hello, My Lady," he bowed stiffly. "I must say I am surprised to see you here."

"I'm sure you are," Edema smirked. "We are here to see Parno. Please tell him we have arrived once you have shown us to visitors' quarters so we can freshen up."

"We?" Harrel felt a knot of dread settle in his belly. Before Lady Willows could answer he saw none other than Stephanie Corsin-Freeman stepping down from the carriage.

"Oh boy," he murmured to himself. To Edema he said;

"Of course, milady. This way."

-

"What?" Parno's voice was low and deadly.

"Sir, I... I had no idea..." Sprigs stammered. "I mean we had absolutely no word whatsoever that she was coming!"

"Relax," Parno told him, waving a hand at his secretary. "I sense Edema's hand in this. I assume they are here to see me?" he sighed.

"She asked that you be notified they were here to see you and then be directed to visitor quarters to freshen up. I took them to the tenting we use for visiting Generals. I... I honestly didn't know what else to do!"

"It's alright," Parno assured him. "Just... bring them in when they're ready," he sighed.

"Yes sir."

-

Jaelle had smelled the food cooking as well and it made her realize she had been working all morning and had not eaten breakfast. Setting her work aside, she rummaged around in Parno's tent and found a pair of hammered tin plates that could double as shallow bowls. Smiling to herself she decided she would surprise him with lunch while he worked.

That decision made, she set out to find the source of the aroma of cooked beef, intent on taking care of Parno to the very last minute she was allowed.

"Duchess Cumberland and Lady Corsin-Freeman, milord," Harrel announced, his voice neutral.

"Parno, dear boy!" Edema swept into the room like a whirlwind, moving to hug him tightly despite knowing he would be less than pleased to see her and her traveling companion.

"Edema," Parno said evenly. "Stephanie," he added with a nod, not bothering to offer her an embrace despite her body language clearly screaming she would gratefully accept it.

"That'll be all, Harrel," he told Sprigs, who withdrew with as much grace as possible so as not to appear as if he were escaping.

"Well, take a seat," Parno extended a hand before returning to his own chair. "What is it that brings you two here, even knowing that this is no place for you?"

"Is that all you have to say?" Edema demanded, an elegant eyebrow raised in open defiance. "After three days in a carriage and one day of layover to wait out the weather? Just to see you?"

"I am not in the habit of receiving social visitors in the Army's headquarters, Edema," Parno told her. "And I am especially not fond of receiving unannounced visitors."

"That's why I asked Harrel to announce us," Edema smiled.

"That isn't what I meant and you know it," Parno replied evenly. "Now, in all seriousness, what is it that has brought you here. Is something wrong with Memmnon?" he asked in sudden concern. "Surely that news would have been sent by Royal Courier."

"Nothing is wrong with your brother, milord," Stephanie spoke for the first time. "I have given him his release, in fact. He is still in recovery but that recovery is no longer in doubt."

"Well, that's good to know," he sighed in relief. The last thing he needed was for something to happen to his brother.

"We simply came to visit, dear," Edema tried again.

"You don't 'simply come to visit' in a war zone, Edema," Parno was beginning to be short even with her. "Moreover, one where we could literally experience an attack of overwhelming numbers at any moment. Now I'll ask just once more; why are you here?"

Edema blinked at Parno's harsh tone. For the first time she was beginning to think Stephanie had been right; this wasn't a good plan.

"Very well," she decided to lay all their card on the table. "I know what happened between you two, and I have brought her here to try and repair this rift before it grows worse. The two of you have to-"

"I don't have to do anything," Parno cut her off cleanly, much to her shock and surprise. "I'm selfish. Haven't you heard? Selfish, self-centered, it's all about me, me, me," his voice was grating. "And I had a safe journey by the way," he addressed Stephanie directly. "Thank you."

Her face flushed at the well-deserved jab but she remained silent.

"That's beneath you, Parno," Edema scolded.

"Beneath me," Parno repeated slowly. "You make it sound as if this 'rift' as you put it were my doing. Is that your intention? Because if it is then you can stop here. Make yourselves comfortable for the night in the visitor quarters because you'll be leaving in the morning," he stood. "Wonderful to see you again and all that."

"You are not getting out of this so easy, Parno McLeod!" Edema leaped from her chair, her voice rising. "This has got to end!"

"It did end," he almost hissed as his temper finally boiled over. "I trusted her," he pointed at Stephanie, "and I trusted your opinion of her. Remember that? And what did I get for it? Did she tell you everything she said to me? Making demands on me that she knew good and well I had no way to fill? Hm? Did she mention how selfish I was to mention hundreds if not thousands of years of tradition that I can't simply toss out the bloody window just because she's accustomed to getting her way whenever she wants it? Did she tell you all of that?" he almost screamed. Edema rocked back on her heels in the face of Parno's sudden onslaught and watched as he visibly made an effort to control himself.

"I wasn't the one who walked out or walked away," he said very quietly. "I wasn't the one who made demands of the other. I wasn't the one accusing the other of insincerity. Did she bother to tell you that she had not even made her parents away of our 'arrangement' at the time she was demanding that I marry her in secret so that I could try and get her pregnant before I returned? Did she tell you that? Or how she attacked me personally because of royal customs that I have to follow simply because I am now the Crown Prince?"

Edema looked at Stephanie who was now a bit pale.

"She failed to mention that her parents weren't aware," Edema admitted. "In fact, I corresponded with her mother under the assumption that she did know."

"Well, she didn't," Parno said before Stephanie could respond. "Now if that's all you came for, this should settle things nicely, wouldn't you say? I-"

Whatever Parno was about to say went unsaid as a wholly unexpected guest chose just that moment to make an appearance.

-

Jaelle had managed to find the nearest mess line and was given two heaping plates of beef stew and bread to go with it. She drew many admiring glances but the presence of a few of the Prince's men in camp was more than enough to prevent anything other than looking.

Almost bouncing, Jaelle made her way to Parno's 'office' tent, intent on sharing lunch with him before she had to depart.

No one had bothered to tell her that Parno had visitors and the guard had been moved back to allow him privacy as he spoke to the two ladies who had arrived earlier.

Arrived without Jaelle seeing them.

-

Harrel Sprigs made his way to Parno's personal tent to check on Jaelle and make sure she didn't need anything. If she was ready to return to the Inn, he could get her an escort and if she had need of anything, he could get it for her. The least seen she was at this point the better it would be.

He knocked on the ridgepole of the tent to announce himself and then opened the flap, stepping on inside… to find Jaelle nowhere in sight, the Prince's clothes still laid on the bed in various states of repair. His frantic looking around the tent would have been comical in any other setting, but as he spied the open mess gear set and the missing pieces, he realized at once what had happened.

A horrible vision flashed in front of his eyes as he started for the tent's entrance at a run.

"No, no, no, no, no!"

-

"My Prince, I have brought you… some…" Jaelle trailed off as she spied two well dressed women in Parno's presence, with Parno himself on his feet and clearly angry.

"Lunch," she finished, unable to think of what else to say. She didn't know if she should run, continue as she had planned, stay where she was or look for another option.

Parno just sighed.

Of course, he thought even as she watched the reaction of Stephanie and Edema. Perfect timing.

"Thank you, Jaelle," he smiled tightly. "I appreciate you thinking of me. Where you able to finish?"

"Finish?" Jaelle repeated, then realized what he meant. "Oh, yes. I mean no. Not quite. I had stopped only to eat and thought if everyone was still busy I would volunteer to bring your lunch as well."

"That is very kind of you, and I thank you," Parno accepted the plate and set it on the table. "As it happens, Harrel was supposed to bring my lunch so I could continue working, but he was sidetracked by a little surprise," he turned to look at his visitors. "If you could let me know when you're done, I can have Harrel get you an escort back to the Inn."

"Of course, milord," Jaelle curtsied without thought and then turned to go.

"No women in the camp, huh?" Stephanie's voice was cutting.

"Don't," Parno warned quietly, his eyes dark. "Go on," he told Jaelle. "Thank you again," he added. She left, feeling as if she had just escaped a lion's den.

"Well," Edema was the first to speak after Jaelle's departure.

"Think before you speak," Parno warned her. "That woman has shown me more kindness than you," he looked at Stephanie, who winced under his glare.

"She repaired my jacket," he showed them where Jaelle had repaired the sleeve. "When she delivered it, she offered to do other mending for me and was doing it when you arrived. When she is finished, she'll be escorted back to the tavern near the edge of the camp where she works as a seamstress and occasional serving girl and cook. Be very careful what you say about her."

Neither woman missed the warning, almost threatening tone of his voice.

"It seems you don't miss me very much after all," Stephanie said stiffly, getting to her feet. When Parno didn't bother to reply Stephanie departed the tent in somewhat of a hurry.

"You know, I assured her all the way up here that you would receive us kindly and hear us out," Edema said finally.

"Then you spoke out of turn," he shot back without pause and she almost flinched. "What did you really expect this to accomplish, Edema?" he asked her more kindly. "If she really told you what all she said to me, what did you expect me to say when you got here?"

"I expected you to give her the opportunity to apologize," she replied.

"Did I miss the part where she apologized?" he asked. "It may have gone by me too fast to see."

"Or it might have been hidden by the skirts of another woman," Edema gave as good as she got.

"To use your own phrase, that's beneath you," Parno's voice was flat. "I was never once in any way duplicitous or unfaithful to her. Ever," he emphasized.

"You seem to have gotten over her in a hurry," Edema mused.

"Anger does that," he nodded. "It burns away pain and leaves you bare. It reminds you why you decided not to trust others in the first place."

"I probably deserve that," Edema admitted after a few seconds. "I did not take into consideration how you would be feeling."

"Too busy being concerned with the good doctor's feelings?" Parno asked, almost sounding solicitous.

"I was furious with her, actually," Edema surprised him. "Furious. When she told me how she had treated you my first instinct was to slap her teeth down her throat."

"Well, thanks for that, anyway," Parno frowned. "I see it didn't last long."

"Stop doing that," she grated. "I am not against you. I am not taking sides."

"You took sides when you brought her up here promising I'd listen," Parno disagreed. "And yes, it hurt, but unlike the rest of you I don't get to show that. I have to hide it, because I'm the damn Crown Prince and the bloody Lord Marshal and whatever else I get stuck with. She gets to cry to you, her mother, Winnie, anyone else that will listen, and I get to ride away like nothing happened. I made the mistake of allowing her to get too close to me and I paid for it. It's an old story for me. I thought I had learned my lesson, but this has reminded me that sometimes I forget things. Like why I stopped trusting people in the first place."

"You trust your serving girl I see," Edema just had to say.

"My serving girl as you refer to her has been more kind to me than anyone I have ever met, and that includes even you, now," he said softly. So softly she had to strain to hear. "And has asked nothing of me in return. Nothing."

Edema reminded herself that Parno had not had the easiest life. She had allowed herself to... not forget, exactly, but to believe that recent events had put that behind him. She could see now that she had been premature in that regard, especially since Stephanie was one of those recent events.

"I'm sorry," she said finally. "I have meddled where I should not have," she admitted. "Stephanie begged me not to make her do this, so don't blame her for it. Blame me."

"I'm not concerned with blame," he told her honestly. "I... I thought I had put her away from me, finally," he said in a fit of honesty. "That I had moved past it. Moved on. Whatever the proper term is. One night I went over to the Inn and had a bit too much to drink with Enri and Cho. On my way out, I saw Jaelle. My serving girl," his voice had only a tinge of scorn to it.

"I... I mistook her for something she wasn't," he had no idea why he kept talking. "Being somewhat inebriated and... depressed... lonely," he admitted finally, "I started to talk to her and one thing led to another. It wasn't until the next night, the night of the storm, that I realized she wasn't... that she's not..."

"She isn't a whore," Edema said softly.

"Yes," Parno nodded. "I... I apologized to her and she laughed. Thought it was the grandest thing that the one man who might apologize for a mistake like that would be the Crown Prince. I... I spent that night with her too, and she was so kind to me," he said softly. "She didn't ask for anything, didn't demand anything, didn't expect anything, just... just was nice to me."

Edema felt like a heel now and was fighting not to cry at the raw pain in Parno's voice. That the mere act of someone simply being nice to him would have such an effect...

"I take it she stayed here with you last evening as well?"

"Yes," he nodded, mouth set in a thin line. "For the last time. It was funny, actually. She thought I was telling her that I didn't want her because she's who she is," he laughed without humor. "That I was sending her away because of what she is."

"You're sending her away to protect her," Edema saw it at once. "Merciful God, Parno, you're trying to protect her," she almost whispered.

"People close to me die," he nodded. "It's a fact of life. She has to go."

"You think you love that girl, don't you?" Edema was on her feet now. Parno just shook his head slowly.

"No. I do like her but it's just because she was nice to me. I don't get much of that, you know." It was as close to self-pity as she had ever seen him get. And since it was the truth it wasn't much like self-pity.

"But if she stays around me she will become a target. For wagging tongues and assassin knives both. I can't protect her, not for certain. So..."

"So, she has to go," Edema nodded, understanding in a way possibly no one else could. "Tell me, Parno, and for God's sake be honest with me, please. Do you love Stephanie? Or, at least did you?"

"Very much," he didn't even consider lying. "Until that night I was certain I had found the one person other than you who would never turn on me and would always support me," he smiled at his surrogate mother sadly. "I was as sure of it as I was of anything, ever. She couldn't have hurt me more if she had run me through. That would have been more merciful. At least that way it would have ended quickly."

Edema suddenly grabbed him and pulled him into a near suffocating hug.

"My dear, precious boy," she whispered. "I am so sorry. God forgive me I am so sorry. We never should have come. And it's my fault. I've hurt you by trying to help. I should not have meddled."

"It doesn't matter," he assured her. "Just... go home," he told her. "Get up in the morning and get away from here. Away from me. Both of you." He released her and stepped back, his mask in place once more.

"It's dangerous here, especially now," he told her stiffly.

"Why is that?" she asked.

"Therron is on the move, free and running," he told her. "Sherron is dead, but he doesn't know it. He could be headed anywhere, but probably is headed to the Coasties. He has friends there, and influence. Once he finds out Sherron is dead, all bets will truly be off."

"He'll come after you," Edema nodded.

"Without hesitation. Now that I think of it, you need to be protected too." The idea that something could happen to her hit him like a thunderbolt. "I'm going to arrange for a detachment to be stationed at your home and go where you go."

"That's not ne-"

"I'm the Lord Marshal and I say it is," he cut her off, his voice one of authority. "I can't remove Stephanie's escort either since the bastard knew we were together before he was banished. She won't be safe either."

"She's staying in the Palace," Edema told him. "Memmnon convinced her to stay on as the Royal Physician and as Winnie's chaperon."

"Really."

"Stephanie actually entrapped her," Edema snickered, explaining briefly what had happened.

"I bet that was fun to watch," Parno actually laughed, but it was a hollow sound.

"I'm going to go back to my tent," Edema said. "I want to see you again before we go, but we'll leave first thing in the morning assuming we don't have a problem."

"It's for the best, I promise," he nodded. "I can't guarantee your safety here."

"I know," she nodded. "I've made it harder on you when I really thought I was helping. I had hoped that even if you two couldn't patch things up you could at least be at peace with one another."

"I am," he nodded. "Tell her that if you want. Tell her whatever makes her feel better, or let her come to me later and I'll tell her. I can make her think we're good. She can go home with that, anyway."

Edema wanted to scream. He was the one hurt so badly and yet Parno was willing to tell Stephanie anything she wanted to hear to help her feel better and move on. On impulse she reached up and caressed his face.

"I do love you so," she smiled at him. "I couldn't love you more if I had borne you myself, and could never be more proud of you, either." With that she turned and left, making her way back to the tent she and Stephanie had been given. Parno watched from the entrance of his tent as a trooper fell in behind her to make sure she got where she was going.

"Harrel!" he called out once she was gone.

"Sir," came the immediate reply, almost from beneath him.

"Dammit, how the hell do you do that?" Parno demanded. "Never mind. I don't want to know. Find Jaelle and ask her to come see me."

"Right away sir," Sprigs nodded. "And sir, I'm sorry-"

"Not your fault," Parno waved his apology away. "None of it. Go on now."

"Sir."

"What a day this has turned out to be," he shook his head as he returned to his now cold lunch.

-

"Stephanie," Edema said softly.

"What," her reply was muffled by the pillow her face was buried in.

"I'm sorry," Edema apologized. "I... I didn't realize how badly he was hurt. If I had I'd not have done this."

"He got over it pretty quick it seems like."

"He's still not over it," Edema told her. That got Stephanie's attention and she sat up, looking at Edema.

"What?"

"He's not over it," Edema repeated. "He's just hiding it. In his position, he's not allowed to show pain. Of any kind. It's weakness. He can't be weak. So, he buries it, whatever is hurting him, and he ignores it. I think one reason he is always so quick to battle is because it's the one place he can release all of that."

"So, killing other people is therapeutic for him," Stephanie shook her head. "Boy can I pick 'em or what?"

"You ungrateful little wench!" Edema hissed. "You want to know how badly you hurt him? Want to know how much he loved you? Trusted you? He said he would rather you had run him through. That at least that would have ended quickly and been merciful. So, spare me your pity party. I may have made a mistake bringing you here, but you have no one but yourself to blame for the position you're in where he's concerned."

Stephanie recoiled slightly under Edema's assault, but in truth it was hearing that Parno would have preferred she take his life rather than break his heart as she had. She slowly collapsed back onto the bed, sobbing quietly.

"I didn't mean it," she told the tent ceiling softly. "I swear I didn't mean it. I was just... I was just scared. So very scared..."

Edema shook her head sadly, remaining silent. This was a right royal mess all right. And she had not helped it.

Nor did she think she could.

-

"You wanted to see me, milord?" Jaelle said softly from the entrance to Parno's tent.

"Come in," he waved to her. "Sit with me. Did you eat already?"

"Yes," she nodded, taking a seat.

"I want to apologize for what you walked in on," he told her. "The blonde woman is... she's the closest thing I've ever had to a mother," he explained. "She was there with my mother when I was born. My mother died about five minutes after I was born, and my family started blaming me for it about five minutes after that."

"That... that's horrible," Jaelle said softly.

"Well, remember I told you for me being like family wasn't a good thing," he gave her a lopsided grin.

"Anyway, the dark haired one was my fiancé of sorts until a few weeks ago."

"Of sorts?" Jaelle's elegant eyebrow rose at that.

"We had reached an understanding between us that if I survived the war, then we would get married. At least I thought we had an understanding. We had a severe falling out the night before I left the Capital to return to the Army," Parno said. "She wanted something I couldn't give her, and when I told her that she... well, she was pretty... ah, hell, she pretty much told me to go and be damned, and then stormed out."

"What did she demand?" Jaelle couldn't help but ask.

"She wanted us to marry in secret and try to make a baby before I came north. The next morning," he didn't hide anything from her.

"She must love you very much," was the first thing Jaelle said, her features soft.

"I couldn't tell from the things she said to me," Parno shrugged.

"If she wanted a child of yours so badly, even knowing that you could die before she saw you again, then she cherishes you, my Prince," Jaelle told him. "She loves you."

"She may have at one point," Parno agreed, reluctantly. "But I have a rule about getting hurt like that. One time per customer," he smiled to take the harshness from his words but the intent was still there.

"Please let me stay," Jaelle said suddenly, completely blindsiding him.

"What?"

"Let me stay with you," she was almost pleading. "I won't make trouble and I won't make demands, I promise. Just... let me stay with you. Please."

"Jaelle, it's far too dangerous," Parno shook his head. "I... my brother is a traitor to the Crown and is running free right now. There's no telling what he may try to do. He wants the throne and I'm in his way. He is as mean and vindictive as anyone you've ever met and wouldn't hesitate to hurt you just to hurt me. And that's leaving out an enemy army not two miles distant. I'm amazed that they haven't tried to infiltrate the camp already in an attempt to assassinate me. Your being here is an invitation for you to get hurt."

"I don't care," she shook her head. "Let me stay."

"Why is this so important to you?" Parno was bewildered.

"I cannot explain," she replied. "I just... I know this is where I belong. Where I must be."

"Jaelle I don't want you in danger," Parno tried again. "You've been so kind to me, repaying you by putting you in danger would be wrong on so many levels."

"I will do whatever you say," she told him. "If you wish me to remain out of sight I shall. If you wish me to serve you I will. Just... do not send me away. I make no demand," she looked up suddenly, meeting his eyes. "I make no demands and I will not beg. I merely ask this one thing of you. Nothing more."

"I'll have to speak to Tinker," Parno temporized.

"I understand," she nodded. "I will wait in your tent," she rose. "Be safe," she almost whispered, bringing one finger to her lips and then placing it on his own. Without another word she departed, leaving a confused and exasperated Prince behind.

"Harrel!"

"Sir," there was an immediate reply.

"Get Berry and have my horse saddled," he ordered. "I need to go see someone."

"Right away, milord."

CHAPTER SEVEN

-

"Sails! Sails north by north-east!"

Commodore Anthony David strode on to the command deck of the Ocoee as the call came down.

"Report Mister Riddell," he said crisply.

"Sail tops to north by north-east, sir," Riddell replied at once. "At least two ships, sir, but not close enough to identify as yet. Colors are indistinguishable at this distance."

"Very well," David nodded. "Steer us an intercept course."

"Aye, sir," Riddell snapped to and hurried to plot their course change. The winds were with them for once, moving from the southwest to the north east. If those ships were Chastain's then the wind would carry David's ships right at them.

Perfect.

-

"Sails to southward!"

"What?" Chastain was startled by the call. "Where!"

"South by south-west and due south, sir!" Commander Hart replied, using the large deck glass to get a look at the ships. "At least three ships in view that I can see, sir. Can't make out colors, but... I'm pretty sure that's the Ocoee judging by her build."

"Come about!" Chastain ordered at once. "Signal the Snake and Dragon to come about in formation. Set full sail with the wind! We're at a disadvantage for engagement with the wind in our face!"

"Sir, if those are our ships then we don't have to-"

"Signal to come about, damn you!" Chastain screamed, shocking everyone on deck. Hart was so shocked he didn't even bother saluting, just moved to prepare the signals.

Down below Major Robert Guilford was coming to a decision. He didn't know what the best course of action was, but he was leaning toward seizing the ship. From there he could order the signal sent to the rest of the small squadron to drop sail and heave to. For that to work he had to wait and see who this was following them.

That did give him time to work, though. Time he decided to make good use of.

-

"They're running, sir," Riddell reported. "Three ships in view from the lookouts. One cruiser and two frigates. They're coming about and putting on full sail."

"We're already at full sail and moving fast," David spoke more to himself than anyone around him. "We'll cut the water better than the Halifax, too. Continue full sail and signal all ships to close in. Reduce spread to five hundred yards and stand by for engagement and boarding action."

"Think it will come to that, sir?" Riddell asked.

"If they don't heave to when I order it, then yes."

-

"Four ships now in view, sir," someone called. "Two cruisers and two frigates. Flying Kingdom colors!" he sounded excited now.

"Ships... all ships in view are hoisting the same signals sir; heave to and prepare to be boarded." Hart lowered his glass and looked as Chastain. "Sir, what-"

"Ignore it," Chastain ordered brusquely. "Signal the others to do the same. Stay this course."

"Sir, those ships are flying an admiral's pennant," Hart pointed out. "If we don't-"

"Stay this course I said!" Chastain yelled. "Do I have to say everything twice!"

-

"They are not obeying signals, sir," Riddell reported. "Continuing under full sail."

"Run them down, Mister Riddell," David ordered calmly. "Lower the signals, add Admiral Semmes pennant to them and hoist them again."

"Aye sir."

-

"Sir, the signals are being repeated this time with Admiral Semmes personal pennant," Hart reported. "We have to-"

"We have to do nothing!" Chastain spat back, eyes almost wild. "We don't answer to Semmes!"

"Sir?" Hart looked incredulous, which was fair since that was how he felt.

"I said cont-"

"Seasnake and Seadragon are falling from formation sir!" a lookout called.

"What?!" Chastain screamed. "Signal them to return to formation at once!"

"They're ignoring signals, sir," a pasty face lieutenant reported seconds later. "Falling astern of us, collecting sails."

"Fire a shot across their bows!" Chastain ordered. No one moved.

"I said-"

"You've said enough," Major Guilford's voice cut through Chastain's screech. The irrational Commodore whirled to face the upstart Marine-

To find himself facing three marines with pikes while others casually covered the sailors on deck with arbalests.

"Commander, I suggest you drop sail and obey the signals being given us by Admiral Semmes," Guilford said calmly.

"Right," Hart nodded firmly. "Drop sail!" he called. "Prepare to heave to! All personnel to topside and in formation! Double time!"

Sailors ran from everywhere on the ship, pulling wind from sails and dropping the tension on them, pulling the sails in and allowing the Halifax to slow toward a full stop.

"Commodore, allow me to show you the hospitality of the chains you offered me earlier, you traitorous sack of shit," Guilford's voice was like frost.

"I'll have you hung for this," Chastain seethed even as two burly Marines took him by the arms and guided him toward the lower decks.

"Then we'll hang together, I'm sure," Guilford nodded. "Get him out of my sight," he ordered his men. As they took the deposed Commodore below decks, Guilford looked at Hart.

"We'll probably be lucky not to be hung," he said casually.

"No shit."

-

"Ships are heaving to, sir," Riddell reported. "Frigates falling astern. Halifax slower in responding but they are now."

"Detail one of our frigates to each of theirs," David ordered. "Order Warrior to take Halifax on the starboard, we'll take port. Close and grapple."

"Aye, sir!"

-

"Eastern Fleet arriving!" the Chief of the Halifax bellowed. "Render honors port!"

The entire company of the Halifax snapped to attention, saluting crisply. David returned it only after a long pause, just long enough to show his displeasure. He turned to see a commander he didn't recognize.

"Where is Commodore Chastain?" he asked quietly.

"The Commodore is currently being held in the ship's brig, sir," Hart replied, his voice calm.

"Is that so?" David raised an eyebrow. Even as he spoke an entire company of Royal Marines were coming aboard and surrounding the crew and Marines of the Halifax.

"I'm afraid the Commodore has suffered some kind of... something," Hart actually shrugged. "He refused to obey your signals and then actually ordered a shot fired on our frigates when they did obey. At that point Major Guilford and I... relieved the Commodore of his command."

"Pity you didn't do that when he was committing treason, Commander," David's voice was scathing.

"We weren't aware he was committing treason sir," Hart replied. "Even after we had our suspicions, we had no proof. As it is we've already committed an act that might be considered mutiny."

David said nothing else. Hart had a point. Naval hierarchy and discipline were rigid and inflexible. Chastain would have had the power and the right to execute anyone who refused to carry out any order not clearly illegal. In the face of a reported or suspected coup attempt, how does one decide what to follow?

"Your men are all under arrest," he told Hart finally. "All three of your ships will be crewed with prize crews and returned to Savannah where you will no doubt stand trial for your crimes. Speaking of which, where is Prince Therron?"

-

"Do you wish to stop for lunch, sir?" the Marine Lieutenant in charge of Therron's escort asked.

"No," Therron shook his head as he tried to get comfortable in his saddle. There had been no carriage available to him in Port Winton, leaving him no choice but to ride. While he had ridden often, he had never done so day following day. The back-country trails they were following had never been maintained as well as even minor trade routes in the more central parts of the Kingdom. To say the going was rough was the height of understatement. He didn't know which hurt worse at the moment, his ass or his legs.

"No, we'll eat in the saddle," he ordered. "We have no time to waste, Lieutenant. Every minute we delay is a minute more that my brother has to secure his power base. We are in a race to prevent the ruin of the Kingdom. We must hurry."

"Aye, sir."

Securing horses and gear had not been difficult once they had made landfall. Therron had simply seized the horses and supplies he needed as an act of the Crown with no effort made at all to provide payment or recompense of any kind.

This was their third day in the saddle, galloping for the Coastal city of Norfok. They pushed the poor-quality horses as hard as they dared, stopping to walk them only when necessity demanded it. They rode until the last dregs of light were gone from the sky and then made a rough camp, rising before dawn to be back in the saddle as soon as it was light enough to see. This was the fourth day of such travel so far and the wear was beginning to show on both man and beast.

But Therron refused to slow. He had only a narrow window of opportunity here because of Chastain's refusal to kill the men of the Inspector General's command that had kept him prisoner. By now word of Therron's 'rescue' would have reached the Capital and his father would be moving heaven and earth to get him back or else kill him.

Every second now was precious.

-

"All ships signaling ready to get under way, sir," Riddell reported.

"Very well," David nodded. "Best speed to Savannah. Maintain formation."

Chastain was in chains beneath the command deck of the Ocoee and would remain there until they returned to Savannah. It wasn't lost on David that the strength of his command had just been increased by a third with the acquisition of Chastain's ships, but his mission had to be considered a failure. Prince Therron McLeod was loose in the interior of the Kingdom, and now on his way overland to the Coastal Capital of Norfok.

There was no way to stop him now. Whatever he had planned, he would be able to accomplish it without further interruption. The Kingdom already at war, marred by scandal and murder of their Sovereign, by regicide and patricide no less, now faced yet another threat.

Silently and only to himself, David wondered if Soulan would survive.

CHAPTER EIGHT

-

Tinker was not surprised when Parno McLeod appeared at the Hogshead Inn. He was not overly surprised that Jaelle had not returned. But the pensive look on the Prince's face made him worry something had happened to her.

"Milord," Tinker said as Berry took Parno's horse and led it toward the stables. Two of Parno's escort remained behind while others led their own mounts, but they maintained a respectful distance.

"What brings you to see me today, and looking so... anxious?" Tinker asked. "Has anything happened to-"

"No, she's fine," Parno shook his head as he took a seat at a table on the far edge of the porch. Tinker sat down across from him. Seconds later Briel appeared as if by magic and set two beers before them before disappearing back inside.

"You look like a man with trouble," Tinker said after each man taken a pull from the glasses.

"I should look like a man with nothing but trouble," Parno corrected.

"I am sorry for such misfortune, milord," Tinker said sincerely. "I sense Jaelle has become one of those problems," he said rather than asked.

"Not in the way you mean," Parno shook his head. "She's a wonderful girl and a joy to be around."

"But?" Tinker said when Parno offered nothing else.

"It's not safe for her to be so close to me, Tinker," Parno said softly and the older man nodded his understanding.

"Only you would take that into consideration where such a beautiful and willing woman was concerned I think, milord," Tinker raised his glass in salute.

"Everyone keeps saying that," Parno shook his head. "I told her she needed to come back here, and to stay away from me. Stay here with the people she considers family. Stay away from me so she doesn't become a target. I thought she had accepted that, but then an hour or so ago she all but begged me to let her stay." He paused, looking at the older man carefully.

"Tinker, it's not that I don't want her to stay," he said finally. "It's just that..."

"You care about her," Tinker finished for him. "You care about her and now you are worried that because you do that she is in danger."

"Yes," Parno nodded firmly. "I don't want her hurt, but I don't want to hurt her myself, either. And no matter how much I might wish it were different, anyone close to me is a target. That would especially include a woman close to me, and more especially a woman close to me in this camp."

"What do you want of me, my Prince?" Tinker asked him. "Do you want me to order her return?"

"No," Parno shook his head. "No, that would be just as bad. And it wouldn't be fair to you. But do you have any idea why she would think that beside me is where she is supposed to be? Why she would be almost frantic to stay there?"

Tinker's face suddenly looked wooden, devoid of emotion.

"Please tell me what she said exactly," he said at last.

"She said she didn't know why but she had to be near me," Parno shrugged.

"I asked you to tell me exactly what she said, milord," Tinker told him. "I need to know exactly."

Startled by Tinker's sudden intensity, Parno struggled to recall the exact conversation.

"She said she couldn't explain it, but that she knew... she knew that was where she belonged. Then she added it was where she must be."

Tinker finished his beer in one long, final drink, then stood.

"I cannot help you," he said abruptly. "I wish that I could," he added softly. "Your needs are beyond what I am capable of, my Prince. You must choose what you do yourself. If I could help I gladly would, but I cannot. If you will excuse me, I must go as I have things to see to."

"Wha-, Tinker! Wait a minute, now!" Parno called, but Tinker had already disappeared back inside, leaving a stunned Parno alone on the porch.

"Go and get Berry and the rest," he told one of the guards. "We're going back."

-

Inside, Tinker watched Parno leaving as he had arrived, at the head of his escort. A fine group, all hand-picked and trained to a razor's edge. Hard, loyal, unforgiving. Good men to face a storm with.

"Jaelle, my sweet child," he whispered. "Be sure. Be content. Be fulfilled. If not in this life, then surely in the next." He said it almost like a prayer. Suddenly he was moving, burning pent up energy as quickly as he could.

No one bothered him, having seen this in him on other rare occasions.

-

Parno returned to his headquarters to find a few reports waiting for his signature and he read them more to have something to do than because he cared what they said. He realized in a dim part of his mind that he was allowing his personal life and problems to intrude into his duties. But he didn't honestly know what to do about it. All he knew was that he was definitely going to have to do something.

"Milord?" Harrel Sprigs' voice cut through his ruminations and he looked up.

"You have a visitor, sir," Sprigs said formally.

"Who?"

"Lady Stephanie, sir," Sprigs was careful to keep his voice neutral once again.

"See her in," Parno sighed. He had told Edema to send her to him after all. He could hardly be upset that she was here now.

This day just keeps getting better, doesn't it?

"Lady Stephanie milord," Sprigs announced, holding the entrance open for her. As soon as she entered Sprigs disappeared, leaving the two looking at one another.

"Well, sit down," Parno said finally, pointing to an empty chair. "Can I get you anything?" he asked, trying to be polite.

"No, thank you," she shook her head as she sat down. Parno joined her, but behind his desk, not beside her. The two sat in silence for a moment.

"I came to tell you I am sorry," Stephanie finally almost blurted. "My words... my actions, the last night we saw each other were... ill-advised," she settled for saying, fighting for a way to keep at least some pride.

"Ill-advised, huh?" Parno fought to keep any disapproving tone from his voice, but 'ill-advised' wasn't much of an apology.

"I was scared," Stephanie kept going now that she had started. "I was afraid that you wouldn't come back. I let that cloud my judgment and... that led me to say things I didn't really mean in an effort to... to punish you for not doing what I wanted," she admitted at last, rushing the last sentence out in one long, rambling and broken stream.

"Punish me," Parno repeated. It seemed as if he was weighing her words.

"Hurt you," she clarified. "I was hurt by your refusal and I... I wanted to strike back."

"It worked," Parno nodded as he leaned back in his chair. Her face went red at the short come back but she kept her head up.

"I would like to think we can still at least be civil to one another," her voice was almost bitter.

"I feel fairly confident I have at no time been anything other than civil,

Doctor," Parno replied evenly, using her title rather than her name, as she had done when addressing him. He could tell it stung her, but he was not going to give any ground until she got to the point.

They simply looked at one another for what seemed to be a long time before she gave in and spoke again.

"I have to know," she said softly. "Parno, was there ever a time when you loved me? When you wanted, truly wanted to marry me?"

"More than anything," he broke eye contact at that, nodding as he looked down. "Looking forward to that time was what I used to keep me going," he refused to lie. "When I didn't think I could go any further or take any more, when I was so deathly sick of this war, when I didn't think I could stand to send even one more man to his death, I remembered what I was doing it all for in the first place. What I was fighting for. I was fighting for a time when you and I could live in peace, together, and hopefully have a good life together. I prayed for it at night when I laid down. It was my one great hope. What kept me getting up each morning." He stopped abruptly, looking up as if realizing he had said too much.

Silent tears were streaming down her face now as she listened, still and quiet.

"So yes," he finished. "I loved you with all I had. You were the only person I have ever done that with. You were the first, and you will be the last. I can't do it again. Go through it again. I won't."

"I am so sorry," she finally said softly. "I am so very, very sorry Parno. If I had one wish I would take it all back and make it like it never happened. I swear it. I hope that one day you can forgive me."

"I already have," he told her, careful to keep his voice cool. He wasn't offering her any false hope. "I can't carry that around with me. It would cripple me. I made a mistake, that's all. But I'll learn from it, and be stronger for it, one day. So, don't let it weigh you down. Let it go and forget it. I forgive you, completely and without reservation."

She wanted to go to him but realized from his body language that he wouldn't accept her. Not anymore.

"What do we do now?" she asked instead.

"You go home in the morning," Parno said at once. "Go back to the Palace and being Memmnon's doctor and I guess teaching or whatever you choose to do. What you do is up to you. You get to choose."

"And you?" she asked.

"I don't get a choice," he replied. "I have to stay here and try to find a way to win an unwinnable war."

"That's not what I meant, Parno," her voice was strained.

"That's all there is now, Doctor," he refused to use her name. Deep down he felt like he was being childish in some way but he couldn't help it. He wasn't going to open himself up to her again. He couldn't.

"So, that's it then," she nodded, getting slowly to her feet. "I make one mistake and we're done."

"It was my mistake, not yours," he told her gently. "Go home. Build a life you can enjoy and be happy with. I... I'll try and make sure you get the chance to do that," he stood as well. "I wish you a safe journey home. I hope your travels go easier than the trip up did."

"Don't just stand there like nothing is happening," she told him. "I came here pouring my heart out to you and asking your forgiveness. And this is all you can give me?"

"I told you I forgive you," Parno tried to sound reasonable. "I don't know what else to say. I don't know what you want me to say. I don't know much of anything anymore," he admitted suddenly. "I can't do this. I can't be so confused. I have too much riding on me. Too many decisions to make. I need a clear head to do it. It's better this way."

"Does the serving girl give you a clear head?" she couldn't help herself.

"Good evening, Doctor," Parno settled for saying rather than sniping back at her. "Captain Sprigs will show you to your tent. Harrel!"

"I know the way," Stephanie told him.

"And it's dark in the middle of an army camp," Parno nodded as Sprigs appeared.

"Sir?"

"Have someone show the lady to her quarters please," Parno said politely. "Good bye, Doctor. I wish you well."

She didn't say anything else as she left, though she did stop and look back at him once from the door. He was already back to looking over the paperwork spread across his desk. She stood there for a minute, knowing that he was aware she was looking at him, but he never looked up.

"Milady?" Sprigs reminded her he was there and she stepped outside. A young trooper wearing the Regiment's colors was waiting and followed at a discreet distance as she walked in silence back to her tent.

Sprigs watched her go before entering the tent once more.

"Milord, your supper is ready in your tent," Harrel Sprigs announced softly.

"Is she still there?" Parno asked, knowing already the answer.

"She has not left since she returned," Sprigs nodded. "I took the liberty of posting two members of the Regiment on guard. Just... in case. A similar guard is set on Lady Willows and Miss Stephanie as well, by her escort."

"Okay," Parno sighed. "Is there any reason I can't retire for the evening?" he asked.

"None that has been brought to my attention, milord," Sprigs replied.

"Then I suppose I'm going to go eat and then try to rest," Parno told him. "Tomorrow has to be better, right?"

"I'm sure today will look differently tomorrow, sir," Sprigs settled for saying.

"You could have just agreed with me," Parno muttered. Sprigs smiled into the growing dark but said nothing else. He looked at the four men following the Prince and laid a finger alongside his nose then shook his head. The Sergeant in charge of the detail nodded and began posting his men around the Prince.

Sprigs decided he would work out and then get some rest himself. Being Prince Parno's assistant could be truly exhausting at times.

-

"Hello, my Prince," Jaelle said softly as Parno stepped inside his large wall tent. The interior was lit with several candles and there was a sweet-smelling fragrance in the air that he thought he knew but couldn't recognize.

"Jaelle," he smiled. "How was your day?"

"I should be asking you that," she said as she helped him out of his jacket. "You have had a very hard day if I am not mistaken. And I have been part of that which made it such a hard day," she said apologetically. "Please do not be angry with me."

"I doubt I could ever be angry with you," Parno admitted with a silent laugh, then kissed her forehead. She hugged him close, just holding him for a moment.

"Jaelle, why would Tinker suddenly tell me he can't do anything for me when I told him what you had said?" Parno asked. She pulled away from him at that, looking up slightly into his eyes.

"What did you ask him?"

"I was just looking for advice," Parno shrugged. "Your sudden insistence that you be allowed to stay with me even knowing it was so dangerous, and that I wanted you to go back, it confused me. He knows you better than I do so I figured I would ask him what to do."

"What did he say?" her head tilted slightly to one side as she continued to look at him.

"When I told him what you said he just got up and said he couldn't help, though he wished he could, and that was that. He left me sitting there and went inside."

"I see," Jaelle nodded. "He has simply allowed me to make my own choice in this matter," she told him. "Had he ordered me to return I would have been almost honor bound to do so. Did you ask him to do that?"

"No," Parno shook his head. "I didn't think it would be fair to him or to you. I wasn't trying to get someone else to do it for me, just... I was just trying to understand."

"Some things cannot be understood, my lovely Prince," Jaelle whispered. "You must not try. And surely there is some way Jaelle can comfort you after such a difficult day," she kissed him softly. When Parno didn't immediately respond she looked up at him, curious.

"Is it because of her?"

"Huh?" Parno was caught by complete surprise at that.

"Is it because of her presence that you do not wish me to be here?" Jaelle asked.

"You mean because of Stephanie?"

"Is that her name?" she asked. It dawned on Parno he'd never told Jaelle either of their names.

"Yes, that is her name, and no, her presence doesn't influence anything between you and I," he shook his head.

"Then stop brooding my Prince, and allow Jaelle to care for you," she insisted. "It is little enough that I can do for you. Allow me to do it."

"Why do you keep saying that?" he asked. "That it's little enough that you can do?"

"Because it is all that I have," she said, her voice happy despite the conversation. "What I have I give you freely."

Parno was confused to say the least. What had he done to deserve something like this? To have such a gentle, beautiful woman taking such good care of him? Never had anyone been so intimately kind to him, whether as a child or a teen or a young adult. Plenty of women had shared his bed, but it had never been more than a tryst to them and normally he was too drunk to care.

This was completely different and it confused him even as he was grateful for it and even aroused by it.

Even as he had that thought he suddenly realized that Jaelle had managed to strip him of his clothes while he stood there, and he was now naked.

"I have a bath prepared for you," her voice was husky.

"I don't have a... tub..." his voice trailed off as he saw a small tub in one corner of the large tent. Small yes, but a bathing tub nonetheless.

"How did you get that here?" he asked.

"A smile and thank you will often suffice where orders will not," she replied. "The water is only warm now rather than hot, but it is warm," she pushed him gently in that direction. "Allow Jaelle to care for you tonight," she almost cooed. "Tomorrow and the worry it brings will be here soon enough."

-

"I want to inspect their hospitals tomorrow," Stephanie said as she and Edema prepared for bed. "While I am here, I want to look and see if things are in good order. That will at least have made this trip productive."

"Very well," Edema nodded. "It would doubtless be a help for them to have your input."

"We should still be able to leave by mid-day or so, assuming I find no glaring problems," Stephanie continued as she brushed her long hair.

"That sounds fine."

-

"Good evening, General."

Wilson didn't start this time but his heart missed about three beats as he finished pouring his drink.

"Snort?" he asked the man in the shadows.

"No, thank you," was the humored reply. "I wanted to tell you that tomorrow might be a very good day for you to attack," 'Smith' said.

"Tomorrow?" Wilson was stunned. "Do you realize how much time and effort go into preparing an attack of that scale?"

"I do, and I'm not saying you have to. Just that tomorrow might be a good day. At the very least a large demonstration to rattle your enemy. They will very likely be confused and disoriented tomorrow. Say... after lunch, perhaps?"

"What have you done?" Wilson wanted to know.

"Nothing as yet," he could see the shadow's arms raised in a gesture of innocence. "But something could happen tomorrow. It was just a friendly warning. You know, I think I will have that drink."

"Of course," Wilson turned to his small bar and set up another glass. "So, what is it you think will happen tomorrow? I've already passed orders for one of my infantry divisions to move out on an exercise in the morning." he asked as he poured. Replacing the stopper, he turned to offer the drink to his visitor only to find that he was gone.

"Should have known," Wilson sighed. "Tomorrow, huh?"

CHAPTER NINE

-

Parno awoke long before sunrise, or even before the bugles began blaring for the Army to rise. A gentle and reassuring presence on his left arm made him smile as he remembered the previous evening. Jaelle had pampered him for much of the evening before 'ensuring' he could sleep. Even in the flickering light of the last burning candles he could see a contented smile on her beautiful face and knew his own probably had matched it.

She had to go. Today. She could not stay any longer because if he allowed her to stay again, he wouldn't be able to send her away. He was already smitten with her and he was smart enough to know it. Keeping her here would distract him as well as make her a target if she wasn't already.

He would send her back to the Inn today. After lunch maybe, when things had settled down. Certainly, before supper.

Decision made, he carefully disentangled himself from her and rose. He bathed himself quickly and then dressed for the day. By the time he had finished, bugles were sounding around the camp, rousing soldiers for another day in Army life.

"Good morning, my Prince," Jaelle's soft arms encircled him suddenly as he finished preparing his uniform.

"Morning," he turned in her embrace to kiss her. "Sleep well?"

"Very," she almost purred against his chest. "You must go, I take it?"

"You take it correctly," Parno actually chuckled. "I must go. I will see you later."

"Yes," she nodded. "Have a pleasant morning."

-

"Morning Captain," Parno said softly. Jeffrey Winters almost jumped in surprise but managed to stop at the last minute.

"Good morning, milord," he said instead.

"How is your company?" he asked.

"They would rather be here, of course, but they do their duty splendidly," Winters replied honestly.

"Still numbering what now, about sixty?" Parno asked.

"Sixty-five, including me, yes sir.

"Have a good second?" Parno asked. "One who could manage a small independent command?"

"Lieutenant Spader, sir," Winters said at once. "He's young but was with us at the Gap and fought very well. Commended twice for bravery in action."

"Sounds like just the man," Parno nodded. "When you reach the palace, I want you to split your command and send one half under Spader's command with Lady Willows. They will become her personal escort and she is to go nowhere without them. Remind him that his job is not to protect her house nor household, but her, and I will hold him responsible for her safety. Understand?"

"Yes milord," Winters nodded. "Milord, that will leave us very weak if Lady Stephanie wanted to do something such as this again," he pointed out.

"She didn't want to make this trip," Parno informed him. "I suspect she will not leave the palace much anymore save for checking on the schools she has started. But, if you see that you can't handle her schedule without help, send a courier and I will send you more help. Spader can send to Cove Canton for help if he finds himself shorthanded. I will include that in dispatches next time."

"It will be done, milord," Winters promised.

"Thanks. Please pass my appreciation to your command as well."

-

"We will be leaving shortly," Edema met Parno at his command tent, already prepared. "Stephanie wants to visit the hospitals to inspect them before she leaves. I thought that was a good idea."

"A very good idea," Parno nodded. "I wish I had thought of it. That's what I mean by distracted," he added. "My thoughts are addled and I overlook the simplest things like that."

"We will be gone before long," Edema promised with a smile.

"Tinker runs an inn near here," Parno thought to tell her. "A friend of his is running a... a..."

"I've heard the word 'brothel' before, Parno," Edema laughed at his discomfiture.

"Well, anyway, the place is a functioning inn as well. If you're late enough getting away then you could stop there for lunch before going. The food is decidedly better than ours," he chuckled.

"I may just do that," Edema nodded thoughtfully. "What are you going to do about your serving girl, dear boy?" 'Serving girl' wasn't meant as an insult this time.

"She has to go back," Parno sighed. "Tinker was notoriously close lipped about her when I appealed to him for help yesterday, but... she can't stay. No matter how much she wants to, she can't."

"My poor, precious, darling boy," Edema touched his cheek softly. "I promise you Parno, it will not always be this way."

"From your lips to God's ear," Parno smiled, catching her hand in both of his and kissing it lightly. "I'm not mad at you," he told her out of the blue. "Don't go home thinking I am. Regardless of how things turned out, you meant it well for me and that's what I care about. You are the only person in this Kingdom that cares about what is good for me. Outside this army, anyway," he added. *And Jaelle*, he didn't add.

"She cares for you too, Parno," Edema shook her head. "I know that the damage is likely permanent, but remember that she loves you desperately. That desperation was what led to all this. She has cried herself to sleep every night I have spent at her side. I have heard her praying when she thought I was asleep, and she prays most of all for your safety and then that you will forgive her and take her back. I'm not trying to influence you," she held up a hand to forestall his comment. "I'm simply giving you information, as I did long ago." She paused.

"Only it wasn't so long ago, really. Was it?" It was more of a statement than a question as she remembered when she had been one of Parno's 'spies'.

"No, it wasn't," he agreed. "A lot has passed since then and much has changed. But I still love you as I would have loved her," he kissed Edema's forehead and hugged her gently. "You are the only mother I have even known, Edema Willows. Take the love of a son with you as you travel."

"You ridiculous boy," Edema hastily wiped a tear away. "You'll make me look a fright."

"You're the most beautiful woman here or anywhere," Parno smiled at her own discomfiture. "It was wonderful to see you, even under these circumstances."

"You look fit and healthy," Edema nodded. "I could not ask for more than that. Do not risk yourself so much, dear child."

"I'm not allowed to," Parno laughed.

"Good-bye my boy. Be safe and be well," she kissed his cheek.

"You too."

-

Parno's morning was usually spent reading reports that had no true bearing on anything to do with the actual fighting of the war. True, worry over supply, troop dispositions, gear allocations and all the rest were important, but there were a great many things that he just didn't think demanded his level of attention.

This morning was a little different. Another Imperial infantry division was apparently on the move at first light this morning, moving west along the same trail that the first had followed. Parno sent for Doak Parsons, who was there in less than fifteen minutes.

"Do you have a man tracking them?" he held up report of the moving Imperials.

"Three," Parsons nodded. "I think General Davies is correct, sir. This smells like an exercise, and like it's designed to get and keep our attention. And it's working if you think about it."

"How so?" Parno asked.

"Sir, we've got three of our best cavalry divisions in the field now, shadowing that first bunch," Parsons reminded him.

"Very true," Parno mused. "I need to think that one over. Please make sure that we don't lose contact with this second group."

"Will do, milord."

-

Stephanie walked slowly through the large collection of tenting and rough buildings that represented Army Field Hospital Eleven. She had visited two others already where former students of her school were doing very good work. Here she was equally pleased with what she found.

"Good, clean conditions, proper sterilization of instruments and supplies, and proper disposal of blood-soaked bandages and clothing. I notice there are very few amputations," she turned to the wiry young physician following her.

"No, milady," he agreed. "The few you do see are usually a result of battle injury. Your treatment techniques have allowed us to save many limbs that Army Surgeons in the past would have amputated without thought. Most of these men will be able to fight another day thanks in great part to your teaching."

"That is wonderful to hear," Stephanie said gratefully. "Not that they will have to fight, but that they will still be able bodied. You've done well. No, you've done very well. Outstanding."

"Thank you, milady."

-

Parno looked up at the knocking of the framed entrance of his tent, expecting to see Sprigs.

"Yes Harrel."

"I am not Harrel, milord," Jaelle smiled at him. "I assumed you would pay no attention to the time, and I know you didn't eat breakfast, so I have taken the liberty of bringing you lunch," she held up a plate in either hand.

"You're right, I didn't pay attention," Parno laughed lightly. His stomach growled just then and Jaelle laughed along with him.

"Come in and join me," he motioned her over. She gladly moved to his table/desk and sat down with him to eat.

-

Harrel Sprigs was an extremely intelligent young man. It was that intelligence that had seen Darvo Nidiad single him out of the application process when the Black Sheep were still just an unnamed penal regiment and make him Parno's secretary. Harrel was not a criminal nor a washout soldier but merely a young man who wanted to serve.

His education was continued in the regiment, though along a different track. Cho Feng had taken the young man as a student and had taught him several combat techniques for use with weapons or in bare handed combat. As he progressed in skill, Darvo and Cho had agreed that he was a good candidate for a bodyguard that could get close to Parno without arousing the young Prince's suspicion. He didn't like to be 'coddled'.

Harrel had become Parno's shadow and was all but indispensable to the Lord Marshal. His education had made him perfect for what he did in that regard and his training, done mostly in secret, had prepared him for his secondary and what Darvo considered his primary role.

Protect Parno McLeod.

It was that young man that was near Parno's tent when the first courier arrived.

-

"Three couriers arriving sir," an aide announced. "All Royal couriers, milord. One from Shelby, one from Nasil, the other from Savannah."

"All at once," Parno frowned.

"Apparently so, milord," the aide nodded. "Should I allow them entrance?"

"Yes, of course," Parno nodded, chewing one final bite of his unfinished lunch. Before he could tell Jaelle she should go, three men dressed as Royal Couriers stepped inside the tent. None of the three noticed Harrel Sprigs step inside behind them.

"So, gentlemen, I understand you have all traveled a very long way," Parno smiled.

"Yes sir," one dust-covered courier agreed. "I have urgent news for you,"

"As do I," another stated. "Very important message," he stepped forward reaching into his bag even as the third, who had not spoken yet, did the same. He spoke as he reached the desk.

"Assassins!" he heard someone yell. Even as that alarm was called out the last messenger to speak reached him.

"My Emperor demands your death," the man hissed and lunged across the desk, a wicked dagger in his hand.

Parno was caught by complete surprise. It had never occurred to him, even once, that someone would be able to impersonate a Royal Courier, let alone three of them.

What fools we are, he thought, as the dagger came toward his chest.

-

Harrel Sprigs' sixth sense was already screaming at him when three couriers arrived at once. He knew there was something wrong about them but couldn't place it. He kept watching their horses as they were led away, knowing somehow that the clue was there but unable to drag it forth. That sixth sense made him follow the three men into Parno's presence.

He eased in behind them without the three even knowing he was there and examined them carefully.

He noticed it just as the second one to speak stepped forward. There was a slit on the back of his jacket. Not much of one really, but it was there nevertheless. That alone would not arouse his suspicions, but the blood stain beneath it did.

"Assassins!" he yelled at the top of his lungs even as the startled man in front of him turned, dagger in hand.

-

Jaelle had kept back at first, realizing that whatever news these men brought was not for her and she had no part or parcel in this business. As the three men stepped forward, she saw Harrel enter behind them, his face a mask of concern. It was then that she realized this was a scene she had observed before.

She closed her eyes for a brief second, her lips moving in prayer, then opened them to watch this play out for the final time.

-

Parno became aware of several things at once even as events played out before him as if in slow motion. First, of course, was the courier coming at him with what looked like a krishank knife. The analytical part of his mind remembered from his training that this was the favored blade of the Imperial Secret Police Special Missions Directorate. It was essentially a hand-held harpoon, with only one real use. They were assassins.

The second was that there was a fight already occurring in the tent somewhere. It had sounded like Harrel's voice that had raised the alarm, leaving Parno to suspect that one of the assassins was killing the secretary.

The last thing he became aware of before he fell was another body coming between him and the assassin's knife.

-

Jaelle leaped from her chair in such a fluid movement that one would think she had practiced it. Without any hesitation whatever she threw herself in front of Parno McLeod, her face almost touching his. She jerked suddenly even as his arms closed around her by instinct as they fell. Her face was frozen in a combination of a painful grimace and a slight smile.

The assassin's blade had struck her in the middle of the back instead of taking Parno in the heart.

"M... my Prince," she whispered then screamed when the blade was abruptly and violently jerked free.

-

Harrel faced the man before him with confidence his appearance didn't justify. He recognized the terrible weapon in the man's hand and realized at once that this wasn't the workings of Therron McLeod but was instead a true act of Norland aggression. These men where Imperial assassins.

The assassin facing him was over confident and took a lazy stab at Harrel, expecting a mere secretary to be easy meat.

The 'easy meat' deflected the blade without difficulty with his left arm even as the web of right hand buried itself in the assassin's throat with a sharp jab. Gasping for air, the assassin managed to grab Harrel's arm on his way to the ground.

The second assassin took advantage of that, sinking his dagger into the exposed back of the secretary. Harrel felt the knife enter his body and knew he had to prevent it from being withdrawn or it would kill him before he could defend his Prince.

Twisting in a windmill motion, Harrel managed to throw the weight of the first assassin off of his left arm as his right knocked the second assassin's hand away from the hilt of the blade. Pain shot through the young man as the knife in his back was jolted by the motion, but he kept turning.

As he faced the man who had stabbed him, he realized that the last assassin was lunging at his Prince. Unable to prevent it without getting rid of the man facing him, Harrel drew his own knife. The assassin had produced another of the nasty krishank blades and came at him with the blade held in a downward grip best made for stabbing.

But not the best for fighting.

Harrel's blade blocked the first swing in a shower of sparks but the assassin had expected that and merely changed the direction of his swing as soon as the blades made contact. The assassin was trained in a method of knife use that was said to be much older than the Empire, and that method had never failed.

Unfortunately for the assassin, he was facing a student of Cho Feng, a master of both armed and unarmed combat. A favored student who was the recipient of a great deal of knowledge, learned the hard way.

Harrel's knife changed direction as well, slicing back down the arm of the assassin's knife hand. The razor-sharp blade easily carved a slab of meat from the assassin's arm, eliciting a surprised scream of pain from him and forcing him to drop his knife. His left hand was waiting and caught the blade, instantly ripping it in a cross slash against Harrel's midsection in an attempt to make him back away.

His own left hand now free, Harrel grabbed the wrist of the hand that now gripped the assassin's blade and forced it down. As he did that, his right hand turned his own blade horizontal and pushed it into the left side of the assassin's chest. As soon as the hilt struck flesh, Harrel ripped the blade across, the razor edge slicing the assassin's heart and part of his left lung.

The look on the man's face was one of stunned disbelief as he fell, blood already bubbling from his open mouth. Harrel, gasping for air himself now, turned to the last assassin.

-

"M... my Prince."

Parno was speechless. Things had happened so fast. One minute he had been having lunch and now... now Jaelle was in his arms, blood streaming from her mouth.

He was dimly aware of the assassin standing over them, but there was nothing he could do. Pinned beneath Jaelle's limp form, Parno had no weapon on his person. He turned, trying to move himself from beneath Jaelle so that he could fight back, but suddenly the assassin was gone.

The attack was... over?

-

Harrel Sprigs saw the last assassin looming over the prince, with Jaelle between them. He realized at once what had happened and was suddenly filled with a terrible rage that he had never felt before. Without thinking he grabbed the remaining assassin and pulled him back, away from the prince and his woman.

Surprised, the assassin nevertheless recovered quickly and twisted to confront his attacker.

With a scream of pure, primal rage erupting from his damaged lungs, Harrel used his left arm to block the assassin's arms down and away while his own blade came up, already coated in blood.

Without the need for conscious thought Harrel brought his blade across him, horizontal and with the edge pointed away. Then with a slashing motion that began in his shoulder he pulled that edge across, aiming for the assassin's exposed throat.

On anyone else it would have worked, but this was not just anyone. The highly trained assassin managed to pull his head back the instant before the slash landed, resulting in a severe cut across his throat below his jaw but preventing the life ending slash Harrel had intended it to be.

The assassin raised his right foot and kicked Harrel's left leg, using that impetus to force the young soldier back. Surprised at the failure of his move against his enemy, Harrel was caught off guard by the kick and stumbled back, staggering three steps backward before he could stop himself.

The assassin was charging before Harrel managed to stop himself, blade once more held in an overhand grip designed to stab rather than cut. Harrel raised his arms as if trying to block the move, but at the very last second grasped the arm plunging the blade toward him and twisted, pulling with all his might as he stepped inside the swing, back now to his attacker.

It was the assassin that was caught by surprise this time as he went flying over the right shoulder of his target and slammed into the ground hard enough to force the air from his lungs. As he was being flung across Harrel's shoulder, however, the assassin's knee hit the dagger still buried in the young secretary's back, almost blinding him as dark spots caused by the pain danced in his vision.

On his last legs and knowing it, Harrel didn't hesitate. His grip on the knife changed in one fluid motion, turning to an overhand grip similar to what the assassin had been using, edge facing back. With no pause in his motion Harrel plunged the blade into the assassin's stomach and fairly ripped the blade back toward himself.

The assassin's body was cut open from his navel to his sternum. Blood rushed from the hideous wound that left organs exposed and, in some cases, sliced apart.

The assassin had been eviscerated.

It was the first still moment in what seemed like a lifetime. Harrel was gasping for air as he managed to get to his feet using the pole near the door to pull himself up, leaving a trail of blood all the way up the pole.

Heaving for air, Harrel staggered toward his prince.

"M... milord, are y... are you alri... right?"

-

Parno, aware that the assassin was gone, looked down at Jaelle. Her eyes were open and she appeared to be smiling,

"Why did you do that?" Parno almost cried.

"W... where I am sp... sup... posed to be... my Prince," she tried to touch his face but couldn't manage it, her small hand falling limp between them.

"M... my Prince, I... I lo...," she managed to gasp, and then she was gone.

"Jaelle?" he shook her, trying to get her awake again. "Jaelle!"

But there was no answer.

"M... milord, are y... are you alri... right?" Harrel asked.

Alright? No, he wasn't alright. He doubted he would ever be alright again.

"Mil... milord?" Harrel tried again, even as other soldiers began streaming into the tent, guards that had been too far away to take part in the fight.

"Mil... lord, I th... think I..." and with that Harrel fell over onto the desk and for the first time Parno realized how badly injured his secretary was as he saw the hilt of a krishank sticking out of his back.

"Don't touch it!" Parno yelled as one man went to pull the knife from his back. "Get a surgeon in here! And send runners to every hospital! Lady Stephanie is still here somewhere! Find her and get her here as soon as possible! MOVE!" he screamed and soldiers tripped over themselves to get out of the tent and start obeying.

"We have to keep him face down, so we have to make sure he can breathe," Parno told two soldiers that had stayed.

"Milord, we need to get you-"

"This man and woman just saved my life," Parno said thickly. "If you think for a second I'm leaving him you are delusional. Now get blankets and roll one up to put to either side of his head! We need to keep his head elevated and still make sure he can breathe!"

"Sir," the man nodded and ran to find one of the boards used to ferry wounded to the hospitals.

"You," Parno grabbed the remaining soldier and pulled him close. "You stay with him no matter what, you understand me? No, matter, what! That," he pointed to the hilt sticking from Harrel's back, "is a krishank blade of an Imperial assassin. It can only be removed by Lady Stephanie. If anyone else tries, you stop them if you have to run them through. Understand?"

"Yes sire!" the man stammered. "I will do so!"

Patting the soldier on the shoulder, Parno stumbled back to where Jaelle's body was lying on the floor of the tent, her blood flowing quickly into the hard ground.

"Why?" he slumped to the ground. "Why didn't you just go home?"

CHAPTER TEN

-

Stephanie had just ended her tour of what had been the very first field hospital at the camp, finding the conditions there much worse than in others.

"The worst cases are brought here, milady," the physician in charge explained. "Also, we use this as a primary evaluation center for most of the seriously wounded. We have three such evaluation hospitals, of which this is the central one."

"A triage in other words," Stephanie nodded.

"Yes, exactly," the physician nodded. "We try to keep similar wounds grouped together, using the personnel that are best in treating that particular type of wound to staff that particular field hospital. Each section of the line is supported by an evaluation center that has several individual hospitals assigned to it for transfer of patients once they are evaluated."

"Do you not lose time that way? Treating the wounds, I mean?" Stephanie asked, intrigued by the idea.

"We do," the man nodded sadly. "But we keep the evaluation centers over staffed to try and stabilize wounds until we can send them to the proper field area for treatment. While we do fail in some instances, recovery statistics have shown this method to be better overall compared to simply having wounded from everywhere taken to whatever hospital is closer. When we do that, hospitals near the worst fighting become inundated and thus we lose patients due to a lack of personnel on site to treat them all. We have people on staff here and at the other centers whose only job is to keep up with how many patients have been sent where for treatment. In this way we avoid overcrowding any one hospital and the staff working there. We also are able in that way to get particular wounds to the surgeons and physicians that are best able to deal with those wounds."

"I'm very intrigued by this, Doctor..." she realized she couldn't remember being introduced to him.

"Bartram, milady," the doctor smiled. "Richard Bartram, at your service."

"Doctor, I'd like to incorporate this idea into the training we are giving future Army surgeons and physicians," Stephanie told him. "Can you prepare a report for me detailing how you organized this method, and what made you think of it? Such innovative thinking is how we will save more lives."

"I'd be glad to, milady," Bartram nodded. "I'll try and prepare it for you in the next few days and forward it to you. Where should I send it?'

"When it's prepared have it sent to Prince Parno's headquarters to be included in dispatches sent to the Palace," Stephanie instructed. "I am now the Royal Physician so that is where my main office is located and we have established two new schools in the Royal City specifically for training field surgeons and military nurses. I also have a school at Cove Canton that trains field surgeons so it will be taught there as well."

"We have several of your graduates here on staff," Bartram nodded. "I must tell you that their training has saved countless lives and limbs milady. A brilliant piece of training that is."

"Thank you," Stephanie blushed under the praise. "But it was actually Prince Parno's idea to establish the school. He merely requested that I do it. I took his idea and made it real. He deserves as much credit as I do."

"He is an excellent Marshal," Bartram surprised her. "He visits the hospitals regularly checking on the wellbeing of his men. Another of the reasons they respect him so."

"He is a good man," Stephanie felt herself getting emotional and knew she needed to end this. "Please send me your report as soon as possible, Doctor. I look forward to reading it and implementing it into our education system. This... you have done remarkably well. To say I'm impressed is an understatement."

"High praise indeed from someone of your lineage, milady," the man smiled.

"I must go, but thank you for your time," Stephanie shook his hand.

"Farewell, milady."

Stephanie walked outside into the warming sun where the carriage was waiting, Edema sitting inside, reading.

"Are you ready to go, dear?" she asked kindly.

"I think so," Stephanie nodded. "It was a valuable visit. I have learned much that I-" she stopped suddenly as a thundering horse approached the carriage from the back. The rider was wearing the livery of the Black Sheep so her escort didn't stop him but watched warily.

"Lady Stephanie, ma'am, beggin' your pardon but there was an attack on the

Prince and he has requested your presence as quickly as you can, milady!"

"What?" Stephanie and Edema echoed on another.

"Get aboard, ma'am," Winters gently ordered. "We have to go." He helped her up and was yelling instructions before the door was secured.

"Get turned around and make best speed to the Prince's Headquarters!" he bellowed as he literally leaped into his own saddle. "Run down anyone who doesn't yield! GO!"

The runner turned to go before them, yelling for a clear road and for everyone to make way. Inside the coach, Stephanie was already going through her bag, mind racing as she tried to separate her duty as a physician with her worry over Parno.

"If Parno asked for you then he is at least alive and conscious," Edema said softly. She was trying to encourage them both.

"Yes," Stephanie nodded. "I should have told them to prepare a place for me to work at that hospital, but... there are closer places I'm sure."

"You may not even need one," Edema was trying to find anything to keep their hopes up. "He may have asked for you simply because he trusts you."

"Or because I'm the Royal Physician," Stephanie nodded. "It sounds as if he was alright enough to make decisions, at least."

They fell silent as the coach bounced its way along the dusty dirt road leading to where Parno was waiting.

-

"Milord."

Karls was standing over Parno who was holding Jaelle in his arms, a stunned look on his face.

"Hey, this one's still alive!" someone called. Enri Willard turned to see one of the assassins moving on the floor.

"Take him and secure him somewhere out of here!!" Enri ordered, taking charge as Parno's Chief of Staff. "I want a minimum of four guards on him and make sure they're from the Regiment!"

"Yes sir," the man nodded, moving to secure the living assassin.

"And get the rest of this trash out of here," Enri added to another soldier as he pointed to the two dead assassins. With a nod the man began grabbing passing soldiers to assist in removing the dead.

"No one gets near him from now on that we don't know personally!" Enri yelled. "We should have been doing that all along!"

"Parno," Karls ignored his brother as he tried again to speak to his friend. "Parno, are you okay?"

"I'm not hurt," Parno assured him softly. "Bring the army to a full alert," he added. "This was an Imperial assassination attempt. If they think it was successful, they may attack. A show of readiness might stop them."

"Sound the alarm," Enri ordered a sergeant that stood by waiting for orders.

"All men to posts, prepare for attack. And have someone find General Davies at once!"

"Sir!" the man saluted and ran to carry out his orders. In less than a minute a bugle began blaring 'To Post', and it was picked up by others and repeated all through the army. In less than ten minutes the army would be ready to receive an attack should it come.

"Parno, you need to get up," Karls kept trying. "You can't keep sitting there. Let me help you."

Parno looked up at him. It was clear that now that things had calmed down, if that was the proper phrase, that he was sliding into shock. Not at his own near death, but that of Jaelle and possibly of Harrel Sprigs.

"Help me?" Parno repeated. "Everyone who helps me dies. Why would anyone want to help me?"

"Because you're important to them, Parno," Karls said gently. "Let me take her, okay?" he asked. "I'll send someone to the Inn for Tinker and let him bring someone to clean her up. Okay?"

"I... she just jumped in front of me," Parno explained, never offering to move. "How is Harrel?"

"He's breathing, but it's ragged," Karls said. "We've sent people looking for Stephanie. They should have located her by now. We've laid Harrel on your desk and tried to make him comfortable. The knife is keeping him from losing much blood from the wound, but he's bleeding from his mouth, which means he has internal injuries. I'm sure Stephanie can fix him, but Parno you have to get up. We can't move Harrel very far in his condition. She will need to try and operate on him in here. I've already got people fetching supplies and equipment for her. Now let me take her and get on your feet."

"No," Parno shook his head. "No, I'll do it." He struggled to get to his feet with Jaelle's limp form in his arms but was unable to manage it.

"Parno," Karls kept his voice soft. "Friend... brother," he said more firmly. "Let me help you. Let us all help you. We failed you today, I know, but we won't ever again, I swear to you. Just let me help you," he extended his hand. "Take my hand, brother. I'm always here for you."

Parno looked at him for a long moment but finally reached up almost timidly and took the firm grip offered him. Karls pulled him to his feet even with Jaelle still clutched to him. She wasn't very big, really.

"She's so frail," Parno said as he gathered her in his arms, princess style. "How can someone so small and so frail be so strong, Karls?" he asked.

"Her spirit is bigger than she is, brother," Karls whispered. "Come on. I'll take you to your tent and we can lay her out there. I'll send a runner to the Inn."

"Yeah," Parno nodded. "I tried to get her to go you know," Parno told him. "Tried to get her to see."

"I know," Karls kept his voice calm. "I know." He looked at his brother as he went passed.

"Send someone to 1st Corps to find Cho. He needs to be here."

"Right," Enri nodded.

-

"All divisions report on line and ready, sir," Britton Sterling reported.

"Very good," Wilson nodded. "Any sign of activity over there?" That was usually how he referred to the Soulan lines.

"They sounded the alarm shortly before we did, sir," Sterling nodded. "They're on line now, apparently at full readiness according to our scouts."

"So whatever Smith was doing failed then," Wilson mused aloud.

"Sir?"

"Nothing," Wilson hadn't realized he had spoken out loud. "Keep the men on alert for an hour or so, then begin a staggered stand down. Drop us by twenty-five percent every hour. If they don't move by then, they aren't going to, not this late in the day," he looked at the sun overhead. "I want to know the minute there's any movement in their camp outside of normal."

"Of course, General," Sterling. "Sir, if I may-"

"You may not," Wilson shook his head. "I'm sorry, but I can't tell you. Just... keep watching."

"Yes sir."

-

Tinker kept his face expressionless as the runner dressed in the Prince's livery dismounted in front of the Inn.

"Mister Tinker," the man nodded.

"You have need of me?" Tinker asked.

"I... yes sir," the man nodded. "There was an attack on the Prince not long ago, sir. Imperial assassins."

"Is the Prince injured?"

"No, sir, but... Miss Jaelle, she... well sir she..." the man was trying and Tinker had mercy on him.

"She is gone," he said softly.

"She saved him," the man nodded. "She jumped in front of him. Took a blade meant for him."

"I see," Tinker sighed. "We will be along shortly," he told the man. "I will bring someone to see to her."

"Sir," the runner nodded. "Mister Tinker, sir, I'm... I'm right sorry, sir. She was a brave girl."

"That she was," Tinker nodded. "That she was."

-

Stephanie had the carriage door open and was outside before it was stopped good, walking straight into Parno's command tent.

And straight into a mass of organized bedlam.

"What is going on here?" she demanded.

"Milady," Enri Willard appeared. "Over here, please," he practically pulled her toward the desk. She was startled to see Harrel Sprigs lying face down on the table, blood seeping from his mouth.

"Is Parno...?" she looked at Enri.

"He's fine," Enri lied only slightly. "Harrel fought off the assassins alone, but..." he held up one of the krishank blades for her to see.

"One of these is buried in his back," Enri explained. Stephanie looked at the knife and wanted to recoil in horror. A long weapon with a blade approaching twelve inches and in the shape of a triangle set over another triangle, somewhat like the design of a warped six-point star. One triangle was a set of razor edges, wickedly curved and meant to slice flesh in such a way as to make repair difficult at best. Along the edges of the overlaying triangle were a series of angled spikes with a sharp edge on the point side. Designed to enter flesh easily enough but tear it apart on exit. Truly an assassin's weapon.

"My God," she breathed. "If anyone tried to remove it-"

"That's why we didn't," Enri assured her. "His Majesty noted the blades being used and directed that no one but you be allowed to touch it. His instructions were very clear. You and you alone were to be trusted with this."

Stephanie felt a quiver in her heart even as she went to Harrel's side. Parno still had this much trust in her, at least.

"I will need assistance and some-" she stopped as the tent opened again to admit a young bespectacled surgeon, two orderlies carrying bags and boxes and two nurses carrying more.

"Milady," the young surgeon bowed slightly. "We shall be ready momentarily," he promised without preamble.

"Very well," she nodded, removing her jacket. "I need a gown. In fact, I need to change," she started for the carriage. "This will hamper me. Have my things taken back to the guest quarters at once. We won't be leaving today after all. I shall return in five minutes," she told the surgeon.

"We'll be ready," he promised, already working.

-

Once Edema realized that Parno wasn't the one they had called Stephanie to work on, she began looking for him. Two stone-faced troopers followed her every step but didn't hinder her. She finally found someone who had seen Parno carrying Jaelle to his tent with Karls Willard alongside him. Edema felt a knot in her throat as she realized what must have happened.

"No, please no," she whispered as she hurried to his tent. She didn't bother knocking or announcing herself but instead walked right inside.

Parno had laid Jaelle out on his bed and was sitting beside her on the floor. One look was all Edema needed to see that the girl was far beyond any help. She looked at Karls Willard.

"She took a knife meant for him," he whispered to her. "Harrel killed or disabled all the assassins but he's in bad shape. Parno is alright," he promised. "No, he's not alright, but he's uninjured," he amended after a brief pause.

"The blood-"

"It's hers," Karls nodded. "He's not hurt."

She nodded and crossed the room to where Parno sat and knelt down beside him.

"How are you my sweet boy?" she asked gently.

"Why are you still here?" he asked. "Oh. If you're here then Stephanie is here, I guess. Is she-"

"She's tending to young Harrel," Edema nodded. "Went right to work as soon as we got here." She turned to Karls.

"Have hot water brought and get an aide to lay him out a clean uniform," she ordered.

"Yes ma'am," Karls didn't hesitate to obey. As he left, Edema turned back to Parno.

"My dear, dear boy," she rubbed his face gently. "We have to get you out of those bloody clothes, Parno, and get you cleaned up."

"I'm fine," he said blankly. "I'm the only one who didn't get hurt. Not a scratch."

"I know, dear child," Edema's voice was soothing. "But we need to get you cleaned up. It's not good for you to sit like this. I'm having water brought and I will help you, but you can't keep sitting here like this. You have to get up, Parno. You have to move and you need to clean yourself up."

The tent flap opened again and she saw Tinker step inside followed by two women she didn't know. One had obviously been crying and went straight to Jaelle's side. The other followed more slowly, tears streaking her own face. Tinker nodded to Edema and knelt beside her.

"My Prince," he said softly. "We will care for her. She is in good hands, I promise you. There are things that must be done and they," he nodded to the two women, "will do them. You must see to yourself."

"Tinker, I begged her to go," Parno said, as if he hadn't heard a word said to him. "I told her she couldn't stay. That it wasn't safe. Why didn't she listen to me? Why didn't she go?"

Edema had never heard Parno sound so desperate and neither had Tinker. They shared a look of concern before Tinker spoke again.

"We will speak of that at a later time, my Prince," he said simply. "It is of no concern at the moment. Let us see to her while you see to yourself. You must take care of yourself, my Prince. There can be no doubt among the Army that you are still here."

"I don't care about the Army," Parno said numbly. "I... I don't care."

"You must care because you have no choice," a new voice filled the tent, ringing with power and authority. Edema and Tinker turned to see Cho Feng standing in the doorway.

"On your feet my Prince," Cho ordered. "Do not disgrace her sacrifice in such a way as to say you do not care. Do not disgrace what Harrel has done for you this day. Get up! Make yourself presentable!"

Edema seemed as if she was about to attack Cho Feng when Tinker grasped her arm. She turned to see him shaking his head, looking at Parno. She looked back at her adopted son and saw his face showing the first sign of emotion she had seen since entering.

"Get up!" Cho's voice raised a bit more. "Get on your feet, Warlord!"

Parno got to his feet, fighting to control his emotions.

"Clean yourself," Cho ordered. "Do not force us to do it for you. It is a hard thing, I know. Our way of life is hard. Easy times make us forget, but war is harsh! Full of danger and loss with death lurking at every turn! But there is an enemy to face and there is an Army that must be led. Now make yourself presentable and allow Tinker and his women to see to this poor child. This young woman who has given herself in your stead, that you may live on. If you cannot live for yourself then you must at least live for her and for young Harrel."

"Alright," Parno's voice sounded alert for the first time. "I hear you." He began to unbutton his jacket. The same jacket Jaelle had patched for him.

"Don't get rid of it," he ordered as Edema took it. "She... she fixed it for me."

"Of course not, my dear boy," Edema agreed, placing the jacket nearby. Next was his blood-soaked shirt, leaving him bare chested.

"Tinker I am so sorry," he said softly, almost a whisper. "I am so very sorry."

"Do not be, my Prince," Tinker patted the younger man's shoulder. "It is as it was destined to be. Do not concern yourself with this for now. Make yourself presentable as Master Feng has said, and then we can speak of this at a later time."

"Come, child," Edema ordered as aides arrived with hot water. She led him to the far side of the tent where a dressing screen was sitting. She instructed the aides to empty the water into the small tub and then sent them away with orders to get his clean clothing prepared.

Tenderly she finished undressing him until he was standing before her in briefs.

"Parno, you need to get undressed and sit down in the water," she ordered. "You're too old for even your mother to undress you like this." A ghost of a smile came to his lips at that.

"Then turn your head, mother," he told her. She did, and seconds later heard the water splash as he got into the tub. She gathered a wash rag and soap and began to help him clean up.

"I am so sorry, sweet child," she whispered. "I cannot tell you how sorry."

"She jumped in front of me," he told her, though his voice no longer sounded like he was in shock. "She took that knife for me. If it had hit me, I'd be dead."

"I know," Edema whispered, her eyes closing for a moment at the horror of seeing him dead in such a manner. In any manner. "I will never be able to repay her," she added a moment later.

"For what?" Parno asked her.

"For being so good to my son," Edema kissed his forehead. "For loving my precious, precious boy. For saving him for me." She felt tears flowing down her cheeks but didn't bother with them as she hugged him close. Anyone not knowing of their relationship might have thought it improper, but those around Parno knew how close the two were, and that he treated Edema Willows like his mother.

"Finish while I check on your clothing," she got to her feet.

"I got your clothes wet," Parno told her.

"I don't care," she assured him. "I have others and these will dry. Now finish up."

"Yes mother," he smiled slightly.

Edema walked around the screen to see Cho Feng standing there still. She walked toward him with purpose and Tinker was sure she was going to strike the man, but instead she hugged him.

"Thank you," she whispered. She didn't have to say what for. She embraced him for only a second before moving on to retrieve the fresh uniform for Parno that Karls had laid out. Cho looked at Tinker for a moment before speaking.

"We must talk someday, good Tinker," he said simply.

"Perhaps we will, Warmaster," was the equally simple reply. And then both had other things to concern them.

CHAPTER ELEVEN

-

"No, no, don't pull," Stephanie said, her voice insistent. "We have to cut around each of these damnable spikes or else make sure they aren't hanging on anything. Sponge, please," she told the man next to her and he wiped her forehead gently with a small sponge cloth.

"Can you sew?" Stephanie asked the surgeon.

"Yes, milady," the young man assured her. "I attended the Royal Dispensary College in Birmingham." He used the old name for the city, she noted idly.

"Excellent," Stephanie was pleased to hear that. This man had received an excellent education in the medical arts. "I have seen no signs of arterial damage. Do you concur?"

"I do," he nodded. "I have seen one small vein that was opened in his right lung, likely the source of his oral bleeding. We are cleaning the blood up now and I'm prepared to sew the vein closed."

"Then do so at once," she nodded. "You," she looked at a nearby soldier. "Go to the main hospital and find Doctor Bartram. Tell him we need another physician here at once. Someone with surgical skills. And at least two more nurses trained in surgical methods."

"Yes milady!" the man ran to obey.

"Please keep the blood wiped away as best you can," she told the nurse that was trying to do just that. "I'm about to cut around one side of these spikes, so the blood flow may increase. There is a vein close by and it's entirely possible that I will nick it so be prepared." The nurse nodded and reached to place more sponge cloth within easy reach.

"Here we go," Stephanie whispered.

-

Parno dressed mechanically and then stepped out from behind the screen. He had bathed and washed himself of Jaelle's blood and then took a minute to see to his grooming. Behind the screen he had some protection and could allow his emotions to show, but now he left that protection behind, his face a carefully schooled mask.

Jaelle's body was gone, as were the bed clothes that had once covered his bed. Tinker and the women who had accompanied him had taken her away to do whatever it was their people did when... when they died.

"Better," he heard a voice say and turned to see Cho Feng examining him.

"Thank you," Parno nodded. Cho returned it, knowing that Parno was thanking him for more than a simple compliment. "What's happening?" he asked.

"The Army is on full alert, and there was activity among the enemy about half of an hour after the attack on you. There's no doubt this was Imperial in nature. Miss Stephanie is currently using your command tent to operate on Harrel, and Brigadier Willard has moved your own command functions to an adjacent, smaller tent."

"What's the news about Harrel?" Parno asked softly.

"His prognosis is not good," Cho admitted. "The knife wound is severe in nature. A horrid weapon, designed only to kill with as much damage as possible. A truly barbaric instrument."

"Stephanie hasn't said anything about him?"

"She has sent for an additional doctor skilled in cutting, as one put it," Cho replied. "It doesn't sound as if it's going well, but then I am not a medical professional."

"He fought all three of those assassins," Parno said as he buttoned the sleeves on his shirt. "He killed the last one with that knife already in his back. Pulled him off of me just as he was about to finish me off."

"He is an apt pupil and a formidable opponent," Cho nodded firmly.

"You taught him all that?"

"I did," Cho replied. "The Colonel and I thought he would make an excellent bodyguard in addition to being a good secretary."

"It put him in harm's way," Parno noted.

"He wanted to be a soldier," Cho said flatly. "Being a soldier puts one in harm's way. And he accepted the job readily and without hesitation. A good man."

"Yes, he is," Parno nodded. "What do I need to do, Cho?" he asked.

"Be seen," was the immediate response. "Let word spread by word of mouth that you have been seen and are none the worse for wear. That will be enough unless the enemy chooses to attack. So long as they do not, there will be time enough later for more."

"Alright."

-

"Sir, they aren't backing down but there's no sign that they intend to attack, either," Sterling reported.

"Very well," Wilson nodded after a moment's thought. "Allow the Army to stand down but keep our scouts on the job. Did the 33rd get off on time?"

"Yes sir, they left this morning before all the activity. Well on their way by now. And without the extra baggage the 16th had to carry."

"Good. Very well. We shall have officer's call in the morning as usual. Until then let things progress as usual."

"Very good sir."

-

Stephanie almost staggered out of the tent she had been using as an operating room and Parno, of all people, was there to catch her.

"Easy," he said softly. "Sit down," he guided her to a chair. "Rest."

She was exhausted, but it gave her a shot of adrenaline to be in such close proximity to him once more. She allowed him to guide her and sat down gratefully. Parno noticed the blade in her hand and carefully took it.

"That thing is evil," she said flatly and Parno nodded silently. "There is no corner of hell hot enough for the man who invented it."

"Allow me," Cho Feng said. Parno passed it to him wordlessly, wondering why Cho wanted it, but he had other, more important things on his mind.

"Stephanie, how is he?" he asked.

"He is alive, but I don't know how," she replied. "He has lost a great deal of blood and there was significant damage but remarkably the bloody thing missed his vitals other than a minor cut to one lung and slight damage to his gall bladder. I had to cut a great deal on him to get that thing out, Parno," she looked up at him. "If he lives, I doubt he will ever be able to serve again."

"I'm sorry to hear that," Parno murmured. "But right now, I'm just praying that he lives."

"Prayer may be all that saves him at this point," she admitted. "I've done all I can for him," she told them both. "It will be several days before we know for sure if he will even live." She looked at Parno then.

"Are you sure you're alright?" she asked softly.

"I'm fine," he nodded slowly. "Jaelle jumped in front of me and took the blade meant for me. Harrel took the assassins down by himself."

Stephanie didn't know what to say to that.

"You should go and rest," he saved her the trouble. "Edema was putting your quarters in order last I heard. You should be able to get at least some rest."

"I need someone with him at all times," she said, standing. "And I need to be called the very second he shows any sign of difficulty."

"I promise we shall see to it, milady," the young surgeon promised as he stepped outside. "I shall arrange assistance from the primary hospital as needed."

"Very well then," she nodded. "I am tired," she admitted.

"Let me walk you to you tent," Parno offered.

"No, that's alright," she said, though she really wanted to accept. "I'm sure you have work to do. I'll talk to you later."

"Very well," he nodded. After she was gone, Parno looked at Cho.

"What do you need that damn thing for?"

"A message."

-

General Davies stood looking at the map, weighing his options. He wanted to strike back at the Nor for the attack on his Marshal, but he had to be limited in what he did. Also, he had to think about over extending his authority.

There was an Imperial Infantry division on the move west, and another had established a camp in a small town called Unity in the last day. He was sure this was just an exercise, but with the attack on the Marshal-

"General," a cultured voice said behind him and Davies turned to see Cho Feng looking at him.

"We should talk."

-

"I want a man on the fastest horse to carry this, understand?" Davies was saying thirty minutes later. "Make sure it gets there as soon as humanly possible, if not a bit faster."

"Got it, sir," his aide nodded and set off at a run. Davies turned back to look again at the map, thinking about what he needed to do now.

"I need to see General Graham," he said aloud, turning to find another aide. "Find General Graham and ask that he come see me."

-

"So, it's true then?" Simmons asked. Karls nodded.

"I'm afraid so. Harrel is fighting for his life, but he took all of them down with him. Killed two and damn near ripped the third's throat out."

"Who would have thought he had that in him?" Simmons said approvingly. "So, what are we going to do?"

"I don't see how we can do anything without the Marshal's orders," Bret Chad said. Since his arrival, the Regiment had been reorganized into three battalions that each numbered just under five hundred men. Simmons commanded the 1st, Seymour the 2nd, and Tom Hildebrand now commanded the 3rd. This put Chad second in overall command behind Karls Willard.

"Bret's right," Karls nodded. "We keep working, training 1st Corps and doing whatever jobs the Marshal needs us for. In the meantime, we're doubling the size of the escort around Parno starting now."

"Berry still in command?" Simmons asked.

"This wasn't his fault," Karls nodded. "Security kept being pushed back for one reason or another when it should have been left as is. That's not going to happen again. We're going to increase his escort to sixty, and they will provide all security for his quarters, command tent, and when he's moving. Period." He paused as he looked at each man.

"We're not going to let this happen ever again."

-

Rosala sat at a small table in the rear lounge of the Hogshead Inn, head bowed slightly.

"She should not have been with him," her voice was soft. "He did not deserve her."

"He said the same and tried to make her come back," Tinker replied, running a narrow dagger down a whetstone. "He tried as late as this morning to get her to return here, and she would not do it. She told him that was where she was supposed to be. Where she must be."

Rosala's head shot up at that.

"She had-"

"Yes," Tinker nodded darkly. "It was her choice. It always was."

"I must go," Rosala got to her feet suddenly. "I have things to see to."

"Rosa, it is as it must be," Tinker said just before she left the room. "As it always is."

"And that is why you are sharpening that... thing?" she demanded without turning.

"It has gone dull," he said simply.

She snorted at the lie. The knives he carried had never known dullness.

"You have your ways and I have mine," she settled for saying before disappearing up the stairs.

"Good Tinker, have I come at a bad time?" Cho Feng's voice was little more than a whisper.

"Now is as good a time as any," Tinker shrugged without turning. He did not express surprise at Cho's presence or appearance.

"I wonder, good Tinker, if you are busy this evening?"

"As a matter of fact, I will be," Tinker nodded, still working on his blade.

"I suspected as much," Cho nodded. "Could I interest you in a proposition, then?"

"I am listening."

-

Aaron Bell was sitting on the front porch of the Hogshead Inn when Briel came outside. Normally shy around him, this time she made no such pretense, coming to sit at his side.

"I will miss her," she said softly, leaning into him. "She was a bright spirit in a dark forest."

"I've never heard that," Bell admitted, placing his arm around her shoulders. "The bright spirit thing, I mean," he added after a few seconds.

"It is just a saying," she shrugged a little. "I heard that she saved the Prince."

"Heard the same thing," Aaron nodded. "If I know him, he'll be looking for blood, too."

"You think so?" she raised her head, looking at him. "For someone like us?"

"Someone like you?" Aaron's brow creased slightly. "What does that mean?"

"You know what I mean," she refused to say more.

"Listen," Aaron removed his arm from about her and leaned forward, straightening slightly. "The Prince doesn't care a single whit of nothing about where you came from or what you look like or nothing else. He don't get hung up on that kind of sh-, crap, and probably ain't never. She was close to him, and she took a knife meant for him. Saved his life." He leaned back again, face tense.

"You can bet he'll want some payback, and so will-" he broke off, about to say 'so will we', but Briel wasn't privy to the fact that Bell was a member of the Black Sheep. While he trusted her, the fewer who knew it the better. Even her.

"Anyway, don't judge him by nobody's standards cause he's got his own."

She settled into his side again, saying nothing. They enjoyed the quiet for a little while.

-

Doak Parsons was angry, but there wasn't much he could do about it at the moment. Parno McLeod had taken Parsons and his men in and made them his own, giving them a place to call home when they were hunted from one end of the Kingdom to the other. To say that Parsons felt indebted to the younger man was to understate the facts by a considerable margin.

Now that same man had been attacked in the most cowardly way possible and that same attack had killed a brave young woman and might yet kill an equally brave young man. Parsons had interacted with Harrel Sprigs on many an occasion and liked the quiet young secretary. And word was spreading now that the 'secretary' had taken out three Imperial assassins alone, at least one of them while a knife was buried in his back.

That just made him more angry.

"Boss, what you thinking 'bout?" James asked, seeing a look he knew all too well on the face of his 'boss'.

"I'm thinking I want to get some payback, that's what I'm thinking," Parsons didn't mince words. "I want to kill somebody over what happened today, and I don't mean just some random Imp, either."

"I'm very glad to hear you say that, Mister Parsons," both men jumped as Cho Feng walked up on them. "I was wondering if you and a few of your associates were free this evening?"

-

"Where is everybody?" Parno asked Enri Willard.

"Here and there, scattered around," Enri replied. "Karls is with the rest over at 1st Corps, I think. I haven't seen Cho since earlier when he was with you so I assume he went back as well. Lady Edema wanted to stay with Lady Stephanie in case she needed anything, but we have a strong guard on their tent. Davies returned to his headquarters to check on the state of the alert and begin standing down once we figured the Nor weren't going to use this as a cover to an attack."

"Sounds like everyone has something to do but me," Parno mused.

"You could rest, sir, begging your pardon," Enri suggested.

"No, I couldn't," Parno shook his head, looking to the tent where even now Harrel Sprigs was fighting to live.

"Have they said anything?" he asked.

"No sir," Enri shook his head. "I'm told it may be several days before they will know anything definitive. Assuming he can pull through anyway."

"What did I do to deserve that kind of loyalty?" Parno asked suddenly, catching the older man by surprise. "What did I do that made Harrel fight so hard to protect me? That made J... her, jump in front of a blade for me? How do I rate that, Enri? Can you tell me?"

The elder Willard paused for a moment, considering the question.

"What makes a man put on a uniform, sir?" he asked Parno finally. "What makes a man decide that the man next to him is worthy of dying with, or dying for? What makes us think that a crown or a flag or anything else is worth the struggle we go through to defend them?"

"We are all a sum of our experiences, milord. What makes us who we are is a combination of everything we've done, been or seen. I joined the military because I grew up in a military family. There was never any question that Karls and I would become soldiers. It was just expected and thus we were raised that way. I fight to defend the realm because it's my home and I love it. I don't want to live under Imperial rule and I'm not going to as long as I draw breath. I don't want my family to do so either, so... I fight. And I'm willing to die to keep my people free."

"Something in you inspired their loyalty sir," Enri told him softly. "Something you did or said, something they saw in you made them want to protect you. And when the moment came, they were ready to do what was needed and necessary to keep you safe. It doesn't matter if you think you were worthy of their sacrifice, milord. They did. They thought you were worth saving. Worth fighting for, and even dying for." He paused for a minute before continuing.

"I wanted to be a hero when I was a kid," Enri laughed softly. "I ran around with a wooden sword killing imaginary Nor, or bandits, rescuing princesses and damsels in distress, hunting Tribals, the sort of thing every boy does I imagine. I told my father I was going to be a hero when I grew up. That I would never be afraid and be the bravest soldier on the battlefield so that he could be proud of me."

"He told me, 'Enri, bravery has nothing to do with the absence of fear'. I had no idea what he meant by that back then, and by the time I had figured it out he was gone. Bravery, loyalty, whatever you want to call it, milord, whatever it is that makes us do the things we do, we aren't born with it. We have to find it. Others have to lead us to it. We learn it as we grow, or else we learn it from someone who inspires us to be greater than we think we can."

"You do that, Parno McLeod," Enri told him. "The first time I actually met you was the day before we met on the dueling field," he laughed lightly. "That day when you could have handed me my head and been fully justified in doing so, but you didn't. Instead, you offered me your hand and pulled me to my feet. Set me back up and told me to live to fight another day in service to my kingdom."

"And that's what I've been doing every day since," he concluded. "You, a spoiled brat or so I believed, not only beat me soundly but then rather than kill me, and make no mistake I would have killed you," he said grimly, "you taught me that day that there was a higher duty than to simply be called a hero or to be admired for my skill with a blade. I will never forget it if I live to be a hundred. That day is burned into my memory not in shame or even humility, but as a new beginning. I would have sworn on my life that morning that there was nothing you could teach me. In fact, I did swear on it, only to have you give it back to me." He stood, looking down at Parno.

"You wonder why an army no larger than ours can hold off one three times our number? I'll tell you why, milord. It's because you inspire us to be more than we think we can. Your dirty tricks, as you call them, help, but they can only help. This army would literally follow you straight to hell and then take the gates if the last man died doing it. That's why you 'rate it', as you put it. That's why people are willing to die for you. Out of love, respect, and to that higher calling that you inspire us all to reach for." He stopped short, as if suddenly aware of how much he had said, and to who.

"I don't think I've ever heard you say so much at one time, Enri," Parno smiled slightly. "I'm glad you did. I appreciate it."

"We all have our weak moments," Enri chuckled. "Me included."

"We'll just keep it between us then," Parno assured him, getting to his feet and giving the older man a pat on the shoulder. "I'm hungry, I think. Have you eaten?"

"I have not, in fact."

"Then what say we see what kind of slop the mess is serving tonight?"

-

"I assume it's clear to all what we're doing?"

Heads nodded around the small circle.

"I'm not the slightest bit interested in their failure. As far as I'm concerned, the fact they made it that far was a win. Now it's our turn. Quietly, carefully. We have all night. Questions?"

There were none.

"Then let us be about our business."

CHAPTER TWELVE

-

Cho Feng was a simple shadow in the dark, a literal non-presence as he stood deep in the shadows of the Imperial camp, a mere stone's throw from what he believed to be their commanding General's quarters. In his hand was one of the despised krishank daggers and a small bag. He watched the guard changing, knowing they would not change again for two hours. He gave those new on their posts a few minutes to get comfortable before moving.

-

Tinker slipped from shadow to shadow as easily as a night bird. It had been a simple thing for him to find what he was searching for as the Imperial Army was lax despite the close proximity to their enemy.

Before him was the personal tent of the general commanding one of the Imperial Army's infantry divisions. There was one guard on the tent itself and another moving between it and a second tent that Tinker assumed was probably where the general did his work. The guard changed every two hours, it appeared, and had changed approximately twenty minutes ago.

Just about right...

-

Anthony Felds had been chosen by Doak Parsons to accompany him on this little jaunt because the younger man was practically a ghost in the woods. If he didn't want to be found, then you wouldn't find him. He had been the scout to detect the approaching Nor army in the cover of darkness on the last day of battle at the Gap, moving far ahead of other scouts and being close enough to hear even the sound of metal clinking in the enemy's movements.

But this wasn't scouting and the young man admitted even if only to himself that he was scared. Not necessarily of dying, or even capture, but of failure. He didn't want to fail.

And he was angry, like everyone else. Where it not for Parno McLeod, Felds would be in prison or dead. The Prince had given all of them a new lease on life, dangerous though it might be. To think that the Prince had been so close to death was enough to anger everyone in the army, but it had infuriated the men of the Regiment. And unlike the rest of them, Anthony Felds had been given the chance to do something about it.

Drawing his knife, he made his way to the nearest line of small tents that sheltered Imperial soldiers from the elements.

-

Cho smiled as he finished his handiwork, pleased with the result. It should certainly create a scene. Davies had instructed him not to try and go after the Imperial commander since they knew how he operated. A change in command would mean facing someone who might use different methods and that would complicate the Royal Army's position. Cho could see the reasoning in that strategy and agreed to obey it.

Setting the final piece of his 'message', Cho decided he had been in the Imperial Camp long enough. It was time to return to their place of meeting.

-

Killing the general had been easy for the Tinker. It had been no task at all to cut his way into the rear of the tent and the plunge the dagger into the chest of the general, covering the sleeping man's mouth as he did so to ensure he could not cry out. The general's eyes had opened and Tinker had taken a malicious pleasure in watching the light leave the man's eyes. He knew that this man had played no direct part in the death of Jaelle nor the attack on the Prince, but he worked for those who did and that was enough.

Finished, Tinker slipped out the way he had entered. He still had time and decided to use it on his way out. He wanted to make sure the Imperials got the message.

-

Doak Parsons smiled grimly as he placed the slow-burning fireplace match near the trail of lamp oil he had left along the Imperial supply area. He had wanted to roll pitch barrels into place around the tents and buildings but didn't see any way to make that happen, so he had settled for setting a fire by the nearest barrels of pitch before he began trailing lamp oil from tent to tent. Inside those tents were boxes and boxes of supplies of all kinds from tent sides to rations to uniforms and all the other sundries that an army could not operate without.

He knew intellectually that this small amount of damage wouldn't really affect the war effort, but it was the thought that counted. This would force the

Imperial Army to change its security, strengthening it against this sort of attack being repeated. While that would make it more difficult to repeat this little project if they needed to, it would still be worth it.

Besides that, he wasn't the only one working.

-

Cho Feng was standing roughly five hundred yards from the Imperial lines, just about where their picket posts were located. He and the others had already disposed of the pickets, so he didn't fear discovery as he waited. He had been the first to arrive. Meeting in these conditions could be tricky without even the light of the moon, but it could be done by men who were good at slipping about, and all of the men with him tonight were indeed good at it.

"Warmaster," he heard right next to him and turned to see the dark outline of the Tinker, identifiable only by his voice.

"Master Tinker," he nodded. "You appear to be well."

"I am very well, thank you," the near mirthful voice replied. "It would seem we finished quicker than the young ones."

"Age brings the wisdom of getting things done with less effort," the oriental chuckled.

"Well, you two are nothing if not old," Doak Parsons joined their conversation, surprising them both, although they hid it.

"Ah, Scoutmaster," Tinker said. "I trust your efforts were successful?"

"Should see signs of it any time," he nodded. "Using a long match is unpredictable, but we used more than one for each location. It should work."

"And the guards?" Cho asked.

"Gone," was Parsons short reply.

"Excellent."

The three waited in the dark as man after man returned, each reporting some level of success. Not all of them had been able to achieve their goals completely, but even then, they had simply chosen something else to do instead. Doak counted heads and came up one short.

"Where is Felds?" he asked.

"Ain't seen 'im, Boss," someone replied in the dark.

"Didn't see him," another spoke at the same time, as did three others.

"Dammit," Parsons muttered. He had chosen the kid himself because of his skills. If anything had happened to him...

"Y'all lookin' fer me?" a quiet voice asked from behind them and all of them jumped slightly, even Cho.

"Felds, you little shit!" Parsons hissed. "I was afraid you was caught or dead."

"No sir," the young man replied. "I did get a little cut, but it ain't bad. And I did for him that cut me, I did," he added.

"Are we all accounted for?" Cho asked.

"He was the last one," Parsons nodded.

"Then may I suggest that we get back to the lines?" Cho offered. "We can get young Mister Felds some medical attention and..."

"Look!" one of the scouts hissed and they could just make out his arm extending in a point toward the enemy camp.

"Fire's going," Parsons said. "Time to go, boys. By pairs so we don't lose anyone. Move it out."

They left an ever-growing glow behind them as the fire began to spread.

-

"Fire! Fire in the Quartermaster's camp! Fire!"

Wilson was roused from his sleep by yells and shouts from outside. He heard the word fire and decided he needed to take a look. If it had been bad enough his guards would have awakened him, but even so he'd have a look. He doubted he'd get back to sleep anyway. Dressing quickly, he stomped his way into his boots and made for the door.

It was dark when he opened the door and that made him frown. There was supposed to be a lantern lit here.

"Sergeant!" he called for the senior guard, but no one replied. Two further calls netted the same results. Assuming they had gone to the fire, wherever it was, he went back inside and secured a lantern of his own, determined to track down his wayward guard force and execute the lot.

As he walked outside he kicked something. Looking down he realized that it was...

"Holy Mother Mary!" he exclaimed, seeing the head of an unknown man at his feet. There was something else there as well and he knelt to examine it.

"A krishank," he said it like a curse, examining the nasty weapon now embedded in his porch. "I guess you were one of the people Smith sent against the southern prince then."

He stood and noticed for the first time the dark forms of his guards, still at their posts at either corner of the house.

"Didn't you idiots hear me calling you!" he demanded. "A man could have been killed waiting on help from you lot!" he spoke as he made his way to the nearest man, intending to chew his ass out good.

"Who in the hell was able to get close enough to me to leave... that..." he trailed off as he realized something was wrong. Why weren't the guards responding to him? In the light of the lantern he could see why.

His guards were dead, still standing by virtue of being tied to the posts by the shoulder and left there. He ran to check the others and found the entire squad, five men plus their sergeant, all dead, their throats cut.

"Son-of-a-bitch!"

-

"Generals Mitchell and Hayworth, Brigadiers Mayborne, Fairfield and

Farnsworth, Colonels-" Sterling stopped as Wilson raised a hand.

"Total?"

"Total command officers so far is fourteen with the nine colonels," Sterling said flatly. "For the other officers and the enlisted we're still counting, but it's up to forty-two, last I heard."

"How in the hell did anyone get into our camp and do all this damage without someone seeing or hearing them?" Wilson demanded.

"I don't know sir, but we found this," he held up another krishank dagger, "in General Hayworth's chest. This is a-"

"I know what it is," Wilson cut him off. "Found one outside my door where every one of my guards was dead but tied in place. This is some kind of retaliation for something the Imperial Secret Police have done, you can bet. There's no telling what else we'll find or have happen."

"Fire! Fire in the artillery cache! Fire!" came the call from outside.

"Of course," Wilson sighed, sitting down. "Why not light the pitch we had ready on your way out?"

"Sir, we-"

"There's nothing to do but wait for daylight and see how bad it is, Sterling," Wilson shook his head. "Let our men be so they can put out the fire. They don't need me yelling and screaming on top of everything else. We may as well have drink," he took two glassed and a small bottle. "Sit down. Give me the rest of what you know while wait for the reports to come in."

-

"Hell of a fire in the Imperial camps it looks like!"

Enri Willard was roused from his sleep by an aide who reported with breathless excitement that the Imperial camp was on fire.

"The whole camp?" Enri asked, rising to a sitting position. "Cause it better be the whole camp after you woke me up."

"Good part of it, looks like," the aide nodded. "And there's more than one fire."

"Very well," Enri decided he may as well get up. He doubted he'd get any more sleep tonight. Five minutes later he walked out of his tent and right into Cho Feng who deftly sidestepped him.

"Master Feng," Enri said respectfully.

"May I suggest you place your troops on alert, Brigadier?" Cho was almost serene as he made his suggestion. "Just as a precaution of course," he added dryly.

"Of course," Enri raised an eyebrow. "What have-" he stopped as he saw the Tinker standing behind the Oriental sword master along with Doak Parsons of all people.

"Do I want to know what you all have done?" he asked carefully.

"Doubt it. Sir," Parsons replied for them. "I'd hurry right along with that alert, was I you, sir," he added helpfully.

"Very well," Enri sighed and began yelling for aides and runners.

"Can I interest you two gentlemen in a rare drop o' Finest Tinsee River Water?" Parsons asked his two cohorts.

"I could be persuaded," Tinker nodded.

"I rarely imbibe alcohol, but this does seem to be an occasion that rates it," Feng nodded.

"Well let's head over to my tents and see what I can find."

-

"What has brought all this on, exactly?" General Davies demanded, still buttoning his jacket as he strode into the Headquarters tent.

"Well sir, there is a great deal of commotion in the Imperial Army camp at the moment, including a number of large fires."

"Ah, I see," Davies didn't appear surprised. "Well then, do we have everyone standing to?"

"Both corps on line report manned and ready, sir," Enri nodded. "General Graham reports that his men are assembled and prepared to march on orders."

"Good, good," Davies nodded. "I had warned him earlier to be prepared for such orders after what had happened with the Prince. Have all regimental commanders drill their men in place while we see what develops with the enemy. Perhaps they'll be so busy with their fire that they have no time for any further foolishness for a while."

"One can hope."

-

Dawn revealed the extent of the damage. The cost in Imperial Sovereigns had yet to be calculated, but it was severe. It would easy enough to replace the supplies, but the loss was still a loss. One that would have to be explained.

"The final tally is over three hundred dead," Sterling said. "Three hundred nineteen, to be exact. Most murdered in their tents. One man killed, the other left sleeping, unharmed. Somehow, we have kicked over a hornet's nest, sir."

"Oh yes," Wilson sighed. "Most definitely."

"We have to at least double our security, sir," Sterling was saying as Wilson mulled over the situation. "If they can do it once, they can do it again."

"True," Wilson agreed. "See to it. Today. I don't think they'll be back, at least not unprovoked, but let's not assume that. And let's get the Corps Commanders together after lunch. Perhaps it's time we consider making a move against the Soulanies, even if it's just to keep them occupied."

"Yes sir."

-

Jaelle's funeral was supposed to be a small affair with just the members of the Tinker's group present, but word of how she had saved the Prince had spread and by the time they were ready to proceed with her ceremony most of the army knew what had happened.

Rosala was still bitter as she stepped outside to follow the wagon that would carry Jaelle to her pyre and stopped short at what she saw.

One hundred men, decked out in their finest uniforms of the Prince's Own, formed in ranks of two, half in front of the wagon bearing Jaelle's body, the rest behind it.

Gathered around and further behind were many hundreds more, perhaps thousands more uniformed soldiers, their ranks looser but still formed and prepared to march.

"What is this?" she asked, looking around.

"This is their way of paying respect," Tinker's voice was quiet.

"For what?" she asked him, puzzled.

"For Jaelle," Tinker explained. "She saved their Prince. That makes her special to them. Were it not for the enemy across the way I dare say all of them would be here to pay respects and render honors."

"But she... I... since when do such as they have anything like respect for the likes of us?" she finally stammered.

"For some of them perhaps just since Jaelle's sacrifice, but most of them take their cues from the Prince, and he does not look down on us. Any of us," he emphasized. "Thus, neither do they."

The older woman was clearly shocked by what she saw and had nothing further to say. Karls Willard suddenly appeared, resplendent in his dress uniform. He stood at attention before them before speaking.

"Sir, ma'am, we are ready to escort you to Miss Jaelle's final place of resting. You have only to give the order."

"We do not bury our dead, Colonel," Tinker said softly.

"So, I'm informed sir," Karls nodded. "In which case we will render honors until such time as the ceremony is complete. With your kind permission of course."

"Gladly," Tinker nodded. "Let us go then. It does no good to delay." Even as he spoke another group of horsemen appeared, smaller, but no less impressive.

Parno McLeod rode at the head of the small column, his face drawn and haggard. He stopped a respectful distance from the group and dismounted, handing the reins to Berry as he strode forward to where Tinker, Karls and Rosala stood.

"Karls, Tinker," he nodded and then turned to Rosala.

"Ma'am," he bowed to her, shocking the woman further. "I have come to pay my respects if you will allow it. I know that Jaelle was special to you, and I wanted you to know that she was to me as well. And not because of what she did for me yesterday, either," he added. "I cannot tell you how sorry I am. I would rather he stabbed me a hundred times as to stab her but once. I... I have never had... no one has ever..." Parno trailed off as words failed him.

Rosala was clearly stunned and looked to Tinker for help.

"Rosa would normally be rather acid tongued, my Prince, but your appearance seems to have..." He trailed off as yet another group of mounted men, also arrayed in Parno's livery, forced their way through the growing mass of men to lead a carriage to the front of the inn. One of the troopers dismounted to hurry over and open the door, letting down the steps.

Lady Edema Willows, Duchess of Cumberland, stepped down with the assistance of said trooper and made her way immediately to where Tinker and Rosala stood.

"Tinker," she embraced him briefly and then turned to Rosala.

"You are Rosala?" she asked politely.

"I am," Rosala nodded warily.

"I wish to join you in paying respect to that beautiful young woman," Edema spoke even as another, younger woman stepped down from the carriage. Stephanie Corsin-Freeman walked to where Edema stood, nodding to all and hugging Parno very briefly.

"Why?" Rosala asked, now thoroughly confused.

"Firstly, because she was so good to the young man I consider my son," Edema didn't mince words. "She showed him nothing but love and concern, and for that I will ever be in her debt. But that debt pales next to the fact that because of her I still have him. She will always be precious in my sight. Always."

"I see," Rosala nodded, though she didn't really. Or at least she couldn't see clearly just yet.

"I would offer you to share my carriage to wherever our destination is," Edema said.

"It is customary that we walk," Tinker explained.

"Then I would ask that we be allowed to join you," Edema didn't hesitate.

"I see no reason that cannot be," he smiled faintly. "But we should start."

Without further talk the group moved to the rear of the wagon. Karls set out leading the procession at a slow walk behind a single man with a small drum that he would occasionally beat. The rest followed quietly.

-

It was a simple affair. A group of six women in black carried Jaelle from the wagon to a small funeral pyre and placed her there with a tenderness that brought tears to many a battle-hardened soldier's eyes. Flowers decorated her body, placed there by mourners, and her hands, pressed together on her torso held a small bouquet of black roses.

There was no eulogy. Those who had things to say would do so later. Once the flowers had been placed, Rosala took the torch they had brought with them and Tinker lit it for her. As she started for the pyre, Karls called out a command;

"Render honors... FRONT!"

Hundreds, perhaps thousands of boots snapped as the soldier came to attention while the honor guard all drew swords and presented them, moving to form a tunnel of sorts for Rosala to walk through. Startled, she almost fell, but Karls was there and offered her his arm as an escort.

After a brief pause, she took it and let him lead her through, emerging on the far side next to the pyre itself. Karls left her there, taking his place among the others.

The older woman spoke a few simple words in a language few present could understand, then gently placed the torch in the middle of the pyre's lower level. The oil-soaked logs caught at once and the fire began to spread. Soon it was burning so hot that anyone near it had to move away.

When the flames finally died down, Jaelle was gone.

-

Parno rode back to camp in silence, Berry and his men surrounding him rather than following at a respectful distance. There would be no more of that. From now forward there would always be a bubble around Parno McLeod. If you weren't personally known, you wouldn't be getting through it.

Parno scarcely noticed. He made it back to his quarters and handed care of his horse off to an aide before entering his tent and removing his dress uniform. After that he did something he rarely ever did.

He laid down in the middle of the afternoon and went to sleep.

CHAPTER THIRTEEN

-

General Gerald Allen looked at the hastily scribbled orders he'd just been given with a combination of rage and satisfaction. He had sent runners to find Generals Coe and Vaughan. They had plans to make and they didn't have a great deal of time to make them.

Things were about to heat up.

-

General Wilson read the report he'd just received from his cavalry force with mixed emotions. He was glad to read that Stone had, in fact, reached the Soulan Royal City and effectively sacked it but he was alarmed at their losses both in combat and due to sickness. This report, sent by a healthy trooper on a good horse had likely reached Wilson before Stone's battered command had returned to Lovil.

One of Stone's commanders was smarter than the others and his command had avoided the food poisoning that had laid low the rest of Stone's command, but then in defending the sick troopers of the other two divisions General Baxter's command had suffered more battle-related casualties than the other two combined as they were forced to fight alone and unsupported. There was no official count of losses as yet, but it was almost certain to be high. Wilson's cavalry corps was out of commission for the foreseeable future.

Wilson wanted to be angry and he was, but... Stone had warned Wilson that he was sending Stone and his men to fail. They had marched without adequate preparation, including rations. Eating that Soulan beef had been too easy, but it had been a way to feed his men when they hadn't had time to acquire enough field rations to carry with them.

"Sterling," he called. "I want you to have a good medical team dispatched to Lovil to help Stone's command. Save as many of them as they can. Provide them an escort and have them carry supplies they need with them in case there aren't sufficient supplies in Lovil."

"Yes sir," Sterling nodded and departed.

Stone's report had mentioned in passing what it called a 'reiteration' of his actions in Lovil as detailed in his report sent before the incursion into the Soulan interior, but Wilson didn't have that report and hadn't seen it.

Except, the next envelope he opened contained a terse report from one Lucas Silven, whom Stone had promoted after executing one Commodore Haskings for rape. Silven's report detailed how his boat force and their escorting cavalry battalion had been attacked by a large force of Soulanie cavalry. The Imperial cavalry had apparently been wiped out to a man and the boat force had been attacked by archers who had killed over two hundred of Silven's sailors. The loss of so many of his personnel had resulted in a large number of lost boats and the loss of their supplies had left them no choice but to allow the current of the northern flowing river to return them to Lovil.

Wilson sighed as he read the tally. What should have been simple assignments turned into massacres. Massive losses of life and war material during what should have been a simple movement. The damned Soulanie cavalry had thwarted him once more.

"Sterling," Wilson called and his Chief of Staff returned at once.

"Send someone to find that heathen savage Blue Dog," he said bitterly. "See if he will come and meet with me. Make sure whoever you send knows to be polite and phrase it as a request. The bastard is brazenly independent and usually on the verge of insolent. Make sure your messenger knows that and is prepared for it. They have to remain calm regardless of what the bastard says."

"Yes sir."

Wilson reread Stone's report after Sterling had departed, wondering in the back of his mind what else would go wrong today. All because of an apparently botched assassination attempt by the Imperial Secret Police.

-

General Ezra Crandall, commander of the 33rd Imperial Infantry division, was not in the best of moods despite his division's good performance. His ill mood had nothing to do with his division's performance, however, and everything to do with why they were out here to start with.

He had received orders from General Wilson the night before last to have his division on the road at first light the next morning, yesterday, on a forced march to a small town some twenty-five miles west of the Army's main position. They were to make the march in three days at most and on arrival relieve Taylor's 16th

Infantry of the position they had established, completing the camp and holding it until relieved themselves.

He knew for a fact that Taylor's division had just departed five days earlier, so what the hell was the rush to get out there and relieve them to start with? Five days was no real hardship for a well-provisioned unit. Crandall considered Taylor a blowhard and braggart, always crowing about his division's 'great and exemplary performance' during the massive Soulanie cavalry attack a few weeks back. Taylor was always more than willing to recount his division's brave stand in the face of overwhelming odds in holding the flank after two other divisions failed to... blah, blah, blah.

Crandall knew he wasn't the only one tired of hearing it and has assumed that was the reason that Taylor had been given the 'honor' of making the march to this Unity in the first place. But Crandall's division had arrived just after the failed attempt to carry the Soulan Army's position and had not been a part of either action. While Crandall had been critical of the policy of Wilson's 'victory through inaction', he had not thought his criticism had been severe enough to warrant his division being forced out of camp with twelve hours notice.

Apparently, he had been mistaken in that as he and his men were now on their second day of march, heading for this Unity township and whatever awaited them there.

At least the weather was better than Taylor's men had endured. He had no way of knowing that his day was about to get very hot indeed.

-

Allen and his cohorts had devised a simple plan to accomplish their simple orders. The terse message from Davies had been short and to the point. Trap and destroy the division now on the road, eliminate all but one piece of evidence, and then proceed to Unity and repeat the process.

Those were orders he could definitely get behind, and both Vaughan and Cole had readily agreed. Their plan was to attack from three sides, cutting the Imperial infantry off from all avenues of escape except for running toward Unity, where they would finish them off later.

Allen would attack from the south. Coe would cross the road ahead of the enemy and attack from the north, while Vaughan would move in behind the Imperials and attack from the east. Simple but effective.

They were to take no prisoners.

Word of the attack on the Prince had spread like wildfire through the whole command and left over twenty-thousand Soulan cavalry troopers seething with anger. They were ready for payback and considered this the first installment. No one other than the chaplains had any problems with not taking prisoners, and the chaplains weren't part of the chain of command. Their objections fell on deaf ears at any rate.

Vaughan would initiate contact since he had to be in proper position in order to prevent any runner from escaping.

Coe and Allen would await his signal before launching their own attack.

-

General Vaughan's family had served the House of Tyree since before it was a House. Vaughan's direct ancestor had been one of Tyree's closest retainers. Service to the Crown was imbibed in the milk of mothers in the Vaughan family.

Well educated in the art of war, Vaughan was a natural at his job and was the perfect choice to start the battle off. His scouts reported the moving Imperial division had passed their position almost twenty minutes ago. Vaughan quickly calculated the distance the column of men on foot could have traveled and decided it was enough.

"Form line of battle with 2nd Brigade centered on the road," he ordered. "1st Brigade to the south, 3rd to the north. Each brigade to keep one battalion in reserve to ensure no one manages to escape back toward the Imperial camp. We'll begin moving in five minutes and will move in silence until ranks are dressed. Bugles will sound Canter and that will be the signal to move forward. Maintain your lines and interval at all times until contact. Remember the Black Flag."

Runners took off at once to pass these orders. Vaughan waited the five minutes and then nodded to his 2nd Brigade Commander, Brigadier Brandon Webb.

"Let's get moving."

"Sir," Webb nodded. "Forward to line of departure and then hold!" he called out. Slowly the mass of horsemen began moving.

-

"Are we on line?" Coe asked.

"We are sir," his chief aide replied. "I've checked the orders myself. All brigade commanders know their missions."

"Outstanding," Coe nodded. "Have the scouts continue screening and let's move into position."

"Yes sir."

-

"Sam," General Gerald Allen said quietly. "Are we ready to get under way?" Brigadier Samuel Walters had taken over the lion's share of work commanding the 9th Cavalry while Allen commanded the newly formed 1st Soulan Cavalry Corps.

"We are sir," Walters promised. "Brigades are all in position and orders passed."

"Let's move to line of departure then and have the scouts keep us out of sight."

"Right you are, sir," Walters nodded and started issuing orders. Thousands of horsemen began moving toward their places.

-

"Do you hear that?" one young company officer asked a counterpart.

"Hear what?" his tired companion asked, trudging along the gravel and dirt-packed road. "All I hear is a bunch of grumbling and cursing."

"You don't... feel, that?" his friend asked. "Like a rumbling feel?"

"No," his companion shook his head. "We're at the back of the entire formation, though, Wil. There are thousands of boots ahead of us tromping on this road. Tens of thousands actually. That's probably what you're feeling."

"No, I... if that was it we'd have been feeling it most of the way, right? This is... I think this has-"

"Has what?" the companion asked without looking. "You're para... noid... Wil?" He looked to see his companion gone.

"Wil?!"

He found him finally, twenty feet or so behind, face down in the road with an arrow sticking out of his back.

"Oh shi-" he managed to get out before another arrow buried itself in his chest. The last thing the young officer heard was a distant bugle call.

-

"What the hell is that?" Crandall demanded, hearing the bugle call in the distance.

"Sounds like a bugle, sir," a young aide mentioned from behind him. Crandall actually stopped his horse and turned in the saddle at that.

"No shit? Well aren't you just fucking brilliant? Able to identify a bugle call after only a few notes." The young man's face flushed but he wisely remained silent.

"That's not an Imperial call, sir," a senior aide said softly. "We've got company."

"Sound the call to form ranks," Crandall ordered. "Probably a raiding force of horsemen trying to inflict some casualties on us. Form ranks and prepare to repel any close-up attack."

"Sir."

-

"That's the signal," Coe's voice betrayed his eagerness. "Have the scouts guide us in and let's move. I want to make sure we're in the right position. Remember, no one escapes. That is very important."

"One battalion from each brigade detailed to prevent that, sir," his aide nodded.

"Then, by all means, let's move to engagement. No bugles until we sound the attack."

-

"Sounds like Vaughan is engaged," Allen nodded to himself.

"Notify the scouts to prepare to guide brigades into place," Walters ordered. "You three remind our rear-guard battalion of their orders. I don't want any screw ups. Meaning I don't want any Imperials escaping. Move it now!" The men took off bearing their reminders.

"Move to line of embarkation!" Walters called.

-

It was a perfect whipsaw. Vaughan's division hit the rear of a column still moving from marching to defensive formation. In addition, the Imperials were expecting only a raiding force, a spoiling attack and little more. Instead, they were facing over eight thousand Soulan horse troopers.

Angry and vengeful horse troopers. And they weren't alone.

-

"We are in position sir," Coe's chief aide reported.

"Then sound Forward, Canter," Coe ordered his bugler. "Let's get this show on the road."

-

"Ready to depart, sir," a scout reported. "We're in perfect position."

"Sound Canter," Walters ordered at once. "Let's move."

-

"I'm hearing other bugles," the young aide Crandall had spoken so harshly to said cautiously.

"From where?"

"Both sides of the road," the aide reported, turning his head to try and hear better. "Sir, I think this is more than just a raid," he risked telling his General. "I think-"

"Stop thinking and get in line," the older aide snapped. "The General is capable of doing the thinking."

Stung, the young aide did just that, moving to the outer area of the group and drawing his sword. Crandall dismounted from his horse, not wanting to be one of the few mounted men in the column and make himself a target for Soulanie archers.

Crandall could hear bugles from north and south of him now as well as behind him to the east. He was torn between thinking it was just a ploy by some very crafty Soulan commander and believing it was a major attack. If he deployed his entire division and there was no attack, he would have wasted the remainder of the day and be forced to make camp far earlier than planned. That would make them late in getting to their objective.

But then, if he didn't deploy his division and was hit with a major attack by mounted Soulanie horsemen then his division would be torn to shreds by lancers, bowmen and mounted swordsmen. The Soulanies were nothing if not masters of horse warfare.

While Crandall was still struggling with his decision, General Allen had already made his and was in the process of carrying it out.

-

Vaughan's troops were already at a gallop with arrows flying before Crandall realized that his men were under attack. While he had archers in his ranks, they were further forward. Orders were passed for the archers to move through the column to the rear in order to engage enemy cavalry. This resulted in a bit of confusion as the division was still in the process of changing from a marching formation to one designed to repel an attack.

The archers as a group were almost to the rear of the column when Vaughan's lancers began to hit the Imperial rear, tearing massive gaps in the hastily formed lines. The archers were just beginning to return fire when Coe's division struck from the north. Another nearly eight thousand horsemen bearing down on the Imperial infantrymen was a rude shock that came from seemingly nowhere.

Shouts of alarm ran down the length of the transitioning column as soldiers who had thought the danger was at the rear of the road column now saw a large group of Soulan horsemen bearing down on them.

"Form up!" Sergeants screamed as they kicked and cursed their men into ranks. "Form up! Archers in back, swords and pikes front!"

But all the archers had begun moving to the rear of the column to help stop that attack. Those still moving stopped and began to hurry back to help defend the front half of the line even as cries began rising from the left flank.

"Horsemen in sight to the south! More Soulanies to the south!"

At that point, even the veteran NCOs weren't sure which way to turn. Who defended what side of the road? Which units would form to the north and which to the south. Conflicting orders were being screamed all up and down the line leaving rank and file soldiers with no idea who to follow and what to do.

When Crandall realized how many horsemen there were in the attack, he realized that no orders he gave would be adequate. There was no way his division was going to survive this as a fighting unit. The only hope any of his men had was to break and run.

"Every man for himself!" he shouted suddenly. "Pass the word, every man for himself! Escape and evade as best you can! Head for the main camp if you can get free! Every man for himself!"

Perhaps someone would be able to let Wilson know what had happened here.

-

"They're running," Walters told Allen quietly. "We've broken them, sir, and they're trying to escape."

"Indeed," Allen nodded grimly. "See to it that none of them do."

"Yes sir."

"And I need their General."

-

It was a dirty business and the Soulan cavalry didn't have things all their own way. There were a number of talented archers in the Imperial Army and some of them occupied the ranks of the 33rd Infantry. Southern horse soldiers began to fall to their arrows even as the southern archers were repaying them in kind. Imperial swordsmen were forming to try and hold their position but many of them had left their shields on wagons rather than carry them on the march in Imperial controlled territory. Pikemen that were supposed to have the protection of shield bearing swordsmen fell victim to Soulan lancers with the advantage of fighting from horseback.

Crandall's order of 'every man for himself' had been a last-ditch effort to save at least some of his men and hopefully have someone survive and escape to warn Wilson what they had run into out here. He doubted he'd be able to himself, but surely someone would be able to slip through.

The battle raged for nearly ten minutes before Crandall realized that all he was doing was throwing the lives of his soldiers away to no gain. Sure, they were killing a few southerners, but for every one they killed at least four of his own men were falling. He hated the thought of spending the rest of the war in a POW camp but comforted himself with the knowledge that the war wouldn't really last too much longer. He looked at his bugler and ordered him to sound the surrender. The bugler did so at once and all down the line Norland troops began to drop their weapons and raise their hands.

All that accomplished was to make them easier to cut down.

At first Crandall thought some were just slow getting the command, or else that the southerners were slow to realize that he was surrendering his command. Then he saw what had to be the southern commander riding forward with his escort and saw that in addition to the Soulan Royal flag the Soulan cavalry color guard was carrying a black flag.

No quarter.

We should have kept fighting was the last thought Crandall had as an arrow found his chest and he fell to the dust road.

-

"Is that him?" Allen asked, absolutely no sympathy in his voice.

"Yes sir," the trooper holding Crandall's body nodded. "Got the stars on," he pointed to Crandall's shoulder board.

"Good. Leave him and drag the rest away, off to the south," he pointed. "Douse them in oil or naphtha and burn them. I don't want them found. Search them and keep anything useful, especially any identification papers, maps or orders. I want all but one regiment of each division on that. Have those three regiments set a guard. We're on a schedule." He started to dismount.

"What about him, sir," one man asked, pointing to the dead Imperial General.

"He stays," Allen said, digging into his saddlebags. "I have a use for him."

-

Major General Brent Stone was still sick as the proverbial dog when his horse brought him in sight of Lovil.

The men of Weir and Blake's divisions were still deathly ill and Stone shuddered to think of what the casualty count would be before it was over. Troopers of his command were strung out for miles behind him as those who were reasonably healthy hung back to try and aid those still sick.

Baxter, the little snot nosed bastard, had not lost any men to sickness, but his men had borne the entire effort of the southern counterattack and had suffered high casualties because of it. Something Baxter would not soon let Stone forget.

Stone could not see any way he would survive this debacle. He had warned Wilson first that he was misusing the cavalry force, and then that he was setting them up for failure by not allowing them adequate time to prepare for operations behind enemy lines. But Wilson would never accept the blame for this, which meant the best Stone could hope for was reassignment to some demeaning post and a probable demotion. Compared to losing his head, however, he'd take it.

Assuming he survived. He was just as sick as any of the troopers following him and had been for days.

The first person he saw was Lucas Silven, who looked like death warmed over himself. As Stone staggered from his saddle, Silven grabbed him to steady the general. The cavalryman nodded his thanks to the sailor.

"Looks like we both ran afoul of the enemy, General," Silven said gently. "Let me help you get somewhere you can rest. There will be plenty of time to tell you what happened to us."

Stone nodded his agreement and let the sailor guide him into a large building that had already been set up as a temporary hospital. Runners sent ahead to order preparations be made had apparently made it.

At least one thing had gone right.

-

"All right, sound muster," Allen swung into his saddle. "We've got a long way to go in order to be in place by nightfall. We eat in the saddle. Time is our enemy for this operation. What about our wounded?" he asked Walters.

"We got hurt," Walters admitted. "Total losses for the entire Corps are still being tabulated, but we're looking at somewhere in the neighborhood of eight hundred fifty dead and one thousand seven hundred wounded. Some of those are slight, others won't likely live out the night."

"Assign an escort to the ambulances and start ferrying the wounded back to camp," Allen ordered. "Don't leave a single man behind. I want our dead handled properly as well. One of the support battalions that came with us can see to them. I want everyone else ready to go in half-an-hour. No exceptions. We have to be within five miles of Unity by nightfall."

"Yes sir."

CHAPTER FOURTEEN

-

Parno woke to the smells of supper. Realizing that he hadn't eaten at all during the day, he rose, washed and dressed, and walked out of his tent following the smell. It led him to the nearest mess tent where everyone tried to allow him to go before them but he refused, waiting in line like everyone else. Once again word passed along through the ranks that the Marshal was waiting in line for the same food they were.

Everyone but Parno noted that there were at least a dozen troopers hovering close by, watching the young Marshal like proverbial hawks. Finally getting his plate full of what looked like the oldest army food ever, chipped beef on bread, Parno headed back toward his own tent. When he arrived, he noticed two troopers outside his tent that weren't normally there. Assuming rightly that he had visitors, he ducked into his tent to see Edema Willows working to straighten out his tent and make it presentable.

"I have people who get paid to do that, you know," he told her as he sat down. "I didn't know you were here or I'd have brought you a plate too. I can share mine with you."

"I don't eat that stuff," she sniffed and then smiled. "What would people say?"

"It's not bad," Parno shrugged as he dug in. "How are you doing?"

"Shouldn't I be the one asking you that?" she walked over to sit down with him.

"I'm okay," he nodded. "Thank you for helping me through that," he told her softly. "Without you, I doubt I'd have made it."

"I'm honestly glad I was here for you," she told him. "I wish it hadn't been needed."

"Me too," Parno nodded. "It was my fault for letting her stay."

"Parno, you may be stubborn, but sometimes we women can outdo even you," Edema smiled. "She meant to be with you and your input wasn't required. Sometimes that's the way it is."

"Still, I knew the risks even if she didn't. She was at risk around me. Just like ..." he trailed off suddenly and concentrated on his food.

"Just like Stephanie?" Edema said kindly.

"And you," he nodded slowly.

"You still love her, don't you?"

"Of course, I do," he replied honestly. "Probably always will," he admitted.

"Then why can you not put aside her one lapse in judgment and make things right between you?" Edema's voice was rife with exasperation.

"She's safer this way," was his reply. "No matter how many soldiers I put around her, or you for that matter, nothing guarantees your safety. Not now. I can't... I can't lose anyone else."

"You can't live your life like that Parno," Edema scolded lightly. "It's not right. You cared deeply for Jaelle but you didn't love her, did you?" It was more a statement than a question.

"No," he admitted. "I just loved an idea that looked like her. But I did care for her very deeply. You're right about that. She... she was so kind to me," he almost whispered. "It was... it was nice."

"My poor child," she sighed. "Of course, something like that would make a huge impact on you. Please accept my apology for not thinking of that. I thought... well..."

"That I was just chasing skirts?" Parno chuckled. "I was," he admitted. "I wouldn't have if I was sober, probably, but... she was so beautiful and I was lonely and... well," he shrugged.

"I know," Edema nodded. "There's nothing wrong with it. I mean there is of course, it's sinful," she chided. "But it's human nature to seek out companionship, Parno. We all do it. You and Stephanie had just had a terrible blow up and here was beautiful young woman who was equally infatuated with you and... well, nature does the rest," she shrugged. "It's as natural as breathing."

"I guess," Parno sounded non-committal. "It's funny. The entire time I was with her, I kept thinking in the back of my head like I was being unfaithful to Stephanie. I wasn't, of course, since I was pretty sure she had said goodbye to me, but it still felt that way."

"Poor boy," Edema laughed quietly. "You really have it bad, don't you?" Again, it was a statement.

"I did I guess," Parno agreed. "But I can't afford to do that again. I was letting it distract me anyway."

"Liar," Edema said at once, though kindly. "You were using to keep yourself going. Don't try to lie to me."

"Did she tell you that?" Parno demanded.

"We've barely talked since we got here," Edema admitted. "I'm not her favorite person at the moment you know. And she's very busy caring for Harrel, too."

"How is he?" Parno felt ashamed he hadn't checked first thing. "I was hungry when I woke so that was what I did first thing was get something to eat."

"His condition is unchanged," Edema informed him. "That isn't good, but it also isn't necessarily bad, since it means he isn't worse."

"I'll take it," Parno nodded. "I miss his steady presence. I don't know how hard it's going to be to get by without him."

"You'll manage," Edema assured him. "You always do. Now, we're going to be here for several days because of Stephanie needing to be here to treat Harrel. This is a perfect opportunity for you and her to try and work out your differences."

"Edema, I was just sleeping with another woman two nights ago," Parno looked aghast.

"We women expect that of unmarried men," Edema informed him frankly. "It's a fact of life. You're only men after all, and you're weak. Even for men who are engaged, if it's a long engagement, no one thinks twice about something like that unless he makes a fool of himself and embarrasses the family. Either family but primarily the bride's."

"For God's sake," Parno was shaking his head. "Even assuming she ever did love me, there's no way she still does. If me refusing to marry her and try so desperately to give her a baby in one night didn't do it, then my tryst with Jaelle certainly would have. And there should be a period of mourning over Jaelle anyway, shouldn't there? Besides which I just told you I need to be concentrating on the Army and the fix we're in and not... that."

"You can do both," Edema told him. "You listen to me, Parno McLeod," she turned deadly serious suddenly. "That girl loves you. She loves you deep down where she lives, so much it hurts. Your tryst won't mean anything to her, more especially since Jaelle gave her life for yours. That alone will make her forever someone Stephanie feels she owes. Just like me," she added quietly. "I don't know what I'd have done had that terrible knife been plunged into you instead of that sweet girl."

"It was supposed to have been me, you know," Parno said quietly. "'My Emperor demands your death' he said and then was across the desk and on me. No way I'd have reacted in time to stop him. But she did." He stood up abruptly as if he could no longer remain sitting.

"They'll try again," he told her. "They'll try again somehow, and they'll keep trying."

"I suppose they will," she agreed.

"I need to go see how Harrel is doing," he changed the subject just as abruptly as he'd raised it. He suddenly reminded her of a caged lion, testing the strength of the bars that held him.

"I will walk over there with you," she decided. Rather than object, he merely nodded. Edema was wearing wool pants and a matching shirt rather than her normal frilly women's clothing. Clothing more suitable to camp living. Comfortable, serviceable and practicable.

The two walked in silence to the tent that had once been used as Parno's command tent. They stopped outside rather than step inside. One of the guards stuck his head inside to announce them. Less than a minute later, Stephanie herself stepped outside.

"Good afternoon, dear," Edema spoke for both of them. "How is he?"

"He's developed a fever," Stephanie sighed. "That's not unexpected but it is undesirable. The problem is trying to find the cause of the fever. Fever normally is a sign of an infection somewhere, but I can't locate the source. It may be a piece of his uniform we missed during his surgery, in which case there's nothing I can do about it now. I thought we had gotten it all but it's possible we missed something and it doesn't take much."

"What else could it be?" Parno asked.

"It could be something those damnable knives were coated with," she admitted. "I don't know. If it was then there's nothing I can do about that, either. Without knowing what was on it, I can't treat it."

"I need to go," Parno said suddenly. "I'll be back shortly."

-

The as yet unnamed surviving assassin was chained hand, foot and neck to a tree and under constant guard by four members of the Black Sheep. Three times he'd attacked them and each time been handed his ass, and in one case a tooth. He had learned that attacking them was not the way to freedom.

He straightened from his position against the tree as he saw his target coming toward him, along with an oriental man and a tall, dark skinned man dressed in gray and black.

"Your knives are unique," the Prince said at once with no pretense at a preamble. "Designed only as weapons of murder. What do you coat them with?"

The assassin smiled up at him but remained silent.

"I have no time for frivolity," Parno warned. "You and your friends have killed already and a good man lies sick even now because of you. I want to know what you coated those damned blades with!"

"Your friend is dying?" the assassin spoke for the first time. "I am his only help, no?"

"No," Parno said. "Merely his fastest. One last chance; tell me what coated that blade."

The assassin remained quiet, studying the Prince carefully as he turned to his associates.

"Find out what he's using," he said simply and then walked away. The oriental looked down at the assassin and smiled slightly.

"I wish to know what it is that your knife is coated with," he said simply. "You will tell me."

-

Screams were heard throughout the camp but word spread that it was nothing to be concerned about. Merely the last Norland assassin paying for his crime. The screams didn't last long. Fifteen minutes at most. Soldiers within hearing distance exchanged money in many cases after having made bets on how long the screams would last.

-

"Nightshade," Cho Feng reported twenty minutes later. "The blades are coated with the juice of a plant that is commonly called Nightshade. Bittersweet to be exact. A coating of the juice of berries that is allowed to dry on the surface of the blades before use."

"Nightshade," Stephanie almost spat the word. "Perfect."

"What is it?" Parno asked.

"Bittersweet can cause convulsions if given in large dosages, but wouldn't necessarily account for his fever. It might, but it's not certain. There's not much we can do for it except keep him hydrated. I'm trying something I learned from ancient texts, but our methods are crude compared to theirs," she pointed to a hanging bottle with a line running to Harrel's mouth.

"In ancient times, they would have done that through a needle into his arm," she explained. "We don't have that ability, at least not yet, but we have run a long tubing down his throat to his stomach and are continually giving him water. Hydration at this point is all we can do. Try and combat both the fever and the poison. This particular toxin is not deadly except in large doses, at least not normally. While coating a blade would ensure someone who didn't know what was done to them more likely to perish, it isn't a sure thing. Normally you would be more concerned with the damage done by removing that horrid blade."

"But thanks to you, we aren't," Parno nodded. "Stephanie, I can't thank you enough for being here," he said softly. "While Harrel may yet die, he'd already be dead if not for you."

"I'll do my best to save him in return for his saving you," she said just as softly. "There is no one who means more to me."

"Even now?" Parno asked, eyebrow raised.

"Forever," she nodded. "There will never be anyone who matters more."

Parno was stunned to hear her say that even though Edema had already mentioned it. He turned and walked out of the tent and back to his quarters, where he simply sat down on the bed. He sat there for a long time, thinking. Not looking for answers, but just thinking.

Just thinking about everything.

-

"His fever has broken," Stephanie reported when Parno next went to check on Harrel. It was early evening, the camp preparing to retire other than those on duty.

"His fever began going down late this afternoon for no reason I can find," she admitted. "I don't know of anything we did that would have helped other than the cold water baths. That is proven to help, but usually not so rapidly. It may simply be that whatever caused it was not as serious as I had first believed. Whatever the cause, so long as it's not some more serious underlying condition, I'll just be happy with the result."

"I have to trust your judgment there," Parno said with a nod. "I don't know enough to make an informed decision one way or another."

"That's what you have doctors for," Stephanie smiled thinly. "If anyone could do it then we'd be out of a job."

Parno laughed lightly at that, but in truth there was very little humor.

"You need to get some rest," he told her, seeing the dark circles beneath her eyes. "You're no good to him if you're too tired to make decisions."

"I was going to tell you the same thing," she raised an eyebrow. "You have to rest so your mind is clear to make good decisions." She was sitting next to him and suddenly laid her head over on his shoulder as she had many times in the past.

"I admit I am tired," she stifled a yawn. "I don't remember how long now I've been awake."

"Then it's time for you to sleep a while, wouldn't you say?" he asked her, a bit of mirth in his voice. When she didn't answer he looked down only to see she was sound asleep.

"Looks like I was right," he said to himself. He looked up at that guard.

"Is that young physician that's been helping here?"

"Arrived about fifteen minutes ago, sir," the man nodded.

"Then tell him that Lady Stephanie has retired for the evening unless there is an emergency," Parno ordered, gathering the sleeping young woman in his arms. "I'm taking her to her tent. Lady Edema can see to her wellbeing."

"Right away, sir."

Parno was careful not to disturb her as he carried Stephanie across the short way that separated the VIP quarters from where Harrel was being treated. One of the guards on that tent saw him approaching and called a warning within which saw Edema emerge, throwing on a shift.

"Is-"

"She's fine," Parno said softly. "Just exhausted. I left word that she would be retiring for the evening barring an emergency." He slipped inside and Edema pointed to a bed. Parno carefully eased Stephanie's sleeping form onto the soft bed and stepped back.

"I'll leave it to you to... well," he motioned to where Stephanie lay sleeping and Edema nodded.

"I can take care of her," she promised. "Good night, dear," she kissed Parno on the cheek and received one in return.

"Good night."

Parno made the solitary walk back to his tent still thinking about all that had happened in the last two days. What had passed between he and Stephanie, the things Edema had told him, the time spent with Jaelle, all of it.

His head was in such a swirl by the time he returned that he had no idea how he would ever sleep. He never remembered lying down, let alone drifting into slumber.

-

Therron was not accustomed to discomfort but he'd had to learn on the fly. Riding until dark and then stopping only for lack of light left little in the way of amenities in camp. His men cared for their horses and his along with the two pack horses they had. There wasn't much selection in the way of provisions, really. Some jerked meat, dry cheese and some bread that had begun to mold three days into the trip. They had gathered a bit of wild fruit along the way and one Marine who was skilled with a bow had taken a very small deer which they had cooked over a fire. Therron had wanted to object to the fire but ten hungry Marines who were already in a sour mood made a good argument.

Another three days, he figured, and the lieutenant agreed with him. Three days until they were well inside the Coastal Province territory, and another ten perhaps until they were in Norfok. What happened between now and then was anyone's guess.

Therron had been out of the loop for a long time and had no idea what news there was from the palace of the war front. For all he knew his inept brothers had already lost the kingdom to the Nor.

No, he shook that thought away. No, say what you would about Memmnon, he would never allow the Kingdom to fall without a fight, even if he had to kill Parno himself. For that matter, his father was not an idiot. While Parno might have 'won' a single, small engagement, that alone didn't mean he could manage an entire military apparatus. Tammon would see that even if Memmnon did not. There would still be a Kingdom, of that he was sure.

That meant his work had to concentrate on removing Tammon and proving Memmnon unfit. Eliminating Parno would not prove difficult once those things were done as no one would defend the youngest McLeod, including the family. So, moving Memmnon out of contention was the main thing. With that done he could ease Tammon into retirement and assume the throne. Tammon was already in ill health so doing something along those lines would work.

So long as he could get the assistance he needed.

A single division of CPC cavalry and he would be King Therron inside a month. Probably less. Sherron would bitch and moan about being 'traded' to Picon, but tough. In four or five years, once she had taken firm control of the CPC and perhaps birthed a son, then she could 'negotiate' for charitable terms by which the Coastal Province Coalition could be incorporated into the Kingdom of Soulan in its entirety. Their commercial contracts with foreign powers alone would be worth making any number of concessions to get them folded into his rule, essentially returning his sister to him once Picon suffered a fatal heart attack. Or whatever.

But all of that was in the far future. Right now, he was leaning against a log somewhere in what he believed to be the Lower Calina Forest. If he was right then he was already inside the CPC, but still well within reach of a Soulan horse unit. It was a gamble, but a good one as most of the best troops were gone north to help with the invasion. It would work. It had to work.

No one but he was fit to be King, Therron told himself as he settled in to try and sleep. His kingdom needed him. So, for their sake it had to work.

-

"Are all our men in position?" Allen asked.

"Yes sir," a dozen voices answered at once.

"This is how I want this to go," he drew a diagram in the dirt with a fire-burned stick. The fire they were gathered around was the only one allowed, and it only by necessity. "Walt will attack first from the east," he made a rough arrow in the dirt. "Once he is engaged, Coe rides in from the north and Vaughan from the south. We hit them just as they're waking up and starting their day. They'll be at their worst. That General we killed this morning had orders to relieve this outfit and send them back to the lines on a three-day forced march."

"It is entirely possibly that there's another infantry division on the way up this road, or will be by the time we get half way home. If there is, we can hit it, too, and do the same thing to them. I don't think anyone is opposed to our returning to the Prince to report three Imperial Infantry divisions destroyed in their entirety, are they?"

Feral grins around the fire were his only answer.

"All right. Catch regiments here, here and here," he outlined where back stopping regiments from each division would be posted. "No one escapes to the east. I want no warning of what's happening to get back to that bunch until it's too late. Preferably no one escapes at all, but it's war; shit happens. Let's just do our best to make sure it happens to them, not us."

"Black Flag?" Vaughan asked, more from habit than need.

"All the way," Allen nodded. He looked around the fire and found no more questions.

"You have your orders, gentlemen.

-

"Your mans say you want talk at me."

Wilson looked up to see Blue Dog standing before him, bow in hand. The savage stank to high heaven but Wilson was used to that by now.

"Yes, I did ask to see you if you were available," Wilson tried to sound as if he considered Blue Dog a near equal. "I was wondering if your men had been scouting any to the west of our position?"

"Saw your mans go out, followed them there," Blue Dog nodded. "Hard move in rain with so much. They did okay." The compliment sounded as if it had hurt him to say.

"Well, that is part of their training," Wilson nodded casually. "What I was wondering was if you had seen any movement among the Soulanies to the west. Have you seen any of their horsemen that far out?"

"Not go far or see much, but no Southmans," Blue Dog shook his head. "Southmans would make battle anywhere they see us."

"What if you outnumbered them?" Wilson asked.

"Southmans still give battle," Blue Dog remained solid. "Unafraid of Painted Warriors." Only proven warriors among their people were allowed to wear more than the basic face paint of their unique tribe, Wilson recalled.

"I was wondering if I could persuade you to make a large showing of yourself in this wide area," he made a circle of about twenty miles around Unity. "Be seen, skirmish the Southerners, raid anyone still there, whatever you choose to do, but make a strong showing."

"How long?" Blue Dog asked, considering. "Moon come soon. Better for night raids."

Wilson thought of that. They were on the new moon now so moving at night meant using torches and lanterns.

"Can you move in daylight for a few days waiting on the moon, and then move at night?" Wilson asked, suggesting a compromise. "That would put you in position already when the moon comes full."

Blue Dog stepped forward and surveyed the map. Suddenly a finger came up and stabbed a spot to the southwest of Unity.

"No here. No tribe go here," he said it quietly. "Here, long ago, many die. Something wrong with land, or maybe water, but many die. No reason, no sign, just death. Some go to see, they die too. All who go there die. We not go here."

"Do you know what-"

"Blue Dog say 'no reason'," the Chieftain sounded irritated. "No sign. We ride, we look, we fight if look good, but we not circle. Stay away from here," he stabbed the spot again.

"Very well," Wilson nodded, making a circle on the map to inform his staff of what Blue Dog had said. "When will you go?"

"Two days, no more," Blue Dog replied at once, already moving toward the door. "We go."

"Good luck to you."

-

"I'm riding in the carriage tomorrow," Winnie said as she gingerly sat down on a log around the fire.

"Why is that?" Case asked innocently. He had tried to get her to ride the carriage earlier.

"My as-, my backside says I'm going to," she shot back and he laughed.

"I told you riding every day is something you have to work up to. Just because you're in good shape doesn't mean you can ride all day, every day."

"I can run further in a day than we're moving," Winnie complained. "Why is riding so much harder?"

"First of all, when you're running what are you carrying?" Case asked.

"Well, my bow, quiver, my knife and possibles bag. That's it I guess," she shrugged.

"So, not much of anything then," Case nodded. "Now how far and fast could you run carrying just what your own horse carries for you? Bedroll, bags, whatnot."

Winnie didn't answer but nodded her head slowly as what Case said made sense. She spoke after a minute of thought.

"Still don't explain why I hurt so bad."

"Different muscles," Case informed her. "You use an altogether different muscle group riding than you do running. Particularly your thighs and buttocks. Not to mention the strain on your lower back if you aren't used to riding."

"How do I get rid of the soreness?" Winnie wanted to know.

"You have to work through it or have it massaged out," Case shrugged. "In your case, I'd say you're going to have to work through it. Well," he paused, clearly thinking.

"You better not be thinking what I think you're thinking," Winnie said glaringly and Case's face flushed slightly in anger.

"I'll pretend for both our sake you didn't just say that," he told her flatly. "I remembered that at least four other women are riding and likely to be in the same shape. It's possible you could trade with them. Scratch each other's back, so to speak. And I'll thank you, milady, not to speak to me so informally in the future if you are then going to take offense to informal speech. I shall make sure you're notified when supper is ready, and I remind you now to check with the wagon train before dark to see if there are any problems. Good day."

And with that Case was away, leading his horse to the picket area after cleaning and inspecting his hooves while talking to Winnie.

"Dang it, Winifred, when are you gonna learn?" she muttered to herself. "You got to stop takin' offense to ever little thing."

She decided she would make her rounds and look for those horse mounted women at the same time. No sense in not being economical with her time. And while she was at it, she'd figure a way to apologize to Case.

Again.

CHAPTER FIFTEEN

-

General Brandon Taylor was an early riser and today was no exception. There remained a bit of work to be done for the 16th Infantry, but he expected them to be finished with their encampment preparations by the end of the day.

Unity appeared to have been a thriving village in the past but had been abandoned ahead of the Imperial advance. He couldn't blame them, really. Having a half-million soldiers of a foreign army in the neighborhood would bring down the property values, that was certain.

The abandoned homes and buildings had made establishment of a facility here much easier than anticipated, and he and his officers had taken advantage of the empty homes to make their quarters in something other than a tent. Thanks to stables and hotels there were actually very few tents needed, but Taylor had ordered roughly half the tents put up anyway in the event they had a visiting unit such as one of Stone's cavalry outfits. He had ordered three modest homes that sat empty set aside as VIP quarters as well, just in case.

Taylor was beginning his day by looking over reports brought in the previous night while he had his breakfast when he heard yelling in the camp. The last time he had heard such yelling, the camp had been under attack so he didn't ignore it. Instead he grabbed his cap and sword and stepped outside to see what was happening.

To find himself and his 'elite' division under attack by Soulan Cavalry once more.

-

Samuel Walters had deployed the men of the Soulan 9th Cavalry as well, if not better, than Gerald Allen himself could have. Despite the predawn darkness they had assembled in, his horsemen were all in position and ready to go by the time it was full light.

"Ready Sam?"

"We are, sir," the brigadier nodded.

"Then have at 'em," Allen ordered simply.

"Pass the word, forward at a Walk, wait for bugles. Two minutes," Walters ordered. Rather than using bugles or whistles, they would pass the order by word of mouth to avoid noise. The two-minute rule was for those at the center of the line. For those at the end, they would begin moving as soon as the order reached them. While it wasn't perfect, it was workable. And a proven tactic.

So it was that two minutes after the order was given, the center regiment of the 9th Cavalry's line began moving forward at a walk, along with the rest of the line.

They were less than a ten-minute walk from the Imperial position.

-

Imperial pickets and guards had drawn their attitude straight from their leader. Like Taylor, they felt they were being punished, given duties better suited for units that had not seen combat. There were no Soulan forces out here, nor was there anything else for that matter. The only good thing about this mission was to be away from the rest of the camp and its incessant drills, inspections and lectures.

All of this attitude also made them a good bit more lax than normal. Alert levels were low among the guard posts and things that should have rated further inspection were ignored. Signs like the night birds going silent. Insect noises ceasing to fill the night, even close to dawn. Wildlife running toward the camp even in the early predawn light.

Yet none of this made an impression on the guard posts surrounding the 16th Infantry as they grumbled to one another about the unfairness of their being given such mundane jobs as establishing a new camp, regardless of who it was for.

And all the while that they spent moping over these and other considerations, three full Soulanie Cavalry divisions were walking right up on them, blood in their eyes and vengeance in their hearts.

-

"I think we're about as close as we're gonna get," Walters said quietly. "I'm amazed they haven't sounded the alarm already."

"Agreed," Allen nodded. "At your command, Walt."

"Bugler, sound Forward Canter if you please," Walters tightened his grip on the reins of his horse as he drew his sword.

With the clear notes of the bugle the line lurched forward, moving much faster now.

-

"What was that?" one Imperial guard said, standing up straighter. As a picket post, his job took him much further out on the edge of the camp than a mere guard post. "Did you hear that bugle?"

"It's time for bugles all over camp, you idiot," his partner said. "They're blowing Rise to Ready all over camp."

"This wasn't Rise to Rea-" was as far as he got before a Southern arrow pierced his chest, stopping him from worrying about what he had heard. A second arrow ended the shock his partner felt at seeing his friend killed before him.

"Forward at a Gallop," Walters ordered at once. "Take them at a run!" he yelled for those around him and the line broke into a slow run.

-

Taylor had for just an instant thought perhaps the rumble beneath his feet was a quake. This area was well known for them so it wasn't uncommon. But the rumble continued and began to grow. And now it wasn't just... it was...

"Soulanies!" the cry rose from all over the camp. "Horsemen! Attacking from all directions! Soulanie Horse-" the cry was cut off and Taylor didn't have to see it to know why. He felt a few seconds of panic as he realized this was the worst time for his men to be hit by such an attack. Then he shook his head and began shouting orders.

"Parade!" he yelled. "Fall back to the Parade Ground and hold! Box in the Parade Ground!"

The Parade Ground was hardly a true parade type field but rather the center of town where the well was located. It was also contained by the square of the town and cut down the angles of attack the Soulan horse soldiers could attack his men as they defended the place. And with access to water, his men stood a better chance there than they would spread out through the small town.

The buglers began to sound Parade in all directions and many of his soldiers knew at once what their general was trying to do. Breaking contact regardless of their position they broke and ran for the center square, hoping to find more support there to form an organized defense.

But not all of Taylor's soldiers would understand, there having been no drills for this eventuality. Some assumed it was the wrong call made by a scared bugler. Others thought Taylor had lost his grip on reality or perhaps didn't realize the scope of their situation. Regardless, many of the soldiers didn't follow the directions, choosing instead to fight or run on their own.

And that actually helped those of Taylor's command who did run for the square as Soulan's horse soldiers were occupied with rounding up and putting down those who continued to fight and move in the town proper and its outskirts.

Leaving Taylor and his men time to erect a sturdy defense around the well by the time the Soulan horse soldiers got there.

-

"Well, this is an issue," Vaughan said as he eyed the closed off streets leading to the town square.

"It's not, really," his senior Brigadier, Charles Lockhart said calmly.

"Oh?" Vaughan looked at Lockhart, eyebrows raised. "What would you do? Burn them out?"

"Exactly."

-

Taylor looked at the collection of men he had to assume was all that was left of his division. Less than a full brigade of soldiers, perhaps two thousand men at most, remaining out of ten thousand and more.

Their position would be a strong one against anyone but such an overwhelming number of Soulanie horsemen. Even then it wasn't bad, but he knew it would eventually fail.

"Sir!" he heard someone call and looked up to see a young Captain coming his way.

"Sir, there is a single rider with a flag of truce waiting for you are the south barricade, sir!"

"Very well," Taylor tried to sound confident. "I suppose I should see what the gentlemen wants, aye?" He accompanied the Captain to the barricade where a horse soldier with black trousers and a green jacket waited for him.

How did they pick those atrocious colors, I wonder? Taylor asked himself.

"You have a message for me?" he said aloud to the trooper, who nodded.

"Surrender or be killed to the last man," he said simply.

"Is that it?" Taylor asked.

"That's it," the man nodded.

"Well, tell your commander he can do a little better than that, I'm sure," Taylor laughed. Rather than take that as an insult, the southern rider merely nodded and rode away, leaving Taylor concerned.

"Let's make sure they can't get in here unseen, boys," he called out. "Archers to stay back from the line to cover engagements!"

-

"He refuse?" Allen asked and the rider nodded.

"Well, figured he would but it was worth a shot. I didn't think on this," Allen admitted. "Didn't see it coming."

"Rider from General Vaughan, sir," an aide galloped up. "Message for you." He handed over a small piece of paper. Allen read it grim faced.

"Well, that would work, wouldn't it," he sighed, passing the note to Walters.

"So, it would, sir," Walters agreed. "Seems a waste, but better than the lives we lose attacking a strong position."

"True," Allen nodded. "All right. Get the orders out. Half-an-hour. God forgive us."

-

"What was that?"

"What was what?" an Imperial infantryman had just been dreaming about the breakfast he had missed.

"There it is again!" the first trooper pointed. "It... I think it's fire arrows! They're burning the town!"

"Fire!" another soldier down the line called. "Fire! Fire in the town and spreading this way!"

"Just when we thought we were in a strong spot," the first Imperial muttered. "Damn that bunch anyway."

"General Taylor, there are fires all around us!" a young Major reported. He was one of the more senior officers to have survived.

"Well, so long as they don't make it to us, we're fine," Taylor said.

"They are coming straight at us, sir," the young major reported. "What isn't being blown by the wind is being fed with fuel. We're surrounded on all sides by fire and it's drawing the net closer and closer."

"Damn them," Taylor swore, bitterness clear in his voice. "Raise the white flag; we surrender."

"Yes sir," the Major looked glum. "Right away."

-

"White flag approaching on foot, General," an aide reported.

"Cut him down," Allen said without a thought. "It's what they'd do to us."

"Yes sir," the man nodded and returned with his orders.

"What do you think of that?" Walters asked once they were alone.

"Of what?" Allen asked, trying to watch the battle.

"The Black Flag," Walters specified.

"I think if we'd done it two wars ago, we'd be at peace right now," Allen replied. "That's what."

Walters nodded in reply and there was no more talk of the Black Flag policy.

-

"Sir, the Soulanies aren't accepting our surrender," the Major appeared to be in a mild state of shock as he was faced with his own doom.

"What do you mean not accepting it?" Taylor demanded. "They have to!"

"Perhaps if you told them, sir?" the Major said. "They have cut down everyone we've sent forward so far."

"That's a violation of the rules of war!" Taylor shouted, jumping to his feet. "Where are they?"

"Everywhere, sir," the Major made a sweeping motion with his hands that including their entire surroundings.

"I'll do it myself," Taylor muttered, grabbing a more or less white bed sheet from the bed he'd been using and walking into the street. He grabbed a pike from a stunned and useless infantryman going into shock and tied the sheet to the pole as he moved toward the southern barricades.

Waving the flag as he stepped through the blockade closing the street, Taylor waved the flag non-stop so that any blind Soulanie could see it. He slowed that waving as he approached a group of mounted soldiers, barely visible in the smoke. Clearing the smoke, Taylor saw a Soulanie general along with several brigadiers and colonels.

"Why have you been cutting down my men who have offered you our surrender?" Taylor demanded to know without preamble.

"You in command of this lot?" the southern General asked by way of answer.

"I am."

"In the leg," the southerner said next. Before Taylor could think he felt a searing pain in his leg as an arrow pierced his flesh. He fell, unable to keep his balance even with the pike pole.

"Wha-" Taylor tried to gasp but the southern general had dismounted by now and was standing before him. The southerner reached down and grabbed the arrow, giving it a little shake which made Taylor scream.

"Know what this is?" the southerner asked. 'This' was one of the nastiest weapons in existence that Taylor knew of. A krishank blade used by the Imperial Secret Police.

"It's a dirty assassin's blade fit only for the fires of hell!" Taylor managed to grit out.

"Well, on that at least we can agree," the southerner nodded. "And because of that I'll grant you a quick and painless death. Which is more than you granted ours." With that the southerner kicked Taylor over onto his back and left him there, slowly bleeding out. But not for long.

A Soulanie Trooper appeared over Taylor, sword in hand and raised high.

General Brandon Taylor, commander of the 16th Imperial Infantry, died in the dusty streets of a small town that had been abandoned in the face of Imperial aggression. He died quickly, and rather mercifully all things considered.

The remainder of his men would, for the most part, not be so lucky.

-

"Report," Allen ordered even as the last of the fires were being put out. All things considered, the damage wasn't nearly as bad as it could have been.

"We lost four hundred seventy-five dead, nine hundred and twelve wounded," his Chief of Staff reported. "Seventeen horses are unfit for use. Six never will be again."

"Place them, the wounded and the dead on the Imperial wagons along with all this gear we've taken and start them for home at daybreak with a one regiment escort. Give them a route south of us that will put us parallel to their movements and keep us between them and the enemy. We will bivouac here tonight and then move east down this trail tomorrow behind a screen of scouts. If we encounter another Imperial division we'll stomp if flat, but otherwise we're returning home. Get the orders out and let's get settled for the night."

"Cold camp again, sir?" Walters asked.

"I don't see the need," Allen shook his head. "Imps were gracious enough to leave us all this, we may as well make use of it and have a good meal and a good night of sleep!"

Morale in the three divisions went straight up at that.

-

"You're in a fine mood this morning," Winnie tried to keep her voice sounding amused as she rode up beside Captain Case. She had elected to ride again rather than use the carriage after she and the other single women had indeed helped each other with massages the evening before. One woman's advice was simple; keep riding or else pay for it the next time. So, Winnie decided to keep riding.

Case hadn't spoken to her all morning unless he had something he had to report, and when he did it was 'milady' this and 'milady' that. The friendliness of his tone was long gone after the damage done by her run away mouth the night before.

"You have a specific complaint, milady?" Case asked her.

"I don't need one just to point out what a rotten mood you're in," she replied, trying to sound teasing.

"If you believe me to be in a 'rotten' mood, milady, you are wrong," Case replied flatly. "I am in no mood at all, to be honest. I am merely attentive to my duties, as I should be."

"You ain't spoke a word to me today you ain't had to," Winnie accused and to her surprise Case nodded in agreement.

"I have not, nor will I in the future," he assured her, catching her by surprise. "You will never again have the opportunity to semi-accuse me of such impropriety as you did last evening. I have gone my entire career without such accusations and you shall not be the first."

"Look, that was just me talking," Winnie tried to semi-apologize. "You can't-"

"Such talk may be nothing to you, but it has ruined more than one good man's career, and I have worked far too hard to get where I am to have my life ruined by the words of one girl who has become accustomed to getting her way regardless of anything else. Now, if you will excuse me I need to check on our scouts." Without waiting to be excused, Case put heels to his horse and galloped to the front of the column where scouts were indeed arriving to report in.

The word 'girl' had automatically put Winifred's back up, but the barb about being 'accustomed to getting her way' had hit home hard. Too hard. She frowned, knowing that Case was right at least in that. She had become accustomed to getting what she wanted. Being the 'King's Intended' had gotten her a lot of attention, and people tripping all over themselves to get her whatever she wanted. And despite her best intentions, she had become accustomed to it.

It was clear that any chance she had of simply apologizing to Case and making good were nil. If she wanted to work her way back into his good graces, she would have to earn it.

Somehow.

-

"How is he?"

"His condition is unchanged, which in this case is good," Stephanie told Parno as she emerged from the tent Harrel was being treated in. "His breathing is less ragged this morning though, so that in itself should rate as an improvement. I am almost to the point where I could say he will definitely recover."

"That's great!" Parno looked as enthused as he had about anything in the last three days.

"Parno, even if he recovers completely... I still doubt he will ever be able to serve you again."

"So long as he lives," Parno made a pushing motion as if to ward away anything else. "I will miss his service and his companionship, but if he lives then if I have to give up the rest, I will. If nothing else, there will be administrative positions at Cove Canton he can fill. I will see him taken care of."

Stephanie smiled mentally as Parno swore to be loyal to those loyal to him. It was one of the things she loved about him, his dedication to those who helped him. Fate seemed determined to take those people from him one way or another, but still he was loyal.

"I'm sure he will appreciate that," she said instead of touching his face as she wanted. "I think I'm going to continue my survey of the army's hospital corps while I'm here seeing to his care. I've been very impressed by them so far."

"If you encounter any difficulty at all let me know at once," Parno nodded. "I appreciate your doing that, as well. It's a huge help to my men."

Always thinking about others. Always.

"I'm glad to do it, Parno," she smiled. "I will be back to check on him after lunch."

-

"We're mounted and ready, sir," Walters reported. Runners from Coe and Vaughan reported the same.

"Change of plans, Walt," Allen said suddenly. "Send runners to Coe and Vaughan to bring their troops this way. We'll all take the southern route home with the wounded and wagons. We've left a pair of nasty surprises for the Imps, so there's no point in ruining that. We've accomplished our orders. We'll be satisfied with that."

"Yes sir," Walters nodded and turned to send those orders out by runner. Once that was done they would move out for home.

-

General Darin Westcott was no more thrilled with his orders than either of the first two generals sent on this snipe hunt. A three-day forced march to a map dot, relieve the division already there and then hold until relieved. If the plan followed the established routine that would be about three days, give or take.

Westcott's 14th Infantry had departed from their place in line early that morning, amid a great deal of cursing and kicking. Why his unit had been given this honor he didn't know, but orders were orders. This road was pretty narrow, being a minor trade route. Worse, he and his men would at some point encounter that idiot Taylor's 16th Infantry and have to share the road with them as they passed each other.

Wonderful.

-

Despite his worry over Harrel and his guilt over Jaelle, Parno did have work to do. He made his way over to the series of tents and buildings that made up the Army Headquarters and found General Davies and Enri Willard pouring over maps and reports.

"So, have the Nor surrendered yet?" he asked, trying to be humorous.

"No sir, I'm afraid not," Enri snorted in amusement. "Scouts have reported that their cavalry have made it as far north as Lovil, where they appear to have encamped for the time being. Many of their men are sick and will remain that way for some time I'm sure."

"That's what I hear," Parno nodded. "What else?"

"Another infantry division on the move at daybreak this morning," Enri replied, passing the report to his Marshal. Parno glanced at the report before handing it back.

"Headed the same way, I see," he looked at the map.

"What are they up to with that?" he asked aloud. "Still think it's an exercise, General?" he asked Davies.

"I do, sir," the older man nodded. "It fits all the data we have. They've been in camp for a long time and moves like this are the ideal way to keep their men in shape. More importantly, it keeps their general officers off balance as well."

"I see," Parno nodded, getting an idea of what Davies was thinking. "You think their generals are getting mouthy. Or antsy."

"Or both," Davies nodded. "This gives them a lot less time for that foolishness."

"So, it does. Well, so long as that keeps them moving in any direction but south, maybe we should be grateful."

"I'm tempted in that direction myself, sir," Davies voice was non-committal. Parno frowned at that.

"General, is there something you'd like to share with the rest of us?" he asked. Davies seemed to be weighing his thoughts before giving a deep sigh.

"General Allen was given orders to eradicate the first two infantry divisions that went on this exercise, milord," he said rather formally. "Those orders were issued after the attempt on your life, in conjunction with other projects designed to show our... displeasure, with the Nor attempt to kill our Marshall. Sir."

"What other projects?" Parno asked. "Or do I want to know?"

"I doubt it," Davies admitted. "Cho Feng and the man called Tinker were the ringleaders, along with Mister Parsons and a good many of his men."

"No, I don't want to know," Parno admitted with a sigh of his own. "We'll just pretend I don't know. Agreed?"

"Of course, sir," both men replied. Enri looked curious but would try to find out on his own.

"What do you expect to happen due to Allen's actions against their infantry?" Parno asked Davies.

"Nothing," Davies replied. "If things went as planned, there will be little enough left for the Imperials to work with. I expect them to take a day or two still to realize what's happened. And when they do, I rather think they will leave well enough alone, at least for now. They think time is working for them when in fact it's working against them. Every day they wait is another day our men get to train. And not just the men here or at Cove Canton, but the new men training at Red Rock. Six divisions of men, all receiving the same conditioning that your original regiment received if not the same martial skills."

"Well, that is a start," Parno nodded. "We'll see what happens I guess. Any word from Raines?"

"Shelby front is quiet since the show of cavalry leaving their front headed north," Davies shook shook his head. "Again, looking more and more like a ruse."

"We have to keep our wits about us, though," Parno warned. "If we allow ourselves to get used to these ruses, then one of them, sooner or later, will be real."

"We're watching, sir."

CHAPTER SIXTEEN

-

"Sir, there are riders approaching."

Therron raised his hand to halt his small column of men, waiting for the Coastal patrol to reach them. The young lieutenant slowed considerably when he saw the uniforms of the men in Therron's group. He halted his men perhaps a spear's throw from Therron signaling them into line abreast.

"Who are you?" he asked cautiously.

"I am Prince Therron McLeod of the House McLeod, ruling dynasty of the Kingdom of Soulan," Therron replied. "I would like to be taken at once to see Governor Charleston. Without delay," he added when the men didn't offer to move.

"I can take you to my commander," the lieutenant offered. "After that it will be up to him. You and your men will follow me," he ordered. He signaled to his sergeant who took half their men and fell in behind Therron and the rest.

"Follow us," the lieutenant repeated, and with that lead off. Therron sighed dramatically but did as he was bid. This would take a bit, but he knew the drill. He would have to see this man's captain, and then likely a colonel, and finally a general who would probably recognize Therron, which would speed things along.

At least the food and accommodations would improve at this point.

-

"Bow lines down and fast!"

"Stern lines down and fast!"

Commodore Anthony David listened as the calls came one after another that signified that the Ocoee was now moored fast in her berth at Savannah. The other ships in his squadron, now including the Halifax and her escorts, were also mooring. The shipyard was as busy as David had ever seen it. Between repairs on those ships deemed salvageable and new construction to replace their losses the entire area was a bee hive of activity.

"Bring him up," David ordered his Marine commander, a Major. The man nodded and repeated the order to those below. Soon Commodore Anthony Chastain was brought on deck in irons. David was offended by the fact that this traitor shared his first name, but there wasn't anything he could do about that.

"Take him ashore," David was suddenly very tired. "Place him in the brig until Admiral Semmes has time to deal with him. We'll have to build gallows, I guess," he added thoughtfully.

"You think it will be that easy?" Chastain demanded. "I was following a lawful command!"

"No, you weren't, and you knew it," David replied calmly. "Take him before I kill him myself," he ordered. The marines half pushed, half carried the still chattering Chastain off ship and down the pier.

"I think he's cracked," Jonathon Riddell said softly. "I mean, here," he pointed to his head.

"He may be," David admitted as he made an entry into his personal log. "We'll see what happens I suppose. I have to finish my report to the Admiral and then get it to him."

"We managed to get him off the ocean and bring three undamaged ships into port, sir," Riddell reminded him.

"And missed the opportunity to put an end to Therron McLeod and the threat he represents to the crown," David nodded. "Yes, we really did a bang-up job."

Riddell had nothing to add to that.

-

"Commodore this report has you accepting responsibility for everything other than the war itself," Semmes said a few hours later as David stood before him. "Will you for God's sake relax and sit your ass down?" the admiral demanded.

"Sorry sir," David sat.

"You were given an impossible mission that shouldn't have even been necessary to start with, Anthony," Semmes said more calmly. "The fact that you managed to capture Chastain and bring his ships in is nothing short of a miracle. I note that most of his officers seemed to be cooperative?"

"I don't think the Captains of the Seadragon or Seasnake even realized what he was doing," David nodded. "While his people on the Halifax figured it out eventually, as Hart pointed out, knowing it and proving are two different things. They had essentially committed an act of mutiny when they refused to follow

Chastain's orders to continue to run."

"That is true," Semmes nodded. "All of that will come out in the court martial. As it is, we have more than enough men to man those ships and we need them, so it will work out. I think for now we will leave the prize crews in place unless any of them want shore duty while we're working up new and repaired ships. Meanwhile, we'll keep the current squadron close by. This place has to be protected at all costs until the fleet is rebuilt. I want this..." he handed David's report back, "...rewritten in a way that relays the facts without your taking blame for everything from the wind direction to the sea currents. Get it back to me by tomorrow."

"Aye aye, sir."

-

"I am-"

"I heard you the first time," the Coastal Captain said, raising a hand to stop Therron's saying it again. "That doesn't change the fact that it's a five-day ride to where my Colonel can take you off my hands. And while he may can get you to the Governor, there's no way that I can do it. So, you and your men make yourself comfortable tonight and tomorrow I'll have a patrol take you to our regimental headquarters, where I feel sure my Colonel can take care of your needs. Sir."

Seeing there was no reason to argue, Therron merely nodded and followed the young enlisted man who guided him to a small cottage used for visiting VIPs. It was at least more comfortable than sleeping against a tree in the forest.

"If you need anything sir, just ask," the young corporal said. "Mess is in one hour, sir."

"Thank you," Therron forced himself to be polite. He was still a long way from where he wanted to be. "I appreciate it."

"Of course, sir."

-

It was dark. So very dark. No, his eyes were closed, that was it. His eyes were closed even though he was awake? That didn't make any sense. There was something he needed to remember, but what was it? For some reason he thought of horses. Was it something about cava-

"Horses!" Harrel thought he shouted but only muttered

"What?" an orderly snapped to attention. "Did he say something?"

"Horses," Harrel repeated. "Wrong... wrong horses..."

"Get Lady Stephanie right now!" the young physician on duty demanded at once. "Tell her he is awake for the moment!"

-

Stephanie ran to the tent, led by the young orderly. She darted inside to find Parno already there but standing out of the way. She went at once to Harrel who was fighting to get up.

"Stop it Harrel," she told him at once. "Harrel!" she snapped and he stopped, eyes focusing slightly.

"Lady Stephanie?" he mumbled. "What are you doing here?"

"Trying to keep you alive, Harrel," Stephanie patted his jaw tenderly. "You've given us quite a scare."

"The horses are wrong," he said suddenly.

"What?" she couldn't understand. "What do horses have-"

"The couriers," Harrel told her. "They're riding the wrong horses. They're not real couriers. Tell the Prince the couriers aren't real."

"Harrel," Parno spoke gently and Stephanie started as she hadn't realized Parno had moved so close to her. "Harrel, I know about the couriers, thanks to you. You saved me, Harrel. You were hurt very badly but you saved me. You can relax, alright? Relax and rest because you did your job wonderfully well. You protected me when I couldn't do it myself."

"My Prince," Harrel's voice was muffled. "Greatest honor, my Prince. To have served... you... Colonel Darvo said keep... keep tha... that idiot al... alive..." Harrel's voice trailed off at that and Stephanie checked him over.

"He's just sleeping," she said finally. "Not unconscious, just sleeping. His subconscious has been trying to get you the message about the horses all this time and now that he has, he can rest." She looked up at Parno. "What does he mean?"

"Royal Couriers use some of the best horses anywhere in the Kingdom," Parno explained. "Two of the three who tried to kill me were riding horses that wouldn't make the cut for a cavalry unit, let alone a Royal Courier. That must have been what first tipped him off. He saw their horses."

"Remarkable," Stephanie shook her head.

"More than," Parno agreed. "I will miss him sorely. But at least he will live. Right?" he asked her.

"He should," she nodded. "His regaining consciousness even briefly is good. Very good, really."

"That's a relief," Parno exhaled deeply. "There's been enough loss. Getting someone back like this is a blessing." He stood up and walked outside the tent suddenly, leaving everyone else behind.

"Keep watching him, but I think we should start to see some improvement," Stephanie ordered. "Start the physical therapy on his legs and arms, but be very slow. All we want is to work the muscle groups, nothing else."

"Yes, milady."

Stephanie followed Parno out of the tent only to find that he had already disappeared among the moving bodies outside. Sighing in defeat, she returned to her own tent, her escort close around her. She found Edema lying across her bed, reading.

"How was he, dear?" Edema looked up from her book.

"He was awake for a good five minutes," Stephanie reported, removing her shoes and lying down across her own bed. "It's a wonderful sign, really. He is improving. I'm prepared to say he will almost certainly recover."

"That is great news," Edema sounded wistful. "We need some good news."

"Indeed."

-

Parno visited Army Headquarters again, where he had established a small temporary desk to deal with the things that he couldn't delegate to Davies or Enri. He resisted the idea of selecting a new secretary, though why he wasn't sure. He just did.

He spent an hour reading and signing bureaucratic nonsense that every military organization seemed to run on, mostly dealing with large expenditures of funds for everything from beef on the hoof to training equipment and supplies. All needed and yet for some reason all requiring his signature of approval. He needed to do something about that. Maybe a brigadier's post. Brigadier in Charge of Bullshit Paperwork. He snorted aloud at the title. It sounded funny anyway.

He looked up to see everyone looking at him in puzzlement.

"Just thought of something funny, that's all," he assured them. All returned to work, unwilling to risk asking what it was that had tickled the Prince's funny bone.

Parno finished the rest of his paperwork in silence.

-

General Westcott was already in an ill mood when his column came to a staggering halt in the middle of the road they were following.

"What now," he mumbled to himself as he and his aides rode forward. At the head of the column he found the commander of his lead brigade and the leader of his scout and picket force in conference.

"What in the bloody devil is going on?" Westcott demanded.

"Sir... sir you should come and see," the captain that led the picket detail stammered. "Begging your pardon, but... you really need to see this."

"Well, then lead me to it so we can get back moving," Westcott sighed. His people were not prone to panic so whatever this was, it was probably important. He followed the captain, the brigadier falling in uninvited and without orders, but Westcott didn't mind. It was a short ride, less than a quarter mile over a small rise. The captain halted at that point and sat waiting.

"Well?" Westcott demanded. The captain raised an arm and pointed. Following the point, Westcott saw ...

"Is that one of ours?" he asked.

"Yes sir," the captain nodded. "As near as I can tell, it's General Crandall, sir, of the 33rd Infantry."

"What? The 33rd is the unit we're supposed to be relieving!"

"Yes sir," the captain nodded. "But... sir, there is sign all around us of a massive battle, yet there's nothing to suggest that battle took place other than the signs on the ground. And here in front of us is General Crandall. And sir, this was left lying on his chest, sir," the man handed over a small object.

"A krishank," Westcott almost spat. "Are you telling me there is absolutely no sign, anywhere, of an entire Imperial infantry division? Ten thousand men plus attachments? Nothing?"

"Nothing sir," the captain nodded. "My men have looked for a mile in every direction including back the way we came in case we missed it. Nothing. We can't find a single sign of them anywhere other than the fact that there was definitely a battle fought here. In the last three days or less."

"And Crandall is all that's left." Westcott made it sound like a curse. "Get him on a horse and back to camp," he ordered the captain, then looked at the brigadier. "We'll continue, but I want a full company on each flank and out as a vanguard. We'll try not to join them," he nodded to Crandall's body.

"Yes sir," the brigadier nodded and rode back to begin issuing the orders.

"Make sure that General Wilson gets that krishank," Westcott ordered. "I'm sure there's a reason for it to be here. Maybe he'll know what it is."

"Yes sir," the scout captain nodded. "I'll see to it."

"When your men are positioned, continue on," he ordered the brigadier. "Our destination is unchanged."

-

"You're definitely doing better at this," Whipple said as he and Beaumont crossed the finish line together.

"Hard not to when I have to do it every day," Beaumont wasn't breathing too hard. "It's definitely made an improvement in our men."

"That is has," Whipple nodded. "While we may not be the equal of the Prince's Black Sheep, we can hold our own I feel sure." He looked at Beaumont more seriously.

"Speaking of which, did you send off your request?"

"I did," Beaumont nodded. "Added it to dispatches last time a rider went through. He should get it in a week or less."

"Well, we'll see what he says," Whipple nodded. "Meantime, about our integration..."

"Are you sure you want to do that before we hear back?" Beaumont asked. "It will mean losing your unit's history if we do. For us it's nothing more than a divisional identity that we no longer really answer to, but your men were a unit apart already."

"There's no particular glory attached to us," Whipple shrugged. "No real unit history, either. Just something I convinced the powers that be would work and be a good idea. And it has. They know it now and should probably be working it into another unit or even two. But saying good-bye to it won't be particularly difficult assuming we can make this work."

"Then we'll call a meeting of regimental commanders tonight and hammer out some details," Beaumont nodded. "The biggest problem will be breaking down who commands what."

"Thought about that," Whipple nodded. "Got an idea that will probably work. If we..."

-

"Milord."

Parno looked up at the quietly spoken word to see Tinker looking down at him.

"I thought this might be welcome," he offered a brown bottle that Parno recognized as the Tinker's own brew. He accepted it with a nod.

"Have a seat," Parno pointed to an empty chair by his fire. It was a lonely place anymore.

"I hear that young Mister Sprigs has awakened, if only briefly," Tinker began.

"Yes," Parno nodded. "Ste... Doctor Corsin says that is a good sign."

"I am glad to hear this," Tinker nodded. "I thought this might be a good time to talk with you, milord," he continued after a pause and a drink from his own bottle.

"About?"

"About why Jaelle refused to leave you," Tinker said evenly and suddenly had Parno's undivided attention.

"Among our people, a very few are gifted in ways that others are not," Tinker began by saying. "Among those few, a very, very rare number are gifted indeed with the ability to see. To actually peer into the future and see certain things. Do not mistake me. I refer not to those with globes of glass and jewels in their foreheads and other such nonsense, but real, true gifts."

"The thing is, milord, these gifts are most usually beyond the control of those who have them. While they may see what is to come, they cannot choose what they see or where or when. All they can do is accept what is given to them. What they get is all there is."

"Was Jaelle one of these rare few?" Parno had a sick feeling in his stomach.

"She was, indeed," Tinker nodded. "Jaelle could occasionally see what was to be. Sometimes for herself, sometimes for others. She could see things almost as they happened, but she could not tell when those things might happen. Do you see what I am saying?"

"She knew it was coming but not when," Parno nodded glumly.

"Yes," Tinker's voice was firm. "She knew. She had seen it. This is why she told you she must be there. She had already seen it happen. It was where she was supposed to be."

"Then why not tell me?" Parno asked the older man. "Why not just tell me so that we could take precautions that might have spared her! Spared Harrel!"

"Would you have believed her?" Tinker asked kindly. "If she had told you 'I have seen you die' would you have believed her?"

"I don't know," Parno admitted.

"Or would you have sent her away and never spoken to her again?" Tinker continued.

"Probably," Parno had to answer. He probably would have done just that.

"So, she did the only thing she could do," Tinker explained. "She stayed as close to you as she could, waiting for the time she had seen in her vision. When it presented itself, she acted."

"I'd rather she not have and lived," Parno said softly.

"And I am sure she knew that, milord," Tinker smiled slightly. "I am sure that she did. Jaelle was a kind-hearted young woman, but she was also a very smart one. You could have even called her beguiling, were her motives less than pure. She was smart enough to know that you would not want her in harm's way, and even that being around you was a threat."

"She also knew that you are important to this Kingdom, and to her people," Tinker went on. "For her, the choice was easy. She wished you to live. Her love for you was no less real simply because it was also better for others if she died rather than you. If anything, it was a greater act of love. She could have been safe yet chose to place herself in danger believing your life more valuable than her own." Tinker stood suddenly, looking down at the young prince.

"I shared this with you not to anger you or sadden you, but to let you know that Jaelle knew exactly what she was doing. I did not know myself until you told me what she said, but at that point it was beyond what I could do to bring her back. I am allowed only so much, and refusing her that choice is beyond my means, my Prince. Even one such as I have limits."

"Take the life she has given you, my Prince, and use it well," Tinker urged. "Bleed your enemies, reward your friends, love those close to you and hold them dear. That is what she wanted. That is why she did what she did." He began walking away.

"If you have need of me, you know where I will be."

-

"Stephanie dear, it's time we talked, you and I."

Stephanie stifled a groan when she heard Edema's voice. She lifted her face from where it was buried in pillows and faced the older woman with a sense of resignation.

"What is it now?" she asked politely.

"I know you are vexed with me and have every right to be," Edema nodded. "I admit as I did earlier that I had not realized had badly he was stung by your argument. However, the simple fact is that he still loves you, deeply. If you are ever going to take advantage of that then it must be now."

"What?" Stephanie sat up straight, not sure she heard right.

"You heard me," Edema nodded. "He told me himself that he is still in love with you. That as much as he might have cared for Jaelle, sweet girl that she was, he did not love her. Nor was she a substitute for you, but more a shelter for him in a time of storm. When everything seemed to be against him and everything he had thought he knew had crumbled, she offered him shelter. She was kind to him in a way few people ever have been and she asked nothing of him. She simply... gave. Practically the exact opposite of everyone he had ever known. It would have been all but impossible for him to refuse such a one. And had he done so we would be preparing his own funeral right now."

"I know," Stephanie nodded, her voice quiet. "I've thought of that more than once."

"Things happen for a reason, Stephanie," Edema told her. "We don't always get to know the reason, but that doesn't mean the reason isn't there. Had you and Parno not quarreled the way you did then Jaelle would not have been a part of his life, and... again, he would be dead. I could go on for the rest of the day about how things happen but I doubt I need to. You're too smart not to understand."

"So instead, I'm going to talk to you the way Margolyn might have, had she lived. If you are going to love my son, then love him completely. If you are going to give yourself to him, do so completely. Because he will return the same to you. It is all he knows. Perhaps that is unfortunate in some things, this all or nothing attitude of his, but in love for that one true and special person I think it is the most fortunate thing one could ask for."

"If you are going to do this then you will have to do it, because he won't. Indeed, I doubt he can. And if you do it then you are creating exactly the problem he refused to entertain when he first became aware of your affection for him."

"If you are successful then there will be a scandal no doubt, but we're in the middle of a war that may last for years and we may yet be defeated. The King was murdered by his own daughter, she tried to kill the Crown Prince, was killed by a distant cousin and her brother is still on the loose trying to steal the Kingdom from the oldest brother. What's one small scandal more or less in times such as these?" Edema smiled weakly.

"You must be sure," the older woman warned her. "I will not tolerate anything less for him, ever. You must be completely and absolutely certain before you act, because you cannot take it back. If you cannot be sure then... then forget this talk and when we go home put this all behind you as he told you. No one can make that decision for you, and that includes him. So, I am telling you now, speaking about a man I love like a son, if you want him then go and claim him, Stephanie. Let nothing stand in your way. Life is simply too short."

"I..." Stephanie was speechless. Struck dumb by this speech.

"I will support you any way that I can regardless of your decision, but remember this," her blue eyes turned icy. "Mistreat him in any way and I will kill you myself. As I said, one more scandal more or less will make no difference now."

Stephanie was still trying to process Edema's first speech when the threat arrived. She swallowed hard at the sudden iciness that seemed to surround Edema Willows and nodded her understanding of the older woman's threat as well as everything else she had said.

"Well," Edema was suddenly all smiles again. "I'm glad we had this little talk, you and I. I feel better about things already. You?"

Stephanie nodded again.

"Splendid!"

-

"We called all of you here together to tell you something we're working on," Beaumont told the assembled regimental commanders and their seconds. "We've worked well together over the last three months or so and have the record to prove it. After this is over, we'll be put back to work wherever the Prince thinks we'll be the most use, I'm sure."

"The two of us," Whipple took over, "have been discussing this for some time, trying to work out the details as best we could and I'm satisfied we've done it, more or less. Our plan is to integrate the two brigades completely, making them one unit in reality as well as name. General Beaumont will continue to command and I'll be his second."

"What about us?" one of Whipple's archers asked, hand raised. "What happens to us?"

"As to your rank, nothing," Beaumont answered that one. "The plan is a fairly simple one but we think it will be effective. We will essentially swap half regiments. The result will be a regiment that has half swords or lancers and half mounted archers. That organization will run throughout the... hmm," he trailed off, thinking. It was too big to be a brigade, but not large enough to be a true division.

"Demi-division," Whipple supplied. "We aren't quite a division, but far more than a brigade. Since we're an independent command that shouldn't matter. Speaking of which, there's one more thing."

"I've sent a request to the Prince," Beaumont announced. "Asking that we be taken into his service in our new configuration and become part of his personal command."

"You mean become Black Sheep?" another man asked.

"I don't know that we'll actually be called Black Sheep, since that name may be reserved for those who fought at the Gap, I don't know. But I have asked that we be assigned to him personally to carry out such orders as he deems needed or necessary. We're already doing it anyway so making it official is just the last step. Does anyone have any objections to what you've heard so far?"

"I don't know much about archery," one of Beaumont's men said hesitantly. "I'm not sure I'd know how to deploy archers."

"You will when we're done," Whipple promised. "Just as my men will know how to deploy horse mounted swordsmen and lancers. We'll also assign ranking officers from each unit in their specialty. Once we get shook down and accustomed to operating together, it should be fine."

"We can do this," Beaumont promised. "We can do this and we can be of great service to the Prince, as we already have. And if we can't be known as Black Sheep then we'll just pick our own name. How about that?" he grinned.

Grins answered him. His men liked the idea.

-

Stephanie took a deep breath, trying to settle her nerves. This was not what she'd had in mind for her-

"Are you sure about this?" Edema broke into her thoughts again.

"Will you please stop asking me that?" she replied in exasperation. "It's difficult enough without that constant distraction!"

"Sorry," Edema apologized. "I will make sure the arrangements are made."

"Thank you," the young doctor nodded. "And yes, just so you know; I'm sure. I always have been."

-

Parno made use of the small tub that Jaelle had arranged for, bathing the dust from his body at the end of the day. His mind ran to many things but mostly hovered over what Tinker had said to him coupled with thoughts about Stephanie and the things Edema had said about her.

How did things get so muddled and messed up like this? Where was the certainty in life that others seemed to enjoy? He often thought of himself as cursed to live in a perpetual state of confusion and unsteadiness. When he did, at least when he caught himself doing it, he stopped, refusing to participate in anything like self-pity. He had taught himself long ago that self-pity was a weakness, and he didn't allow himself such weaknesses. He couldn't because others would take advantage of those weaknesses, exploit them, use them against him. He shook his head at a life that made a small boy adopt such ideas in order to protect himself.

He stood up from the tub and took his towel, drying himself off, shaking out his short hair before ruffing it with the towel. He went to the small table where his few toiletries were found and combed out his hair, then applied a small amount of cologne he had received as a gift long ago from a woman he should not have been associated with. Whose name in fact he could not remember. How many women could he say that of? He didn't know, to be honest. So many of them had been drunken trysts that meant nothing to him because he couldn't remember them.

"I really am a mess," he said aloud, blowing out a long exhale.

"I've said the same thing more than once about both of us," a female voice said behind him and Parno twisted at once, hand going to a small blade he kept hidden beside the dressing table.

Standing behind him in the shadows thrown by his shuttered lantern was a cloaked figure, silent and still in the face of his sword.

"You won't need that particular weapon tonight, Parno McLeod," the figure said softly as feminine hands emerged from the cloak to lower the hood, revealing Stephanie Corsin-Freeman, her hair pulled up into a bun that could be concealed by the hood.

"Stephanie?" Parno's surprise was complete. "I have to say you are the last person I was expecting," he managed to add despite his astonishment at her presence.

"I can see that," she nodded, a faint smile on her face. At that point Parno realized he was holding a short sword pointed in her direction. A second later he realized he was also completely naked. He placed the sword on the table and grabbed the towel, hastily wrapping it around himself.

"Don't do that on my account," she told him.

"It's not on... that's not... what are you doing here?" he finally managed to demand.

"I'm here to claim what's mine," she told him simply. "Sit," she pointed to a straight-backed chair near the middle of his large tent. For a second she thought he would refuse, but then he moved to the chair and sat down.

"I love you," she told him plainly. "I think I have since the second time I met you, but I'm not sure. I just know that at some point you became the one person I can't live without." She moved closer to him.

"I placed a great demand on you, a great burden at a time when you already had more on you than you could handle. That was wrong of me, selfish of me I suppose, and I am so very sorry. I said hateful things to you that I didn't mean because I was hurt and angry and I wanted you to see it. You left Nasil thinking I no longer loved you and didn't want to be with you. You could not be more wrong. You could never be more wrong." She stopped in front of him and opened the cloak, revealing that she was wearing the scantest of lingerie beneath it and nothing else.

"Wha-"

"I'm here to take what's mine," she told him again. "To claim what is mine for now and all time. I don't care that you had a fling with Jaelle, more especially since her being with you kept you alive. I will never be able to repay her for that. I don't care about the scandal this will cause. I don't care about the customs, about the danger or about anything else. You are mine, Parno McLeod and you always will be. And I'm here to make sure you don't ever forget it."

Before he could speak, she had straddled him and lowered herself almost to the point of joining them. At some unknown point he seemed to have lost his towel. She held herself off him by the strength of her arms and legs, looking him in the eyes.

"If you can't be sure, then now is the time to say so," she told him simply. "After this, there's no going back. I won't share you and I won't be second in your heart to anyone. Understand? No one."

"Ah-" Parno still hadn't managed to form a real word.

"Look me in the eyes and tell me that you don't love me and I'll go, and we will never have this discussion again," she continued, still hovering above him. "Look me in the eyes and tell me that you do love me and we'll never *need* to have this discussion again, because I'll belong to you for the rest of my life. Second to no one, forever and ever."

She was so close. He could feel the heat from her body, smell the hints of perfume she had dabbed in delicate places, but... it was her eyes that hypnotized him. Even in the lantern light the almost predatory look in her eyes was intense enough to take his breath away and leave him gasping for air.

"So, which is it to be, Parno McLeod," she whispered huskily. "Choose."

Head still swimming, Parno said the only thing he could under the circumstances.

"I love you Stephanie," he replied honestly. "I always have."

Hearing that, she bent her head and kissed him furiously. As their tongues fought for supremacy, she began to slowly and gently lower herself on to him. Carefully, bit by bit, so slowly that it actually heightened the sensations both were feeling, she descended upon him until she was completely astride him, enveloping him, her weight now firmly on him and her cloak now encompassing them both. There was a slight bit of pain which she had expected, but...

"Oh my God," she whispered as she broke the kiss. "I-"

"Shh," he whispered in her ear. "You brought us this far. Let me do the rest."

CHAPTER SEVENTEEN

-

Parno woke slowly, almost reluctantly, his eyes blurry enough that he wondered if he'd gotten drunk the night before and forgotten it. As he started to move he became immediately aware of another presence in his bed and suddenly his eyesight was completely clear as he gazed down at the peacefully sleeping visage of Stephanie Corsin-Freeman spooned up against him. Naked. Naked and rather obviously...

"Oh, this is so not good," he whispered to himself.

But it was. It had been. As he replayed the events of the previous evening over in his mind, he realized that for all intents and purposes he'd just had his wedding night. Their wedding night.

In the middle of an army camp, in the middle of a war.

Recognizing the number of things he needed to see to, Parno eased his way from the bed, leaving behind a blissfully sleeping woman to go and start seeing to those things.

He bathed himself in the water that was available, then quietly called for warm water to be brought while he drained the tub. He noted a small bag set outside his tent and rightly guessed it was for his guest, pulling it inside before too many people could see it. By the time he bathed and dressed the hot water had arrived and he took it himself and poured it into the tub. The sound of water splashing was enough to wake his house guest because as he came from behind the screen with the last bucket she was sitting up in the bed, smiling. Her hair was somewhat tousled, loose and flowing around her in a sexy way he'd never seen or imagined seeing, almost like a dark curtain of hair surrounding and embracing her. She was easily the most beautiful thing he'd ever seen.

"Good morning, Parno," she purred.

"Good morning, Stephanie," he smiled back at her. He crossed to the bed and kissed her gently before drawing back...

"There is fresh hot water in the tub, and your co-conspirator has left a bag with clean clothes outside my door sometime during the night. Lord knows what she heard," he sighed.

"Not much since I kept biting you to keep from screaming," Stephanie giggled. *Actually giggled*. He'd never heard her do it that he could recall. Maybe he had, but at least never in this situation.

"Yes, I do seem to be covered in sores this morning," Parno rubbed his shoulder. "But I'm sure they will heal and if they don't I know a good doctor."

"A good doctor?" she looked at him with a frown. "You know an excellent doctor, I'll thank you to remember."

"That is, of course, what I meant," he agreed with an amused snort of barely contained laughter. "In the meanwhile, your bag has toiletries inside and I have just filled my small tub with hot water for you, so you are all set. I need to go over to Army Headquarters and make sure no one stole the Army from me during the night but I will be back probably by lunch."

"It's a date then," Stephanie nodded, rising from the bed completely bare and kissing him again. Parno drank the sight of her in, already regretting getting dressed. Stephanie let him go for several seconds before clearing her throat.

"Going to check on the Army, weren't you?" she asked with a raised eyebrow.

"Right!" he nodded, tearing his gaze away. "I was indeed. I will see you for lunch."

She was humming as she went to immerse herself in that hot water he had so sweetly provided her.

-

"Well?" Edema asked as Stephanie arrived 'home' to their tent in the late morning.

"You already know how it went since I didn't come back," Stephanie teased. "But if you must know, it went perfectly. Could not have been better in fa-."

"Let's not get into too much detail, dear," Edema caught her before she could go further. "A simple worked or didn't will suffice. Good for you. For both of you."

"I never imagined my wedding night would be in the middle of an army camp on the front lines of a great war," the younger woman sighed. "My life has the strangest turns in it."

"A product of falling for Parno, no doubt," Edema laughed.

"I have to go and check on Harrel," Stephanie said as she picked up her bag. "I'm having lunch with Parno. What are you doing today?"

"I... have an idea I'm trying to put together," Edema was almost mysterious. "No idea if it will work or if it's even practicable, but once I've got it sorted a bit further, I'll probably want you to look at it. See what you think."

"I'd be glad to."

-

"Are you telling me that the only sign you can find of an entire Imperial Infantry division is the body of its commanding General and this damn dagger?" Wilson was yelling by the time he finished his sentence.

"The ground is littered with sign of a battle, sir, but... just that. Nothing else. No equipment, no bodies, nothing. Just General Crandall's body in the road with that... thing," he pointed to the krishank.

"Damn you, Smith," Wilson muttered to himself. "This is all your doing." He looked at the man in front of him.

"Get a fresh horse and head back to your unit. Tell General Westcott that when he reaches Unity he is to overnight there and then return with General Taylor's 16th Infantry. Write that up for him to carry with him," Wilson told Sterling, who nodded and started writing.

"Can't even hold a simple exercise," Wilson muttered, looking out the window. "What else is this going to cost us?" he wondered.

-

General Westcott examined Unity with a clear look of distaste, his mind fighting to take in the sight even as his lead brigade deployed around him.

"Looks as if the town caught fire during a battle sir," one of his scouts reported, returning from riding through what was left. "There are still a few smoldering embers spread around but the fires are mostly out. I found a few bodies here and there but... identification just isn't possible. They're burned too badly."

"Any sign of Taylor and his men?" Westcott asked quietly. He already knew the answer but had to ask, for form's sake if nothing else.

"Afraid not, sir," the scout confirmed Westcott's thoughts. "It looks like the most of the fighting was done in the town square. Most of that area is pretty well tore up."

"Sir!" another voice broke in as a second scout came galloping up to him, a small cloud of dust following.

"Sir, I... I think we found General Taylor. Sir," the man saluted as if he didn't know what else to do.

"You think?" Westcott repeated. "Did you find him or not?" he demanded.

"We found a body in a general's uniform, sir," the scout replied. "He was hanging from an arch over the main street leading in from the north, sir. And he had this tied to his hand," the scout handed over the second krishank that Westcott had seen in as many days.

"Perfect," he muttered. "Cut him down," he ordered. "Get a detail together to dig enough grave space for what we found. Keep one brigade on watch and ready at all times. As soon as we can clean away this mess, we're on the road out of here. We're going back."

"Sir?" his second in command was startled. "Sir, our orders-"

"This place is a damn death trap," Westcott said softly. "Hell, this whole road is one long abattoir. We are not going to sit inside it one second longer than we have to. Understand?"

"Yes sir," the man saluted and started issuing orders.

"Wilson can come out here himself if he doesn't like it," Westcott ignored the colonel after that, thinking of the things he had found. He wasn't about to lose his entire division the same way Crandall and Taylor had. Not if he could help it.

-

Parno looked at the proposal in his hands with more than a little appreciation. He and Karls had discussed whether or not to allow inclusions into the Black Sheep and had never come to a decision they were happy with. Now Beaumont and Whipple might have solved that problem, or at least given Parno a litmus test.

Beaumont and Whipple were loyal to Parno, and more than that they were loyal to the Crown. He had twice sent them on special missions, one of them distasteful in the extreme, and both times they had performed brilliantly. Both had likewise done extremely well during the cavalry engagement Parno himself had led. They were smart and capable, and their men were loyal.

"You wanted to see me?" Karls asked, entering the small tent Parno had appropriated as his 'office'.

"Take a look at this," he handed the proposal to Karls. "Tell me what you think." Karls read quickly, then looked at Parno.

"House troops?" he asked. "You can't roll them into the Regiment. There's too many of them. And their plan is to create a short division, combining their two brigades. The idea itself has merit but... how do you apply them? And this still doesn't answer the question of whether or not we're going to allow applicants for placement into the Regiment itself. We're getting more and more requests all the time from officers and enlisted alike. Have been since we arrived, to be honest."

"I still don't know about that," Parno admitted. "I do know that Beaumont and Whipple work well together and their men were already a cut above. They're breezing through the workouts at the Canton I'm told and will graduate far ahead of schedule. Having such a unit at my beckon call that isn't attached to a parent unit or doesn't have to be pulled from a line unit... it has a certain appeal."

"I'm sure it does," Karls almost snorted. "Up until now that's what the Black Sheep have been for."

"I think we'll need to keep the Sheep close to home for a while," Parno commented. Karls nodded at that without comment.

"So, what is your opinion?" Parno asked again.

"I don't have a problem with them being called Black Sheep if you don't," Karls admitted. "But we need a special badge to identify those who were at the Gap. They deserve that much and more."

"Agreed," Parno nodded. "I've considered using ribbons or badges for every major engagement that can be added to a uniform. What do you think of that? To help build morale among the line units."

"Make those who don't have badges want them," Karls nodded. "That's not a bad idea. But how far do you intend to extend the name Black Sheep inside the Army?"

"I don't know, but if I do this then not much further," Parno admitted. "It needs to be small enough to make men work for it."

"Agreed," Karls nodded once more. "Will the Regiment be rolled into…"

"No," Parno was quick to shake his head. "No, the Black Sheep, and you, answer directly to me and no one else. No one else," he emphasized. "That doesn't change, I don't care who it is. Very well, I think I will approve this and see how well it works." He made a few quick strokes with a pen, then looked up.

"How is Graham and 1st Corps hanging in?" he asked.

"Quite well," Karls nodded. "They will finish far ahead of schedule at this rate. They didn't need any basic instruction at all and were already proficient with sword and lance and horse. Archery for all is presenting a training issue but we're working it and it's coming along. Hand-to-hand is a bit slower, but none of us caught on any faster. I'd say no more than another month and you'll have an entire Corps trained nearly to our standards and ready for service."

"That might be the best news we could get on the war front," Parno breathed a sigh of relief. "Now if the enemy will give us that month, we'll be in much better shape."

-

"Any more word from Westcott?" Wilson wanted to know.

"Nothing so far, sir," Sterling shook his head. "I can send-"

"No," Wilson shook his own head, cutting the younger man off. "No, let's don't jog his elbow any. We expect him to command, so let him command. Besides, if he is in trouble one courier won't be of any help."

"Very good sir."

-

"It's almost dark," Westcott examined the sun. His men had just force marched at least five miles back to the east of Unity. They had to be exhausted and he felt for them, he did. He also feared for them. Something had happened to both Crandall and now Taylor's entire divisions. He didn't want the same fate falling on his own men.

"We'll make a cold camp here," he told his assembled commanders. "Regiments to camp in line of battle down both sides of the road. Double watches with pickets no further than fifty yards out. Get it done so they can be settled in before dark."

The various commanders broke away, headed back their units to pass along those orders. Westcott watched them go, hoping he hadn't passed his fear along to them. The night would be long enough as it was.

-

"Large body of horsemen approaching from the west," a picket courier announced to the Sergeant of the Guard.

"Report up the line," the sergeant ordered. "Likely our men returning, but we'll take no chances. Sound the alert!"

Men began running to their posts, positioning for an attack. The sergeant knew that the Norland cavalry was supposed to be in Lovil, sick as dogs, so any large body of horsemen should be their own returning. But with the heathen Tribals attached to the northern army, it paid not to take chances.

"Hello the camp!" a voice called from the dark. "1st Corps, Soulan Cavalry returning!"

"Come forward and be recognized!" the sergeant bellowed back, hand caressing his sword. That hand relaxed as men wearing the army of the Soulan Army appeared into the torchlight, one wearing the stars of a general.

"General Gerald Allen, commanding 1st Cavalry Corp, returning from mission," he reported, returning the sergeant's salute.

"Welcome back sir," the guard replied. "You'll be heading to your old billets?"

"Yes, but we have a train of captured goods and wagons of wounded as well that we need to see to," Allen nodded.

"I'll notify the Hospital Corps then, sir."

"And I will be riding to see General Davies."

"Sir."

-

"One thousand three hundred and fifty-nine dead, two thousand, six hundred seventy-two wounded. Some of the wounded will return within the week or less, some won't return at all," Allen finished his report.

"But you destroyed completely two Imperial Infantry divisions, General," Davies nodded. "According to your records that amounts to just over twenty-two thousand men, all of them dead and the bodies disposed of in such a way as to make it look as if they just disappeared!" Davies hand slapped his desk. "I'd give a pretty gold coin to see the look on the face of the Imperial commander when he hears that, I would!" He looked up at Allen.

"I know you feel your losses, General," his voice softened. "I felt every one of mine as we retreated from Lovil. It never seemed to stop. But remember that we didn't start this war and did all we could to prevent it. You have thirteen hundred and fifty-nine dead but they have over twenty-two thousand! That's the damage you did to them, General. Remember that. Try to always remember that. You spent your men well and that's all a soldier can ask. That his commander spends him well."

"Yes sir," Allen nodded, actually feeling a bit better.

"I will expect your full report day after tomorrow," Davies returned to business. "Until then your men are on rest depending on enemy action. Dismissed, General."

"Thank you, sir," Allen snapped to and departed.

"How do you bastards like that, ay?" Davies turned to the north and asked the dark.

-

"There was a lot of activity tonight as I was coming in," Stephanie said as she brushed her hair. She was seated at her own nightstand which now occupied Parno's tent. She had apparently meant what she said about not caring about scandal or anything else.

"Cavalry returning from a raid," Parno nodded. He was restless and didn't know why. Perhaps it was having her so close. It wasn't that he was uneasy but rather... he didn't know what to do or say. He'd not been in this exact position before.

"Calm down," she told him, running the brush through her long locks. She normally kept her hair swept up if not in a high bun to keep it out of her way, so she brushed it out each night.

"I'm calm," Parno tried to assure her.

"No, you're not," she replied. "Are you that intimidated by my being here?" she turned to look at him. "Is my presence causing you so much fluster?"

"Yes. No!" he stammered. "I don't know!" he finally admitted. "I... this is new to me," he admitted.

"Really?" she raised an elegant eyebrow.

"You know what I mean!" he exclaimed at the implication in her voice. "I... I don't..."

"Relax," she told him again, putting her brush down and standing. She crossed the room to stand before him. "It's alright." She put her arms around him and pulled him in tight.

"It's not... I don't..." Parno struggled just to speak but finally gave up and just returned her embrace.

"I'm the one who will have to deal with the looks and the talk and the innuendo," she reminded him. "And I will. I told you, I don't care." She pulled back to look at him.

"My God, Parno McLeod, have you truly no idea how much I love you?" she asked him softly. "Had I been where Jaelle was I would gladly have done the same thing she did to keep you safe."

"Don't say that!" Parno closed his eyes, trying not to picture what Stephanie had said. "Don't say anything like that again! I can't stand it!" he tried to turn away but she tightened her grip around him, pulling him back to her instead. She pulled his head down to her shoulder and held him.

"I'm sorry," she whispered. "I didn't mean to make you think of it. Of her."

"You're so foolish to be so smart," Parno's muffled voice was plain nonetheless. "I wasn't thinking of her. I was thinking of you in her place. Maybe I don't realize how much you love me, Stephanie, but I don't think you know how much I love you, either."

Stephanie was startled by that admission. It had never occurred to her. She had always assumed that hers was the greater love because of Parno's distance. She was learning that Edema was right and that his distance was a defense mechanism, nothing more. He didn't show love because he was afraid to. It had been used against him too many times. She reminded herself once more that despite all Parno had accomplished, all that he was responsible for, he was still only twenty years old. Twenty years old and emotionally crippled by his family and those around him during his formative years. Having someone actually care for him wasn't something he'd seen much of.

"I'm right here," she whispered. "I will always be here when you need me. I will never desert you. You are the great love of my lifetime and I will cherish you always."

They stayed that way for a long time, the two of them. They had both learned something this night.

CHAPTER EIGHTEEN

-

General Westcott looked at his ragged infantry plodding along and knew their suffering. He had walked much of the way with them, leading his horse rather than riding.

"Just five more miles," he said aloud but to no one in particular. "Five miles back to the main camp and we can rest," he promised anyone who could hear. He stopped as a horse mounted officer rode up to him and halted.

"Sir, we aren't going to make it," the man said. "The men have covered almost twenty miles today and that may well be a record for a forced infantry march, but it's an hour, hour-and-a-half at most before full dark. We can't make the main camp by then, sir. We've got to stop while we can still see to make a safe camp."

Westcott sighed, admitting defeat without actually surrendering to it. He had known pretty much all along that he couldn't, that his men couldn't make this march in one day. They had done damn well, though, and he was proud of them.

"Call the halt and make camp," he ordered. "Scouts out to take a look around and pickets posted as before. Guard is still doubled but cut guard watches to one hour. Let everyone get a least a little sleep."

"Yes sir," the man saluted and went on his way. Five minutes later words moved down the column; halt and prepare to camp.

"Thank God," was the most muttered phrase in the entire division as the men fell out.

Westcott spent an hour walking down the line, alone and leading his horse, telling his men how proud he was of them and why it was so important to get back to camp as quickly as possible. Why is was so important to keep the guard doubled and everything else that was the cause of all this trouble.

By the end of his walk, Westcott's esteem and reputation had risen much higher in the eyes of his soldiers.

-

General Brent Stone was seated at his desk, still feeling the effects of that rotten beef. He was getting treatment as were his men and they were all recovering nicely, but... Stone was looking at the figures for his divisions and could not see this foray as anything other than a disaster.

He had departed Lovil with almost twenty-five thousand troopers, all well-trained and equipped. Between the battles against the Soulan army and the losses to illness, he could now muster only sixteen thousand three hundred and twelve men.

Almost ten thousand casualties. Of those, roughly one-third were combat casualties. The rest were lost to the dysentery brought on by eating that ruined beef. Some would recover, others would not. Many had already perished on the return trip. Even now temporary hospitals overflowed with sick soldiers who were losing water at both ends and couldn't keep anything down. He tossed his pen down on his desk and rubbed his head.

He had burned Nasil, the Royal City. Maybe that would count for something, but he doubted it. He was meant to draw troops away from the main battle front, but the troops he had encountered were either in place already or had come from the east, not the west. His mission had failed but he was still faced with these horrendous casualties.

Like it or not, his unit was out of action for the foreseeable future.

-

"I've taken the majority of the troopers who aren't sick from the other divisions and added to yours," Stone told a wooden faced Baxter. "It should put you just over your nominal strength, but then you'll have to shake down and train again to make sure they can work as a unit. So, take them, and this," he handed over a sheaf of reports, "and head for the main army camp and report to General Wilson. I'm sure he will have use for your men. The rest of us will follow once we are sufficiently recovered."

"Yes sir," Baxter nodded, accepting the reports. "Will there be anything else"

"No," Stone shook his head. "It's entirely possible that you will end up in command of the remaining cavalry of the Imperial Army in this sector," he said quietly. "If that happens, learn from my mistakes. Take better care of your men than I have. And try to get some mounted archers."

"Yes sir," Baxter wasn't quite so wooden now. "I will do my best. I'm sure the rest of you will be back with us soon."

"From your lips to the Emperor's ear," Stone nodded. "You have your orders."

-

"Harrel was awake this evening but has gone to sleep now," Stephanie reported as Parno returned to 'their' tent for the evening. "His condition is much improved. In another week I think we can look at getting him off that table without tearing anything."

"That's good news," Parno nodded. "How long do you intend to stay?" he asked, removing his jacket.

"I will stay until I'm certain of his recovery or until I'm summoned by the King," she replied.

"I'm glad," Parno told her. It was clear that he was tired.

"Why don't you get cleaned up and try to get some rest?" she suggested. "Even an easy day for you seems more than enough to tire a man out."

"Doesn't it, though?"

-

"So, regimental commanders will remain the same while the seconds will move with their respective battalions and take over as Executive Officers for the new regiment. Is that clear?"

"Yes sir," chorused back twelve voices. Beaumont nodded in approval.

"I expect regimental commanders to make full use of their new Seconds in order to get the maximum use out of their combined regiments. I won't tolerate anything less and neither will General Whipple. Is that also clear?"

"Yes sir," the chorus sang.

"Now, off the record and without reprisal, are there any of you who have a problem with this arrangement. Any of you who don't think you can manage this or make this work?"

"I don't have a problem but I do have a question," an archery commander raised his hand.

"Go ahead then."

"We're going to have to completely relearn how to deploy our men and how to use them to the greatest advantage. That's going to take some time and a lot of training. Do we have that kind of time?"

"We have some time," Whipple answered that one. "We are far ahead of schedule on the retraining regimen and because of that we can dedicate some of that time to retraining, which is what we will be doing starting tomorrow. Does that answer your question?"

"Yes sir."

"Anyone else?" Beaumont asked. There were a few looks around the room, but no more questions.

"You are elite soldiers," Beaumont told them. "You lead elite soldiers in battle. You can do this. So can they. And we'll be better for it. If there's nothing else then you're all dismissed. And good evening to you all."

-

General Westcott had his men up an estimated one hour before daylight to break camp and be ready to march. There was general grumbling through the ranks but not nearly as much as there might have been without Westcott's walk through the day before. His men now realized their precarious situation and wanted out of it as quickly as he did.

As soon as it was light enough to see properly, the 14th Imperial Infantry was on the march again.

"We can march easier today and still make it by noon," Westcott repeated over and over as he rode his column, trying to raise the morale of his men. He would dismount on occasion and walk alongside them, laughing about how his feet ached and how much he looked forward to a hot meal and soft blanket in his tent. His men agreed, all wondering at how they could or would consider army food a delicacy, but three days of cold camping made almost any hot food appetizing. Even army food.

"Just three miles now," Westcott promised as he remounted. "We should be hitting picket posts any time now!"

Just three more miles.

-

"You're telling me we have lost two entire infantry divisions?" Wilson demanded of a bedraggled Westcott four hours later.

"Yes sir."

"Nothing to find from any of them?" Wilson demanded.

"We found Generals Crandall and Taylor, sir," Westcott reported. "Taylor had this tied to his right hand" he produced another krishank dagger. "There were a few remains in the burned area of the town but nothing we could identify as being definitely Imperial. And not nearly enough bodies for an entire division. Sir."

"So, you just turned around and came back," Wilson said, eyeing Westcott carefully.

"Yes sir, I did," Westcott didn't flinch. "Two Imperial infantry divisions disappeared along that road or in that town. That tells me that whatever did them in is going to require a larger force to deal with. I had one division and that obviously wasn't enough on at least two occasions. I saw no reason to give them the chance to destroy another."

Wilson continued to examine Westcott for a full minute, then nodded.

"I agree," he stood, walking around his desk and patting Westcott on his shoulder. "We'll have to see what's happening out there, but you were right to preserve your command. Give your men two days stand down before putting them back on the line. I'll examine the information you've brought me and see what I can come up with."

"Yes sir," Westcott saluted and then departed. Wilson sat down again, *slumped down* would be more accurate, looking at the krishank.

"Damn you, Smith."

-

"We need to be especially alert to enemy movements the next few days," Davies told Doak Parsons as the two studied the large wall map of the engagement area. "We've stung them hard and hurt them. We have to expect them to hit back, somewhere. They don't have the cavalry for a raid in force, at least not yet. Truthfully, I expect them to hit us head on, right here," he slapped the middle of the colored lines depicting Soulan positions.

"I've got men strung out for several miles to our west," Parsons showed him. "And a second line about three miles south of them. They can get through but doing it without us seeing them will take some doing. I can try to push forward more toward their lines, but... that really puts my men at risk."

"No, let's not do that," Davies shook his head. "Let's instead maintain the positions we've been using, though consider beefing them up a bit. Instead of trying to push further toward their lines, we add men into the areas we already cover. We can't keep them out there forever but we should be able to manage for the next week or so. Yes?"

"We can do that, sir," Parsons nodded, already thinking about deployments. "I'll start working it out right now."

"Very good," Davies nodded. "And don't forget to use our regular scouts as well as your own men," Davies said. "No reason for your men to carry the entire burden."

"Thank you, sir."

-

Parno was still restless and he knew it wasn't entirely because of his new situation with Stephanie. He was sure that played a part, but it wasn't it. He visited Harrel briefly only to discover that he was asleep, then made his way over to Headquarters to meet with Davies.

"Something is up," Parno said without preamble and was surprised when Davies nodded his agreement.

"I think you're right. I spoke with Mister Parsons earlier and we've strengthened the scout line. We're going to raise our alert level among the scouts for the next week. We can't keep that up indefinitely but we can go for that long anyway."

"Has there been any further movement out toward Unity?" Parno asked.

"No sir, and the third division they sent out returned today around noon," Davies replied. "The stories they're telling by now should be rocking through their entire camp."

"That could work for or against us," Parno mused. "Have to wait and see I suppose. What shape is Allen's group in?"

"Splendid," Davies reported. "A day or two of rest for them and their horses would be ideal, but their losses, while substantial, were in no way crippling. And they killed over twenty-two thousand Imperial infantry in two days."

"Few more battles like that and we could call the war and go home," Parno couldn't help but grin.

"It would be helpful," Davies agreed. "But I don't expect them to offer us that opportunity again. And if they do, it's almost certainly going to be a trap."

-

"I want a meeting of all corps commanders this evening at one hour before mess," Wilson told Sterling. "They should bring their seconds, and their chief of staff. Expect a long meeting and a working dinner."

"Yes sir," Sterling immediately went to get those orders out. Wilson was still examining the map before him.

"Is there something out there you don't want us to see?" he traced the route to Unity where two of his best divisions had been completely destroyed. "Or was it just an attack of opportunity?"

That had been bothering him to no end since this all started. Were the krishanks left to indicate that this was somehow payback for whatever Smith had tried to do, or was that just to throw him off his stride and make him think that while they were, in fact, hiding something from him out on his western flank?

If I hadn't sent Stone on that ill-advised raid then I could send my cavalry to take a look, Wilson thought to himself. That savage Blue Dog might return with something useful but I doubt it.

Blue Dog's usefulness was limited at best, and Wilson had asked him to take his men west more in hopes of messing with the Southerners' heads than in their actually accomplishing anything worthwhile. If he got lucky and got something out of it then so much the better. But he didn't count on it.

He had decided that it was time to shake things up. They had sat on their asses long enough. He had a formidable army collected here, and estimates were that he outnumbered the available Southern soldiers almost three-to-one if not better. While they still had those damned exploding weapons of theirs, Wilson thought he had a counter for that. Something that would reduce their casualties anyway.

Tonight, he would explain his plans and ideas to his Corps Commanders and get their input. They were so smart, after all, knowing far better than him what to do and how to do it. He'd give them a chance to prove it.

-

"Do I wanna know what that is?" Whip Hubel asked cautiously.

"Ah, Master Archer!" Roda Finn rubbed his hands together as he saw Whip. "I'm glad you're here. You're just in time to see my latest invention. Or at least a prototype of said invention."

"And just what is it?" Whip asked reluctantly, looking at the long iron... tube?

"In ancient days, artillery was capable of striking targets miles away," Finn began to lecture. "Tens of miles in some few cases. They did this by using explosives more powerful than my own as a propellant for an exploding warhead as the term was used back then."

"Okay," Whip nodded.

"While we can't possibly duplicate such feats, my failed ballista rounds sent me back to the drawing board to see if I could improve that particular weapon or at least make use of it another way. That research led me to this!" he waved proudly to the... tube?

"And 'this' is?" Whip asked again.

"Well, I don't have a name for it as yet," Roda almost sputtered. "But in ancient times weapons similar to this one were referred to as cannon."

"Sounds fancy enough," Whip nodded. "So, what's it do?"

"Well, in a perfect world, it will use black powder to propel an iron ball many yards," Roda sounded more sure of himself now. "Once I can perfect that, then I believe that I can use that to hurl iron balls set with a burning fuse that will explode somewhere within the enemy lines."

"So... how does it work?" the archer rubbed his jaw, a sinking feeling in his stomach.

"This hole, here," he pointed to a small hole on top of the rear of the tube, "will hold either the fuse or a small trail of powder or other propellant that will touch off the larger charge below," he patted the tube. "That in turn will ignite that powder, creating a force powerful enough to propel the iron ball in front of it out of the muzzle and toward the enemy!" Roda finished in grand fashion, waving his arms and talking like a circus ringmaster.

"Well," Whip said slowly. "What did you need me for?"

"Well, good Archer," Roda sounded less confident suddenly. "For the first experimental firing, I thought it prudent to take precautions as we are dealing with a great deal of destructive force here, never before tried in our tim-"

"Roda, I ain't got all day," Whip cut into the lecture. "You want me to try and hit that hole up there with a burning arrow? That it?"

"Well, ideally, yes," Roda nodded.

"Alright," Whip nodded. "From where?" he looked around.

"Well, from there," he pointed to a log wall almost fifty yards away.

"That's a hell of a shot to have to make, Roda," Whip looked at that small protection. "Even with no wind."

"I had considered that good Archer, and made provision for it," Roda agreed, moving in his fussy little way over to where a trail of oil ran over and down the tube.

"All you need do is ignite the oil," he promised. "Essentially hitting the tube anywhere in this area," he indicated the rear portion, "should set off the main charge. That will be most satisfactory for our first experiment."

"Uh huh," Whip was under enthused. "How do you know this whole damned thing ain't just gonna... blow plumb up and shatter?"

"Well, I don't," Roda admitted as he made his way toward the small shelter in the distance. "That's why we need protection, good Archer."

"How do I get roped into this kinda thing?" Whip shook his head as he followed Roda up the small hill. When he got to the small shelter, which wasn't that small now that he was standing behind it, he found six cloth-wrapped and oil-soaked arrows along with a flint and steel.

"Six huh?" Whip grunted. "Got a lot of faith in my aim, do ya?"

"Is this not enough?" Roda looked puzzled. "I thought surely this would be-"

"Shaddup and gimme that," he grabbed the first arrow from Roda Finn's hand and held it toward him. The fussy inventor struck flint and steel together and on the second try the arrow flamed to life.

"Anywhere along the back ed-" Roda was saying when Whip let the arrow fly and ducked behind the wall.

"Oh, yes indeed," Roda ducked as well, watching through a tiny prism.

The arrow lofted into the air and flew straight and true, bouncing off the back end of the tube and setting the oil on it ablaze. It burned... and burned... and kept burning.

"I... I don't understand," Roda looked at Whip and then back to the 'cannon'. "The fire should have set off the charge." He stood, walking around the edge of the wall.

"I shall have to go and see what-"

Whip grabbed Roda just as his 'cannon' erupted, yanking the smaller man back and down behind the barrier. A gout of flame longer than the inventor was tall belched from the end of the tube and cracked the pipe all the way down. Pieces of hot iron were falling around them as Whip pulled Roda to his feet.

"Well, I must say this is a serious setback," Roda said as he brushed himself off. "Perhaps the tube isn't damaged too severely and we can-"

He stopped as the tube in question split apart and fell in two more or less equal pieces to the ground. Roda sighed deeply, then shrugged and turned to Whip.

"Ah, well, I suspect not. Good Archer, I thank you for your time and your expertise. Once I can get a new tube cast, I will call upon you again!"

"How are you gonna change things after this?" Whip asked.

"I shall have to lessen the charge, I suppose," Roda was already on his way down the hill to check on his experiment. "It will lessen the impact but should still work."

"Or you could make the walls o' that there tube thicker, you know," Whip called and Roda came to a halt.

"Maybe even put one tube inside another?" Whip continued. "After that inner tube gets to going back you may could pull it out, replace it like?"

"Good Archer you have once again shown that intelligence comes in all forms and packages," Roda beamed. "A tremendous idea. No! Pair of ideas! Yes, I shall see about this. About both! Two tubes, a liner and outer layer, with the..." Roda was still talking even as he went out of earshot. Whip shook his head as he started back to the Foundry where he had been helping with a new version of the arrow that carried his name.

"I hope he don't kill his fool self before the war is over."

-

"This is a good place to make camp," Case ordered. "Circle the wagons and prepare to make camp for the evening!"

"We've still got three or more hours of light left," Winnie objected.

"We cross the river tomorrow," Case told her. "About two miles from here we should find a ferry. Whether anyone is still manning it or not, I don't know. If that ferry isn't there then we have to head south to one of the old bridges. I really don't want to do that, but if we have to, then we have to."

"Anyway, we don't camp right at the river or the ferry landing," he continued. "Too tempting a target for raiders or for Tribals either. We're close enough as it is to be on the trail in the morning and there in time to cross, assuming all goes well. We can get things taken care of early tonight and be ready for a hard day tomorrow. If we can cross the river and make another two or three miles besides, I'll be happy."

"I don't see why we shouldn't camp near the river," Winnie said. "We could at least get clean there."

"Creek about one hundred yards that way," Case pointed north. "Be careful of water moccasins this time of year. And copperheads. Both are venomous and can kill with a single bite. If you decide to go, all of you ladies should go as a group and take five men as escort. They can stay back far enough to give you privacy while being close enough in case of trouble."

Winnie didn't say anything else as Case finished with his statement. He had been nothing but cold and proper to her since she had run off at the mouth earlier in the week. She recognized it was her fault, but he could give a little she figured. She looked at Case who was checking the hooves of his horse, patting the giant war horse and talking calmly to him.

"I wanna go to the river!" she demanded suddenly.

"Two miles, that way," Case pointed without looking at her. "Help yourself. Try to be back by dark. Stick to the trail as it's easy to get lost around here."

"I want the train to go to the river," Winnie insisted.

"Not going to happen," Case assured her. "This is where we stop for the evening, milady. Your options are already laid out. I would suggest you stay in camp but can't order you to do so. I can only warn you against going. But the train stops here tonight and tomorrow crosses the river, if the ferry is still there."

Fuming, Winnie went to speak with the other women in her party, some of whom were equally eager to wash. Collecting those who were, she set off to find the creek without informing Case or taking the escort he had required. Case noticed them go and sighed, shaking his head at the stubbornness of their future Queen.

"Lieutenant," he called his nearest officer.

"Sir?"

"Take a detail of four and follow Her Royal Sassyness," Case ordered. "Stay far enough back that they have their privacy but be close by in case of trouble."

"Sir," the lieutenant grinned at Case's nickname for the future Queen. All of them used it at one time or another as the girl was a handful and then some. He quickly rounded up four men, two of them archers, and set out to follow the women.

"Why me?" Case sighed, feeling somewhat sorry for himself. "What did I do that was so wrong to get stuck with this duty?" he asked the sky.

He felt a raindrop on his nose in reply.

"Perfect."

-

There were nine women who served in the battle of Nasil as part of the Auxiliary Archers on the train along with seven other civilian women serving different functions other than driving wagons. Four of the archers had readily agreed to go with their 'commander' to wash away the dirt, dust and what have you of several days on the trail. The other civilians as well as three women wagoneers had all refused, the latter suggesting that doing so was foolish and foolhardy, particularly in a time of war and with Tribals known to be about. Winnie had ignored that and then she and her cohorts had left for the creek. She decided against telling Case about it to punish him in some way.

It never occurred to her to consider that he was right.

There was a trail, little more than a deer path Winnie thought, that led them straight to the promised creek. The water was slow but clear, and with recent rains the creek was full. In mere seconds the women had stripped off their dirty and dusty clothing and plunged into the inviting water. All screeched as they hit the cold water, laughing at how foolish they were not to have checked how cold it was first.

The lieutenant and his men stopped well back from the creek and slipped off the trail. They could hear but not see the five women which was good enough. They could be where the women were in a matter of seconds if there was trouble.

-

Pitch Magee had never had a real job. He and his three friends, Hack and Tucker were known in most towns in a fifty-mile radius as thieves that would take the coins from a dead man's eyes. The three of them made their way on their 'rounds' as they called them, looting, stealing, raping and murdering for a living.

They were moving through broken country near the river, hoping the ferry was running, when they heard the unmistakable sound of femininity. The three stopped cold at that, exchanging glances.

"Sounds like a party," Pitch grinned, unsightly though it was.

"And we didn't get an invite," Hack grinned just as wide.

"That ain't neighborly is it?" Tucker's face was colder. He, by far, was the worst of the three. And the deadliest.

The three moved by unspoken agreement toward the sound of feminine happiness, intending to join in, invitation or no. That was what they did, after all.

-

Winnie was usually more aware when in the woods, having been raised in the mountains in a rough and tumble world. But she was enjoying the water a little too much as well as the satisfaction of doing something that Case had told her not to do. Which meant she was not the first to recognize the danger.

She was looking at Bethany Wright when Bethany's face had gone from joyful to terror in a mere flash as she looked over Winnie's shoulder. Even as Bethany screeched in fear Winnie was turning to see what had frightened her. She saw three rough looking men on the far side of the creek, blades already out.

"You ladies wasn't gonna leave us outta the fun, was ya?" the ugliest of the three smiled a blood curdling smile. "That just ain't neighbor... ly..." he trailed off as an arrow appeared in his chest as if by magic. Another cut down the man next to him, the one who had looked like the most predatory of the three. The third didn't bother to check on his friends but took off running for the river.

Before Winnie could react, soldiers were on her side of the creek bank, one snapping orders to the others.

"You two, run him down, get rid of him," he ordered the archers as he pointed the escaping figure. The two nodded and took off without a word. The lieutenant looked at his two remaining men.

"Get those two out of the water," he ordered. "And you, all of you," he turned to the women. "Out of the water and back up the trail. Now!" he shouted when they didn't move. All of them, Winnie included, moved that time.

"Turn your head!" one woman called.

"We don't have the time for that foolishness," the lieutenant said coldly, though in truth he wasn't looking at them but at the other side of the creek. "Now get out of the water and get back to the train! For all we know those three were scouts for a larger group! Move!"

Reluctance showing in every move, the women did as ordered, each woman grabbing the nearest clothing whether it was hers or not in order to cover herself. Winnie stopped by the lieutenant to protest only to be pushed up the trail without so much as a 'milady'.

"Get moving," he hissed at her. "There are only five of us and two are running that third one down. We can't cover this much territory and I don't have time to argue about it, now go," he shoved her along the trail and almost added the flat of his blade to her backside but she was already out of reach.

"Get them up here and into the bush," he ordered his men. "All we need to do is hide them."

-

Pitch Magee wasn't sure if he was good or just lucky, but Hack and Tuck had taken them arrows and let him get away. He was running quick as a deer he thought, wishing he could have grabbed his two friends' possibles bags and the goodies they held. A lot of loot was lost.

And what in the hell were Royal Soldiers doing out here in the middle of nowhere with a war on anyhow? This was supposed to be the best time for his line of work. He paused for a minute as the trail forked, trying to remember which way was the quickest way to the ferry landing. He felt a wasp sting him between his shoulders and tried to reach over his shoulder to pull it off. In doing so he looked down and saw an arrowhead sticking out of his chest.

Now where did that... come...

-

"Did you get him?" the lieutenant asked as the two archers came running back.

"Yes sir," one nodded, tossing the officer the bag they had taken. "Pulled his body about fifty feet off the trail and covered the sign of our movement. His friends won't find him soon enough to matter."

"I'm not sure these three had any friends," the lieutenant was going through the third bag. "I think these three were just garden variety thugs and thieves who thought they had just got lucky."

"Wasn't for the Captain, they just might have," one of the swordsmen nodded. "What now, sir?"

"We're done here. There's no one else around or sign of anyone else either. Back up the trail. Let's get back to the train."

-

It was a comical affair to see the women running back to camp, barefoot and wringing wet, trying to cover themselves in whatever best way they could and still carry their things. The wagon train members all laughed at the sight, the three women wagoneers laughing the loudest, having warned the other women not to go. The archers who had not gone along were careful not to be seen laughing right along with the others but did laugh when no one was looking.

To say that the five women's feathers were ruffled was to put it mildly. By the time the lieutenant and his men returned a very angry and still very wet Winifred Hubel was waiting for him.

"Don't you ever talk to me like that again!" she said at once.

"Very well," the young lieutenant nodded. "Next time I'll just leave you to it." With that, he ignored her completely and turned his attention back to Captain Case to finish his report.

"All three are accounted for and there were no indications of a larger group that we could find either on the ground or in their effects," he held up the three bags. "Honestly, sir, it appears they were merely low-class thugs who thought they had stumbled across a target of opportunity."

"I am talking to you!" Winnie grabbed the young lieutenant's arm, intending to force him around to face her. It worked, in a manner.

The young officer's adrenaline was still running on high and his instincts took over when Winnie grabbed his arm and yanked on it. He moved without conscious thought, spinning faster than she had intended to force him around. She held his left arm so it was his right hand that rose, palm out and flat, to strike her in the sternum. The young man managed to get control of himself at the last possible second to pull the punch, but it still was enough to put Her Royal Sassyness on the ground, flat on her ass.

The laughter had pretty much ceased after that.

"Sir, I... milady... sir. I didn't mean..." the young officer was beside himself at what he had done, but Case merely patted him on the arm.

"Easy Lieutenant," he calmed the young man. "You were still hopped-up from combat and she was asking for it. It wasn't your fault. She knows better than to assault someone like that. You and your men go and get dried out. You're excused duty tonight, all of you," Case called to the other four. The men nodded their thanks and eased away from what was sure to be a confrontation.

"I want him-" Winnie wasn't even off the ground before she started making demands.

"No," Case's voice was flat and brooked no argument.

"He hit me!"

"You grabbed him first and did so when he was only minutes out of a combat situation and still in that state of mind. That entire incident was your doing, milady. Yours and no one else. You refused every piece of advice given you, not just from me but from anyone else, and went off to do as you damned well pleased because you've become used to getting your way."

"Had I not sent the lieutenant and his men after you, where would you be now?"

A sullen and angry Winnie didn't reply, but merely tried to stare Case down, glaring at him with her arms crossed.

"Nothing to say? Then I'd suggest you do something about your clothing," he looked her over from head to toe. "Buckskin is known to shrink as it dries and yours is drying."

It took her almost a full ten seconds to realize what he was saying. Looking down at her rapidly drying buckskin pants and shirt, she realized that it was skin tight and showing enough that she might as well still be naked.

She managed to maintain her dignity, what was left of it anyway, as she stomped her way across the campsite to her carriage to change. She pretended not to notice the way the other members of the train were looking at her after what she had just done.

Case looked up at the sky to ask again why him and was rewarded with another raindrop, this one right in the eye.

"Right."

CHAPTER NINETEEN

-

Therron was almost beside himself. The young lieutenant in charge of his escort seemed to be in no real hurry to reach their destination. Each night they halted in designated areas complete with small huts and even a caretaker! While Therron could appreciate the comfort, the time lost was killing his soul and possibly his chance at the throne. Three days of travel had seen them cover less than fifty miles.

"Lieutenant... Stanley wasn't it?" Therron tried tact. "There are at least two hours of good light left for us to travel by. Surely, we should take advantage of that, no?"

"Protocol says we stop here overnight, sir," Stanley was adamant. "So, we stop here. There's no real good place to make a cold camp further along and we'd never reach the next station before full dark. So, we stop here. We won't risk the horses or my men along these trails after dark, sir."

"Look here, Lieutenant," Therron tried sterner tactics. "I am Crown Prince Therron McLeod of Soulan! It is urgent that I reach your governor as soon as possible, and I can't do that stopping every fifteen miles to make camp! Now I insist that we press on!"

"Protocol says we stop here, sir," Stanley would not be swayed. "So, we stop here."

Almost apoplectic at this point, Therron realized he was getting nowhere and gave up. This man, Stanley, clearly had no initiative of his own whatsoever.

While he would spend the night in relative comfort, Therron would pass it in misery.

-

"So, gentlemen, what do you think?" Wilson asked, having laid out the situation before his six commanders.

"What happened to wait them out, sir?" Darrell Thomas, commander of 3rd Corps asked.

"Nothing at all," Wilson replied. "This has nothing to do with the general war effort but rather what to do about this situation to the west of our position. There is something out there, a force powerful enough to completely wipe out two Imperial infantry divisions. Now, either the enemy is making a move, or else there is something else out there they don't want us to see. I am asking for your suggestions on just what we should do about it?"

"Isn't Stone back yet?" Joel Vanhoose, commander of 2nd Corps asked. "Why not send him out there? Be much quicker than having infantry do it."

"I hope to get at least part of his command back in the next few days, but... Stone's raid into the central high country was of limited success. While he and his men did sack and burn much of the Southern Capital, his force has suffered almost fifty percent casualties. Many of those are from eating bad beef and they will in time recover and hopefully return to duty, but in the meanwhile his forces, what remains able to take the field, may not be sufficient." That information was met with several seconds of stunned silence.

"Could we wait and see how much of his force we can use before making a move?" Abe Springfield, Commander of 5th Corps was the first to speak. "Using the cavalry to screen our infantry movements would possibly prevent any more of these disasters, at least. If there is something out there then we find it, screen our movements with cavalry until we're set, and then we engage them on our terms, not theirs."

"That is one possibility that I'm considering," Wilson nodded. "With a sizable enough cavalry force, an infantry Corps in support would or should be able to meet and suppress any threat that can be out there."

"This is all assuming anything at all is out there," Peter Venable, commander of 1st Corps spoke up. Venable had been promoted after Milton Fairmount, a long-time friend of Wilson's had been killed in action not many weeks ago. He was a smart and able commander, but he had the tact of an elephant.

"Is it not more likely that these two divisions fell victim to southern cavalry?" he asked, walking to the map and circling the area in question. "Without our own cavalry to screen our flanks, we don't really know what might or might not be here. It's entirely possible that a large force of Soulanie cavalry happened upon two isolated and unsupported infantry divisions and... cut them to pieces," he said the last part a bit lower. "If the force were large enough, say as large as Stone's force was for his raid, then destroying a lone infantry division would be well within their capabilities."

"Your point?" Vanhoose asked.

"That is my point," Venable replied. "If it was Soulanie cavalry then for all we know they're back in their tents sleeping tonight behind enemy lines. Hell, for that matter they could be sleeping behind our lines and we'd never know it. I'm just suggesting we don't throw good money after bad by sending still more unsupported troops to the west. If you want this... Unity, so badly, then send an entire infantry corps out to seize and hold it. Wait for whatever cavalry we get back from Stone to give us at least some screening element and then we just go and take it. Fortify it and dare them to come and take it away from us."

Murmurs of agreement ran through the room and Wilson was nodding as well. He liked this idea.

"Very well, General Venable," Wilson said. "I will assign 1st Corp to take and hold this village. You will have three days to prepare your men and their gear. The Quartermaster Corps will see to it you have provisions enough for three weeks with you and we will plan to resupply after two weeks. You will move out as soon as we can get you a rested and ready force of cavalry sufficient in size to screen your movements. Once your preparations are complete, you will hold your men ready to march on one hour's notice, but they may stand down after two o'clock each afternoon. They will also be excused watch detail during that time. Brigadier Sterling will deliver your written orders tomorrow."

"Yes sir," Venable nodded, returning to his seat. He didn't look pleased, upset, satisfied or angry or anything else. Venable simply looked as if he were prepared to do his duty.

"With 1st Corps coming off the line in the morning we will be shifting the rest of the line west to maintain our anchor on the river. That will mean opening the gaps between the corps slightly because I do not want to reduce the front in length. This will mean widening the distance between regiments to cover more ground. This should not cause a difficulty since we are already squeezed in tightly, but I also do not want to commit our reserve to the line. We need a force ready to fill any hole in case of attack or else to launch a counter attack should the opportunity arise. Questions?" No one spoke.

"Orders will be forthcoming tomorrow afternoon for new positioning. If you have any relevant points to add to it, bring them to me at that time. If there are no questions, gentlemen, then we are adjourned."

-

"Sir," Sterling began once everyone was gone, but Wilson held up a hand to forestall his comment.

"I know. Not what I had planned. Still, this may work to my advantage."

"How so, if I may ask, sir?" Sterling looked puzzled.

"What will the Soulan Army do when an entire corps of infantry is seen marching off to the west, escorted by a cavalry screen?" Wilson asked.

"They will undoubtedly attempt to... I see," Sterling caught on.

"Good. Not a word, mind you," Wilson warned. "I want even our own people to be surprised. We may be on the verge of getting this war over with sooner than we thought."

"Yes sir."

-

"I could get used to this," Parno said as Stephanie lay collapsed on top of him, their breathing more or less back to normal.

"Oh?" she asked teasingly.

"If it weren't for the war," he nodded. "Being with you like this every night, waking up next to you every morning. Spending every day with you, all day, every day-"

"Okay, you're starting to sound creepy," she laughed. "Besides, even if we were at home, we'd still have work to do."

"I know," he grinned back. "And I couldn't have you following me around as I visit my favorite haunts."

"Your haunting days are over, Prince," Stephanie sounded amused. "Count on it." She got up and went to take care of her ablutions and then returned.

"Harrel is almost well enough to transfer him to a regular hospital, but I'd much rather carry him back with me," she told him.

"How long before he could make that trip?" he asked.

"Maybe two weeks. And it may be longer," she admitted.

"I'll give you the two weeks, but no more," Parno said after a moment's thought. "I want the best for Harrel but... your being here is not safe. Edema's being here isn't safe. We could literally be attacked in the morning."

"Do you think we will be?" she asked, frowning in concern.

"No, but I've been wrong before," he shrugged. "I think they are up to something, but I don't know what. And I don't think they're ready to move just yet. Things just feel... off," he struggled to explain.

"If Harrel can't make the trip at the end of the two weeks then I'll have him moved to a regular hospital and we'll go back," she promised.

"Good."

-

Brigadier Jerome Baxter mounted his horse, still sore from hard riding the day before. With any luck he and his command would be back to the main camp in three days, give or take. Better food and sleeping conditions than they had enjoyed in a long while.

"We're ready, sir," an aide reported. Baxter nodded and raised his hand, then let it fall.

"Move out!"

His scouts were already out and roaming as were his flankers. He might well lose his entire command to the Soulan Army, but it wouldn't be because he didn't take precautions.

"Three more days," he murmured. "That's all."

-

Three days could seem like an eternity to some and go by in a blink for others.

For Therron McLeod, that three days would be hell. Stopping at every station regardless of time of day because 'protocol says we stop, so we stop' was about to drive him insane, but there was nothing he could do about it and his own marines were clearly not willing to complain about it. Nor were they acting very much like 'his' marines when it came to that.

The third day would see him arrive, finally, at the regimental headquarters only to learn that 'the Colonel is out' and would not be back for two days. Therron tried to bluster his way over the young Major who delivered this message, only to be told 'protocol demands that anyone sent to the Governor must have the Colonel's approval, so please, make yourself comfortable as our honored guest', so forth and so on.

Therron was all but certain he would lose his hair to worry before he reached the age of forty. He consoled himself with two bottles of wine that had a very good appeal and left him numb. 'His' marines looked at him, shook their heads, and cautiously made friends among the Coastal soldiers.

-

In the main Imperial camp, General Venable would be using his three days as expeditiously as he could to ready his men for the march ahead and the anticipated combat he might fight at the end of it. He drew his divisional commanders together and emphasized the threat along with their mission, and then they set about devising a strategy that ensured they had everything they could possibly need with them. Their own artillery battalion would accompany them, four catapults and four trebuchets, along with their own engineer battalion and their equipment.

Venable doubted very much if Wilson had intended him to take all of that, but he had said 'take your corps', and 1st Corps included those units and their gear. And, it was easier to get forgiven than to get permission. Three frantic days would be spent readying all of that equipment ready for travel.

Also necessary was the need to carry supplies enough for fifty thousand men, plus an estimated ten thousand horse soldiers. Wagons had to be loaded and placed in line of march, ready for horses to be hitched to them at literally a moment's notice for preparation to move out. Spare gear for any lost in combat, mobile forge and blacksmith equipment for repair of equipment and shoeing horses. Canvas for tent repairs, medical supplies for a major battle, the list was almost as long as the marching column would be, it seemed. Yet all this and more would be needed for such force to survive and to fight in a foreign land.

Something had destroyed two entire infantry divisions. Venable would not see one of his divisions suffer the same fate.

-

"Sir, I'm not arguing against your plan, but to take one sixth of the army, and the most experienced in some cases out of play-"

"Sterling, I've considered all of that," Wilson held up a hand to stop further comment. "This is a gamble, but a gamble worth taking. Start preparing the orders."

"Yes sir," Sterling knew he was defeated and surrendered gracefully. Full of apprehension and dread at what his general was planning, he began drafting orders for the army.

-

"Poll the Regiment," Parno ordered Karls over breakfast. "I need another escort force, identical to Stephanie's. We'll need someone who can exercise an independent command."

"For Lady Edema?" Karls asked.

"Yes, and Dhalia," Parno nodded. "In fact, make Edema's escort large enough to detail a squadron to stay with Dhalia when Edema is traveling. Their only mission is to protect the two of them. Not the house, the grounds, the staff. Make sure that is understood."

"I'll take care of it." Karls knew what Parno was thinking. Among the Black Sheep were all men he could trust absolutely. Soon, he would have Beaumont's command to send on the errands that Karls and the Sheep were doing now. That would allow him to allocate the men he trusted most with the missions most important to him.

Like protecting the only people that were important to him that couldn't protect themselves.

-

"The ferry is still there, sir, but no one appears to be around."

Case nodded at the report, considering his options. Finally, he turned to the lieutenant immediately behind him.

"Fain, take one squad and investigate the ferry. Make sure it's safe to take the wagons down."

"Yes sir," the younger man nodded. "Second Squad, on me!" he called and started down the trail to the ferry crossing followed by eleven others. It seemed to take an age but was actually less than a half-hour before a single rider returned.

"Sir, Lieutenant Fain reports that the ferry is in place and operable. The caretaker's shack is still standing but doesn't appear to have seen any use in some time. The rope looks a bit dry but there is grease available at the shack. Old, but usable. The raft itself is solid sir. He believes we can cross with minimal difficulty."

"Very well," Case nodded. "Advise him we will be down shortly. Prepare the ferry and be ready to cross ahead of us and establish a beach head on the western bank."

"Sir," the man gave a brief field salute and raced back down the road. Case turned in his saddle and looked back down the line.

"Ferry is in working order!" he called. "We're heading down now! Pass the word!" The call was repeated down the small train as Case started his horse down the road. One at a time the wagons began rolling, teams straining to get the heavily loaded wagons moving.

Winnie was silent, having literally shown her ass the day before. Her chest was still sore where she had been struck by that lieutenant, whose name she had learned was Rucker. The man had not so much as looked her way since and Case had ignored her, but... she was sensing an underlying resentment now from the men of her escort, something she'd never felt before. Her behavior was slowly turning the men assigned to protect her against her.

Had she changed so much in so short of a time? Had she really become someone to be resented like that? It was definitely easy to do with everyone bowing and scraping to her because of Memmnon, but these men... King or no, they had their own pride and she was apparently trampling on it. She had overheard Rucker and two others last evening discussing asking to be transferred to a line combat unit upon their return to Nasil. Her face burned in shame to think that men who had worked hard to be assigned to a unit as prestigious as the King's Own would give that up to get away from her.

Her horse stopped and she realized with a start that she was on the ferry landing. The 'ferry' was actually just a large log raft joined with iron bands instead of mere rope. Side boards rose perhaps four feet on either side with the ends being eight-foot ramps that would be pulled up when not in use to serve a similar function.

The ferry was kept in place by a long, thick rope, the strands of which were also secured with iron bands. The rope ran through rings of iron secured on the posts of the right hand or 'starboard' side of the raft. Men would have to haul on the rope to pull the raft across the river. Another, similar rope was attached to the end of the ferry to allow it to be pulled across the river empty if necessary. It was slow and hazardous, but no less so than some of the ancient bridges, few of which were still standing and all of those that were could hardly be trusted with the weight of the wagons they were pulling.

"Captain Conway, you and Lieutenant Fain will board first platoon of First Company," Case ordered. "Cross and establish a safe beach head. Lieutenant Rucker, your men will stand by to pull the ferry back across. Captain Conway and all of First Company will cross first and establish security, then we'll start sending wagons across."

"Sir!" the younger men replied in unison before issuing the orders needed to carry out Case's wishes.

Winnie watched as twenty-four men and horses, all that the ferry could safely hold (if 'safely' meant 'without sinking') loaded on board. The ramp was taken up and then half the troopers manned the ropes while the other half held the reins of the horses. One man had a towel soaked in axle grease and would use it to moisten the rope as they went. One of the wagoneers stood by to do the same thing to the return rope to protect it against the water. She pitied the men who would be forced to pull that rope and the smell they would have to endure.

As the ferry began to move under the pull of twelve men, Winnie realized that Case's hope of managing to cross the river and gain two or three miles from the river was more accurate than she had realized. She had crossed rivers before but... nothing like this.

The river at this point was almost a mile wide and the current as deceptively swift. Ripples in the water showed the presence of a strong undertow that would be difficult for even a strong swimmer to resist.

This was going to be more dangerous than she had imagined.

-

"Scouts are reporting a big kerfuffle among the heathen this morning, milord," Doak Parsons reported quietly before lunch. "Large movement among the divisions on the line. Looks like some are being pulled and the rest are side stepping to take up the slack."

"No new troops coming into the line?" Parno frowned.

"Not as yet," Parsons shook his head. "We can't get close enough to see if they're leaving or just being taken off line. I do have men behind their lines, but their orders are to report only in the event of something major. Men just coming off the line won't be enough. Should those men head out somewhere other than west, they'll report, though."

"Why other than west?" Parno asked without thinking.

"We could see 'em headin' west, milord," Parsons smiled faintly and Parno sighed, shaking his head.

"Lack of food must be addling my brain."

"I'm sure that's all it is milord," Parsons nodded. "I'll let you know if anything else changes."

"Do that Mister Parsons," Parno nodded. He looked back to the map again, trying to see something that wasn't there.

"What are you up to?"

-

"What are you up to now?"

Winnie jumped slightly at the voice behind her but turned to see Case looking down at her from his horse.

"I'm gathering honeysuckle, jasmine and pine needles," she replied, adding what was in her hand to the bag she was carrying.

"Dare I ask why?" Case's tone indicated he didn't think so.

"It's for the men who have to pull that rope," Winnie explained. "They're gonna stink of grease and it's hard to get rid of. This will help so they don't have to smell that stuff for days."

The look on his face was so incredulous that it made Winnie a combination of angry and embarrassed. Had she been such a pain in the ass that even doing something nice seemed a shock to them now?

"I appreciate it that, milady," Case's voice was gentle. "I'm sure the men will too. Thank you."

"You're welcome," she nodded.

-

"Morning milord," Davies said as Parno walked into the main command tent.

"Morning General," Parno nodded in return. "Any news? Mister Parsons reported there was some unusual movement among the enemy this morning."

"That's all so far, milord," Davies admitted but looked troubled.

"Something you want to add to that?" Parno asked.

"It... it's just a thought, milord," Davies admitted. "Thing is, I'm wondering if we've kicked over a hornet's nest with our actions the last week or so."

"Instead of making them think the same?" Parno raised an eyebrow.

"Yes," Davies wasn't being humorous. "We may have given them reason to think there's some reason we don't want them out there on the west, when in reality it was just targets of opportunity. We saw a chance to eliminate a large force of enemy soldiers and we took it. Granted it was in reprisal fo-" he stopped short, realizing he had said perhaps too much.

"It's alright, General," Parno said softly. "I already knew."

"Yes sir." Davies looked surprised though not shocked. This Prince had an uncanny ability to know what was happening around him.

"I appreciate it," Parno added. "But your worry might present an opportunity for us, no?"

"Well, yes sir," Davies admitted. "That is what I was thinking about."

"It's too large a gamble, General," Parno said after a minute of examining things a little longer. "For now, anyway. Once we get the other two corps back on line, and especially once we have the new soldiers on line, then we'll see."

"That was my assessment as well, milord," Davies sighed.

"We won't always be on the defensive, General," Parno slapped the older man's shoulder lightly. "I promise."

"Yes sir."

-

Three of the twelve wagons were across along with a third of the escort. It was possible, barely, to load two wagons and their teams, but then when enough men were added to pull the weight the ferry was dangerously overloaded. The wagons were fully loaded save for the few supplies used since leaving Nasil and they were heavy. Case watched as members of Lieutenant Rucker's Company pulled the ferry back for a fourth wagon and realized that this was not working fast enough.

"Lieutenant Rucker," Case called and the younger man crossed to where his commander was watching the crossing.

"Sir."

"We need to speed this up," Case said quietly. "I'm open to suggestions if you've thought of any."

"Without a pull rope on the western shore, sir, I don't have any," Rucker admitted. "If we had that, we could load two wagons and pull them to the other shore with horses. Even use the trace teams already across for it if we had to."

"Has anyone checked for another rope?" Case asked.

"Not specifically, sir, but a mile-long rope of that size would be difficult to overlook," the younger man pointed out.

"True enough," Case nodded. "Suppose we were to take this rope to the other shore and then use our men to walk the ferry back across?" Case suggested. Rucker considered that, looking at the river as he did so.

"If there are lugs on the far end of the ferry to hook to, yes sir," he said finally. "We would still need to make a crossing once in a while just to get enough men back to start over, however."

Now it was Case's turn to consider that.

"In your opinion there is no way to safely cross with two wagons and the men needed to pull them," Case said finally, a statement rather than a question.

"Not with their horses si..." Rucker trailed off, looking back at the ferry now nearing the shore.

"Lieutenant?" Case prompted.

"Sir, if we... if we could load the wagons without the horses, then... I think so, sir. We can unload them with the horses already across."

"Still have an extra trip for the horses Lieutenant," Case reminded him.

"Horses are lighter than the wagons, sir," Rucker pointed out. "We can load... four teams at once. That means getting four wagons across in the same time we're getting three across now, assuming we can load them quick enough by hand."

Case thought that over, then looked at the sun. It wasn't midday yet, but they weren't half finished, either.

"Let's try it once and see if it works," Case ordered. "Send another wagon alone this time with this plan along. We'll be ready on the next return trip to try it."

"Yes sir," Rucker nodded and ran back to his command.

Case hoped this would work. They needed to speed this along or else his command would spend a night separated by the river and that was completely unacceptable.

-

It took an hour to make another round trip and that left Rucker's men gasping for air once they got the ferry to shore. Case had two wagons in line and ready to go and was using half of Lieutenant Garrett's company to load them against his better judgment since they were providing security on this side of the river.

Fifteen cursing-filled minutes saw both wagons on board, sans horses, along with thirty men to pull. With a sergeant calling the cadence, the men set out across the river.

Case watched with bated breath as the ferry crossed, but the trip went smoothly. Teams were standing by to unload the wagons and in much less time than it took to load, the ferry was empty and on the way back. The thirty men who had pulled it across could now rest while the seventy remaining men in Rucker's company pulled them back as Garrett's men readied two more wagons.

This might just work.

-

"I thought we could have lunch in the shade," Stephanie said as she displayed the table setting under the large fly of Parno's personal tent. Edema had agreed to join them for lunch, happy to see the two reunited.

"This does not look like Army food," Parno mentioned as he sat down.

"That's because it isn't," Edema snorted. "Benson is almost as good a cook as my chef at home. He gathered the ingredients and prepared this feast."

"Nice," Parno rubbed his hands together. It was ridiculous in a way. The second most powerful man in the Kingdom of Soulan, Parno could easily have a staff of chefs preparing his meals as he ran the Army from Tinker's Tavern in comfort. That simply wasn't how Parno did things and the Army knew it. Parno ate what they ate and complained about it just as loudly. The few times he ate better than they did bothered no one.

"The water came from the well at Tinker's Tavern," Edema added. "It's cool and rather sweet."

"Works for me, let's eat," Parno sounded like a child at Christmas, pleasing Edema to no end.

"Splendid!"

-

It was working, Case decided, but at a price. At this rate Rucker's men would be too tired to pull themselves across at the end of the day, and far too tired to stay awake on watch tonight. He made a snap decision at that point to keep the train still the next day. This exertion had been difficult on all of them as the day had heated and they would need a rest as well as an opportunity to bathe. They had earned it. All of them had.

He looked to where the last four wagons sat waiting to go. Two were loaded and starting the trip across, then the horses for four wagons would cross. Three more trips for the wagons would still leave a minimum of six trips to get the rest of the command and the ambulance that served as Winifred Hubel's carriage across, but Rucker had been fudging that number by sending his men's horses across in small batches with the wagon teams. It would only eliminate one or maybe two trips, but that seemed like a golden egg at this point.

Meanwhile, the sun continued its trip across the sky without pause.

-

Jerome Baxter looked to the sky, seeing the sun high overhead. He turned to his lead brigade commander.

"Pass the word. Dismount, lead horses, eat while we walk."

"Yes sir," the man sketched a salute and turned to issue the order. The column slowed, then stopped. Baxter dismounted, stretched his back and then rummaged in his saddlebags for a bite of jerky and the hard camp roll hardtack that his men carried in the field. Looping his horse's reins through his elbow he took his canteen and started walking, leading the horse along.

It wasn't as good as giving the horses rest, but it would help. They would stop a half-hour early if they had to water the horses and they could rest overnight, but Baxter was anxious to get back to the main army. His men needed rest as badly as his horses did and they needed to refit. Being unable to carry the proper support along with them had made caring for their horses difficult at best. If they didn't get that care soon, some would become lame.

He shook his head at the problems that seem to be mounting in his head as he thought about everything that needed to be done. It was enough to give him a headache.

-

"Smelling that grease is giving me a headache," Winnie said quietly. "I can't imagine what it's doing to them," she was looking at Rucker's men, pulling on the rope to return the ferry. "They look tired."

"They're bordering on exhausted," Case agreed.

"We should rest tomorrow," she said suddenly before he could mention it. She turned to look at him. "We should take a day and let them rest and clean up. We have the time to do that don't we?"

"Yes, milady, we do," Case agreed softly. "That would be much appreciated by all I should imagine."

"You don't have to tell them it was my idea," she shook her head. "Just make sure they get to rest." With that she walked off, trailed by four soldiers at a respectable distance. Case watched her go, shaking his head slowly.

No way to understand her. None.

-

Anthony Felds sat in tall grass on the far left of the Imperial Army, looking at a picket post through his spy glass. The Royal Army had given him all kinds of toys as a scout and that glass was just about the best one that he couldn't use to fight with.

The cut on his arm was bandaged and already showing signs of healing so he was able to return to duty. Right now, he was watching past that picket toward the very far edge of the Imperial lines. There was a lot going on but mostly it was hidden by trees. He was too far away to hear anything but once in a while he would catch a shout. No way to make out what was being said, but to his thinking that meant something was definitely going on.

He placed a small bit of cracker into his mouth and waited for it to soften, just listening for a bit.

He'd figure it out.

-

"Have a nice tea party?" Karls teased as Parno walked into the Black Sheep camp area.

"I did indeed," Parno refused to rise to the bait, he was in too good a mood. "And you?"

"We don't get tea much, over here," came the acidic reply. "Someone has to actually work or else the Nor will cart away the Kingdom."

"And you're doing an excellent job," Parno assured him, patting him on the shoulder. "Find a good man for that new detail?"

"Captain Antoine Pike," Karls nodded. "Multiple generation Army. His uncle is actually General Vaughan."

"Milton Vaughan?" Parno asked and Karls nodded.

"Pike's mother is Vaughan's sister."

"Interesting," Parno nodded. "I'm sure he is not thrilled to be leaving."

"No sir, he is not," Karls replied. "But he wasn't thrilled with being initially assigned here, either, so there's that. He was one of my Lieutenants in the original command."

"I remember," Parno nodded. "Tall, broad shouldered?"

"Takes after the Vaughan side of his family," Karls nodded. "But he is duty oriented and squared away."

"Let me talk to him."

-

"Captain Antoine Pike, reporting as ordered."

"Relax, Captain," Parno said, being informal. "Take a seat."

"Yes milord," the young man sat stiffly. *Young* was relative considered Pike was at least five years older than Parno.

"You were noted for bravery twice at the Gap and a third time at the cavalry engagement when we arrived here," Parno noted. "Promoted from Lieutenant, Second, to Captain since we began this adventure. Has Colonel Willard explained your orders, Antoine?" Parno asked.

"I'm being detached with a small independent command for escort duty, sir," Pike replied. "That's all I know."

"Don't like it much, do you?" Parno said casually.

"Permission to speak freely, milord?"

"That's what I'm doing," Parno nodded.

"No sir, I don't like it," Pike then replied. "But I will do it to the best of my abilities. I simply wanted to stay where I could fight."

"That's commendable, but I have to admit that I hope where I'm sending you,

you never have to draw your sword save in training."

"Sir?" Pike looked puzzled.

"You're familiar with my relationship with the Duchess of Cumberland and Viscountess of Wolfe?"

"Lady Edema and The Colonel's daughter?"

"That's correct," Parno nodded. "Colonel Nidiad's daughter lives with Lady Edema at the moment, though she has her own steading now. Lady Edema might as well be my mother. In fact, she is the only mother figure I've ever known. And Lady Dhalia is my sister in all but blood. Your independent command will be to lead their permanent escort. Dhalia's escort will be a sub-detail under your command in fact."

"I... see," Pike's entire attitude changed. "Sir, I... I apologize," he said softly.

"For heaven's sake, don't apologize," Parno laughed quietly. "I'd be disappointed if any of you didn't want to stay here where there's action to be had. But the truth is, anyone close to me is in danger. You realize that, don't you?"

"We all know what happened to Harrel and to Miss Jaelle, sir," Pike nodded.

"Well, your job is to make sure nothing of that sort can happen to Edema or Dhalia. I want you to understand that your mission is not to protect property or servants or anything else, just them. They are your only priority. And that's not a priority that I would trust to just anyone."

"I know sir," Pike nodded. "Thank you."

"You may pick your detail yourself, within reason. Colonel Willard will set the restrictions but they won't be too demanding, I imagine, since Lady Dhalia is his fiancé."

"I had heard that rumor, sir," Pike's face actually cracked a smile at that and Parno laughed.

"I asked Colonel Willard to pick a man I could trust with two of the most important people in my life, Captain," Parno continued. "He chose you. I expect you will do fine."

"Thank you, sir," Pike's voice wasn't terribly deep, but was resonant.

"We won't leave you there forever," Parno promised. "I plan to allow most of the men in the Regiment to rotate through the various escorts from the lines, but even here the days of our seeing much action are growing less."

"I'm aware of the changes, sir."

"I appreciate your time, Captain, and your service," Parno stood, offering his hand. "Don't fail me, please."

"Not so long as I draw breath, sir."

"Good man," Parno slapped his shoulder. "Carry on."

The young Captain saluted and left, Parno following him out of the tent to find Karls waiting.

"He looked a lot more happy when he came out," Karls noted.

"Well, he said you hadn't told him anything about what he was doing," Parno said. "Apparently, being trusted by even the lowest member of the Royal Family is a big deal to some people."

"Some people are just too easy to impress," Karls said dryly.

"Speaking of which, you can use your imaginary authority to go and tell Simmons he won't need to divide Stephanie's escort after all. And we probably need to find another squadron or so for it, too."

"I'll just imaginary that up for you while I've got all this other imaginary work to do," Karls promised.

-

"Last wagons, sir," Rucker sounded tired. Case knew the young Lieutenant had been helping his men with their labor. He shouldn't have, but then a good officer led by example.

"So, I see," Case nodded. "You've done well Lieutenant and so have your men. I want you to start leaving squads of your most overworked troopers on the other side with this trip," he continued. "The last men across will be the men in Garrett's company and they can pull themselves over. Your men, when fully across, will mount up and proceed to the nearest available campsite that will serve our needs, preferably with a good clean creek nearby. We will camp for two nights before continuing, allowing your men time to rest and bathe. Lady Winifred's orders," he added softly. Rucker's eyes showed his surprise but he said nothing.

"Carry on," Case ordered.

"Sir," Rucker was so shocked he almost forgot to salute before returning to work.

CHAPTER TWENTY

-

Therron was 'summoned' just at sundown by an orderly informing him that 'the colonel has returned and will see you now'. Incensed, Therron gathered himself and followed the aide to the Colonel's bungalow, an actual bungalow of all things, to 'be seen.'

"Prince Therron McLeod, Colonel," the aide announced after knocking. He opened the door and ushered Therron inside.

"Ah, Prince McLeod," said the middle-aged man just starting to gray that met him. "I am Colonel Nathan Cavendish of the-"

"Yes, yes, delighted I'm sure," Therron waved him away. "I need to be taken to see your Governor at once. At once do you hear? I have been shuffled around for over a week only to get here and find you 'out', forcing me to wait another two insufferable days for you to return while my Kingdom is in the throes of revolution!"

The colonel had grown more and more red-faced at Therron's dressing down until he matched one of the lobsters that Therron had always heard of from the northern coastal areas. Good, he had the man's attention.

"Now, I demand and require a suitable and immediate escort direct to the Governor's Palace! Do I make myself clear?"

"Quite clear, Prince," Colonel Cavendish nodded, his voice strangely soft. "Is that all?"

"Yes, that's all!" Therron snapped.

"Then be prepared to leave in the morning," Cavendish said. "I shall have a suitable escort ready to carry you directly to the Governor's Palace without delay. It will be a ten-day journey to the Palace from here by the most direct route. I must warn you that it is a rugged trip to take that-"

"It can't be any more rugged than getting here was!" Therron interrupted yet again. "Just have them ready to go at sunrise! And inform my marines of that as well!"

"As you wish," Therron missed the odd light in Cavendish's eyes as he was so busy berating the man. Without even the barest hint of courtesy Therron turned and stormed out, returning to his small bungalow. He sat down at the desk and continued to write his formal request for assistance. The wording had to be just right.

It was the last group. Garrett and his last twenty-five men and horses, working their way across the river. Rucker's men were already gone ahead as Case had ordered, leaving Fain's Company still with the wagons. Case had almost sent them all on ahead but had decided against it. Rucker's men deserved the rest, but he wanted to maintain as much security as possible for the wagons and for Lady Winifred.

"Lieutenant Fain, let's make sure all the wagons are ready to roll as soon as this last-"

It was an odd noise that cut him off and Case had no idea what it had been. Fortunately, one of Fain's troopers did.

"Line break!" the trooper shouted. "Grab the line! It broke free on the other shore! Ferry's free!"

The ferry was indeed free, already moving north with the river and gaining speed every second. Garrett's men were not nearly so exhausted as the others were but the rope was coated with grease and that made it hard to hold.

Garrett knew at once what had happened, having been looking back at the eastern shore when the rope separated from the post it had been anchored to. As rope began whistling through the iron rings, he grabbed the rope trailing behind and began to pull it on to the raft.

"Hand over hand!" he called to his men. "Get the end into the boat and then we can jam it up. They can pull us in if we can keep hold of the line!"

The men not engaged in trying to hold and calm the now skittish horses began to do just that, helping their commander haul the greasy and wet rope in as quickly as they could.

One especially alert trooper at the 'front' of the ferry, the western side, grabbed the steel bar used to pull the ramp up and jammed it into the last ring on his end of the ferry, using it as a pry bar to pin the rope to the rail beneath the rings. While it didn't stop the rope from moving it did slow it down. Seeing that, Garrett ordered two men to go help the trooper, seeing that it would give them more time.

And right now, they really needed more time.

-

On the shore, men had grabbed the rope but Case stopped them from hauling on it as yet.

"Wait!" he called, hand out in a holding motion. "If we pull before they secure the line then it will just make it harder. Use this time to get everyone lined up. The more hands we can get on that rope the better. If we have to we'll cut it and tie it off to the horses to help."

Every available man scurried to be ready to haul the ferry in, assuming Garrett could manage to stop the rope.

-

Back on the raft, Garrett could see the end of the rope coming toward them, still too quick but slow enough perhaps to make his idea work.

"We need to make a big knot in this thing," he told his men. "Big enough that it won't pass the rings, and maybe even big enough to ram that bar into against the rings. If we can do that then the men on shore can pull us in."

His men grabbed the heavy line and began trying to bend it into a knot but between the thickness of the line and the grease it just wasn't working.

"What if we cut into the line?" an industrious sergeant asked. "Make a slit in it and use that bar in there?"

"Try it!" Garrett yelled at once. The sergeant produced a massive knife and had two troopers stand on the rope to steady it. Using the knife like he would sword the sergeant rammed the blade into the line. It made a deep cut but didn't go through. Swearing the sergeant tried again but missed as the boat jerked just before impact.

"Dammit!" he yelled and jammed the knife into the slit he had already made and began to hammer at it with his bare hands. A nearby trooper grabbed a saddle ax and knelt before the sergeant. Turning the blade flat he used it like a hammer against the grip of the knife while the sergeant held it steady.

Behind them rope was running out. Garrett and the others had done all they could and now hurried carefully to the front to assist with trying to slow the rope down.

"Got it!" the sergeant called suddenly as the knife went through. A few more seconds and he had managed to open the gash substantially without weakening the rope too much. The trooper with the ax didn't hesitate a second waiting for the steel rod, using the handle of the ax instead and shoving it through the gash, using the head of the ax as a stop for it.

With seconds to spare they had managed to make a stop-gap brake for the slipping line.

"Gettin' awful far away there, boys," Garrett tried to sound calm.

"We got it sir!" the trooper yelled as he and the sergeant worked the rope around just in time. The ferry jarred suddenly as the ax head slammed into an iron ring. For a terrible second the wood of the handle creaked and the sergeant hurriedly worked his now-ruined knife into the gash, using the still strong steel of the blade to strengthen the temporary break. The two men looked at it for several seconds before the sergeant dared to look away.

"I think it's working, sir."

Garrett sighed in relief as he turned toward shore and swept his hat off, swinging it around his head in a circling motion.

-

"There's the signal, boys!" Case called excitedly. "Pull! Everyone who can, get in there and pull! The rest of you let's get horses ready in case we need them!"

By the time the ferry reached the dock and the ramp came down, everyone on both sides of the affair had calmed down and all tried to act as if it were just another ordinary day in the Army. Men laughed, joked about Garrett and his men joining the Navy, ignoring the fact that twenty-five men and horses had almost been lost.

Case was the last man up the trail. As he topped the rise he looked back at the ferry, still docked and docked it would remain until the rope could be restrung, something he lacked the ability to get done.

They would have to find another way home.

-

It was a tired and disheveled group that staggered into camp that evening. Rucker's men had established the camp but done little else and no one blamed them. As soon as one of Fain's squads had shown up Rucker's entire company was off to the nearby creek to bathe. Tired though they were, it was a happy bunch who made use of that creek, returning to camp just as supper was starting. Excused duty for the evening, Rucker's men relaxed and even dozed waiting on their evening meal.

Winnie prepared a cook pot over her own fire and added the herbs she had gathered slowly, making a sort of flower 'broth' to help wash away the grease smell. She would allow it to steep overnight and then tomorrow there should be enough to add to the soap the troopers would use to wash out their gloves and uniforms in the creek downstream from the camp. The added flower scents would effectively eliminate any remaining smell of the grease. She didn't ask for any help doing it other than for four troopers to get her the needed water and set the pot on the stones she set about the fire herself.

Once the broth was finished, she pulled all but a few coals from under it, allowing the concoction to cool slowly while she made her rounds and spoke to the civilians of the wagon train. She was careful to be courteous to everyone and especially the troopers of her escort. She didn't attempt to speak with Case as there was nothing she needed, and after supper turned in without asking for anything.

Fain's men, as the most well rested, stood the watch for most of the night, with Garrett's men taking the last and the train settled in for the evening.

"Sir, are you ready to-"

"Yes, of course I'm ready!" Therron snapped. A night of sleep had not improved his disposition.

"-depart," the Coastal Captain finished, eyes flickering to his Colonel. Cavendish merely nodded slowly, his eyes somewhat hooded. The Captain returned the nod and made a hand signal to his men who instantly mounted their horses. Twenty-five troopers and five pack animals prepared to take Therron and his ten marines on their trip.

"Your orders are to escort the Prince McLeod directly to the Governor's Mansion using the Ginia Road, making no deviations in your travel, regardless of whatever other orders you are given save from a higher Coastal Province authority than mine." He handed the Captain a pair of rolled scrolls sealed with wax and a family crest that Therron couldn't make out, nor did he care to.

"Yes sir," the Captain saluted, placing the scrolls in his shoulder bag. "Permission to depart."

"Be on your way and Godspeed, Captain," Cavendish returned the salute. "Safe travels for you and your men." The young Captain mounted his horse and turned to his column.

"Move out!" he waved them on their way.

"I'll be sure and mention your cooperation favorably to the Governor," Therron promised as he passed by Cavendish, offering what he considered a boon to a lesser life form.

"You do that," Cavendish's slight smile should have alerted Therron but again he had already looked away, uninterested in Cavendish's response.

In ten days, he would finally be at the end of his journey. The end of his journey and the start of his quest.

The quest to be King.

It was not always good to be King.

That was a truth that Memmnon's father, Tammon, had kept to himself until the trouble with Therron had arisen, and Memmnon was almost certain that had said trouble not erupted then Tammon would have went to his grave laughing that he had not warned his oldest son of the difficulties associated with ruling Soulan.

Like this, for instance.

"Milord, placing women in the militia, even the unorganized militia, is a far cry from simply using women in a limited role for defense of the realm!" Sebastian Grey was on his feet. "I cannot sit idly by while-"

"Sebastian," Memmnon's voice was soft. "I grow weary of this. Very, very weary," he emphasized. It was not lost on the Palace staff, save perhaps for Grey, that Memmnon's attitude had grown steadily worse since Winifred's departure. Grey seemed to have missed that memo.

"Milord," Grey proved that with his next sentence, "we have never in all the years of this Kingdom placed women in comba-"

"ENOUGH!" Memmnon's shout, coming as it did from someone who rarely raised his voice in any setting, was enough to stun even Grey to silence.

"Read your history, Sebastian," Memmnon's voice was almost a growl. "The very foundation of this Kingdom was forged in part by women who were capable warriors! Does the name Donovan not ring a bell from your history lessons, or are you so far removed from them to have forgotten that she was one of the very people who first served Tyree in your own capacity!"

"There were women in combat roles from the very beginning of this Kingdom," Memmnon reminded him. "It was only the institution of silly traditions and customs that eventually removed women from such roles, and then later on from most positions of authority. Women were restricted in their roles not by lack of ability but by men such as yourself who refuse to see their true and complete value to this Kingdom!"

"I warned you once and I will not do so again," he brought the argument to a close as brutally as he had opened. "Raise this objection again at your own peril. Are we clear, Sebastian?"

"Very clear, Your Majesty," Grey fought not to swallow loudly into the silence around him. "Please accept my apology," he bowed.

"Sit down," Memmnon waved his apology away. "Now, on to other business. How are the repairs to the city progressing? And how are we doing on the refugee problem?"

Just another day in the life of the King.

-

The troopers were very appreciative of a day off, and Rucker's men were even more appreciative, as were Garret's for the flower 'broth' that Winnie had made to go with the soap they used to wash their uniforms. All went out of their way to give her thanks for thinking of them.

"Nice work," she heard Case say and turned to see him watching from the shade of a tree. "I appreciate it."

"Didn't think you needed it," she said lightly, smiling ever so slightly. It was the first more than civil thing he had said to her in several days.

"My men did," he said simply. "You did something good for my men and I'm appreciative of that. Thank you."

"You're more than welcome," she nodded back. "That little bit of rain last night maybe settled the dust for a day or so?" she changed the subject.

"Hopefully," he agreed. "We'll have to see once we're back on the trail. If it rained harder further west it may complicate our travel, but it will be nice to have a day or three without eating dust."

"How long you think before we hit Jason?"

"We'll hit a major trade route tomorrow afternoon, barring any severe problems," Case replied, taking a small map from his tunic pocket and opening it to show her.

"We're here," he placed a finger near the river. "We'll follow this route through two other towns to reach Jason. Four, maybe five days at most. We should make Cams Den before lunch tomorrow. I suppose we could overnight there, but with the light growing longer it would mean a big loss of travel time. The most ideal situation would be to stop there for perhaps..." he trailed off, an idea forming.

"What is it?" Winnie asked when he didn't say anything.

"We're not far from the front," he told her quietly, still thinking. "There may or may not be anyone left in Cams Den. We came this far north to avoid crossing more than one major river. We'll have to swing far south to return home after losing the ferry behind us. That won't be a problem since our ultimate stop is in Shelby, or rather just outside there to be more specific."

"We could overnight in Cams Den, assuming there's anyone left, and start your objective there. The engineers can get them started on their own earthworks or palisades, whichever they choose, and you can demonstrate how good it would be for the women to know the bow and perhaps to a lesser extent the sword. Any who wanted to go to Jason could follow along with us in better safety than if they traveled on their own. They'd be on their own returning, but it's better than nothing."

"So, what does that do to our schedule?" Winnie asked.

"Very little in terms of loss," Case replied. "And it could mean more people will take part. I don't know. We can do the same thing the day after in Carroll, which is on the trade route to Jason. From Carroll to Jason will take three days in good weather and with no other difficulty. So.... five days, six at most so long as we don't have any major trouble, and we can be in Jason and still have accomplished a good deal more than if we just passed through. The choice is your milady. It will take at least another two days if not more for the riders we dispatched to reach all the towns in their assigned areas, and still more time for people to travel there. In terms of that, we do have time to spare."

"Part of what we do in Jason will be to help with their defenses," Winnie mused. "Waiting for others to arrive wouldn't be a hassle since we'd be using that time anyway. I don't see why we can't do this," she tapped the map to indicate she meant Case's idea. "And it might mean helping more people."

"We have to be careful, milady," Case warned. He traced a finger up the map, not nearly as far as he'd like, and tapped another spot.

"The lines are near here," he told her. "We are less than two days ride behind the lines at this point for a fast-moving cavalry raid such as the one that hit Nasil. Probably only one day for a Tribal raid. We will have to be extremely careful on the trail. Returning from Shelby we will follow a different route that will be at least as difficult terrain wise but much safer in terms of enemy activity. On the return from Shelby our most dangerous obstacles will be a few bandits and perhaps another river crossing. But at least being so much further removed from the war we stand a better chance of finding an operating ferry that's manned. That would help immensely. We may even find a ford somewhere."

"With our luck?" Winnie raised an eyebrow.

"We managed not to lose anyone or anything despite what happened yesterday," Case reminded her. "You can't say we didn't have good fortune there."

"Well put," she nodded in agreement, smiling. "Thanks for reminding me of that. Very well. Let's adjust our plans according to what you've just laid out. If we have to change them again, we can, but I do like trying to use at least a little time helping those close to the front."

"Very well, milady."

-

"How are you feeling, Harrel?" Parno asked as he sat down so that Harrel could see him without looking up.

"I have felt better, milord," the 'secretary' admitted. "I am sorry I could not prevent-"

"Not another word," Parno told him, holding up a hand to silence the young man. "Not one word about anything that even resembles failure. None of that was your fault, and if not for you I'd be dead. If anything, I owe you an apology. Had my personal life not resulted in lax security for my privacy then those three would never had been able to do the damage they did. You're laying where you are because of me, so I don't want to hear anything resembling an apology from you. Understand?"

"As you say, milord," Harrel nodded.

"Now, do you want the good news or the bad news?" Parno asked.

"Is there any good news?" Harrel asked.

"You're alive," Parno nodded. "And you're going to recover, barring any unforeseen problems. That's the good news, and so far as I'm concerned it's very good news."

"So, what's the bad news then, milord?"

"It's doubtful you will ever be able to return to service with the Regiment," Parno dropped the boom all at once rather than draw it out. "There was a great deal of damage to your back, though thankfully not to any of your internal organs. Still, the muscle damage will almost certainly prevent you from being able to serve in the field. I'm sorry."

"It's alright, milord," Harrel said softly. "Many men have died in the war so far. I'm already more fortunate than they are."

"Well said," Parno nodded. "You are not without options, Harrel. But we can discuss those once you're back on your feet, okay? For now, I want you to concentrate only on your recovery. Nothing else. For the next few days at least, there's not much more you can do anyway. It's likely though not yet certain that you'll be heading home to Nasil in the next few days. Once there you will be a guest at the Royal Dispensary until such time as Doctor Corsin-Freeman deems you cleared for limited duty. Once that happens then I'll be putting you back to work."

"I thought you said-" Harrel began but Parno stopped him.

"I said you wouldn't be able to return to service with the Regiment, Harrel. That doesn't mean I don't still need you. I'm Crown Prince and Lord Marshal now. There's more work to be done on my behalf than what you can do here. And, I need someone I can trust to represent me in Nasil when I'm in the field. Someone who can weed out all the ass-kissers who want to bend my ear, that sort of thing," he grinned and Harrel laughed slightly only to have it end in a fit of coughing. An orderly was there at once to wipe his mouth and offer him some water.

"Look, we can discuss this stuff once you're back on your feet," Parno sensed that Harrel was tiring and that the orderly wanted him to go. "Just worry about recovery for now. You're awake, but a long way from being healthy." He stood and carefully patted Harrel's shoulder.

"Rest and try to sleep."

-

"He took it better than I thought he would," Parno said to Stephanie later on in the day. "Service in the Black Sheep meant a lot to him, even as just my secretary. Still, there's plenty of work for him at home once he's well."

"I think another week, perhaps week-and-a-half and he can make the trip home," she told him. "He's doing remarkably well considering his injuries."

"Probably because he has an excellent doctor," Parno smiled and she laughed.

"Ten days then," Parno declared. "Ready or not, in ten days at most you and Edema are headed back to Nasil. I'd rather you go now, but I'm willing to wait if it means he gets better care."

"You know, the proper thing for you to have said was 'if it means I get to spend more time with you'," she raised an eyebrow as she gave him a sour smirk.

"I'm hoping to spend many a long year with you," Parno replied. "But not on a war front. You've been here too long already. And being with me makes you a target. You have to go."

"I know," her voice was soft. "I will."

-

"Why are we stopping?" Therron demanded of the Captain commanding his escort. "There has to be at least two hours of light left!"

"Protocol says we stop here," the Captain said stiffly. "We don't take these trails at night and this station…" he indicated the small collection of buildings, "is where we will billet for the evening. There is a small stable and-"

"We should keep moving!" Therron said in exasperation.

"Protocol says-"

"Can you say anything that doesn't begin with 'protocol'?" Therron demanded. "Now I said we keep moving!"

"And I say we won't," the young Captain said stiffly. "I'm following my orders, sir. We will be staying here overnight. We're on schedule. Now if you will excuse me I need to issue orders for my men."

Therron almost screeched but caught himself at the last second, realizing that he wasn't looking very much like a King's candidate. He resigned himself to another wasted afternoon and dismounted.

Behind him the Coastal troopers exchanged a look with the Royal Marines, who merely shrugged as if to say 'what can you do'.

-

"Orders are written and ready to be dispersed on your say so, General," Sterling reported.

"Very well," Wilson nodded. "Remember, this is between you and I alone, Sterling. If our own people are surprised then the Soulanies will be as well. Right?"

"Hopefully sir," Sterling nodded.

"That is not the proper attitude, Britton," Wilson sighed.

"I'm working toward it sir, I promise," the younger man replied. "I can't help but worry, that's all. General Venable-"

"I don't really like or dislike Venable, but he is at the least a capable commander," Wilson said. "He's no Milton Fairmount, but few are. Still, he should be more than able to pull this off. Let's do our best to have a little faith."

"I will sir."

CHAPTER TWENTY-ONE

-

Jerome Baxter led a tired and dirty group of men into the main Imperial Army camp, limping slightly as he led his horse. Almost twenty percent of his horses were missing shoes and a good number of others were lame from over use. Walking helped the horses but was hard on the men.

"Get us settled in," he ordered his senior brigade commander. "And have the wrangler collect our worst-off horses right away," he told a senior aide, a Lieutenant Colonel. "I want smiths working on their shoeing before the sun sets. Take the others to the vets' encampment and have them looked at. Hopefully they aren't too far gone to be saved."

"Sir," the men said in unison, the aide then taking Baxter's own horse, save for his saddlebags and courier bag. Baxter caught a ride by wagon to Wilson's headquarters.

"Lot of movement going on," he noted to the driver as they made their way through camp.

"Big movement on, sir," the brawny corporal replied. "Don't know the particulars but all of 1st Corps has been pulled off line and put on stand-by to move. They won't be ready for another day or so at least but they're working into a tizzy getting ready."

"Nothing about where to?" Baxter asked.

"Nothing I've heard, sir," the man shrugged. "But then I'm just a corporal, so that don't mean much."

"Don't feel bad," Baxter told him with a dry laugh. "I'm a brigadier and I don't mean much either." The two shared a laugh as the wagon slowed and Baxter dropped to the ground.

"Thanks for the ride," he nodded.

"Anytime, sir." The wagon bounced on its way as Baxter made his way to the house where Wilson was headquartered.

"Halt!" he was surprised to be challenged.

"State your business!" the sergeant bellowed.

"Sergeant, I know I'm a little trail worn, but I'm still a damned Brigadier of the Imperial Army," Baxter growled. "You damned well better show me a little more respect than that. I'm going to assume you didn't see my rank, since it was so dusty," he brushed his collar tabs off, making a show of it, then looked back at the non-com.

"Now what say you try that again?"

"State your business, sir!" the red-faced sergeant barked, coming to attention.

"That is only marginally better," Baxter replied. "Inform General Wilson that Brigadier Baxter is reporting. With a report from General Stone."

"Sir!" the sergeant nodded and disappeared inside. Baxter looked around as he waited, wondering what had happened to make all this necessary.

"The General will see you, sir," the sergeant opened the door to allow Baxter entrance.

"You work on that attitude or I'll see you up on charges," Baxter whispered as he walked by and the sergeant's face got even redder, though he dared not say anything. Baxter moved inside to find Wilson standing, waiting for him.

"Brigadier, welcome back," Wilson smiled slightly.

"Brigadier Jerome Baxter reporting sir," he snapped to and saluted. "My men are still coming in but I'm fairly sure we will all be in before dark. This is from General Stone, sir," he handed over the reports he had been given, having included is own as well.

"Thank you," Wilson handed the reports to Sterling without so much as a glance. "Tell me, Brigadier, how many men do you have at present?"

"Sir, General Stone removed the bulk of healthy troopers from the other two division and placed them with me," Baxter explained. "We are running about twenty percent or a little more over nominal strength due to that. Last count was fourteen thousand, nine hundred and twelve."

"Good, good," Wilson nodded, liking what he was hearing. "How soon can you be ready to ride?"

"Sir?" Baxter blurted. "Ride where?"

"I need you to screen a major troop movement, Brigadier," Wilson seemed oblivious to Baxter's incredulity. "How soon can your command be prepared to move out?"

"Sir... sir we need days to be ready for movement, and that's not even taking into consideration how exhausted my men are," Baxter tried to be tactful.

"They've been in the saddle for weeks and in combat for much of that. Our horses have got to be seen to properly and many of them are quite possibly lame beyond service at this point. Over twenty percent have lost shoes somewhere and over half have shoes that are threatening to come off. My men have had one proper meal in the last twelve days, sir, and have eaten many of the bad meals either in the saddle or else while walking and leading their horses. We'd be lucky to be able to be ready to move in less than a week, Sir."

"A week?" Wilson looked shocked. "Why so long?"

Baxter had to fight not to goggle. Had Wilson not heard a word he had said?

"Sir, I just told you," he said respectfully. "Our horses are shot, sir, and my men aren't far behind. I'd wager that if you put them through a physical at least a quarter of them would be ruled unfit for duty without at least two days rest. We walked the last two miles because we honestly didn't think some of our horses would make it. I've already ordered all the horses to be re-shod, and the lame horses to be carried to the veterinarians. I hope we don't lose too many of them, but I know several have hooves that have cracked because we didn't have an opportunity to shoe them properly before our last mission."

Wilson winced at that, stung by the fact that he was responsible for forcing the cavalry out into the field absent proper preparation.

"I see," he sighed. "I can give you three days, Brigadier, but that's all. I want your men in the saddle in three days."

"We can't do it, General," Baxter didn't hesitate. "You may as well relieve me now because I can't make that happen. I doubt using every blacksmith in this camp we could get our horses prepared to move in three days. And some of those horses simply can't make another trip like that without some rest and proper care. We didn't have feed bags with us and foraging was poor in those highlands. Some are so gaunt I was ashamed to have to use them it was so much like animal cruelty. We simply can't do it."

Wilson was frowning mightily at this 'refusal' by the time Baxter had finished, but Baxter himself had already robbed him of the 'find someone who can' argument with his mention of being relieved. He had made the same threat to Stone to force him out when his men and horses weren't properly prepared.

"My men and horses have been on constant duty in the field for nearly five weeks, sir," Baxter continued. "The last two or better without support of any kind, let alone the proper support we need for field operations. They are shot, sir. Without proper rest and recuperation, they are unfit for duty. Those that might be able to get into the field would be defeated in the first engagement they had with a properly prepared enemy. Our horses have a hard enough time in combat against Soulanie war mounts as it is. Underfed and exhausted we may as well just slaughter them ourselves. It would be faster and we'd at least preserve the men to use as infantry."

"Enough," Wilson said, raising a hand. "I'll give you an extra day but in four days your division will take the field."

"Then I request relief, sir," Baxter said at once. "I just led my men into one debacle that cost roughly a quarter of them their lives. I may not can prevent it from happening again but I won't be the one to lead them to slaughter like that."

Wilson's face reddened at that but he held his tongue rather than speak in anger. Few knew it, but Jerome Baxter was a favored nephew of the Emperor. It wasn't widely known because Baxter neither wanted nor had asked for any special or favored treatment. Unlike Daly, who has simply been some distant cousin, Baxter was close to the Emperor. If he were relieved, the Emperor would want to know why. Explaining that would be problematic at best.

"I'm not accustomed to being told 'no', Brigadier," Wilson settled for saying.

"Maybe if General Stone had said no last time, sir, we'd not be in this mess," Baxter decided he had had enough. "Our men were put into the field already in poor shape. Honestly, we're fortunate to be in as good a shape as we are. I will not sacrifice my men like he did, sir. I won't. My education as an Imperial officer taught me that my men and horses are assets of the Empire and are not to be wasted or used frivolously. While your mission may not qualify as frivolity, it will qualify as wasteful, sir. I will not be the one to throw away my trooper's lives. Sir."

Wilson almost rocked back on his heels at that declaration. To have the Empire's military diction thrown back at him like that came as a surprise, and an unwelcome one at that. It did serve to remind him once more, however, that the state of the cavalry in his army was one almost entirely of his own making. He thought through his options rather than speak off the cuff.

"I will put every blacksmith in the army to work ensuring your horses are shod correctly," he said finally. "Any horses that cannot be deemed serviceable I will replace even if it means stripping officers of their horses. Moreover, your entire division will be granted three days leave with no duties of any kind, followed by two days of preparation in order to move out. On the sixth day, you will depart, screening 1st Corps as they move west to take and hold the township of Unity," Wilson walked to the wall map and placed his hand on the town in question.

"We have lost an entire infantry division, as in gone to a man save for the body of its commander, in that town. We lost another in the same exact way on the road between here and there. All this in the span of three days time." He turned back to face Baxter.

"I'm not sending you there alone, or even to necessarily fight. I'm sending an entire corps along with all support functions to this town. What I need from your men is to screen that movement so that they are not caught unprepared and demolished while they're in column of march, as what happened to at least one division. Now, given those five days, starting tomorrow, with all the resources I've promised, do you still believe your men incapable of doing their duty?"

Had he not added 'their duty' he might have won Baxter over right there. But he did.

"Sir, my men are not, when used correctly and given the proper support, 'incapable' of doing their duty," Baxter almost visibly fumed.

"Poor choice of words," Wilson raised a hand in supplication. "I should have said 'incapable of carrying out that assignment'. The question remains just the same, however."

"Will the infantry train carry proper supplies for my men and horses with them?" Baxter asked.

"Yes," Wilson nodded. "Forage, rations, even the blacksmith units assigned to their corps, and I will ensure that General Venable gives you their complete cooperation."

"Then... probably," Baxter nodded. "Three complete days of rest will go a long way to restoring my men's health and strength. As to the horses... I don't know," he admitted. "It may be that we can field enough horses for one full division but not all the troops at my disposal. But that's better than nothing. Assuming we can get the horses ready, then we can probably make that. And get the job done."

"Then see to your men," Wilson ordered. "I'll have Sterling make sure you can get anything you need from the Quartermaster without argument or beating around the bush. And the order will go out this evening for all blacksmiths to lend their complete effort to seeing that your mounts are properly ready for duty in the field. You will report back in four days with your estimate of readiness." He decided to soften his tone slightly to try and mollify Baxter.

"I did make a mistake sending you out unprepared this last time, and that was mostly due to my anger with Stone," he said quietly. "That is not to say he deserved it but nevertheless it was there. He made the argument that you could not be ready to move and I said he would do it or I would find someone who could. Your men would have gone regardless, just with someone like Weir in command instead of Stone."

"I need this move to take place, and I need it soon. Just delaying this six days may make the entire operation fail, but it can't be helped. I put us in this position so I have to bear the responsibility and I will. I will also do all that I can to rectify it, starting tonight. Go, rest and eat. Let your men get cleaned up. I will send over enough beer from the Quartermaster to help them have a good evening of it, though I expect you to keep them in check. Meanwhile, I will start doing the things I've promised. I will see you in four days time. Say, one hour before evening mess."

"Yes sir," Baxter saluted and Wilson straightened and returned it. Without another word Baxter spun on his heels and left, leaving Wilson feeling as if he'd just bearded a lion in its den.

"Sterling!"

-

Six days. Venable read the note and shook his head in disbelief. All this running and scurrying about and now six days while the cavalry 'rested'. He tossed the note down on his desk and sat down wearily. At least this would give him more time to prepare his own men.

He had already planned to carry stores for the cavalry contingent but would use his latest orders to gather still more in the way of supplies for both the horse soldiers and his own. The more he studied his orders and the overall situation around him, the less at ease he felt. The more stores and equipment he could have on hand, the better. Since he'd been given this extra time, he would make the best use of it he could.

-

A day of rest had helped more than just the exhausted troopers, it seemed. Well before the sun was fully up the wagon train was once more under way. Winnie chose to ride rather than use the carriage. It looked like it would be a pretty day and the dust had settled thanks to the brief light rain the night before last.

She had never been so far west and the heat and humidity surprised her. It wasn't yet oppressive to those used to it, but for someone who had spent her entire life in the rugged mountains of the east, it was definitely different.

True to Case's prediction they had been on the trail no more than an hour when they turned on to a well-maintained trade route headed west.

"This is a good road," she noted in passing when Case had rode beside her for a bit. "Where does it run?"

"It actually runs to the Royal City and then on further east," Case told her.

"Really? Then why not use it all the way down?"

"Because of the raid, milady," Case replied gently. "We went as far south as we could without having to make two river crossings. As it is, we'll have to make two on the return trip."

"Right," Winnie nodded. He had hinted at that before but she had not thought it through.

The trip into Cams Den was not a long one on such a good road and true to Case's prediction once more they hit the edge of the small settlement just before lunch. Scouts met them on the eastern edge to report the town still had some residents though others had reportedly fled already. There was a good camping location on the way out of town, west of the town itself but still on the route, with clean water and ample room for so many. Case ordered Conway to take half of First Company and follow the scouts to the location and claim it for the night.

The train slowed on its way through town and let the residents get a good look. Winnie decided it was worth an extra day just to let people see soldiers in their part of the kingdom. It would bolster morale if nothing else. Case waved her over to where he was speaking to a small group of people just off the town square.

"Milady this is Mayor Benton," Case introduced her to a slightly balding middle-aged man with a short beard and politician's smile.

"Welcome my lady," Benton tried to kiss her hand be Winnie deftly prevented it by turning it into a handshake.

"Thank you, mayor," she smiled at him, though what she really wanted to do was wash her hands. "What a lovely town," she added.

"Thank you, milady," he bowed slightly. "These gentlemen are the town aldermen," he introduced three other men. "Alderman Brown, Alderman Wicket and Alderman Farris. Together we r- govern the town and area immediate surrounding it."

She suspected he was going to say 'rule' but thought better of it. She decided to ignore it for now.

"I want to meet with your townspeople after lunch, Mayor," she said instead. "If you could have a messenger make the rounds and ask everyone to attend it would make things go much faster and easier."

"Easier than what?" Benton's smile had faded.

"Easier than my men doing it for you," Winnie replied, maintaining her smile. "That would give them time to get settled and eat. I have an announcement to make and I'd like everyone there to hear it."

"Well, we could certainly ensure that everyone heard what you had to say," Benton told her.

"I can ensure it myself so long as you ensure that everyone is there," Winnie held her ground. "Please see that they are. Now if you'll pardon me I have duties to see to but we will return after lunch." With that she spurred her horse on, leaving the greasy man behind. Case caught up to her perhaps two minutes later.

"Was it just me or-"

"It wasn't just you," Case replied before she finished. "He's hiding something. He's as greasy as the kiddie pig on E-Day."

"Kiddie pig?" Winnie asked, puzzled.

"Each year on Establishment Day there's a fair in Nasil," Case explained. "One of the competitions for the younger crowd is to catch a baby pig coated in grease. The child who succeeds in catching the pig wins and is allowed to keep it."

"That's a good prize," Winnie nodded. "Nice comparison too," she made a face and Case chuckled.

"He definitely doesn't want us around, and he really doesn't want us talking to the townspeople," he said. "We'll just have to see if we can flush out whatever it is he's hiding."

"Works for me."

-

Anthony Felds was confused.

Up until this morning the Imperial lines had shown all the signs of impending movement. Now, they had stopped. True there was still some movement, but there had been a sense of urgency about the movements as late as yesterday afternoon that was gone now. He spent a good hour looking over the west flank of the Imperial position before crawling back out of sight to where his horse was picketed. Felds saddled his horse quickly and mounted up, heading to report in. Normally he didn't report when nothing was happening. This time, the report was that nothing was happening.

Even though is seemed as though it should be.

-

"It's a beautiful morning," Stephanie said as she sat out under the awning of Parno's tent.

"It is, indeed," he agreed as he read over a report. He heard Stephanie sigh in exasperation and looked up.

"Harrel used to do this for me," he semi-apologized. "Now, I have to do it for myself."

"You poor man," Stephanie dead-panned. "So much hard work, whatever will you do," she placed the back of her wrist to her forehead in theatrics.

"Funny," Parno nodded. "*Funny*," he drew the word out. "Meanwhile, if I don't read this extremely important report from the Quartermaster regarding the apparent loss of up to five percent of the weight of the current herd of cattle held in readiness for slaughter as rations, the war effort may be adversely affected."

"You have to be joking," she looked appalled at the waste of time.

"Only about the war effort," Parno sighed. "And if I don't reply, I'll just get another report tomorrow 'reference my report, yesterday' and asking if I had seen said report and if so could I please advise him how to prevent the cattle from losing so much weight when all they're doing it standing around, chewing."

"You have to be exaggerating," she looked really appalled now.

"Such is the army that I have inherited," Parno assured her.

"My God, how do we not lose the war?" Stephanie was aghast. "How does anything ever get done!"

"Very slowly, I assure you," he answered her as he scratched out a reply and set it aside for an aide to deliver.

"What did you tell him?" she asked.

"Feed them better grass," he shrugged. She looked at him for a moment then suddenly her head rocked back and peals of laughter rocked across the morning. He waited until she had managed to get her laughter under control before saying;

"No, seriously."

He managed to read through three more reports before her laughter was under control again.

-

The town square filled slowly. Too slowly, Winnie thought for a town this size. According to Benton, very few if any of the townspeople had fled, believing that the Royal Army would prevent any further incursion by the Nor, as they had through history. It made a decent story and was fairly convincing, but Winnie had been fed a line of crap before and knew when she heard one.

So did Case.

"There aren't many women in this crowd," he said quietly. "Young women I mean," he added as a group of older women sat off to the side, acting as if they were fighting not to be noticed.

"I want to know what the hell is going on around here," she muttered back. "Have Lieutenant Fain and his men make a circuit through town and maybe the surrounding area, say a mile out of town. Anyone not here is to be pointed in this direction. Is that alright?" she asked him.

"I would have suggested if you hadn't," Case nodded his agreement. "There is something wrong here, milady. In time of war like this, the population of a town this small should be predominantly old men, which it is, and far more women they we're seeing. I see children," he nodded toward a group of children playing together just off the square, "but not the women I'd expect to be watching them. It looks more as if their grandmothers are looking after them."

"Have Fain find out what's going on," Winnie ordered. "And make sure Benton and his cohorts can't leave. I'll try and keep everyone occupied. You left half of Rucker's men to guard the wagons?"

"Yes," Case nodded.

"Have the other half maintain order here then," she suggested. "By which I mean keep Benton and any of his lackeys under control," she added wryly.

"We'll do just that, milady."

-

Winnie wasn't a public speaker but having been placed in the position she was in, her education in recent weeks had been much better than before. As a result, so long as she concentrated, she could do fairly well. And these were working people she could identify with far more readily than the people in the palace.

"You may or may not know it," she told the assembled crowd, "but Nasil was raided just a couple weeks gone by now." Starting with that proved to be a good idea as it brought her the riveted attention of most everyone over the age of twelve.

"Imperial Cavalry riding down from the central highlands managed to get into the Royal City and burn a great deal of it. Not enough to destroy the city," she stressed, "just enough to make a mess. They paid dearly for it as our own cavalry pretty much routed them from the city the next morning and sent them home hanging from the saddle." That drew strained laughs from the crowd.

"The thing is, though, that if they can do it there, they can do it anywhere," Winnie went on. "Worse, the Nor have made a treaty of some kind with the tribes out west and their men are riding in some kind of alliance with the Imperials. More with those opposing Shelby than here, but there are still a large number of them running loose here on the western plains." This caused a much greater stir among the people.

"So, my project is to make sure that people can defend themselves in towns like this. I have Royal Engineers who can show you how to properly prepare a defensive position, soldiers who can tell you how to stock for a siege and how to fight one, and others who can lend what assistance they can in the time we have."

"The problem being that our time is limited," she went on to explain. "So, I want the most experienced builders to meet with my engineers as soon as this meeting is over, and let them show you how to make this square, right here, the ideal place for you to defend yourself should a raid occur. Atop that, some of the men from our escort," she indicated the soldiers who were slowly surrounding the crowd and didn't mention they were actually just her escort, "will be showing you rudimentary sword techniques that will let you be better able to defend yourselves. And finally," she smiled, "myself and these ladies here," she indicated her Auxiliary members, "will be showing the women of this town how to wield a bow effectively if they don't already know. That will let the women fight back instead of merely hoping that the men alone can prevent the town from being sacked in the event of a raid."

"What's that?" Benton said suddenly. "Women?"

"Yes," Winnie nodded. "Women. These ladies and myself assisted in repelling the attack on the palace in the Royal City, using the bow. The women of your town can do the same thing here. Just because women aren't part of the army doesn't mean they can't fight. And neither the Nor nor the Tribals will care that women aren't supposed to be fighters. That's a proven fact."

"No woman in this town is going to be taught to use any weapon whatsoever!" Benton erupted, his face red. His fellow 'aldermen' were standing with him, nodding their agreement. "We say what goes on here and not some... some..."

"Some?" Winnie's voice was deceptively mild. "And are you saying that your orders outweigh those of the King himself?"

"Absolutely our orders... what?" Benton shut himself down as her words registered.

"Perhaps my escort commander didn't properly introduce me," she smiled sweetly. "I am Winifred Hubel, fiancé and Queen-Designate of King Memmnon McLeod, leader of this expedition. It is on his own orders that we are conducting this training. Since you've chosen to oppose the King's orders, I have no choice but to place you under arrest for sedition. Lieutenant Garrett, could you have some of your men escort the good mayor and his aldermen to the local constabulary for confinement?"

"Wait one damn minute-" she couldn't remember which alderman it was that started to object.

"With extreme pleasure, milady," the stone-faced Garrett nodded. He pointed to a junior sergeant who took the eleven men in his squad and surrounding the 'aldermen' and leading them away even as they continued their protests. Once they were gone, Winnie looked at the remaining people who stood in the square looking uncertainly at one another.

"I want to know what the hell is going on in this town, and I want to know right now," she said. Her voice was quiet, but every person in the square heard her. It took a minute for it to sink in that Benton and the others were no longer a threat to them. After that, it was like a breaking dam. First one, then two, and soon all of them were talking. All but five men at the rear of the group who were trying to edge away.

"Stop them," Winnie ordered and Garrett's men collapsed on the five before they could get more than ten yards.

"Confine them with the others," she instructed. "And get my secretary up here. We're going to need sworn statements, I think."

-

"Milord," Doak Parsons arrived after lunch.

"Yes, Mister Parsons?" Parno smiled.

"Sir, I've had a man sitting on the western flank of the Imperial line for three days now," Parsons reported. "There's been a great deal of activity there, always just out of sight of where he could get to. Every day now for three days, he's caught glimpses of wagons being brought up in line and left sitting as well as large numbers of men on the move, but again always behind cover of trees as much as possible."

"Sounds as if they're going to make a move," Parno nodded.

"It stopped cold as of this morning, milord," Parsons said simply. "Nothing. No activity at all. Either they've changed their minds..."

"Or they're waiting for orders," Parno finished, nodding. "Very well. Have it marked on the map and then ask him to keep a sharp eye on that area. Give him some help. Pull it from elsewhere if we have to. They may be going to make another westward movement, only in much greater force this time. Make sure we know when they leave or when there's any movement along their line."

"Will do, milord," Parsons saluted and hurried on his way.

"Trouble?" Stephanie asked once they were alone again.

"Probably."

-

Darby Hayhew had a good life. A good thing going even if he did say so himself. A large and thriving business on a decently traveled trade route and a good, thriving sideline business run from his tavern and inn besides.

'Tavern' was a loose term, as most of his rooms were dedicated to his brothel. A brothel where none of the employees were actual willing prostitutes, but that was okay. There was a war on and business was good and the locals were actually making a good bit of coin from Hayhew himself, so they didn't interfere. Most of the better constables were off with the Militia fighting the war and those who were left either lacked the courage to oppose the current people running things or were making money off of it themselves.

Occasionally, he would sell off some of the younger women to traders headed south to the coast. There they would be put aboard ships and sent off somewhere that women with fair skin and complexion were popular and in demand. He didn't know where exactly and had anyone asked, he'd readily admit he didn't care. What he cared about what his bottom line and that line was pretty solid. He had control of a good chunk of the surrounding area and was as safe as he could possibly be while doing pretty much anything he wanted.

So, it came as a rude shock to his system to be awakened in the middle of the night by shouts and even screams echoing through his 'tavern'. Struggling out of bed over the slave he'd enjoyed before falling asleep he was still trying to get his pants on when the door to his room literally splintered apart in front of him, revealing a huge Soulanie Army trooper standing there, back-lit by the low burning lamps in the hallway.

"Darby Hayhew?" a woman's voice asked from the hallway. "I'd like a word with you."

-

"You'll never get away with this!" Hayhew screamed as he was dragged bodily from his own building by two very angry troopers. "I'm a powerful man in this part of the world and I'll see you pay for every bit of this!"

"I seriously doubt it," a man's voice answered and Hayhew looked up to see a hard-faced Army Captain holding a lantern. "Darby Hayhew, you worthless pile of shit, you are under arrest."

"You can't... you aren't allowed to arrest me!" Hayhew protested. "You're military! I'm a civilian!"

"There's a war on, Mister Hayhew," it was the woman again, a pretty redhead, speaking as she walked up to stand beside the Captain. "Maybe you heard? I'm going to assume you have since it's the same war you seem to be exploiting. In time of war, particularly in time of invasion, there is a general declaration of Martial Law. That's been true since the time of Tyree by the way. And that means that you can most definitely be arrested by the Army. In fact, you can even be tried by the Army and sentenced as if you were a soldier yourself, since by Royal Decree of Tyree himself all citizens are called upon in time of war to defend the realm."

"Wh-what?" Hayhew stammered. "What sort of-"

"Didn't know that?" Winnie leaned down and looked Hayhew in the eyes and tough man that he was, Hayhew flinched. He was certain he could see the fires of hell flickering in those eyes.

"You're about to get a harsh lesson in history, then."

-

"You can't do this!"

Winnie had stopped counting how many times she had heard that over the last three days. For three days she, Case and two companies of her escort had been rounding up the perpetrators of some of the most heinous crimes she had ever encountered. Considering where she had spent the year before coming to Nasil that was saying something.

Benton had been only the tip of the iceberg and he had broken as hard as the ferry rope. Winnie's secretary had filled an entire ledger with sworn testimonies and witness statements as well as Benton's confessions of his willing participation in slave trading, racketeering and dozens of other offenses. Based on the information taken from him, she and Case began their crusade against all things criminal in the surrounding ten miles or so. Hayhew had been the worst, but far from the only one that men like Benton had been guilty of peddling flesh to.

There would soon be warrants out for the men who had purchased women from Hayhew, Benton and a dozen more just like them, and three men on good horses were now tearing their way south to the coast with orders for the local militia, and more importantly the Royal Constabulary and the Gulf Squadron of the Royal Navy, to try with all vigor to find and halt any such shipping currently in progress. Anyone caught in the act was to be hung on the spot. Winnie had ordered that herself in Memmnon's name, knowing that he would agree. Even Case said so when she asked.

Now all that was left was to clean up the mess. The women had all been treated by the doctor riding with the wagon train. Some were in pitiful condition and Winnie had ordered that every nickel seized from Hayhew, Benton and all the others be divided among them to help them recover. Case has been especially castigating when speaking to the men of the area, "and I use the term 'men' loosely" he had said more than once, for turning a blind eye to what was happening. He had sent word on to Jason, the nearest major city, requesting a squad of militia and a competent Constable be sent to police the area until further notice. Winnie had again signed the order in Memmnon's name as his representative to make sure 'competent' wasn't conveniently misunderstood.

Finally, anyone who wanted to follow with them was welcomed to do so, most especially the women rescued from places like Hayhew's, several of which were reunited with children that had been left behind them when they had been taken.

Now, after three hectic days, this was all that was left.

Case hadn't bothered with gallows, as they were too many to hang. He had simply hung ropes from every nearby tree. A total of thirty-one men and three women were now sitting horseback with nooses around their necks, screaming everything from curses to cries of innocence and everything in between. Winnie had long grown deaf to such pleas or such curses.

"Captain, please carry out your orders," she said flatly, her voice devoid of any emotion.

"With pleasure, My Lady," Case's voice was the exact opposite. His pronounced use of "My Lady" showed the renewed and perhaps even newfound respect that Case and all of his men had for their primary. She had not hesitated to do the right thing, no matter how hard it might seem.

"Gentlemen!" Case called out loud and the soldiers holding the horse's reins came to attention.

"Execute!" A fitting command, he decided. Each trooper released the horse he was holding and slapped its hindquarters, sending it flying out from under his or her occupant and leaving said occupant literally 'swinging by the neck until dead'. No one cared if the death was slow and by strangulation rather than a broken neck.

"Leave them until sundown," Winnie ordered the townspeople. "After than you can cut them down. Do with the bodies what you will. I honestly don't care." With that she turned and rode toward where the train had already started down the road to Carroll. Case waited until she was out of earshot before looking at the men of the surrounding area who had been ordered to attend.

"If I ever hear that you've allowed something like this to happen again, decide if you want to die fighting it, or die like they did," he pointed to where some of the criminals were still kicking. "Because if they don't kill you, I will."

And with that he galloped away, following his liege lady down the road.

Who he was now absolutely certain would indeed make an excellent Queen.

CHAPTER TWENTY-TWO

-

Brigadier Jerome Baxter made a walk around of his men the morning of their fourth day in camp, mostly just looking over the shape his men were in. Three days of complete rest had done wonders for them he had to admit. Gone was the gaunt, hollow-eyed look that many had begun sporting before their return and all of them were stepping a bit more lively now. In truth they should have had at least double that time off, but there was a war on and needs must and all that.

His horses were another story.

"We've had to put down over one hundred mounts," the chief vet had told him angrily. "Good horse flesh driven into the ground for no gain," he growled.

"Speak to General Wilson," Baxter had told him evenly. "I agree, just so you know. We walked much of the way back to spare them all we could. We left men behind because the horses wouldn't carry them any further. I honestly did the best I could with what I was given."

The older man's eyes had softened at that and he nodded his understanding.

"What about the rest?" Baxter asked.

"You brought in nearly fifteen thousand horses," the vet told him. "Of that number all were underfed. Aside from the horses we were forced to destroy there are..." he consulted a small notebook, "one thousand, seven hundred ninety-two that are currently unfit for duty of any kind and will be for at least another week. And that's at best. The rest..." the old man closed his notebook and sighed slightly. "The rest can be used, but it should be a crime."

"They have until day after tomorrow before we ride," Baxter told him.

"Hopefully that will help. My men will form them into smaller herds to make saddling easier the morning we leave but otherwise they can be still, eat and drink, and have no work on them."

"Then, so long as you take it easy on them, they should be okay," the vet seemed to hate himself for saying it.

"We're traveling only twenty-five miles or so, and doing that with some infantry, so we'll be moving slowly," Baxter pointed out. "Will that help?"

"Most definitely," the vet nodded firmly.

"Do you have spare mounts to replace what we've lost?" the Brigadier asked.

"A bit less than half," the man replied. "I can give you seven hundred head, plus or minus. I won't know for sure until tomorrow, but I will have a hard number for you before lunch. I may can come up with a few more but not without a bunch of screaming Generals."

"Direct them to General Wilson," Baxter grinned. "It's his idea."

"I'll do just that," the man nodded. "Come see me before lunch tomorrow. I'll have your information by then."

Baxter was pleasantly surprised by how many of his horses were able to go out. In truth he had expected it to be much worse. He sorely regretted any having to be put down, but there was nothing for it now. He wasn't in command and while he had stood up to Wilson over trying to make them move so quickly, there was a limit to what he could do without calling on family favors that he was determined not to use.

Not unless he had no other choice.

-

"Still nothing?" Doak Parsons had traveled out to where Anthony Felds and now Dagger Earl were making their small camp while watching the Imperial right.

"More activity, but nothing like before," Felds reported. "It's like... it's like there's more of them now, instead of them doing more work," he tried to explain.

"Maybe their cavalry has returned," Parsons murmured, more to himself than to Felds, but the younger man nodded.

"There was a good bit of dust four days back," he reported. "It wasn't so much as it was most of the afternoon," he amended, thinking about it. "Would have fit a long column dragging into camp, like."

"Their cavalry took a shellacking in Nasil, plus got sick eating bad beef before they left," Parsons informed him. "That would make them slow to return probably. Horses and men both worn down by fighting and sickness. I want you two to try and work around their right a little more," he told them. "Stay back and use your glass. I don't want you to try and get into camp, just try and get a picture of what's happening. If you happen onto something important then hurry back and report in. If we have to we can launch a bigger reconnaissance later to see what else is there. Right now, we can't be sure this isn't all a ruse before they launch an attack on the main lines."

"Could be meaning to make another jaunt out to the west," Earl said, squatting beside the two with his bow strung across his back. "Reckon what it is out there that's so important to them?"

"I'm not sure that ain't what they wonder about us, now," Parsons replied. "We think they started out just doing an exercise. We destroyed the first two divisions they sent and then pulled the bodies away. Didn't leave anything for them to find except the commander's bodies. Now I'm wondering if they think we're hiding something out that way and they're determined to see what it is. All we were really doing is taking advantage of catching isolated divisions and eliminating them."

"So, this is all just a great big misunderstanding," Felds snorted. "Kinda like war, huh?"

"Ain't no misunderstanding this war," Parsons reminded him. "They want to rule us and aim to do it. We aim not to allow it. All there is to it."

"Damn straight," both younger men murmured in unison. "We'll head that way in an hour or so," Felds continued, looking to Earl for confirmation and getting a nod. "We'll head west for a bit and then cross over to their side of the line before trying to creep back where we can see."

"Sounds good," Parsons clapped the smaller man on the shoulder. "How's the arm?"

"Doing fine," Felds showed the small scar, already showing signs of new skin growth. "Ain't but a bit of a cut."

"A cut that damn near went to the bone, the doctor said," Parsons raised an eyebrow. "Mind that next time you mix it up with one o' them heathens," he nodded toward the Imperial lines to the north.

"I plan to," Felds almost growled.

"But not this time," Parsons got back on track. "This time the two of you are looking and that's all. Get me?"

"We get you sir."

-

"Harrel is able to sit up for a bit now," Stephanie reported as she, Parno and Edema Willows sat down to supper. "I think we'll be able to take him home in a few more days. My timetable looks pretty accurate."

"I'm glad to hear it," Parno nodded. When Stephanie looked at him with that raised eyebrow he hastened to add "That Harrel is better, I mean. I will, of course, be very sad to see you go." Even though he meant it, it still sounded somewhat comical and Edema couldn't hide a snort of laughter.

"He's getting better," Stephanie sighed dramatically. "Slowly, but there is progress."

"Are we still talking about Harrel?" Parno asked.

"No," both women replied in unison.

"I made quite a mess, didn't I?" Winnie said later than evening as she sat around the fire with Case, Conway and the three lieutenants. Doctor Reginald Bragg was also there along with one of his nurses Winnie didn't know.

"More like cleaned one up," Conway replied. "Milady," he hastened to add as he remembered who he was talking to.

"Indeed," Bragg nodded firmly. "Those women had been horribly mistreated and that leaves out being taken like that to start with."

"Are they going to be alright?" Winnie asked softly.

"Physically? Probably," Bragg nodded slowly. "Here?" he tapped his temple. "I'm sorry milady, but I just don't know. Several of them are still having trouble accepting that they're free. All of them are cautious of everything. I'm not surprised they chose to come with us, but most are suspicious of even us," he indicated himself and the nurse. "I don't know how long it will take for them to get through that. Or even if they will," he shrugged helplessly.

"How does something like that happen? I mean here, of all places," she clarified.

"Why not here?" Lieutenant Fain asked her respectfully. "What's so special about us?"

"Lieutenant!" Conway growled before Case could.

"No, I want to hear," Winnie held up a hand to stop Conway's objection. "I'd think someone in your position would know how special we are, Lieutenant," she said to Fain.

"Begging your pardon, milady, but while Soulan as a Kingdom is special, extraordinarily so actually, people are still people no matter where you go. And some people will always prey on others if they can find a way. As a group we are a mighty people, and I'm fighting or at least willing to fight to prove it. As individuals, many of us aren't worth the air we breathe. We have prisons in every province to prove it."

"That's actually very insightful," Bragg said as Fain fell silent. "And he's absolutely correct. We as a people, as a whole, are strong and forthright. It's part of what makes us proud to be part of the realm in whatever fashion. But there are individuals among us who terrible people. People who represent all that this Kingdom stands against. I would wager," he leaned forward, elbows on his knees as both hands cradled a mug, "that the Imperial people think the same thing to a degree. We think we know them, but really, what do we know? Almost everything we know we've learned in war or from the Nor themselves in times of peace. How much can we trust what they tell us? And how likely is it that their soldiers, even the good ones, represent their Empire as a whole?"

"We tend to think of the Nor as evil, influenced by their aggression against us. Their *continued* aggression I should have said. We likewise tend to think of their men as heathens because of their behavior during such aggression. But what do we truly know of the Norland people that we haven't learned from a suspect source? I would venture to guess there are some very good people among them, even though I've never met one. Very few societies in history have been comprised of entirely evil people." He paused and looked at Winnie, then looked at the others in turn.

"Just as none of them have been entirely comprised of good, either."

Silence reined around the small fire for a few moments.

"Well, I didn't mean to kill the conversation," Bragg said finally, a rueful grin on his features.

"Just the opposite I think," Case spoke for the first time in the discussion. "And you're right. History is full of tyrants overthrown by their own people due to their rule. No society is entirely either good or bad. You can have a perfect blueprint but that blueprint has to be executed by imperfect people. There will thus always be imperfections in whatever they do, and that includes society." He turned to Winnie.

"As to how it happens, that we can also blame on the aggression of the Nor for the simple fact that most good men who would have prevented what we just encountered are away fighting the invasion. All that is left behind are the dregs of society. That unfortunately includes the few men remaining in positions of authority. There are a few constables, good ones I mean, who are still on the job, usually supported by small militia contingents, but those few men have a huge territory to cover. And they can't do it all. Can't be everywhere at once."

"How do they miss something like that, though?" Winnie demanded.

"It's not what they're looking for," Case replied. "They're looking for things out of the ordinary. Men like Benton and his cronies, all the others we apprehended, they fight like hell to maintain the illusion of ordinary. Normal. With threats, with bribes, with whatever it takes to get the job done. Had you not mouse-trapped Benton into committing sedition and removing him and his men from their spot, it's unlikely anyone would have had the courage to speak to you about what was happening. It would have been their word against Benton's, and in their place whose word do you think they would expect to be believed? While I castigated the men who had allowed those things to happen, a man has to think of his family's safety as well. If he tried and failed then his family pays the price for it."

"And ma'am, if I may," Rucker spoke, "you caught what was wrong, you and Captain Case, right off the bat. Not everyone can see through a ruse like that. I know that I learned something. From now on I'll be more aware of who is where. But had it been me, I might not have noticed. I would have camped and then rode on. Not because I wouldn't want to stop it, but because I'd not have noticed it to begin with."

"He's right," Conway nodded slowly. "Awareness comes with experience as well as training. And while training is necessary, it can never replace experience and that is especially true when we're talking about experience dealing with people. For us," he motioned to himself and the other soldiers, "we don't often interact with civilians other than to ask them to please make way. We're trained to look for assassins. To look for an attack on the Royal Family. Not the palace, not anything other than the Royal Family. That is our responsibility. So, our training dictates that is what we concentrate on. And we separate that in our minds by remembering that there are constables to take care of criminals and they can call on the militia when needed. It isn't our responsibility."

"I made it your responsibility," Winnie pointed out.

"And you are, or will be the civilian authority," Conway replied as if Winnie had just made his point for him. "You can do it. We're trained not to."

"I see what you mean," Winnie nodded after thinking that one over. "That makes sense."

"And on that philosophical exposition, I am for bed," Bragg stood. "Good night milady, gentlemen."

"I have the watch," Rucker stood. "I should check on that. By your permission, sir?"

"Carry on," Case nodded. "I think I'll turn in myself. I might sleep tonight for a change."

"Good night all," Winnie said. "And thank you."

A chorus of 'welcome milady' came from a half dozen sources. She smiled as she made her way to her carriage for the night. For perhaps the first time she felt as if maybe, just maybe with a little work and a lot help she could do it.

Maybe she could be Queen.

-

Morning came on Jerome Baxter's fifth day. He could feel exhaustion still trying to hold on to him and knew his men would feel it as bad or worse than he had. But there was nothing he could do about it. Tomorrow morning, he had to be leading his men west.

He had called a meeting of officers down to regimental seconds for an hour before mess. He arrived just as the last of his officer trooped inside his command tent and made short work of the meeting.

"You already know this, but I'm telling you officially that we leave tomorrow at sunrise to screen 1st Corps as they move west to a map dot called Unity. Two infantry divisions have completely disappeared either in the town or on the road between here and there and nothing was found of them other than the body of the commanding General. Let me say right now that if someone discovers my dead body anywhere, all of you better be found next to me." A chorus of chuckles met his demand as he smiled.

"Seriously, 1st Corps moves out in the morning planning to take and occupy this small town and then make the Soulanie come take it back. Wilson thinks there's something out that way the Soulanies don't want us to find, or to see. I think he's full of shit, but he outranks me so we're going." More chuckles at that along with head nodding.

"It is an almost certainty that we won't have sufficient horses to mount everyone who made the trip back with us," he informed them. "We're looking to be down roughly one thousand horses all totaled. Nothing to be done about it and I won't have the actual figure from the wranglers until just before lunch. If there are men in your command that you're concerned about making this jaunt, remove them from the roster and leave them here. We'll place them in charge of the camp so they can't be stolen and some lucky officer will get to stay behind and command. Volunteers for that job will not be considered, by the way, because if they were I'd take it myself." Again, he got the hoped-for response; laughs.

"We will not collect our horses until one hour before dark," he told them. "Allow them every last bit of rest and care we can before moving them to our own holding areas. In the morning we will wait until the very last minute to saddle up. Saddles and gear can be set ready to use, but we will do everything else before saddling to ride. Make that clear. Our horses are still questionable so save whatever strength they still have for any encounter with Soulan cavalry. Our orders will post after lunch when I know for certain how many horses we will have. Any questions?"

"I don't suppose there's a way to get another day or two before we go, is there?" one brigade commander asked.

"I had to risk court martial to get these last five days," Baxter replied evenly. "I'd say it's safe bet the answer is no."

"Figured," the man nodded. "Our baggage train going this time?"

"It is, but we will not require moving camp. Otherwise bring or load everything we normally would need. Our wagons will fall in with the infantry which will make them marginally safer. Anything else? If not, then I will see you at evening mess for final orders. See to your commands and expect runners after lunch. Good day, gentlemen."

-

"I really threw our schedule off, didn't I?" Winnie said as she rode with Case at the head of the train. It was still early, but the advantage of using a well-maintained trade route was that it was easier to navigate even in the dim light of early morning.

"Had to be done," Case shrugged. "And it just gives the couriers we sent off a few more days to get to their destination and for people in those towns to send representatives to Jason. It will work out."

"I wish after what we seen before that we were going through those towns ourselves," Winnie sighed.

"Not our responsibility, milady," Case reminded her. "I know you don't want to hear that, but you have to learn that you can't do everything. You won't even be able to do most things. Pick your battles wisely and delegate the lesser things to others. In normal times you would have been able to count on the local constabulary to deal with what we just saw. What you're doing is more important than police work, our most recent adventure notwithstanding."

"How can you stand to know something like that is happening and not do something about it?" Winnie asked. Not accusing but asking for advice.

"You have to concentrate on what you're supposed to be doing," he replied after a minute. "What I'd like to do has nothing to do with what the King expects of me. He expects me to do my duty. Counts on me to do it in fact, having delegated it to me in the first place. I can't go off and change what I'm going to do on my own orders. The King will be counting on me to be where I'm supposed to be and if I'm not, then what? So, I do my duty as it has been given to me and I hope that others do the same."

"Even when you know you should do something else?" Winnie asked.

"Milady, you will, Lord willing, be my Queen one day," Case had a sudden attack of frank discussion. "When that happens, you will be able to do something about these things, or even order me to do it. You will be the power in Soulan save for the King and Crown Prince or Lord Marshal. I, however, am a mere Captain… Senior Captain," he corrected, "and I cannot. I don't get to decide what orders I follow and which I change or ignore altogether. That isn't how this works."

Winnie blinked at that, turning her head back to look down the road ahead. She had never thought of it that way. She was accustomed to being free to do as she chose so long as she could accomplish it that it didn't always occur to her that not everyone had that option.

"I'm sorry, Captain... Senior Captain," she grinned at him as she corrected herself. "I didn't think that through. I am so used to doing as I please, and I mean all my life not just since... since," she clarified, "that I don't always think about being constrained by orders or duty or anything else. Before, the only thing that limited me was my ability. Was I strong enough to climb that high? Was I good enough to take that shot? Could I track that animal? It all depended on whether I could actually do it and nothing else. It takes some getting used to," she admitted.

"I should imagine," Case nodded slowly, rethinking what he knew of the young woman at his side. She had grown up in a rough and tumble environment that had forged her into a strong, tough and independent young woman. He had known her background of course, but knowing something and realizing what it meant were two different things.

"War won't last forever," Winnie said finally. "Things will get better. And we'll help."

"Yes," Case smiled slightly. "We will."

-

"That looks like their cavalry but... where are their horses?"

"I don't see any," Dagger Earl shook his head as he used his own glass to scan the enemy lines.

"Reckon they made them infantry now?" Felds chuckled, then turned serious. "I wish we could hear what they're saying," he indicated a small knot of men within sight.

"Can't get no closer," Earl shook his head.

"I know," Felds sighed in disgust. "Sides that, I don't want to get caught out by this bunch."

"Me neither," Earl agreed. "Do we report in?"

"Ain't nothing to report as yet," Felds shook his head. "We'll keep watching. I got a feeling they're gonna do something soon."

"Like what?" Earl asked as the two crawled through the tall grass over the ridge behind them where their horses were hidden.

"I knew that, I'd be a general," Felds replied.

"Like hell."

-

"Morning, General," Parno walked in the main command tent to see Davies already at work. "How do things look?"

"Fine at the moment, milord," the older man nodded. "We're still watching the Imperial lines closely. All indications are that there is a move coming, but nothing indicates how many of them or where other than the location of the activity. Because it's along the enemy right, we believe they are preparing a movement in strength to the west, possibly back to Unity. It could be a ruse of course, but a large number of their men have been pulled from the lines. It's the only thing I can think of that makes sense at the moment. I can't find another single reason for them to do any of this."

"Well, when you've eliminated everything else then it has to be what's left," Parno shrugged. "All we can do is wait and watch. I've been concerned myself. I've been restless the last few days and that has usually been a precursor to action. I don't want to sound like a soothsayer but I've learned to trust my instincts."

"Nothing wrong with trusting instincts that have proven accurate," Davies agreed at once. "How is the training of 1st Corps coming along?" he asked.

"They're almost done," Parno informed him. "Why?"

"Allow me to recommend that they be given some time to stand down," Davies ventured. "A week perhaps, to make sure equipment is in good shape and the men are well rested. Assembly each morning before mess, camp duties, general drill, the sort of routine things we do every day."

"I can order that," Parno agreed. "Why?"

"I have instincts too, milord," Davies looked grim. "And mine are screaming that we'll need those men and need them soon. I'd rather they be rested and refit when we do."

"That makes good sense," Parno nodded. "I will see to it right now. Anything else before I go?"

"Not at present, milord," Davies was still looking at his map. "We have things well in hand so long as they remain unchanged." Implied in that was the idea that things were about to make that change.

Parno nodded and left to send a courier to 1st Corps.

-

General Graham looked at the message and felt his brow crease slightly. They were supposedly almost done, so why this sudden stand down to camp routine, with 'all material preparations sufficient and necessary to enter combat'?

That was an odd turn of phrase if he had ever seen one. He thought about it for just a minute and decided it could mean only one of two things; they were being tested... or they were about to be needed.

Either way he had a great deal of work to do and not much time to see to it. He summoned runners to him and sent them to find division commanders as well as Colonel Willard and Cho Feng.

It looked as if things might be heating up soon.

-

"Milady, I'm grateful for all you have done..." Harrel began, then stopped, seeming to weigh his words.

"But?" Stephanie prompted him with a smile. "I sense a 'but' in there somewhere."

"But I would like you to be straightforward with me," he continued. "Will I ever be able to return to duty? With the Regiment, I mean? The Prince said it was unlikely, but..."

"Harrel, it's too soon to say for sure one way or another," Stephanie replied. She had been dreading this question. "You have a great deal of muscle damage in your back, Harrel. We were incredibly fortunate that horrid thing didn't hit an organ or we'd likely not be having this conversation right now."

"I know," Harrel nodded. "I knew what it was as soon as I saw it."

"I will promise you this," Stephanie looked him in the eye. "I have given you the absolute best care I can, and I will continue to do so until you are healed. If there is a way for you to be fit enough to return to duty, we will find it. I won't promise you that it will happen because I honestly don't know. I do know that the odds are against it, I won't lie. The damage is likely going to be permanent. Not this," she indicated his current condition. "Not like this. You will walk again and be able to dance with your bride at your wedding someday. But service in the regular army is hard enough, Harrel," she added softly. "Service in the Black Sheep..."

"I know," Harrel sighed. "It was the greatest thing," he sounded as if he wasn't talking to her anymore. "It was the greatest achievement I could have attained. For a short while, I was... special."

"Harrel," Stephanie almost breathed his name. "Harrel you defeated three Imperial assassins single handed, killing two and incapacitating another, saving the Crown Prince in the process. I don't know how much more 'special' you can be."

"I suppose that is something, isn't it?" he nodded absently. "Thank you, Doctor."

"Try and get some rest," Stephanie stood.

"All I do anymore is rest."

-

"I don't know you," Edema said, looking up at the young Captain standing before her. He wore the uniform of Parno's personal regiment but that didn't mean anything if she didn't know him.

"Captain Antoine Pike, Lady Cumberland, at your service," the young man snapped to attention and bowed slightly.

"For?" she asked hesitantly.

"I... I assumed the Prince had informed you, milady," Pike looked confused.

"About?"

"I am the commanding officer of your escort, Lady Cumberland," Pike told her quietly. "And I have under my command a smaller separate escort specifically for Lady Dhalia as well. My charge from the Prince himself is to maintain your and her safety above all else."

"What?" Edema was getting pretty good at one-word sentences.

"Where you go, we go," Pike said simply, shrugging ever so slightly. "When you depart this camp and head for home, we'll be following you, ma'am."

"You will, will you?" Edema mused.

-

"Yes, he will," Parno was scratching through the papers on his desk while a fuming Edema Willows stood in front of him shaking her head.

"No, he won't," she replied. "I told you I don't need-"

"And I said you did," Parno cut her off smoothly as he finally found what he needed. "Ah-hah!" he crowed as he spread the map across his desk, weighing it down with odd and end pieces of equipment.

"I am not going to be followed around everywhere I go by-"

"You want to spend the rest of the war confined to the palace?" Parno didn't look up as he spoke.

"What?" the screeched reply was just bordering on outrage.

"Those are your choices," he told her, still pouring over the map. "Pike and his men go with you, or you go to the palace where Memmnon can look after you."

"I have been looking after myself since before you were born, young man!" she snapped. Parno stopped what he was doing with a sigh and looked up at her.

"You weren't close to me then," he said softly. "Your kindness toward me will mark you. Has marked you. You'll be in danger now because of me. From Therron, from Imperials, from enemies of the Crown, the list is long but distinguished. Pike is non-negotiable, Edema," Parno said firmly.

"I need you to be safe," he almost whispered. "I can't lose you."

A sudden awareness of his fear swept over her and she felt a rush of sympathy swell within. She smiled faintly and nodded.

"Very well then," she gave in with grace. "It will be as you say."

"I knew that," Parno nodded as he returned to the map.

-

"This is Carroll," Winnie said as they rode across the flat plain leading toward a collection of buildings. There were farms all along the route as well as small markets selling everything from early produce to meat from livestock.

"So, it is," Case nodded. They had made excellent time through the morning and were arriving just after lunch. They had planned originally to make this trip in one day but with new people added to the train, some of whom were still not quite settled, it had made more sense to spread the trip over two days.

Winnie didn't mind. They would be able to meet and plan this afternoon and evening and then would spend all day next helping lay out defenses and giving some rudimentary training to the locals that they could continue working with on their own.

"This is lovely country," she told Case. "I don't think I've ever seen so much flat ground in my life."

"These plains and the area south of here are our breadbasket," Case nodded. "That's why it's so crucial to get the Nor back across the Ohi. Until we do, they're squatting on millions of acres of prime farmland."

Winnie didn't have anything to add to that and so stayed silent. She knew from sitting in meetings with Memmnon and Parno how bad things were, and how bad things would be come winter. She shook her head slightly as if trying to rid herself of the thought. She had her work before her. Stick to that.

"Let's take one company and ride ahead into town," she said suddenly. "We can find the leaders and start talking to them now."

"Very well."

CHAPTER TWENTY-THREE

-

Thirteen thousand, two hundred and three.

That was how many Imperial troopers saddled horses in the predawn darkness. It was less than he had wanted and still more than Baxter had hoped for. And he was pleasantly surprised to see the horses looking so much better. He had spotted troopers the night before checking hooves and shoes as well as back and skin while they were walking the horses to their regimental corrals to be ready for this morning. So far none of them had reported any problems. The wrangler and vet had been true to their word.

"Sir, all regiments are reporting ready to move," an aide told Baxter just as light began to show in the east.

"Very well. Scouts out, van and flankers. Let's make sure the infantry are safe," he chuckled. The aide grinned in the growing light and went to carry the orders. Baxter mounted his own horse, patting his neck after he was seated.

"We'll try and take it easy today boy," he promised.

-

General Venable was doing much the same thing as Jerome Baxter, just on a larger scale. His aides were reporting in as the huge procession began to shake down in preparations to move.

"Wagons are all hitched to their teams, sir."

"Division commanders report all in readiness for march, sir."

"Wagon Master reports all wagons are manned and ready to travel, sir."

"Medical officer report..."

And so forth and so on, over and over until suddenly it was quiet. Venable waited a few seconds to make sure of what he was hearing, then turned to face them.

"Is that it?"

"Yes sir," his Chief of Staff nodded. "All preparations are made, sir. We are ready to proceed."

"Then let's get this show on the road," Venable ordered simply. "Are the cavalry moving?"

"Ten minutes ago, sir," the staff officer nodded. "They're on the road."

"Then pass the orders and let's get moving. I'd like us to be moving by the time the sun comes up. Ideally, I'd like for us to make this trip in three days and have time to at least get a look at the town before dark. So, let's shake a leg and try to make that happen."

"Yes sir!"

-

Scouts all along the Imperial lines recognized the sound of tens of thousands of men moving. They had been expecting it anyway but even had they not it would have been hard to miss. During the night Soulan scouts would crawl to within one hundred yards of their enemy in many cases and just listen. This morning as they prepared to return to their own lines, they could hear orders being passed and wagons rumbling along the road that ran through the Imperial camp.

The enemy was moving.

-

"Well, we wondered where their horses were," Earl said as he and Felds ran their own mounts flat out trying to outdistance the Imperial scouts that had just almost caught them.

"We need to get ahead of this crowd and back where we belong," Felds said as he looked over his shoulder. He couldn't tell if the scouts had actually seen them or if they were just clearing the way for the others. They would have to chance it.

"When we get to the next cut, we head south," he told Earl. "There's a small rise there. Up and over, we'll be out of sight of the road at least. From there it's straight on south for a mile and then back east to our lines."

"Good deal," Earl nodded. While he probably knew the area south of the road better than Felds, he knew that Felds was more knowledgeable of the northern side. The two urged their horses on, looking for the small dip that would indicate the cut was ahead.

-

"I think I hear horses."

"You can't be serious," the Imperial scout turned to look at the man next to him. "Are you still asleep?"

"I meant besides ours, idiot," the first man replied angrily. "Didn't you hear that?"

"There are over ten thousand horses behind us Jake," the second scout shook his head. "I'm lucky to hear myself think over that noise."

"That's true," 'Jake' nodded. "Probably just an echo."

"Probably."

-

"I think we're clear," Felds said after ten minutes of hard riding.

"Looks like it," Earl agreed. "What now?"

"Head for camp and report in," Felds ordered. "I'm gonna keep watching. See what else happens."

"What do I tell them?" Earl asked. Before Felds could reply they heard bugles blowing.

"Hang on," Felds said, pulling his glass out. Earl kept watch on their own surroundings. After a minute Felds lowered the glass.

"Their cavalry is moving," he told Earl. "At least a division I'd say and maybe more. And there's something else behind them, maybe a wagon train or something, I can't see yet. Head back and report that in and see about orders. I'll be on that little rise yonder," he pointed to a small clump of trees on a low rise behind them. "Should be able to still see but maybe be away from their flankers. I'll meet you there."

"Got it," Earl nodded and set off at once, bearing south to avoid Imperial patrols.

"Come on, boy," Felds patted his horse's neck. "We need to move."

-

Baxter had one brigade remain behind to bring up the rear of the column of infantry. They would be responsible for ensuring that Soulan cavalry didn't come up on the column from the rear, riding over the foot soldiers.

Company strength flankers were posted along the road and would shadow the infantry as they moved, ensuring a clear flank. A full regiment was devoted to the van, with company strength flankers for them and scouts crawling everywhere ahead of them.

Ahead, and not on a small slope just over a mile distant to the south.

-

Felds let his reins trail on the ground as he slipped off his horse and made his way through the thin brush to where he could see. Behind him the horse pulled fresh green grass from the ground, content to wait there for his master.

Felds used his glass from inside the shade of the brush to avoid any flash of glass that might give him away.

"Good thing we moved so far back," he murmured to himself as he saw Imperial scouts a scant five hundred yards away. "They'd have rode right over me." He scanned the road, so far seeing only the cavalry. He would lower his glass every few seconds and take a look around him. Being alone meant he had to split his attention so as to ensure no one could take him by surprise.

He tried to calculate how long it would take Earl to return to camp and explain their situation. Then Captain Parsons would have to report in and that would take several more minutes and then a decision would have to be made and that could take who knew how long. In the meanwhile, he needed to try and see what that cavalry was screening, if anything at all.

"Maybe it's just them," he thought aloud. "I doubt it, though. Now with all this." He resigned himself to wait and see what happened. He didn't have to wait long.

-

"We're moving, finally," Venable said to no one in particular. He was mounted as were his aides and several runners, but the majority of his staff were riding wagons or empty ambulances, their horses pressed into service to mount as many cavalry as possible.

"Yes sir," several of his aides answered and Venable sighed. No one around him could tell the difference between him simply making an observation and him asking input.

Well, that wouldn't make any difference now. His men were moving. They had a small trip ahead, probably three nights camped in the open and then reaching Unity by lunch the fourth day. At least that was his plan. He had said he wanted to make it in three days hoping the extra motivation would help them keep the actual schedule he had in his head. It might not work but there was nothing lost in trying it.

He was impressed by the cavalry commander, Baxter, for the disposition of his men, including leaving what looked like a full brigade to bring up the rear and screen the vulnerable column from being overtaken by enemy cavalry. Venable has made a similar move by placing one division behind his wagon train so that his stores and equipment would not be straggling without cover. In a few hours they would be beyond support of any kind that would arrive in time to matter. Caution was the word of the day so far as he was concerned.

It would take over an hour for the entire column to get out on the road, but once it did, they would move more quickly. It was a good road and good weather. Once they shook down things would be fine.

-

"That's a lotta Imp soldiers," Felds whispered as he watched yet another division emerge from the tree line, the third so far as near as he could tell. He fished in his shoulder bag for a piece of hardtack and broke a piece off, placing it on his tongue to let it soften. He and Earl had of a necessity missed breakfast as they were running from Imperial scouts. Hunger was now scratching at his belly.

He continued to watch as regiment after regiment appeared. Finally, after a fourth division had shown, came the wagons.

"Look at that," Felds breathed as wagon after wagon rolled down the road from behind the trees. "I guess that's what all the noise was," he decided. He had his notebook out and was keeping careful count of how many units he had seen, and had written down any units he had managed to identify. Now he counted the wagons, and when the artillery rolled from the trees as well, he made special note of that.

"They ain't kidding around this time," he decided.

-

"Milord, we have a report of movement in force on the enemy right," an aide said softly as Parno sat eating breakfast.

"How much force?" Parno asked.

"It's still coming."

"Excuse me ladies," he stood, taking a pastry from a dish on the table. "I better check on this."

Having made his manners, Parno hurried to the command tent where Davies was already looking at the reports coming from all down the line.

"What's happening, General?"

"Large enemy force moving out to the west, milord," Davies handed over a handful of hasty reports. "Likely the group they removed from the line earlier but we truly can't be sure. Confidence is high though that it is. And it's a lot of movement. Our reports so far haven't gotten a look yet but-"

"Beg pardon, Milord," Doak Parsons walked into the tent already speaking, cutting Davies off. Parsons walked to the map as he spoke,

"My men have identified a large cavalry force emerging from the Imperial line in the trees here," he indicated the Imperial right. "Infantry coming in force behind them. They were just emerging when one of my men left to report in. Another is still there trying to get a better look. This is a major movement with a heavy cavalry screen. From the look of it, I'd say it's probably every cavalryman they have left."

"I need you to go and check on this," Parno said softly. "I need accurate information so I can make a decision. It sounds as if they're just making a move for Unity again, but if a force that size turns south, we could be in real difficulty."

"We'll be in the saddle shortly, milord," Parsons nodded and departed. Parno took a deep breath to collect his thoughts.

"Have General Wilbanks assemble his men near our left," he told Davies. "His men and mounts have been through the new training regimen and passed with high marks. I don't want them pursuing, at least not yet, but I do want them ready to respond if this is an attempt to flank us." He paused, gnawing his lip, then spoke again.

"And send a runner to Graham instructing him to keep his men ready to march with fifteen minutes notice. I don't want them standing in line but I do want him to be able to get moving as soon as we need him."

"Will do, milord."

It was all Parno could think of for the moment. He needed to know more before he could commit his troops.

-

"I'd give a pretty penny to know what's being said in their command tent," Wilson mused as he watched the last of Venable's men heading out. Sterling stood beside him, nodding. Wilson looked at the younger man.

"Orders written and ready?" he asked quietly.

"Ready to post on your say so, sir," Sterling promised for the third time.

"Deliver them tomorrow after noon mess," Wilson ordered, a decisive tone in is voice Sterling hadn't heard in a several days.

"Sir, I have to caution you again about-"

"I know," Wilson held up a hand. "I've heard all your arguments and you're right to make them," he said to make sure Sterling knew he wasn't being reprimanded. "Follow your orders, Brigadier."

"Yes sir," Sterling nodded.

Wilson reined his horse around and began moving. He had a lot of work to do today.

-

Felds tensed at the sound of horses and hurried through the brush to his own horse, expecting to see Imperial scouts running up on him. Instead he found Earl returning with Captain Parsons and ten other men of their group, all good scouts and horsemen.

"Anthony," Parsons nodded as he dismounted, passing his reins to another man. "Show me what's happening."

"Yes sir," Felds nodded, motioning for Parsons to follow him. The two made it back to Feld's hiding place just as the wagons finished coming from the wood. Felds did a hasty count from the wagon he had marked in his memory and showed the total figure to Parsons.

"All in this one move?" Parsons asked.

"Including eight artillery pieces, sir," Felds nodded. "I never seen so many wagons."

"And now more infantry," Parsons muttered. "What have you seen so far," he looked again at the notebook, copying Felds' information into his own. "Damn," he muttered as he finished. "That's a serious move."

"Yes sir," Felds nodded. "Lotta men and supplies and what not. Wherever they're headed, they aim to stay there."

"So, they do," Parsons nodded. "Keep them under observation until they're done," he told Felds and Earl. "I'm going to start sending men further west to screen that bunch. When they stop coming, you two report to me at headquarters. Got it?"

"Got it," the two younger men replied as one, nodding as they did.

Parsons walked back to the men who had came with him.

"Spread out westward," he pointed. "Keep an eye on that bunch. Stay close enough to each other that no one is lost, and don't let their scouts see you. I'd like them to think we're not looking. If they turn south for more than a mile I want to know it as soon as a horse can get you to me. Hear me?"

"We hear you, sir," the senior man nodded. "Let's go, boys," he said over his shoulder and the five men began moving, angling away to avoid being seen. Parsons watched for a minute, trying to decide if he'd missed anything. Satisfied he hadn't, he hit his saddle and began running back to make his report to the Prince.

-

"An entire infantry corps, plus attachments, screened by a reinforced cavalry division," Parno listened as Davies read off the total. "We're looking at somewhere around fifty thousand infantry and another twelve thousand or so cavalry, all headed west of the line," he traced it one the map.

"They're going to take Unity again and intend to hold it this time," Parno mused. "Why, I wonder?"

"I still think it's because they've decided there's something out there we don't want them to see," Davies was shaking his head. "It's the only thing that makes any sense. There is nothing out there for them to try and take."

"What if they're just looking for a position advantage?" Parno asked, looking at the map alongside his General.

"What do you mean?" Davies asked, frowning.

"Look," Parno began tracing lines. "From Unity there's a major trade route straight to Jason, and another equally good one that runs directly into Shelby," he traced another line. "This force is large enough to present a threat we can't ignore. Do you see what I'm saying?"

"Yes," Davies nodded. "And that would hurt. We would need to divert enough manpower from here that it would severely weaken us on this front. And while they're weakened as well, it's not enough to keep them from attacking even if we maintain our current strength level and trust that they won't strike south."

"Something is off about this," Parno shook his head. "It's too easy."

"Milord?" Davies asked.

"It's too easy," Parno repeated. "It's like they don't care if we see this move. Almost as if they're daring us to do something about it. Or maybe even trapping us into it," he thought back to the first time they had seen Imperial soldiers moving west along that road.

"Would they sacrifice two infantry divisions to set that up?" Davies sounded incredulous. "Even for them..."

"No, I think you were right about those," Parno was shaking his head. "I think that was just an exercise. Meant to let their men work off some steam and keep their generals from raising too much hell. But the fact that we destroyed those two has lit a fire under them. That's not a bad thing," he added as Davies began to apologize. "I'm just saying that was the catalyst for all this. Maybe it is that they're just going to set up shop to show us that if they want something, they'll get it. Or to get us to split our forces." Parno paused, hand on his chin as he studied the map.

"The thing is I've had this uneasy feeling for several days now," he said finally. "As if there was something I was missing, somehow. I'm not saying that's what it is, just that's what it feels like. I get those feelings when things are tense and I'm in a position where I can make a bad mistake. It's like an intuition, I suppose."

"Is it usually right?" Davies asked, interested.

"Usually," Parno nodded. "But is that a strong enough guide to commit so many men to what may be a snipe hunt? I honestly just don't know," he admitted. "But there is something wrong here, General. I know there is, I just can't put my finger on it." Abruptly, he turned away from the map.

"Have scouts continue to watch that column. And send someone for General Wilbanks, please. Oh, and I need a Pioneer company prepared to ride. Horse mounted with pack animals only. They'll need to move fast. They need to be prepared to destroy the bridges here, and here," he tapped two places on the map. "Ideally, they'll be ready in the morning, but definitely the day after."

"I'll make those arrangements now, milord," Davies nodded.

"I need to walk," Parno said absently. "I need to think."

-

Parno walked through camp without really paying attention to where he was going. A screen of Berry's command kept him inside a bubble as he moved, ensuring that he wasn't disturbed and occasionally that he didn't walk into a tent or a wagon. Parno took no note of that as his mind worked the problem before him.

If he ignored the large troop concentration moving west right now, they would certainly be in a position to strike south. The infantry would move slowly and the artillery wouldn't move any quicker. He estimated it would take them at least five days of good travel time and a minimum of two river crossings to reach Jason. To reach Shelby would require a minimum of three river crossings and take at least twice that long, even with good weather.

A scout riding from Unity would need most of a day riding hard to reach Parno at headquarters and let him know that the Imperials were striking south from Unity. Assuming he could prepare a response to march by the next morning, he would need a minimum of three days for a cavalry force to reach Jason, and that was in a perfect world where they got away before full dawn and rode until it was too dark to see. Four days would be more accurate, which would be cutting it very close.

Next was the fact that in order to counter such a big move he would need to commit almost all of his cavalry to the action, leaving him perhaps one division to spare that would have enough mobility to guard his flanks or respond to an emergency. He wasn't sure that was enough, even if it was Wilbanks' newly trained outfit. And he really thought he would need Wilbanks' division to aid the cavalry sent toward Jason, but he wasn't sure.

Allen, Coe and Vaughan had done very well, and their men had done wonderfully. He could always add Fordyce and Bellamy's divisions to Allen's 'corps' and send them all hurtling toward the enemy incursion. With the Pioneer company ahead of them, damaging or destroying key bridges, the enemy's rate of advance would slow considerably, especially with the river crossings. He couldn't recall any easily reachable fords along those rivers, which would mean they would have to either build a log bridge to cross on or else build a ferry. He would go with log bridges himself, floating on the water and lashed to the shore, but would that allow for so many wagons to cross? Would it support the weight? He needed to ask an engineer that question. He turned to tell Harrel to make a note of that and stopped short.

Harrel isn't here any more, he reminded himself sadly. He had come to depend on the very capable secretary, never realizing that he was much more capable than he let on. Shaking his head, he continued his walk, making a mental note to ask an engineer about the weight issue.

They would lose at least a day constructing new log bridges, and perhaps as much as another day getting everything across the river on such a flimsy construct. Floating bridges, no matter how well constructed could not support the same weight and speed that a solid, embedded bridge could handle. While they could make many floating bridges with the manpower at their disposal, the bridges themselves still wouldn't support the weight. No, at least a day would be lost. Maybe two.

Extra time in which his men could maneuver into position. Perhaps even strike the enemy as they sat against the river, waiting for new bridges to be constructed. That could prove decisive, catching the enemy unprepared. But how likely would they be to simply leave their forces in line of march instead of deploying them into defensive postures while they waited for the brides to be finished?

"Not very," he murmured, unaware he had spoken out loud.

"Not very?" he almost jumped out of his skin as Cho Feng spoke from beside him. "Not very what?"

"Wha-, when did you get here?!" Parno demanded, looking around. His escort were all looking anywhere but at him, some obviously fighting not to laugh. They looked away guiltily when he glared, but were unable to smother their humor.

"I have been here for some time," Feng's face was stolid. "Watching you walk and think. Amazing how you cannot do one without the other. It is a wonder you get anything done."

"Oh, you're a funny guy, aren't you?" Parno growled.

"You have not answered my question," Cho Feng said.

"What question?"

"You said 'not very', and I asked what you meant."

"I did?" Parno frowned. "I don't remember saying that."

"Well, you did," Cho assured him. "Now what did you mean?"

"I was thinking about how likely the enemy was to leave their troops conveniently in line of march while they stopped to build bridges. The answer was 'not very'."

"An excellent observation," Feng nodded. "And an accurate summation no doubt. What does this do to your line of thought?"

"I have to figure whether I can afford to ignore this movement or not," Parno continued. "Can I move troops in time to oppose them if they head south? If they turn toward Jason then I would have at most five days to get a force large enough to stop them in place. Jason is the largest city in this region outside of Shelby, but unlike Shelby it has no garrison at all, just a small militia detachment. There are no defenses, nothing. If they get that far they can destroy everything and everyone and unless I can get a large enough force there in time, I can't prevent it."

"Can you?"

"Technically," Parno nodded slowly. "But it would all but strip us of cavalry on this front. And if they can't bring the enemy to a decisive engagement then they would have to stay there, holding them at bay. Which would leave us permanently weak here. Our defense of this position would be reduced to tenuous at best and make any offensive movement completely impossible, even if we got 2nd Corps back and factored in the new men now being trained. We would face a permanent standoff, almost."

"What do you know of your enemy?" Cho asked. Parno considered that before answering.

"So far my enemy has not shown any real creativity but... he hasn't needed it. He had the strength to bull his way this far south before we could stop him. While his past behavior indicates he won't do anything bold or rash, I can't count on that. His recent failures and partial successes will make him want to take some kind of action. The question is what he will do, and where."

"What can you do short of moving so many troops to counter this new development?" Cho prodded.

"I could send my cavalry in force to try and wreck the entire expedition, but again that leaves me without their presence here. In addition to that, our own losses would no doubt be considerable in both horses and in men. Otherwise, all I can do is keep an eye on them and have men standing by to be prepared to make their move south as difficult as possible. Destroying bridges, laying traps, that kind of thing."

"What are you overlooking?" Cho asked him, eyebrows raised. Parno thought about that, knowing that Cho had already found something lacking. It hit him like a brick.

"The Tribals," he almost breathed. "Where are they and what are they doing?"

"Very good," Cho nodded. "They may not be a large force but they are ruthless and fast moving, correct?"

"Yes," Parno nodded.

"Do not forget to factor such a group into your thinking, young warlord. If you do, they will appear and surprise you at the worst possible time."

"Any time right now is the worst possible time," Parno admitted. "I had hoped for just a little more time."

"The enemy has apparently decided to refuse you that time. You must examine realistic options. This is open ground, no?" Cho coached.

"It is, but it is also desperate ground," Parno replied. "We had to fight and try to hold them here refusing them further entrance into our Kingdom."

"Why?"

"Why what?" Parno looked puzzled. "Why fight? I just told you."

"What is here but ground," Cho motioned around them. "What do they gain if you withdraw?"

"They gain the field and can go where they please," Parno pointed out. "Not least of which is to out maneuver me and head for Shelby, catching Raines between this force," he pointed north toward the enemy lines, "and the one across the river. I can't allow that to happen."

"The further the enemy encroaches into your territory, the more difficult his position becomes, yes?" Cho asked.

"Possibly," Parno nodded. "I chose to fight here because the army was already here and the enemy gave battle. I had weapons that could turn the tide so I used them."

"To what advantage?"

"To buy time," Parno replied, trying to see what Cho Feng wanted him to see. "I needed time. I still need time. I was buying that time here."

"A wise stratagem while the enemy is still and offers no more than straightforward battle. But that time appears to have ended, no?"

"It appears to," Parno nodded.

"So realistically now, what are your options?" Cho pushed. "Not just with the mobile force moving west, but overall. What options lie before you?"

"I can wait and let the enemy have the initiative, I can retreat and let them have more ground, or I... or I can attack," he said suddenly. "I can attack them even as they are preparing to attack me."

"Can you though?" Cho asked. "What does your enemy number?"

"With that bunch gone... around two hundred thousand I should think," Parno chewed on his lip. "All of it infantry, apparently, since we think they sent all their available cavalry west with that column."

"And what can you muster?" Cho asked.

"We can muster around half that with 1st Corps, plus another... forty-five to fifty-five thousand cavalry, depending on what I have to send to screen against a movement south."

"And you think that is sufficient to attack an entrenched and prepared enemy?" Cho asked.

"Not in most cases, but if they're preparing to hit me then they will be occupied with those preparations!"

"And if you are wrong and they are not distracted but are in fact inviting you to attack in hopes that you will?"

"Then my army will be badly hurt if not destroyed and we lose the war," Parno lost his enthusiasm all at once. "But Cho, I can't withdraw," he added. "This is a good position and we're in decent shape. Entrenched fairly well behind good barriers and with our artillery sighted and set. We need to hold this position if we can."

"Is there any way that this enemy movement can make your position here untenable?" Cho asked.

"Only by striking south toward unprotected towns or threatening Raines' flank and rear at Shelby," Parno replied.

"So," Feng put his hands behind him, looking at the ground as they walked, clearly in lecture mode. "You cannot risk attack on a grand scale for fear of losing not just the battle but the war. You can interdict the moving column but only by weakening your position here. But what if they do nothing?"

"Which ones?"

"What if this column seizes this small town?" Cho asked. "It is abandoned, is it not, according to your cavalry leaders?"

"Yes."

"Then it is of no consequence," Cho made a shooing motion with his hand. "It means nothing. The importance of the position for the enemy is the intersecting roads that lead south. Yet there is no guarantee they will use those roads. They may simply occupy the town and surrounding area for no other reason than to distract you and pull troops away from this front."

"Yes."

"So, what are you plans?" Cho stopped abruptly. "You know all of these facts, young warlord. You have a great deal of information. You know the capabilities of your army, and you are familiar with the capabilities of your enemy. So, what is the most prudent move, considering your options and your requirements. Are you on desperate grounds?"

Parno considered that for a moment before shaking his head.

"It isn't so simple this time," he said finally. "The ground is open, allowing maneuver warfare, but... if we allow them to start moving forward while we're retreating, we may not be able to stop them again. We have to hold them here if we can. Just a few miles south they're planting crops and growing beef that we need to feed this army and the rest of the people. We can't give up any more. Right now, we have to tighten our belt and do without as you said. Lose more and... we face starvation. My army can't fight if it's starving."

"A hungry army faces defeat at the hands of a well-supplied enemy," Cho nodded. "Again, I ask you, what will you do? You know your options and the disposition of the enemy forces. You know that offensive warfare, while tempting, is not feasible. Your answer lies before you."

"I think this movement is one of three things," Parno ticked items off on his fingers. "One, it's a feint to draw my cavalry away before they attack my position. Two, it's just a dare. We destroyed two divisions that tried to take that town and now they're going to take it in force and dare us to come and take it back. And three, it's in preparation for moving south."

"Of these which is most likely?" Cho queried.

"Either the feint or the dare," Parno decided. "Even though a force that large could be a threat in open ground, it's slow and ponderous. The enemy knows if they head south our cavalry can interdict them."

"And of those two, which would you expect?"

"I..." Parno paused. "What if it's a combination of the two?" he had a sudden inspiration.

"What?"

"What if their general is being crafty?" Parno explained. "He sends this group to take the town as a dare, and if I respond to it then he launches an attack on my position here. If I don't react then he has established a strong position independent of his main lines and will have time to harden it in a way that would make it almost impossible for me to eradicate."

"An independent position that must be periodically resupplied, no?" Cho prodded gently.

"Yes," Parno nodded slowly, trying to see what Cho was hinting at. "I can isolate that new position and prevent resupply, perhaps. And," he began to warm up, "the likelihood of that relatively small force heading south on their own, so far from resupply, is unlikely as well."

"Excellent," Cho nodded firmly. "I ask you again; what can you do? There is one way to prevent the enemy from occupying the town," he suggested. Parno looked at him in puzzlement, but slowly realization dawned.

"I can destroy it," he sighed, shaking his head. "Homes, businesses, personal belongings..." he trailed away thinking about what he was considering.

"I would submit to you that any who fled would have taken their most important possessions with them when they departed," Cho said softly. "And the loss of even a home outweighs losing one's life or losing a war upon which rests your very existence."

"I know," Parno said sadly. "I just hate to do it."

"Of course, you do," Cho agreed. "No good ruler would gleefully engage in destruction of his own people's homes and livelihoods. Yet no good ruler would allow his nation to be overrun when he could by any means prevent it."

"I need to get back."

-

"General, summon General Allen," Parno ordered as he walked back into the headquarters tent. "I need to see him as soon as possible. Has General Wilbanks reported yet?"

"Here, sir," Wilbanks said from behind him. Parno motioned for Wilbanks to join him at the wall map.

"I need you to detach one battalion from your division and send them here," he indicated Unity on the map. "Upon arrival they are to ensure the town is empty and then burn it to the ground. I don't want the Imps to find anything but ashes when they get there."

"Yes sir," Wilbanks was surprised but didn't offer any objection.

"After that, select another battalion and have them return here to stand by for orders. I may need to send them on a harsh ride escorting a Pioneer company. Have their commander report to me here. He needs to be someone who can exercise independent command in the field and make decisions on the fly," he stressed. "A lot may depend on him and his men."

"Yes sir," Wilbanks said once more.

"Inform the battalion commander you send to Unity that as soon as their work is done they are to return to your command with all due haste. Scouts will be in the area to watch what the Imperials do when they find the town destroyed. Questions?"

"No sir," Wilbanks replied. His orders were clear and simple.

"In the event we are attacked, I want you to move your division here and await orders," Parno indicated a place on the map. "I have something I want you to do for me, General." He explained over the next five minutes. By the time he was finished Wilbanks was grinning from ear-to-ear.

"Any questions? Problems that you can see?" Parno asked at last.

"No sir," the reply had much more enthusiasm this time. "I understand perfectly."

"Then get it done."

CHAPTER TWENTY-FOUR

-

"Do you understand?" Parno asked. Allen nodded slowly, examining the map.

"You want me to move west and allow Imperial scouts to see us go, but then isolate them as we loop around," the cavalryman nodded. "Once we do that we're here," he indicated a place on the map.

"Exactly," Parno nodded. "Remember that it's important, no... no it's vital that you be seen," he stressed. "I know it goes against everything we're taught, but this time it's different. I need them to see."

"Then they will, milord," Allen nodded again. "How will I know -"

"I will have a runner standing by," Parno promised. "And you'll know we're engaged if you hear thunder when the skies are clear," he added.

"Very well, milord," Allen rolled his own map. "You want us to leave at first light?"

"Yes, but make sure there's enough light to be seen," Parno nodded. "Remember, until you reach your destination, nothing is more important that allowing the Imperials to see you moving."

"Understood. With your permission, I have a great deal of work to do."

"Carry on," Parno nodded. Next, he turned to the man commanding the battalion that Wilbanks had sent him, a tough looking Lieutenant Colonel by the name of Winburn who looked like he knew his business.

"Colonel Winburn, I need you to escort a Pioneer Company here," he indicated a place on the map, "and await further orders. The enemy has sent a very large infantry column escorted by a strong cavalry force in this direction, we believe with the intention of occupying and fortifying the town. But there is a chance, slim though it is, that they may instead strike south. From here you can move to allow the Pioneer Company to destroy these bridges to prevent an easy river crossing. The enemy will still be able to cross, and you aren't to expend your troops to stop or even slow them. Just let the Pioneers do their work and then move on to the next job. Understand?"

"I do, milord, but... if we aren't to fight the Imperials, what need is there for us to be there?"

"There is a moderate size force of Tribals somewhere on this side of the Great River," Parno replied. "Your battalion will be there in case the Tribals show up. Pioneers wouldn't last any longer than a snowball on a hot stove against them, but you and your men can."

"Yes sir," the man almost growled. "We can."

"Good man," Parno slapped his shoulder. "You and your men will leave in the morning. The Pioneer Company should have all their necessary gear loaded on horses by then. Make sure to make all your own preparations as well so that you're ready to go at first light. Scouts will be observing the enemy at all times. If they head your way, you should know it with plenty of time to spare. It may be that you have to make decisions of your own, so err on the side of caution. Allowing the Imperials to get such a large force behind us will hurt, Colonel. Don't let it happen."

"We won't, milord," Winburn promised grimly.

"Then see to your men, Colonel."

-

"What do you think?" Parno asked Davies thirty minutes later as the two studied the map before them.

"I think it's at least as likely as anything else we've come up with," Davies replied slowly. "I suggest we double our watches and security around the camp. We could see some saboteurs."

"See to it," Parno nodded. "I think we're right on the edge here, General, but edge of what I don't know," he admitted. "There is definitely more going on than seizing one little town in the middle of nowhere."

"I believe so as well, milord," Davies agreed. "We are as prepared as possible for any eventuality, and you have taken every precaution I can think of. Have you advised General Raines of your concerns? So that he can have scouts watching his rear and flanks?"

"Now that you mention it, no," Parno frowned slightly. "I'll see to that right now. Thank you for mentioning it."

"It's what I do, milord," Davies smiled faintly. "It's what I do."

-

"What's going on?" Stephanie asked, seeing all the activity going on around camp.

"Nothing as yet, just a lot of movement," Parno admitted.

"But you think something is going on," she stated rather than asked.

"I think something may happen soon, yes," he nodded. "But I have little to no evidence to support that theory. Just a lot of uneasy feelings. What about Harrel? Is it safe for him to travel yet?"

"I'd prefer another few days," Stephanie admitted. "The two weeks is almost up and I'm confident that by that time he can travel so long as proper precautions are taken."

"Good," Parno nodded absently. "That's good."

"What's really going on?" she asked him, noting his unease.

"Nothing at the moment other than some movement among the Imperials," Parno told her. "As I said, I have no evidence or reports to indicate enemy intentions, just a lot of supposition. And that isn't good enough to act on." Though he had acted on it, he wasn't going to mention it to her.

"I see," she nodded, knowing she wasn't getting the entire story, but also realizing she wasn't actually entitled to it, either. She had promised herself she would not impose on her relationship with Parno to get something she wouldn't normally have had, and that included access to information. She had worked too hard to gain back his trust to throw it away again. She would never take that risk.

"I'm glad, because I don't," Parno mused, still studying whatever he was reading. "I have to just wait and see."

"You do a lot of that, don't you?" she asked sympathetically.

"Far too much for my liking," he agreed, setting the paper aside to give her his attention. "So. What are you and I doing this evening?" he smiled at her.

"We're having dinner with Edema in her tent," she replied.

"Benson cooking?" he asked, almost licking his lips and she laughed.

"I'm sure he is," she nodded.

"Great!"

-

"Carroll is actually built on the ruins of another small city," Case said that evening as he sat around the fire with Winnie, Conway and a few others, including Doctor Bragg and Lieutenants Fain and Garrett. Rucker had the watch and was working.

"Oh?" Bragg asked.

"In the days before the Kingdom was formed, Tyree fought a battle on these same lands," Case nodded, looking into the fire. "A pair of them actually, but in the final battle he was triumphant and discovered he was in a battle with foreign mercenaries in the pay of a crime lord. Men who were, among other things, trafficking in women slaves," he added, thinking about their own recent discovery.

"What did he do?" Fain asked, curious.

"He executed everyone who surrendered, impaled the bodies on pikes around the town square and decorated them with signs that declared them to be rapists and murderers and promised the same end to anyone else he caught in the same or similar acts," Case replied calmly. "There was a great deal of consternation amongst the government of the time in what is now Nasil," he added with an amused snort of understatement.

"I should imagine," Bragg chuckled. "What happened to the town?"

"Burned to the ground by the crime lord's men to erase what had happened here," Case said. "In the end it didn't matter. Tyree eventually put an end to the crime lord in question and executed the remainder of his men who had not been killed in battle. A few years later those who had migrated to Nasil with him returned to rebuild. It is their descendants in great part that you met today."

"Tyree led an exciting life, didn't he?" Winnie mused.

"That's one way to put it," Case agreed. "Our current Crown Prince is said to be a great deal like Tyree himself," he added. "Of course, he is a direct descendant of Tyree, so there's that."

"I hadn't thought about that, but... that isn't inaccurate," Winnie said slowly, mulling what she knew of both men over in her mind.

"How well do you know the Lord Marshal?" Bragg asked.

"Fairly well, I guess" she said after considering the question. "My father and I worked for him at Cove Canton teaching archery to what is now the Black Sheep regiment. A lot of what is said about him is untrue or at least not very accurate. He is a handful, no doubt, but... the idea that he isn't intelligent is ridiculous. He is very smart. Even crafty after a fashion."

"What do you mean?" Fain Garrett asked respectfully.

"He never attacks head on," Winnie said after a few seconds to think. "He's always looking for the angle, as he calls it, or at least as my father refers to it. Always looking for the best way to make his attack at the least cost to his men. Regardless of what the problem may be, he is always looking for a way to be on the offensive. Consider that his first move upon reaching the front was to lead a cavalry attack against the Nor. Did that himself mind, and not ordering it done. I doubt it's widely known but his skill with a sword is second to only a handful in the kingdom, and I personally know of only one who can match him."

"Colonel Willard?" Fain asked.

"Colonel Willard is Karls," Winnie shook her head. "And no, he can't. You're likely thinking of Brigadier Willard, Karls' brother, Enri. He's the holder of the King's Sword. And no, he can't do it either. Parno beat him in a duel a little over a year ago I guess."

"Not quite, but close," Case nodded. "You're talking about the foreigner."

"Cho Feng," Winnie nodded. "I've seen him wield two swords at once and do so with ease. It's almost comical to watch even the Black Sheep try to match him, and man for man the Sheep are probably the best taught swordsmen in the

Kingdom. Of course, Feng and Darvo Nidiad taught most of them, so there you go."

"Two swords at once?" Fain mused. "That must be something else to see."

"It is," Winnie nodded. "Cho Feng is to the sword what my father is to the bow," she added. "They are a large part of why the Black Sheep are so strong. They got beat up by Feng on a daily basis during training," she chuckled.

"I've wondered about them from time to time," Garrett admitted. "If they were as deadly as advertised. We of the Royal Regiments like to think we're a grade above the rest."

"Look, there's nothing wrong with you guys," Winnie told the young officer. "It's just... the Black Sheep were a hard lot to begin with and the training they went through made them harder still. The weak and the worthless, those are Parno's words by the way, were weeded out in training. After the Gap, what was left was the hard core in the center of the Regiment. They can take on four and five times their number and win, and have done it. In fact, during the cavalry battle the Black Sheep had watched from the flank near the end of the engagement. Tribals tried to attack the read guard regiments as the army withdrew, only... well, the Black Sheep were there, and they hit the Tribals in the flank before they could attack. There were a little less than five hundred Black Sheep against an estimated eight to nine hundred Tribals. I think the estimates were that the Tribals lost around three hundred men either killed or wounded."

"What were the Black Sheep's losses?" Conway asked, frowning.

"Four men injured, three of which were treated and returned to service the next day," Winnie replied evenly. "They lost a few horses too."

"Are you serious?" Conway had apparently never heard that.

"She's serious," Case nodded. "I read the reports. Not from them but from the others in the battle. The Tribals never knew what hit them."

"Damn," was all Garrett could think to say.

"So, you see," Winnie smiled faintly, "it's not that anyone else isn't very good. It's that they're just that much better. But it's all a matter of training," she emphasized. "Any of them will tell you the same thing, too. They know how they got where they are, and it was through pure hard work."

"Same as you, gentlemen," Case pointed out. "When you put your mind to it and back into it, you can do anything you set your mind on. Remember that going forward."

"Yes sir."

-

Gerald Allen looked at the five men in front of him as they finished eating their breakfast. All five division commanders had been briefed the night before and their preparations started. Allen had chosen to have this brief meeting to iron out any problems.

"Has anyone encountered any difficulties in preparations?" he asked. All responded in the negative.

"Does anyone have any questions concerning our orders, order of march rally points or rendezvous point?"

"I don't understand what we're doing," Fordyce admitted. "We're deliberately allowing the Imperials to see us start in pursuit of that outfit that left yesterday, and then riding no more than a day at a walk, which means there's no way to catch up to them. After that-,"

"After that we follow our orders," Allen nodded. "You've participated in operations similar to this one, though not on this scale. Our orders are clear and the areas we're responsible for are clearly marked and relatively easy to find. Our divisions," he indicated Coe and Vaughan at that, "have already conducted similar operations in the last two weeks, both in Unity and on the road between here and there. By now the Imperials likely expect us and that could be why there are so many in this movement compared to others. As to why we're allowing ourselves to be seen, that's upon the Marshal's orders. We'll receive any updates to those orders he wishes to give us by courier. Any more questions?"

There were no more questions.

"I want us ready to leave when the sun has cleared the trees," he told them. "If we're to be seen, we need good light. Remember to remind your men that Captain Parsons' scouts will be weaving in and out of our column and will help screen our movements as the day progresses. They have their own orders and are to be given every courtesy and not to be interfered with. If there's nothing further, you may be about your business."

The five men rose and began to exit his small tent, but Milton Vaughan stayed behind.

"Milt?" Allen asked. "Something wrong?"

"This is a big gamble," the man said softly. "All of us out of position like this. More than a day's ride away. It's risky."

"It is," Allen nodded, not wanting to say more. "We'll talk more about it tonight, but for now see to your men."

"Right," Vaughan nodded and ducked out of the tent. Allen sat there a bit longer, a faint smile on his face.

-

Imperial scouts and pickets were treated to quite the sight that morning. In the distance, nearly a mile in some cases but much closer in others, a long line of Soulan Cavalry trailed out of the woods and into the open, following the road parallel in apparent pursuit of the Imperial 1st Corps and their escort. For perhaps an hour the horses emerged, a few bearing packs but most carrying men, moving at a steady gait that would eat ground but preserve the horses.

Imperial Army scouts kept a careful count of what they could see, much as Felds and Earl had done the day before for the Soulan Army. Soon a rider was galloping for General Wilson's headquarters to inform him of the development.

Wilson received the notice stoically and sent orders back up the line to try and get as much intelligence as possible on the column, then ordered a courier to be sent to inform Venable and Baxter of the situation. A concerned Sterling started to comment but a hand stopped him. Wilson merely repeated his previous orders and that was that.

Through the day the Imperial scouts were amazed at their good fortune in being able to follow and spy on the large column. Usually the Soulanie scouts and cavalry screens would be able to keep them at a distance but through at least noon of that day such wasn't the case. They were able to identify five different Soulan Cavalry Divisions and get a rough estimate of forty-two thousand men and horses.

As noon approached and the trail the horsemen were following veered into a more rugged and tree lined terrain, enemy scouts seemed for the first time to realize that Imperial scouts were watching and began to take action. Movements by screening elements and scouting arms began to drive the scouts back further and further from the disappearing column until sight of them was lost altogether.

But the damage was done. Imperial scouts had for once performed their jobs magnificently, gathering the kind of information their generals needed to get their own jobs done.

-

General Abraham Springfield looked at the paper in his hands in astonishment, reading a second time. He had to have read that wrong.

Nope. Still said the same thing. He looked up at the courier who was waiting for the acknowledgment he had to take back to Sterling.

"Is this for real?" Springfield asked the young lieutenant.

"Sir, I have no idea what that message says," the much younger man replied. "My orders were to bring it personally to you and await an acknowledgment."

"Acknowledgment?" Springfield repeated as if amazed. "Acknowledgment that Wilson has lost his fucking mind?" he all but bellowed. The young courier blanched at that but held his ground.

"Sir, I'm afraid it would be entirely improper for me to comment on that... comment," the young man hid a grimace at how stupid that sounded but it was all he could come up with.

"Give him a message acknowledging receipt of orders," Springfield told his Chief of Staff. "Then assemble all division commanders. Half an hour from now."

-

"This has got to be a joke," General Joel Vanhoose looked at the orders he'd just been handed. "Got to be."

"I took it from Brigadier Sterling's hand myself, sir," the courier informed him.

"I'm going to Wilson's headquarters," Vanhoose got to his feet. "I have to make sure this is accurate. That's not a reflection on you, Lieutenant," he informed the young courier who was about to make a protest. "Assemble all division commanders here in one hour," he ordered his staff. "I'll be back by then."

-

Gerald Wilson sat behind his desk, pleased with the effect his orders had on his command. Three of the five available corps commanders had arrived at his headquarters within fifteen minutes to 'check on the accuracy' of the orders they had received. He had assured them all that yes, the orders were accurate, and suggested the should be carrying out those orders rather than wasting time in Wilson's own office complaining, whining and moaning.

All had realized the truth of that and hurried back to their own commands to begin making preparations. Preparations that would last deep into the night for those who had allowed their commands to sink into complacency.

That was their problem, Wilson decided. If they couldn't maintain order and discipline in their commands, then they had no business being in command. Simple as that.

-

"What are we doing now?" Fordyce wondered as the column drifted further and further to the south. A young lieutenant came galloping up to him and saluted before handing over a small roll of paper.

"General Allen's compliments, sir," the lieutenant saluted and then was off again, galloping further down the column. Fordyce opened the scroll and read through it quickly, then read it again, slower.

"Well I'll be damned," he chuckled to himself. He stuffed the scroll into his tunic as his second in command looked on, puzzled.

"We're going a little further," was all Fordyce would say.

-

"All right, remember now," Parsons warned the assembled scouts and the archers from the Black Sheep. "No Imperial scouts get through. We sew this side of that road up tighter'n a virgin's skirt. Get me?"

"Yes sir," a multitude of voices replied.

"Then get going and get it done," Parsons ordered. "No one gets a look at this cavalry no more!"

-

"Word from Parsons," Davies handed over a small slip torn from a notebook with a message scrawled over it. "They're working to isolate the Imperial scouts now. Allen has turned his men south and the battalion you ordered to Unity is still on the move, projected to pick up speed and allow themselves to be glimpsed this evening late and again tomorrow around noon."

"Excellent," Parno nodded. "Killing two birds with but one stone."

"So long as the Imperial cavalry doesn't try to intercede," Davies nodded.

That was a real risk.

"I don't think so," Parno mused. "If they believe it to be the same heavy column they saw moving west then they will know that their cavalry stands no chance against them in open battle and unsupported. They won't risk it. Instead they'll plan to deploy their men as they arrive in Unity and attack with their entire force. Infantry supported by artillery should be able to drive an unsupported cavalry column out of the town. Everyone knows that."

"Except it's not an unsupported column," Davies interjected.

"True," Parno nodded. "But it's what they think that counts. If they think it is, then we're in good shape. Hopefully, anyway."

"Hopefully," Davies echoed with a sigh.

-

Major Sven Andreasen rode at the head of his small battalion, keeping his horses at just under a gallop. He had to make sure he and his men arrived in Unity at least a day before the Imperials, and preferably longer. His orders concerned him, more like dismayed him, but he acknowledged that the Imperials were just as likely to destroy the town when they left it. If doing it themselves denied the enemy the use of the town then... well, so be it.

He and his men had completed their training along with the rest of Wilbanks division just in time to race to Nasil and help put out fires. Now here they were, racing to start one. He shook his head at the irony but didn't slow down.

He had his orders.

-

Gerald Allen was tired when his horse made the rendezvous point. He hadn't gotten a great deal of sleep the night before and this had been a hard day to say the least. He dismounted and stretched before looking to his Chief of Staff.

"Send runners to the division commanders and have them report here as soon as possible. General Davies has men already here to set up camp, though we have only a few tents. Let them set the divisions into order since they lined this up. They should be cooking for us as well."

"Yes sir," the man nodded.

"It shouldn't be necessary but issue general orders through the column to check all horses and report any problems up the line." The man nodded again and hurried to his post. Allen watched him go and handed his reins to the corporal behind him.

"There's an apple in my saddlebags," he told the young man. "Give it to him when you're done."

"Yes sir," the young man smiled, leading both horses away. Allen looked at the tent set up for his use and felt a twinge of guilt, but only a twinge. His men would sleep on the ground tonight, but he would work deep into the night unless he was uncommonly lucky. He imagined they would sleep better than he did.

-

"What's got you so stirred up?" Stephanie asked as she brushed her long hair out. It was a nightly ritual that Parno was becoming accustomed to. He had enjoyed watching her go through the exercise more than once, but tonight his mind was much further away than merely across the tent.

"What?" he asked her.

"I said why are you so stirred up?" she repeated. "You're walking like a cat in a room full of rockers as my mother would put it."

"I didn't notice," he admitted. "I'm just thinking, that's all."

"What about?" she asked.

"About... stuff," he shrugged. "There's a lot going on and I'm trying to keep it straight."

"Can you tell me about it?" she asked, putting her brush down.

"No, because I don't know myself," he replied after a long pause. "All I have is still guesses and conjecture. I'm trying to move my troops to counter the Imperials moves, but they have a lot more troops than we do."

"How bad is it?" she asked softly.

About two to one," he informed her. "And that's with probably fifty or sixty thousand more on the road west right this minute. We don't know the actual number, but we've identified over twenty-five divisions in the last two months. Two of them have been completely eliminated, but... twenty-three is still a lot. Well over two hundred thousand infantry. I have a little less than half that."

"That is a lot," she nodded.

"I have a lot more cavalry," he hastened to add, less she be worried for nothing. "They have about fifteen thousand cavalry, while I have over sixty thousand all totaled. Still, it leaves us outnumbered two-to-one. And with such a large force on the move I have to make plans to counter their movements."

"Have you?" she asked him.

"Yes," he replied with a nod.

"Anything more you can do about it tonight?" she asked, her hands rubbing his shoulders now.

"Not that I can think of," he admitted. "I was just wondering that myself."

"Then come to bed," she whispered in his ear. Without waiting for an answer, she turned the shuttered lamp very low, leaving just enough illumination to see by. She took his hand and led him where she wanted him.

"Let tomorrow take care of itself," she told him softly. "If you can't do any more, then you can't. Let it go. You have to rest," she told him, her real concern showing now. "You're exhausted. Doctor's orders," she gave him an impish grin.

"Lay down," she told him. "Hold me close and sleep," she ordered.

He followed the doctor's orders.

-

"We don't have to leave first thing in the morning," Allen informed his generals as they sat around his fire. A watch was posted to prevent eavesdroppers from getting close enough to overhear anything that was said.

"What?" Vaughan asked, frowning. "How will we catch up-,"

"We aren't going to," Allen replied. "The Marshal thinks the Imperial move to the west is a feint, intended to draw us," he indicated his fellow generals, "away from the lines. If so, he now thinks he has done it. It's entirely possible that we will hear sounds of battle by sunrise. If we do, we will move behind a screen of scouts to a position about two miles west of the lines and hold there, waiting for orders. As the Nor hit our lines, we're going to hit theirs," he grinned.

"And if they don't attack?" General Bellamy asked, leaning forward. He commanded the 6th Cavalry and he, like Fordyce, wasn't thrilled at being 'attached' to a command like Allen's.

"That's up to the Marshal," Allen spread his hands. "He will tell us when to move, if we move at all. Meanwhile, if there's no battle tomorrow, we rest our men and horses here and enjoy a little fresh air and sunshine."

"And some smoked beef," General Coe nodded, rubbing his hands together.

"Indeed."

-

"All corps commanders report preparations completed," Sterling reported at nearly midnight. "All qualify that with 'as much as is possible in the time allowed'," he added.

"If they were on their jobs then there would have been only a few preparations to see to and they would have been prepared and ready for any orders they received," Wilson replied flatly. "We have an opportunity here and I intend to make use of it. We have maneuvered the enemy into a situation of our choosing, at a time and place of our choosing. It doesn't get better than that."

"That is true, sir," Sterling nodded. He wanted to argue but could not find a flaw in Wilson's logic.

He would keep looking into the night.

-

"Aaron, you are up late this evening," Tinker noted as he walked out onto the porch of the Hogshead Inn. The tavern had long since closed for the evening and whatever visitors were still upstairs had no impact on them.

"Can't sleep," the younger man admitted.

"Something in particular that keeps you from your rest?" the older man asked.

"Just jumpy," Aaron admitted. "Something feels off, that's all."

"I see," Tinker nodded. "You have these feelings often?"

"No, I don't."

Tinker frowned in the dark. Aaron was not normally so taciturn. While never talkative he was at least sociable. Not so, this evening.

"Do you trust these feelings?" Tinker asked after a few moments of quiet.

"I do," Aaron admitted. "But just cause I got a feeling don't mean I know why."

"I understand that all too well," Tinker nodded. "Perhaps... perhaps we should be prepared in case things... change, so to speak."

"We already are," Aaron told him. "Wagons is packed with food and water already, lined up in the barn. Anything happens, we hitch the teams and go. Ladies can grab their stuff while we get that done."

"I see," Tinker didn't let his surprise show. In truth there wasn't much of a surprise. Aaron Bell was always ahead on things of that nature.

"Nothin' don't happen I can always unpack it," the younger man added a few moments afterward.

"Indeed," Tinker nodded in the dark. "Very well, Aaron," he stood. "I believe I will leave things in your capable hands then."

"Night Mister Tinker," Aaron nodded absently, still looking into the dark at nothing.

CHAPTER TWENTY-FIVE

-

Doak Parsons had faced a manpower shortage as he tried to both keep watch on the Imperial Army and still keep the Imperial Army from keeping watch on them. The Marshal had solved that problem by giving him a company of archers from the Regiment to supplement the scouts screening the cavalry, which had allowed Parsons to pull his best men back to the lines.

Anthony Felds was one of those men. He had spent the early morning hours crawling to within one hundred yards of the Imperial lines, where he had laid quietly, listening. He had no way of knowing exactly how long he had laid there but suddenly the Imperial camp was lit up, torches and lanterns burning down the line. Felds sat up in the dark and used his glass to try and get a look into the enemy camp using their own lights to see by.

There was a lot of movement. He couldn't make out individual ranks but he could see men bellowing at other men, and those men moving into position. He watched for several minutes, moving every so often to look at other areas. Satisfied, he made a bird call in every direction around, but for a bird that would not be active in the night, at least not here.

He heard the call repeated even as several returned his sign with another letting him know they heard. Soon someone would be hurrying to tell the Marshal what was happening. Meanwhile, Felds would watch as long as he could safely do so.

Something big was going on for sure.

-

"Why can't we do this without so damn much noise!" Wilson almost shouted but caught himself just in time. Wouldn't do for the General of the Army to be bellowing loudly about keeping the noise down.

"Too many men moving, sir," Sterling said softly. "A teeny bit of noise for one man becomes a symphony of noise for so many."

"Very poetic, Sterling," Wilson's reply was acidic. "You should write that down."

"Yes sir," Sterling fought the urge to sigh.

"Please send a runner to the artillery line and make sure they are ready to support this movement," Wilson asked.

"Right away."

Wilson went over a mental checklist, trying to see if he had missed anything. As far as he could tell, he had not. He had succeeded in drawing the enemy cavalry away while he still had the bulk of his army in camp, ready to go. He was about to send four corps, over one hundred and fifty thousand men against a southern line estimated to have roughly half that. And would still have a full corps of nearly fifty thousand in reserve.

And he had issued orders that should lessen the impact of the Soulan Army's new weapons as well. It wouldn't stop them from hurting his men, but it would help. At least some.

Besides, if his plan worked, they wouldn't get off too many salvos.

-

"Milord!"

Parno had slept deeply. He slowly swam up from the depths of that sleep to an incessant and insistent knocking noise which he finally realized was someone knocking at his 'door'.

"What is it?" he called out as he got to a sitting position.

"Massive movement among the enemy milord," his messenger informed him.

"Where at?" he asked as he grabbed his pants.

"Everywhere, sir," came the answer. "All along the entire line."

"I see," Parno felt his stomach drop a little. "Very well, then. Please have someone alert Captain Simmons and Captain Pike for me. Ask them to ready their men and bring the carriage for Lady Edema. You should wake her staff as well."

"Right away milord," came the reply. "General Davies is waiting in the command tent."

"Tell him I'll be there straight away," Parno promised. He stood into his boots and held his pants as he hurriedly drained his bladder, not knowing when the chance would come again. Then he walked back to the bed and gently shook Stephanie awake.

"No," she rolled back into a ball. "Not now."

"Get up, Stephanie," Parno said quietly but urgently. "You have to get up. Your time is up."

"What?" she sat up, blinking. "What did you say?"

"You time here has ended," Parno told her softly. "The enemy are about to attack. Gather your things. I've already sent someone to alert Edema and her men, and alert your escorts. You have to make a decision about Harrel, now. Do that as you get ready to leave. You have until it's light enough to safely travel to get ready."

"What?" she was still working on getting awake. "What about you?" she demanded.

"What about me?" he repeated. "I have to go and command the army, Stephanie," he stroked her hair softly. "That's what I do, remember? Now hurry. Gather your things and be prepared to depart as soon as they can safely see to get you out of here. If you can take Harrel with you then do so, otherwise he will have to stay. But you and Edema are leaving. And I mean as soon as it's light enough to see."

"But I... I..." she tried to find something to say, to protest, but Parno was shaking his head.

"No. You're going. And I don't have time to argue about this. Your time is running out and if you aren't packed by the time the carriage can leave then you'll be loaded on it without whatever you didn't pack. Now move."

"Alright," she nodded, getting to her feet. "Please come back to see us off?" she pleaded.

"If I can, I will," he promised, and with that she had to be contented, because he was out the door and gone.

-

Edema Willows awoke to Benson's voice.

"Milady, we must arise and away," he told her softly. "The enemy is upon us and Prince Parno has ordered us to depart. You must prepare. The carriage is being hitched to the horses now and the escort are preparing to leave as well. You must ready yourself. Quickly now," he urged as Edema resisted.

"I'm awake," she promised. "We're being attacked?" she asked.

"Yes, milady," Benson nodded. "We have to go. And we must do it quickly. We are but in the way, here."

"Very well," she nodded, getting to her feet. "It won't take long. Please see to it that our luggage is on top, in case young Harrel can travel with us," she ordered. "But make sure to ask Stephanie what of her things you may need before loading her up. She will want her medical bag, I know."

"Very good, milady," Benson nodded. "If you need help, please call."

"I will. Hurry to your duties while I prepare."

-

"General," Parno said as he walked inside. "Trouble on the horizon?"

"It does appear that way, milord," Davies agreed. "Movement and racket all along the line and men running to get into formation. It's not just one division or one corps, but everyone. We have runners moving to every command to get our men up and into position as quietly as we can. I've already sent a runner to General Graham as well."

"Good," Parno nodded. "Our artillery alerted and standing by?"

"Major Lars is already making the rounds, sir," Davies nodded.

"Then all we can do is wait," Parno mused. "I need to get a runner off to General Allen and let him know we're under attack."

"Already done, sir," Davies nodded. "Our rider is waiting for enough light to see and then he's off."

"You don't need me at all, do you?" Parno grinned.

"I'm sure we'll find a use for you, milord," Davies chuckled dryly. "Meanwhile, as you said. We wait."

-

Abe Springfield watched as his men moved forward, slowly shaking down into line as they prepared to advance. Bellowing sergeants walked the lines, moving troops where they needed to be and fussing over alignments and distances.

"This is a giant clusterfuck," he sighed quietly. Beside him, in the dark, his Chief of Staff nodded silently.

"Ten minutes and we start moving, sir," the man reminded him.

"Yeah. Ten minutes," Springfield sighed again.

-

Joel Vanhoose watched as his 2nd Imperial Infantry Corps staggered to their lines as division commanders got their men into position. There was no point in yelling for them to hurry since it was the 'hurrying' that was preventing them from getting things done. Men who knew better were bumbling around in the dark instead of moving where they needed to be.

"What a frigging mess," he almost spat. "Twelve hours to prepare a move of this size! Men moving on four and five hours sleep. We'll be lucky if this isn't a giant disaster."

No one around him spoke one way or another, not wanting to draw his ire or say something that was derogatory of General Wilson. Such things tended to be remembered, after all.

"Sir, all division commanders are reporting on line and ready to go," an aide reported finally. Vanhoose checked his watch by the light of a lantern and nodded.

"Eight minutes to spare," he said quietly. "That will be a short eight minutes for some and an eternity for others," he put his watch away. "All divisions to move forward as the dawn breaks," he ordered. "We want to be on them before the sun is fully up."

-

"All positions are manned and ready, sir," a runner reported. "Scouts are returning, lighting the bonfires as they move."

"Very good," Davies nodded. "Lets... hmm," he broke off, clearly thinking of something.

"What?" Parno asked. "What is it?"

"I was just examining the board, sir," Davies replied. "If we can get them to commit, then we can use 1st Corps against their right, allowing Allen to sweep in from behind them. It's a risk, and if 4th and 5th Corps can't hold then it will be a problem, but it could present an opportunity to crush their army completely."

"I would love to do that but... it's too much of a risk, General," Parno sighed. "If Freeman and Herrick gave way at any point then we would lose our own lines and our camps be overrun. I think we need to stick to using 1st Corps to reinforce our line and allow Allen's men to move into the enemy rear and strike from there. We may not be able to roll up their entire flank but we should be able to do a great deal of damage. And at much less risk. I know it's tempting, but the risk is too great, General."

"You are right, of course," Davies nodded in resignation. "I just... I saw an opportunity to..." he trailed off and Parno nodded sympathetically.

"I know. A chance to end this. As I said, it is tempting, but we have to accept that we have limitations and live within them. This is one of those limitations. Our infantry is outnumbered two-to-one and that's after we factor in 1st Corps helping with the line. We will have to depend on Allen to do all the damage he can instead."

"As you say, milord."

-

Wilson looked to the east as the light grew. Satisfied, he turned to the men waiting to carry his orders.

"When they hear 'Rise and Ready', they will wait one minute. After that, start moving. Noise is not a factor since there's almost no way they don't know we're coming. Remind them of their order of march," he stressed. "Off with you." The six runners saluted and hurried away, their horses carrying them as fast as safely possible in the low light.

"Five minutes, Sterling, and you can start the call," Wilson told the younger man at his side. "Today we break the Soulan Army."

"Yes sir," Sterling tried to sound enthusiastic. Wilson might be certain and sure of his moves, but Britton Sterling had felt a tendril of unease the first time he had heard this plan, and it had done nothing but grown since then. He was certain and sure this was a mistake, but there was no way to stop it.

And now he would, in fact, be the one to start things off.

-

"This is so needlessly complicated considering how fast it was laid on," General Darrell Thomas muttered. His Imperial 3rd Corps was once again listed as the reserve, something he was growing weary of but didn't dare say so. Right now, his men were spread behind the main line, ready by division to plug any hole or take advantage of any break in the Soulan lines. He supposed he should be honored by that, since it meant his men were being trusted to prosecute the attack to the fullest.

"Get runners to all division commanders with these stupid orders," he told his Chief of Staff. "No telling how long we have, so hurry." Thomas' divisions were necessarily more isolated from their brethren than the assaulting units, since they needed to be able to respond quickly anywhere on the battlefield. It was necessary but it also made his issuing orders and keeping control of his troops much more difficult. Again, he shook his head, but resisted the urge to curse Wilson. Son-of-bitch just might have someone listening, after all.

"Stand by."

Anthony Felds touch flint and steel together and lit the final bonfire between the two armies, one closest to the Imperial lines. As soon as it was going, he turned and disappeared into the darkness behind him even as he heard an arrow impact the ground where he'd just been.

"Definitely time to go," he nodded to himself. He had overstayed his welcome.

Parno had taken the time to return to his tent and saw the carriage pull in just as he was making his way there. Benson and several men in uniform were throwing bags on top of the carriage and lashing them down. Even as he watched, Stephanie emerged from the tent that Harrel had been recuperating in, two stretcher bearers following her with Harrel Sprigs.

"I can walk," Sprigs was saying.

"You need to save that strength, Harrel," Stephanie told him. "Captain!"

"Milady?" Simmons was there at once.

"I need someone to pack Captain Sprigs' belongings as rapidly as possible," she told him. "His tent is the smaller one closest to Pa... the Marshal's tent," she pointed. "Please have two good men collect his things. Ask them to leave nothing behind."

"At once, milady." Simmons hurried away, calling names as he went.

"Thank you, milady," Sprigs told her softly.

"Of course," Stephanie smiled down at him even as Parno walked up.

"Milord," Sprigs nodded.

"I'm glad you're able to leave here, Harrel," Parno smiled. "I'm already missing your steady presence, you know." He took Harrel's hand gently in his own.

"Yes," Stephanie tried to lighten the mood. "Poor man has to do his own reading and paperwork now." Sprigs laughed in spite of himself and Parno chuckled as well.

"Concentrate on getting well," Parno told his secretary. "I'll need you back to work as soon as possible. Be safe, Harrel," he gave him one final pat on the back.

"Thank you, milord." The two orderlies were gently assisting Harrel to his feet and they bodily loaded him into the carriage that had once been an ambulance anyway. Soon he was nestled in a pile of cushions and heavy quilts that made a soft bed. The simple movement had exhausted him however, and soon he was asleep. Stephanie turned to Parno.

"I wish I were staying with you," she said softly.

"And I'm glad you're going," he shook his head. She sighed sadly as she shook her head.

"You really do need to work on how you say things, my dear husband-to-be," she told him. "You should have said something like 'it's too dangerous, love of my life, and I need you to be safe so that I can save the realm and come home to you as soon as it's done'. Or... something like that," she made a shooing motion with her hand that reminded him of Edema.

"I've said all that and more many times over," Parno reminded her, hugging her close. "I love you," he whispered into her hair. "Please, be safe. Pay attention to those around you and use your escort. I'm begging you, both of you. All three of you counting Dolly. I need to know you're all safe. You three and a few close friends are literally all I have, Stephanie Freeman-Corsin. Or is it Corsin-Freeman?" He asked suddenly. "I've been meaning to ask since I've heard both before."

"They are literally interchangeable. All the way back to the original Freeman and Corsin under Tyree. They married and here we are. There was always a mild rivalry between them and each always insisted their last name was the 'legal' name. Hence the hyphen, and even that didn't work as they began then to argue over whose name was to be on the back of the hyphen. So, from the very beginning it depended on who was talking. As for me, I answer to either, especially if it's you calling," she smiled softly at him.

"Soon you'll need another hyphen," Parno smiled. "To add McLeod."

"No more hyphens," she shook her head. "Just McLeod is fine. Please don't do anything stupid," she changed the subject abruptly.

"I'm afraid those days are definitely over," he promised. "Now load up. He comes Edema. You have to go."

"Goodbye," she kissed him quickly but gently on the lips. "Please, please take care," she added one last time before stepping up into the carriage. Parno turned to Edema, who despite the urgency looked as fresh and put together as she always did.

"Even though you shouldn't have been here, it has been a joy to have you visit," Parno smiled at his surrogate mother and received a brilliant smile in return.

"Please be safe, dear boy," she caressed his face gently. "Don't take so many chances. Promise me?"

"I promise," he nodded, a faint smile this time, but still there.

"Then we must be away," she blinked back tears. "I love you child," she whispered as she kissed each cheek. "Remember that always."

"I love you too," Parno promised. "We'll see each other soon."

"From your lips to God's ear," Edema nodded and then without another word turned and took the hand offered her, stepping into the coach. Benson secured the door and bumped it with his fist.

"Ready!"

Simmons' men were already moving slowly forward, a small screen of scouts already on the road while another squad was standing by to flank the column as it left the camp. Behind the carriage came Pike's men, the young Captain nodded in silence as he passed Parno, an unspoken promise from the professional soldier. Parno returned it and then turned away, unwilling to watch them out of sight.

He had work to do this morning.

-

"Nor are moving, milord," Davies informed him as he arrived at the observation tower. "And there may be a problem," he added with a frown.

"What kind of problem?" Parno asked. Davies indicated the telescope mounted on the tower.

"Have a look." Parno did that and saw at once what Davies was concerned about.

"*Well*," he drew the word out. "Smart buggers aren't they then? That's all right, though. We have a plan for that."

"We do?" Davies asked.

"Oh, indeed we do," Parno nodded. "Runners!"

-

It was a simple plan, but Wilson was rather proud of it. To counter the explosive weapons being used by his enemy he had ordered the front ranks of every advancing division to open their intervals and place more room between each man. Moreover, each succeeding rank would be off center to the rank before and behind it. Wide open intervals would prevent those damnable new weapons from ripping his men apart before they could close with the enemy.

"I feel good about this Sterling," Wilson smiled. "I really do."

"Yes sir."

-

"Archers to the fore!" the call went all down the line. "Cross bows front!"

At that call, every man trained to use a bow, even if it wasn't his primary weapon, moved to the front of the fortifications. They realized at once what was happening even without explanation. The Marshal had anticipated this and had made a plan to counter it. Now it was up to them to see it done.

The first volley would be the Hubel arrows, fired from thousands of bows all down the Soulan lines. Parno wanted the Nor behind the first ranks to realize they weren't actually safe. If they saw the men in front being torn apart even with the wider interval then they would hesitate. Slow down, perhaps even stop in confusion.

At least, that was what he hoped would happen.

"Crossbows! Take aim!" The call was repeated all down the line as every cross bow on the line appeared atop the fortifications.

"Now," was the simple command and a bugle began to blow. The signal to fire crossbows.

Over five thousand crossbows from the eight divisions along the line fired more or less in unison, their firing lanes restricted to only what was in front of their position within a ten-degree arc.

"Longbows!" the call came next, before the sound of the cross bows had even halted. "Take aim!"

Thirty thousand long bows give or take were raised now, each with one of the deadly Hubel arrows nocked and ready. Parno watched from the tower, the battle out of his hands now.

"Now," the simple command was repeated and a higher tone was produced by the horn. This was the signal to commence firing and open the battle in earnest.

The sound of bowstrings being released was audible all along the fortifications as a cloud of arrows lofted from the line headed for the Imperial soldiers. Thousands of arrows carrying the small but deadly 'warheads' developed by Roda Finn and Whip Hubel.

A second volley, this one of regular arrows, was in the air before the Hubel arrows landed, and the battle was truly joined.

-

"Why aren't they using their artillery?" Wilson asked. No sooner had the words left his mouth than thousands of small explosions rippled along his front ranks, felling Imperial soldiers in windrows.

"What the hell was that?" Wilson demanded. In the din of the last battle no one had heard the smaller explosions or even noticed them other than those unlucky enough to be struck by one. Soldiers who survived and reported the strange impacts were written off as being in shock from the rolling barrages that had claimed so many of their brethren and never reported up the line.

The Imperial Army was paying for that mistake now in blood.

-

"You hear that?" Gerald Allen asked, looking at Milton Vaughan.

"Sounds like thunder," he nodded. "Didn't the Marshal say-,"

"Rider coming!" Vaughan's question was interrupted. "Rider coming!"

Two minutes later a courier literally slid to a stop before Allen, producing a note from Davies. Allen took is and read quickly, nodding in satisfaction.

"Please tell the General we'll be moving in ten minutes," Allen instructed the rider. "I estimate we can be where he wants us in less than two hours."

"Sir," the man snapped a salute and reined his horse around, galloping away.

"The line is under attack by the entire Imperial Army," Allen told Vaughan. "Everything. We're to ride to this location and prepare to take them in flank. Get your men moving now while I brief the others as they pass. Stay out of sight, with a good gait just shy of a gallop. We need to conserve our horses for the battle. If we play this right, we may start ending the war today!"

"Sir," Vaughan nodded and then looked at his bugler.

"Canter forward," he said simply and the bugler raised his horn to his lips. Vaughan didn't wait but set off for the battlefield, his small escort following along with his staff. His soldiers followed in column of four.

On their way to war in earnest.

-

"Compliments to Mister Lars and he may open fire now with one salvo before switching to a mixture of pitch and stone. Remind him not to use my reserve without my orders."

"Sir," the runner nodded and took off, replaced at once by another man standing by for orders.

"They aren't holding anything back," Davies estimated as he viewed the battlefield. "I think they have one corps spread along the rear in reserve, but they've left little to nothing behind."

"Good," Parno nodded. "That's excellent."

"Sir?" Davies turned to look at Parno.

"I have a little treat for our northern friends, assuming they emptied their camp," Parno gave him a predatory smile. He turned to the man waiting behind him. He pulled a small map from his tunic and opened it, showing it to the runner.

"Think you can find this?" he asked, pointing to a spot on the map.

"No problem, sir," the runner nodded.

"Then tell General Wilbanks to give them hell," Parno slapped the man's shoulder. "He'll know what it means. Ride like hell, now. Time is important."

"Sir!" the man actually slid down the ladder and leaped onto a waiting mount, tearing off to the west of the lines.

"Milord?" Davies asked.

"We're going to see how well Imperials fight when they're hungry," Parno said cryptically.

-

Wilson jumped when the ripple of explosions tore down the length of his lines, throwing bodies into the air and shredding men who were close by.

"It's working," Wilson said grimly. "We're still losing men but not nearly as bad as the first time."

"We're losing a lot of men, sir," Sterling noted as yet another salvo of smaller explosions erupted along the entire advance.

"We're going to lose men no matter what we do, Sterling," Wilson nodded. "The thing is to not lose them for nothing."

"Yes sir."

-

"We're not scoring as many hits with the bigger stuff," Enri Willard had climbed the tower at some point and spoke for the first time.

"No, their General has managed to find a way to at least partially counter our weapons," Parno agreed. "But our counter to that is hurting them badly. Not to mention the psychological aspect of watching the men in front of you be cut apart, knowing you have to take their place."

"That is true, but they are still coming and there are a lot of them," Enri reminded him.

"I don't want to break them," Parno told him. "Not yet. I need them to keep coming for now. I need them to keep coming and get as far away from their own lines as I can get them."

"Milord, what are you doing?" Enri asked.

"I'm trying my damnedest to end this war," Parno replied flatly. "I'm trying to push this bunch back where they belong. If we can rout them, then we stand a chance of pursuing them all the way to the Ohi. I want to crush their spirit so that any who survive will unwilling to return."

Enri frowned at how savagely Parno was speaking. Not because he disagreed but simply because it was unusual for him in Willard's experience. He glanced at Cho Feng who had yet to speak at all, but the older man's face was inscrutable, impossible to read. Feng caught Enri's glance and nodded slowly but remained silent. Enri turned his attention back to the battle.

"They're slowly making their way to the line," Davies noted. "They haven't yet because of our archery. The front rank was decimated and the few survivors stalled to wait for the next rank. We've managed to do that three times so far, but each time we have more survivors who add themselves to the next rank. Eventually they will hit the line."

"So, they will," Parno nodded. "There's really no hope to prevent that with their numbers. But we're doing fine right now," he said with satisfaction.

"We're taking losses from their archers as well," Enri observed.

"It's a completely uneven exchange," Parno said. "The only thing that worries me at this point is-," he was interrupted as a flaming half-barrel of pitch slammed into the log fortifications below.

"Their artillery," Parno finished. "They can hurt us. Inform Mister Lars to concentrate on counter-battery fire for the time being," he told a runner. The man nodded and ran to find the artillery commander.

"They have a lot more artillery than we do," Davies said grimly. "And they're using it all this time."

"It won't last," Parno promised. "I need red and yellow pennants up here," Parno told an aide. "Another runner to Mister Lars, reminding him to watch for pennant signals, as well." He had almost forgotten that. He had to start concentrating. The aide nodded and descended the tower to find said pennants while a runner as given the message to pass along.

"Something we should know, milord?" Enri asked.

"Just preparing to make sure we can lift the artillery fire quickly if we need to."

Below them, the battle continued to rage.

CHAPTER TWENTY-SIX

-

Gerald Allen could hear the sounds of battle much better now. His command was arrayed for miles to his left and right, some still moving into line. By Allen's watch they had made it to their assigned position about twenty minutes shy of his estimate. He was now less than a mile from the Imperial Army's right flank as they assaulted the Soulan Army's lines.

"What are we waiting on?" Coe asked as he rode up to Allen trailed by a small knot of horsemen.

"For the Prince to send word," Allen replied calmly. "He has a plan and we have our part in it. He says we wait here, so we wait here."

"Mind letting the rest of us in on this plan?" Coe asked.

"Once the Imperial Army is completely committed, we're going to roll them up like a blanket," Allen looked and sounded predatory as he replied. "The Marshal will hold them by the nose why we kick their ass."

"I can get behind that," Coe nodded. Wilbanks snorted as he turned to his runners.

"Have the other division commanders report here as soon as they can," he ordered. The men took off at a gallop carrying his orders. It was time to let them all in on the plan.

-

Wilbanks took the message with a nod, looking at his brigade commanders who were clustered around him.

"Give them hell, huh," he grinned suddenly. "Well, we can damn sure do that, don't you think?" he asked his Brigadiers.

"Damn straight," one muttered as all of them nodded in agreement.

"All right," Wilbanks said abruptly. "We know what we're doing. We've been over this more than once. Watch the time," he warned grimly. "And for damn sure listen for the 'Recall'. We can't afford to get pinned. Get it?" They all nodded.

"Then we ride in five minutes so get to your commands," he ordered. All of them took off, galloping toward their own individual commands. Wilbanks looked at his watch, his own impatience written all over his face. He wanted to move, to strike out at his enemy.

This would be an excellent opportunity to do that, but Wilbanks didn't kid himself. This was a dangerous mission for his men, well trained or not. If he didn't keep a sharp eye on things he could end up losing a huge chunk of his command.

But if they were successful...

-

Anthony Felds wiped his knife on the clothing of the Imperial scout he had just killed before sheathing his knife. He rifled through the man's bag checking for anything of use or value, like a map or an order book, but other than a nice knife and a telescoping glass all he found was a notebook. He flipped through it and realized it was merely the same kind of notes he himself kept when observing the Nor. Still, it was something, so he slid it into his own bag for someone else to examine.

Removing his hat, he stood and surveyed the area around him before raising the hat above his head and swirling it to the left. Half a minute later Dagger Earl appeared, leading Felds' horse from the back of his own, bow in hand.

"Anything?" Earl asked as Felds mounted up.

"Nothing worth riding back for," Felds told him. "Seen anything else?"

"Not so far," Earl shook his head. "Little rise yonder with some trees," he pointed north. "We can try there. If there ain't no Imps there we can see what's about."

"We can for a minute but we got to hurry," Felds nodded. "We got to clean this area out. Boss says no Nor scouts anywhere around here."

"We'll get 'em."

-

Wilson watched the attack develop from his own observation tower built just inside the tree line of the Imperial fortifications.

"Excellent," he lowered his scope, nodding in pleasure. "Our dispersed formation is preventing them from doing so much damage to our ranks. And our own artillery is playing a greater role this time as well."

"They're also taking losses, sir," Sterling noted. "We've lost just over twenty percent of our artillery in the exchange so far. And their fire is continuing as well."

"We won't have to withstand it much longer," Wilson was confident. "Once we break their line, their artillery will have to withdraw or be overrun. It won't be long now."

"Yes sir," Sterling hid a sigh. Wilson was seeing what he wanted to see rather than what was actually happening, but Sterling was merely a Brigadier and there was only so much he could do. Unlike Baxter, Sterling had no family connections so there was no way for him to stand up to Wilson's attitude, be it right or wrong.

He would have to endure. Just like the men Wilson was throwing away were enduring a terrible end at the hands of a well prepared and dug in enemy. Early reports had shown casualties already equal to an entire division, and that was just from two of the four corps engaged, the two attacking the enemy center. He didn't expect any better news from the flanks.

Worse, so far as Sterling was concerned, there were very few troops left in camp. The reserve was following the attack, already in echelon to support any breakthrough. As a result of that, their camp was essentially undefended. And warnings to Wilson about leaving their camp so vulnerable had fallen on deaf ears.

He hid another sigh as he raised his own scope to view the battlefield. There was nothing else he could do but wait.

-

Joel Vanhoose ducked instinctively as another volley of explosions rippled all the way down his front ranks, tearing his soldiers apart.

"Damn that Wilson," he muttered under the sound. "We're walking right into a hornet's nest."

His 2nd Corps was attacking the Soulan right flank which was anchored on the river, just as his own left had been until this morning. Already his losses were staggering as his front-line divisions had been ripped to pieces by volley after volley of archery, some of it much worse than others. And his aide reported that Abe Springfield's corps was in much worse shape attacking the middle on Vanhoose's right.

"This is going to end in a disaster," he promised himself. "Wait and see."

-

"Time to bring General Graham's men to the line," Parno ordered suddenly. "Have his divisions line abreast behind the main line, prepared to respond to any breach in the line. And have his archers report to the front ranks of his own lines and engage targets as they can. Add their fire to what we're already putting down range."

"Yes sir," Davies nodded and began issuing the necessary orders. "Do you want to commit any of his troops to the fighting?"

"Not yet," Parno replied quietly. "Not just yet."

"Very well."

-

Henry Herrick was not a happy man. His 4th Corps was taking a beating defending the line and so far, he'd seen no signs of reinforcement. He knew Graham's men were somewhere behind him, and that at least some of the cavalry was still around, but he'd seen no sign of any support as yet.

He was about to send a runner to the Marshal asking what he was doing when a runner appeared out of the crowd with a short note. Herrick tore it open and read it quickly.

> *I know how bad it is. Hold for just a little longer.*
> *I promise it will be worth it. -McLeod*

So. The Prince had some kind of plan at least. Herrick just looked at the runner and nodded. The man snapped off a salute and was gone back into the mass of bodies surrounding the fight. Herrick returned his attention to the battle and his men. He would have to trust that everyone's confidence in the Playboy Prince was warranted.

If it wasn't then his men would pay the price.

-

Felds and Earl had ridden through the small copse of trees and found no sign of Imperial scouts or pickets there. They had taken the time to use the cover and slight elevation to survey the fields before them but hadn't seen anything definite. One flash of color had caught Earl's eye however, so the two were now headed for it.

They were still some distance away when a man wearing what looked like an Imperial uniform jumped to his feet and began running toward the Imperial lines. Both youngsters immediately spurred their horses into a run to pursue.

Anthony Felds knew that Earl was a decent archer, but he'd not seen Earl actually use a bow. He didn't even notice the other man pulling an arrow or lifting his bow. He did hear the string snap as Earl launched the arrow from horseback when they were still a good fifty yards away.

Bouncing on horseback wasn't the best way to ensure accuracy from a bow shot, especially when the target was running. Earl cursed as his arrow hit the man in the leg, causing him to tumble to the ground. They continued to close and found a man not much older than they were crawling for Imperial lines now that he couldn't walk or run. Felds dropped from his horse as Earl kept a look out.

"Get away!" the Nor screamed, trying to kick out at Felds off his back. "Stay back," he drew a knife and held it out before him in a shaking hand. For the first time Felds noticed that while the clothes the man was wearing looked similar to an Imperial uniform, there was no insignia of any kind on it and the man wasn't armed beyond the knife he was jabbing the air with.

"You really reckon that's gonna help?" Felds sounded amused. "Who are you and why are you out here?"

"I don't have to answer you!" the man declared.

"No, you don't," Felds admitted. "And we don't have to leave you alive, neither. Dag?"

"What are yo-," the Norlander's question ended abruptly as another arrow hit him, this one tearing through his heart and silencing him. Felds knelt and once more rummaged through a dead man's belongings, taking anything that looked important.

"Let me see that bag when you finish," Earl asked and Felds passed the rather nice leather shoulder bag to his friend. Earl examined it, nodding as he dumped out the contents, keeping a good knife he found as well as a nearly new tin cup.

"I'm keeping this bag, happens you don't need it," he told Felds. "Lots nicer than mine."

"Help yourself," Felds nodded as he remounted. "Make sure it ain't marked as Imperial, in case we get caught with it."

"Ain't got nothing on it, actually," Earl sounded surprised. "What'd you find?"

"A thick notebook with a lot of writing in it," Felds said. "I don't know what this fella was up to but he was keeping a good record of it, looks like. Reckon the Boss would want a look at it."

"I imagine," Earl was stuffing his new bag into the roll behind his saddle. "Meanwhile, we gotta keep moving." Felds nodded but then held a hand up to stall.

"Hear that?" he asked. Earl turned his head a bit but then nodded.

"I imagine that's General Wilbanks and his lot," Felds said. "We better get going or they're gonna overtake us."

"Well, let's get on, then."

-

Wilbanks rode near the head of his division, recounting his rather simple orders;

"Get in behind them, into their camp, and tear the hell out of it," the Marshal had said flatly. "Carry torches and set everything you can on fire. Kill anyone you come across, I don't care who they are or what they're doing. And watch for their army to come streaming back. If we can rout them then they'll be headed straight for you. When you see or hear that, retreat at once and do whatever extra damage you can on the way out. Head north out of their camp if you need to and then bear around to the west to return. I'll leave that up to your judgment since I don't know what you'll find. Above all, take care to protect and preserve your command."

Simple orders, but in no way easy. His division was short two battalions and now headed deep into enemy territory. But if the Prince was right and the Nor had all of their troops in this, then their camp, their rear area, would be incredibly vulnerable.

And his men were the perfect outfit to take advantage of that.

-

"When the Marshal's runner gets here, we're taking this entire outfit and hitting the enemy right," Allen said to approving nods and growls all around. "You wondered why we were out here, well, that's why. Once the Nor are committed to attacking our lines then we hit them as hard as we can. General Bellamy, General Vaughan, you will take your divisions far to our left and wheel around and take the enemy infantry from the rear. General Vaughan, you will be the extreme left, on the flank of our entire line. Be especially mindful of enemy infantry in retreat trying to cut you off. I suggest keeping at least one regiment behind on the eastern edge of your line to guard against it, but the final disposition will be up to you. General Bellamy, your division will be on the angle from the rest of us, so lock in tight on the wheel and stay connected to us." Both men nodded their understanding.

"I want all brigades on line as we attack, each with one regiment in reserve in the event we need a reserve. I don't expect to if things go right, but when do things ever go completely right?" he asked and got a handful of laughs.

"General Fordyce you will be our right," Allen continued. "We will move forward and try to connect to our lines on their extreme left. They are supposed to be expecting to see us so there shouldn't be any problems. Once you've reached that position you will continue pushing forward and if the enemy breaks, we will give chase until and unless we hit unexpectedly strong resistance. Our own scouts are clearing the way for our advance so there shouldn't be any warning other than the noise of forty thousand southern horses coming to kick some northern ass."

"If there are no questions then return and brief your brigade commanders. We have about twenty minutes at most, so don't waste it."

-

"Milord," Davies sounded hesitant.

"Yes," Parno replied, more of a statement than a question.

"Sir, our losses are mounting," Davies told him. "They aren't crippling as yet, but this next rank is almost certain to reach our lines. General Graham-,"

"Not yet," Parno said quietly. "Just a few more minutes and we'll begin. I need them committed. I need them completely committed."

"I don't know how much more committed they can be, milord," Davies semi-argued. "They've thrown even their reserves at us, it appears, and their artillery is hurting us despite our own return fire. Our line won't stand against such a wave attack as we're about to be hit with."

"It won't have to," Parno assured him. "Go," he said to the man behind him. "Tell him right away."

"Sir!" the man snapped out and was gone, sliding down the ladder in what had become the accepted way of runners leaving the tower.

"Milord, what are we doing?" Enri asked.

"We're about to destroy our enemy, Lord willing," Parno replied simply. "And if we don't, we'll at the very least hurt them very badly." He looked at Davies.

"You can send Graham the order to move in five minutes. Take his men forward and support the line."

-

"We're going to do it, Sterling," Wilson said excitedly. "We're going to break their line, and Thomas' men will go pouring into their camp. By sundown there may not be much of an Army of Soulan left!"

"Sir, I am obliged to remind you that our own losses are mounting," Sterling said calmly. "Artillery losses are now at thirty-five percent and our forward divisions have literally been decimated. Both General Springfield and General Jurgen are reporting losses nearing twenty-five percent overall, and much higher in their forward ranks." Calisto Jurgen commanded the 4th Corps, lined up to Springfield's right and assisting with the attack on the Soulanie center. He was a quiet but tough professional soldier, respected by his men and peers alike.

"Yes, yes," Wilson nodded impatiently. "I know. There are losses in war time, Sterling and I know of no way to prevent them. I've planned this for three weeks, trying to find a way to destroy or at least cripple the Soulan Army. I've got them outnumbered and their cavalry are nowhere near here. Even assuming McLeod sent a rider for them the minute we attacked there is no way they can reach us before dark. And this engagement will be decided long before dark, I assure you."

He had no idea how right he was.

-

"Here we go then," Allen motioned for his buglers. The two of them looked barely old enough to shave but had served him well.

"Sound forward walk," he ordered. "Give it one minute and blow Canter." The two teens nodded and raised their horns, one facing north and the other south. In unison they blew the desired call. In seconds they could hear other horns taking up the call up and down the lines, passing it along. Allen counted to sixty and started his horse forward just as the rest of his old division did the same thing.

Over five miles of horsemen began walking their horses slowly forward, waiting for the next call which would be Canter. It wasn't long in coming and even the horses were excited, hearing the calls that they knew meant they were about to charge. Twenty thousand lancers readied their weapons, easing to the front while their bow-armed companions fell slightly behind and into trail.

In what seemed like seconds, the Canter call blew and the horses could be heard blowing up and down the line as they began to fight their reins just a bit, wanting to run. The expert horsemen held them tight but allowed their speed to increase. There would be two more calls and then they would be engaged. Grips tightened, hearts quickened, boots twisted in stirrups looking for the best purchase. Generals played their orders over in the heads looking for anything they had missed. Regimental commanders watched their men for intervals and checked to ensure their place in the brigade lines. Captains watched their companies to make sure no one was out of place, and sergeants yelled at those who were, kicking and screaming at them to get their asses in line.

Then came the call; Forward, Gallop. Horses recognized the call and strained harder at the bit, longing to lunge ahead. After one minute, they were allowed to do that as a wave of motion from the center ran both ways. Soon they were galloping forward at an ever-increasing speed. Some of the cavalrymen could already see the battlefield and those who couldn't see could hear it.

It was obvious that the Nor had not yet noticed, but they would in another few seconds. There was no real way to hide so many rampaging horsemen and even as Allen contemplated his next call, he could see a ripple of surprise pass through the enemy ranks.

"Charge!" he yelled and his buglers instantly began blowing the call.

Thirty seconds later those twenty thousand lancers dropped even as twenty thousand bows were nocked and made ready.

Thirty seconds after that the entire line went tearing forward, dirt flying from the hooves of southern horses as they carried screaming and vengeful horse troopers toward their hated enemy.

-

"Sir," Sterling was watching as the southern cavalry came into view. "Sir we have a problem, sir," he managed not to stammer.

"What? Sterling what are you babbling about now?" Wilson demanded. Sterling did a good job at his position but his 'obliged to tell you' routine was wearing thin.

"That southern cavalry that's nowhere near here, sir?" Sterling pointed with one hand as he continued to look through his own scope. "They're hitting our right flank right now." He was amazed that he managed to keep his voice calm and detached.

"What?" Wilson yelled, turning his own glass toward the right... where waves of southern cavalry were indeed streaming out of the grass and trees, lances already pointed at his helpless infantry as they were on the very cusp of hitting the southern fortifications.

"What?" Wilson's voice wasn't a yell this time but more of stunned disbelief. "They... their cavalry pursued Venable. Our scouts saw them!"

"Our scouts had to be wrong, sir," Sterling was again amazed at how calm he managed to sound. "Sir we have to do something or else our men-,"

"Thomas," Wilson still sounded as if he were in shock. "Send a runner. A runner, yes. That's the thing. Send a runner to Thomas. Order him to reorient his men to handle their cavalry. The others can continue on. We are close to breaking them and still outnumber them. Even if their horsemen are here we can still win." Sterling wondered if Wilson was trying to convince the staff or himself. He turned to find the runners all looking pale. He chose three of them to find General Thomas and relay General Wilson's orders.

"Report back when that is done," he added, hoping the relief that they could return at once would steady them up. All three nodded shakily and climbed down from the tower. Sterling watched them hurry on their way, a little surprised that they didn't just run away. Shrugging, he turned his attention back to Wilson who was still pretty much talking to himself.

"Have to get that done," the General was saying. "Once Thomas turns, things will be fine. Just have to hold a few minutes, that's all. A few minute. Five minutes, probably at most. That's all."

He's lost it, Sterling thought to himself. This has sent him over the edge.

"Have to get Thomas in there and things will be fine. And send for Venable!" he turned to Sterling. "Send runners west after Venable and Baxter right now! Yes! Have then turn around at once and return as quickly as possible. Push men and horses as hard as necessary to get it done!"

"Yes sir," Sterling nodded and began scribbling said order in his notebook. Once he was finished, he handed it to the last runner on the platform.

"Get the best horse down there, whoever it belongs to, and get this down the west road toward Unity until you find General Venable. Put this in his hands yourself. Understood?"

"Yes sir," the man took the message and hurried down the ladder, no doubt happy to be going. Sterling sympathized. He wished he was going. Instead he turned back to more of Wilson's babbling, wondering how long he should allow it to continue before notifying the corps commanders that their General was off his rocker.

-

General Eric Metz commanded the 6th Corps of the Imperial Army. While an effective commander and a stickler for orders and regulations, he lacked imagination. He was an excellent organizer and even better trainer as his men's conditioning proved, but he simply could not see past what was in front of him. That hampered his ability to exercise independent command somewhat but he preferred his position rather than one of any higher authority or responsibility. Let others worry about the war and he would concentrate on the battle in front of him.

The problem this time was that the battle was not in front of him anymore. Metz's corps was on the extreme right of the Imperial attack, his orders to eventually turn the Soulan left flank in on itself when he reached it, pushing the enemy back in and against itself. He was expected to meet only light to moderate resistance this far out and not run into any serious problems.

The Soulan archery fire had come as a rude surprise and had already cost him heavily but his men had continued forward, pressed by follow-on divisions as they moved up to assume the assault. Metz was pleased so far with his men and with his part in the attack. He knew that Springfield and Jurgen were being hard hit, but Metz was certain that if he could attain the enemy flank that he could relieve the pressure against them and allow their men to carry the attack over the southern fortifications.

At first, he thought it was thunder and scanned the sky in search of any approaching storms. Oddly, he found the sky mostly clear other than a scattering of thin white clouds at high altitude. He noticed the sound was sustained rather than ending or coming and going. Before he could process that thought, he felt the ground trembling beneath his feet. He knew this was earthquake country and with the luck they had been having so far it would be just like an earthquake to strike in the middle of their biggest offensive since they had crossed the Ohi River.

He felt an aide shaking his arm and turned to see a look of shocked surprise on the younger man's face as he pointed westward. Turning nearly a complete circle, Metz followed the pointing finger to see the absolute last thing he expected to see.

Thousands of Soulan cavalrymen were at that exact moment hitting his right flank. He followed the long ling of lancers to see that thousands more horsemen were wheeling in behind his men as well as Jurgen's, lances already lowered for their attack.

"Dear God," he whispered even as his staff started garbling about orders and dispositions. *Fools!* the word shot through his head. There were no formations or orders for this. His men were neatly boxed on three sides and squeezed on the fourth by their own brethren. The cavalry line was collapsing on his rear elements now and getting closer to his own position with every passing second.

"We are so screwed," he said aloud just before a southern arrow pierced his chest while another struck him just above the belly button. He was already on the ground when his Chief of Staff was struck in the sternum with a Soulan lance which splintered upon hitting him. Neither man saw the cavalry trooper release the now useless lance and draw his sword.

The 6th Corps had just lost the bulk of its command staff, including its commander. Worse was yet to come.

-

General Darrell Thomas listened to the orders from the runner with a growing sense of panic. The right? Soulan cavalry hitting the right? What the hell?

"Why are they here?" he demanded of the hapless runner. "They're supposed to be out to the west chasing Venable!"

"I'm sorry sir, I don't know," the young lieutenant stammered. "All I know is that there is a wave of horsemen rolling up the right and General Wilson wants you to stop it!"

"Wants me to stop it?" Thomas looked scandalized. "My men are spread all the hell over back here and he wants me to go to the right and try and stop how many cavalrymen?"

"I don't know the number sir," the lieutenant shook his head. "It honestly looked like an entire corps of nothing but cavalry. And they are hitting our right flank and appear to be bending around to hit at least part of the rear areas. General Wilson wants you-,"

"To stop them, yeah, I got that part," Thomas was shaking his head. "Look, go back and tell Sterling that we'll try, but we are so far out of position for something like that that we'll be lucky to get even half way over there before it's over. Wilson has my men spread across the entire rear of the formation. Some of my men are two miles from where they need to be and my runners are all on foot!"

"Yes sir!" the man turned his horse and sprinted for the tower, glad to leave the irate General behind, not to mention the battle that now threatened to turn against them.

"Get to your respective division commanders and tell them our right is under attack by southern cavalry and Wilson has ordered us to intercept them. We can't do that because they've already hit the right, so we'll try and form up to the east of General Calisto's men and meet them there. All divisions are to head toward General Springfield's rear area and form up on General Garner's division!" He looked at Garner's runner. "Tell Garner to hold in place and orient his men toward the west to prepare to resist the enemy attack." Ogden Garner commander the 17th Imperial Infantry and was one of his better and more reliable division commanders.

"Sir!" all of them saluted and began to run in different directions, looking for their respective division commanders. Thomas stood there a minute longer shaking his head before explaining to his staff what was happening. The reactions were about on par with his own.

"We'll never be able to do it," his own Chief of Staff was shaking his head. "We're spread out over two miles with too much ground between our men. We'll never be able to just reform and stop so many enemy cavalry. We don't even have pikes!"

"Whether we can do it or not we have our orders, so we have to try," Thomas replied. "Let's start getting things organized. Grab some extra runners from the ranks and let's start getting our men over there as quickly as we can. The slower we respond the more damage they can do before we get there."

Reluctance screaming in every move, his staff officers began to move, trying to carry out his orders.

"We're right on the edge of a disaster," his Chief all but whispered as the others departed.

"Edge of it?" Thomas raised an eyebrow. "The disaster started the minute those horsemen appeared."

The young lieutenant chosen by Sterling to carry Wilson's message to Venable had followed his orders to take the best horse he found at the base of the tower, in this case General Wilson's mount. Smiling to himself at the opportunity to do something that any other time would have earned him a court martial, the young rider wasn't really paying attention as he galloped through the camp on his way to take the road west.

Which was probably why he died with a look of shocked surprise on his face when he was unseated by a southern lance as it crashed through his chest and toppled him from his lucky choice in horses. He bled out quickly, unable even to yell in pain or surprise as he lay on the ground, broken and bleeding.

The message in his tunic undelivered.

General Wilbanks ignored the dying dismounted Imperial and surveyed the camp before him with grim satisfaction. His troopers were already tearing through the camp, killing anyone they saw and setting fire to anything that would burn.

"Make damn sure we're keeping an eye to the south and what's happening there," he pointed to the battlefield as he addressed his small staff.

"One company detailed to shadow our movements with orders to sound recall the minute it looks like the enemy is returning in anything like strength," his aide promised. Wilbanks nodded, trusting his men to watch for them. He turned his attention back to the action in the Imperial camp.

"Don't leave anything we can manage to get to!" he yelled to those around him. He wanted to destroy all he could. If they couldn't destroy the enemy themselves then he at least wanted to destroy their ability to make war on his people. Burning their camp and their stores would go a long way toward doing that.

"Burn it all!"

CHAPTER TWENTY-SEVEN

-

Britton Sterling's attention had been riveted to the enemy cavalry attack on their right flank since he had first seen the horsemen moving in from the west. There was no doubt in his mind that this engagement would be decided, if it hadn't been already, by whatever happened on the right in the next few minutes. He had observed Thomas' efforts to re-orient his wide spread corps to meet the threat and was impressed by the General's skillful deployment.

Sterling was also aware that regardless of how well Thomas managed to organize, there was no way he was going to stop that tide of horsemen from rolling all over his men as well as the rest of the army. The Soulan cavalry had caught them neatly in their flank, allowing them to engage in detail rather than face the Imperial Army's larger numbers at a disadvantage. It was classic military strategy.

"Sir," his own aide said softly, tugging lightly at Sterling's jacket.

"What?" he turned.

"Look," the man said simply, pointing south. Sterling turned his own glass to the south to see newly arrived Soulan infantry pouring to the line, engaging the few Imperial troops who had managed to make it that far. He also noted that southern artillery was taking a greater toll now on Imperial infantry as the latter bunched together for mutual support. It was the age-old problem of 'when in danger, bunch together'. The problem being that too often that was exactly where the enemy wanted you.

"What the hell is that?" he heard one of Wilson's aides ask and turned to see the man looking westward.

Sterling moved to the rear of the tower and looked in that direction, wondering what the man had...

"Oh, shit," Sterling whispered. "Sir!" he turned to where Wilson was still looking stunned by the changes, occasionally babbling about new orders. "Sir, there are enemy horsemen in the camp!"

"What?" Wilson seemed to snap out of his stupor at that, turning to look at Sterling. "What did you say?"

"We're being attacked in camp by Soulan cavalry, sir!" Sterling pointed.

"Their cavalry are all hitting our flank," Wilson scoffed but turned to look and see what was happening only to find that at least some Soulan cavalry was indeed ransacking their camp.

"Tell Thomas I need him to detach one division to return and protect the camp!" Wilson started panicking again. "Tell him to do it right away!"

"Sir, General Thomas is fully engaged with -," Sterling began but Wilson cut him off, yelling.

"I don't care what he's doing, he needs to get someone back here to stop that!"

Sterling lowered his head in resignation and turned to see the returning runner just getting to the top of the tower.

"Go back and tell General Thomas that Soulan cavalry are in the camp and destroying it as they go. General Wilson has directed him to break off one division from his corps to return and defend the camp and deal with the incursion. Understood?"

"Yes sir," the man nodded tiredly and immediately started back down the ladder. Sterling steeled himself before returning his attention to the most recent problem. The problem of everything in their camp now being laid waste with only minimal resistance.

-

Major Greg Tandy had decided that he was a fairly lucky man. Chosen by General Baxter to remain behind in charge of the men who had not been selected to go west, Tandy had figured he and those same men would have an easy day or two with camp duties, and perhaps with other duties as their horses were able to return to work. Maybe courier duty or something else similar.

The attack had come as a rude shock to him since there had been no warning to Tandy or his men. His own corps commander was far to the north still and no one had thought to let the few cavalrymen still in camp know what was happening. Since all of them had been ruled medically unfit for duty, they were not considered as part of the attack and had thus been ignored.

Which meant they were practically the only men still in camp when the southern cavalry had come riding through it, killing anything that moved and burning anything that didn't. Tandy's first warning had been a young corporal limping up to him as fast as he could.

"Sir! Enemy in the camp! Coming from the west, sir!" the excited young man pointed over his shoulder. Tandy had followed that point to see smoke and flames already billowing from a number of places as well as the occasional flash of Soulan uniforms or horses.

"You have got to be kidding me," he shook his head. His men had not a single horse available to them. They also had no archers among them. That left them with the prospect of taking on mounted cavalry with swords and maybe a few lances. Using a lance on foot was a recipe for disaster from the jump, let alone trying to engage a charging horseman with one.

"Sir, there are -," a young lieutenant ran up, arm extending in a point.

"Enemy in the camp, I know," Tandy nodded. "Alright, gather everyone together and we'll try and at least defend ourselves." He looked around for a good place and saw something that might let at least some of them live through the next few minutes.

"See that bramble over there?" he told the two. "Those trees with the dense thicket? That's where we'll make our stand. Tell everyone to gather there with whatever weapons they have at hand. At least the Soulanies won't be able to just ride through it line abreast. Maybe we can fight back against them from there."

"Yes sir!" the two men replied in unison and began to run in different directions yelling his instructions.

"'This will be an easy duty, Gregory'," he repeated Baxter's words to him as he grabbed his sword and other gear. "'Be a good chance to get some well-deserved rest.' 'Just watch after the lads and keep them out of trouble, yeah?'" he shook his head. "What a crock of shit." He looked to where the men under his temporary commander were starting to stream his way.

"Over here!" he waved, then pointed to the thicket. "Bring whatever you can with you, especially pikes and lances! Deep into the thicket, boys! Make the bastards work for it!"

Make them work for it. Make them work to kill them all.

-

Wilbanks' men had been through perhaps half the camp so far when a sergeant came galloping up to him.

"Sir, we're seeing signs that some of the infantry are turning back," the man said without preamble. "They aren't headed this way yet, but it looks as if they will be shortly."

"How far out are they?" Wilbanks asked.

"Four, maybe five hundred yards from the line, sir," the sergeant reported after a moment to think. "They're at the very rear of the enemy formation already sir. Likely part of the reserve as near as we can tell."

"Very well," Wilbanks nodded. "Keep an eye on them, let me know when they start to move. We need to be on the way out before they get here."

"Yes sir." The man raced away, leaving Wilbanks to think. He summoned a runner with a wave of his hand.

"Find Brigadier Hammond. Tell him to detail at minimum one regiment to do nothing but search for and destroy any supplies he can find. Ideally, if not engaged with the enemy, he will use his entire brigade for that duty. Anything that looks like a supply depot or cache is to be burned if possible. Understand?"

"Yes sir!" the runner nodded and set out to find Brigadier Hammond. Normal Jared 'Norm' Hammond was Wilbanks' senior brigade commander. He hated to be called Normal and for some unknown reason despised his middle name, so it was 'Norm' unless you were trying to piss him off. Which wasn't a good plan since Hammond was large enough to wrestle a bear and an above average swordsman as well. He was also tough, dependable and smart. Wilbanks was fortunate to have him, and figured he was the perfect one to get the most damage done.

-

"Sir, our camp... our stores... all appear to be on fire," Sterling said gently. "It may be for the best if we move off this tower and shift east a bit. Get you away from the enemy."

"Don't be preposterous," Wilson scoffed, sounding more like his normal self than he had since the Soulan cavalry had appeared. "Thomas has orders to send a division here to deal with that and he will. Meanwhile our attack is still going well on the left it appears."

"Sir, General Metz's command has been shattered," Sterling pointed out. "General Jurgen's men have lost almost a third of their strength and are now caught between the Soulan cavalrymen and the archery fire from the Soulan infantry. And the Soulanie line has received a massive influx of new soldiers. Reinforcements estimated to be at least corps strength. We've lost the equivalence of an entire infantry corps in this attack plus we are losing all our stores and much of our equipment, including our men's tents and belongings. Sir, I urge you to send runners to recall all of our troops that can disengage from the enemy and let them defend what's left of our camp."

"Disengage?" Wilson looked aghast. "You want to stop just as we're on the cusp of victory?"

"Sir, we are on the cusp of a disaster!" Sterling was losing his fake patience. "Have you heard a word I've said?"

"I've heard every treacherous word," Wilson nodded grimly. "And once this engagement is over and we've crushed the enemy, I'll be bringing you up on charges. Until then I suggest you keep your mouth shut and do as you're told. Perhaps that will encourage me to overlook your impertinence."

"Sir, you are slaughtering your men for no gain," Sterling said in a soft, defeated tone. "We had a magnificent army this morning," he murmured to himself. "Splendid troops. Gone. Wasted."

"Get down, Sterling," Wilson said without looking around. "This is no place for cowards. Get down from here and out of my presence. I shall deal with you later."

"Very well," Sterling nodded and moved to the ladder. Without another word or backward glance, he made his way down to the ground and mounted his horse. Without a word to anyone he began moving east, grabbing what he needed from wherever he could as he went. He didn't know how bad things would get, but he did know things were going to be very bad.

Gerald Wilson had been, Sterling thought, a great general. A man of vision and forethought. A thinking man who did not waste his men on frivolous attacks. All of that had ended today. Actually, it had begun days earlier when he hatched his plan. Detaching a full twenty percent of his army on a herring chase and then attacking almost before they were out of sight. Sterling had admitted even as he tried to stop it that Wilson's plan had merit.

But somehow, someone on the other side had seen through his ruse. Had, in fact, used that very ruse against him. The enemy cavalry had been seen streaming out of the Soulan camp for well over an hour, in pursuit of Venable's column. They had ridden for hours before their own scouts had managed finally to form a barrier that Imperial scouts couldn't penetrate. And at some point after that had merely turned around and returned to a point from which they were able to launch this counter-attack.

Sterling had argued against dispersing the reserve in such a fashion, he had argued against four corps abreast instead of three, he had argued against the attack leaving their rear areas so exposed and open, he had argued against all of that and more but to no avail. Wilson was locked into this plan of his and would not be swayed from it regardless of what kind of disaster it led to.

Shaking his head in disbelief, Sterling kept his horse headed east. Away from the Soulan attack. He didn't delude himself that he was headed for safety, because he didn't think there was any safety to be found. Not here, anyway.

Not anymore.

-

General Darrell Thomas had received the news from Sterling with no more than a nod. First, he was supposed to somehow keep his men organized on a two-mile front, then he was supposed to pull them in to resist a cavalry attack with numbers equal to his own, and now he was somehow supposed to miraculously send one of his infantry divisions to defend the entire camp from still more Soulan cavalry.

"Can this day get any better?" his Chief of staff muttered at his side.

"Tell me you didn't just say that," Thomas looked at him. "Get General Bissette's men on the way back to camp. Tell him just to do what he can to save as much of the camp as possible. It's all we can do."

"Right," the other man nodded and ran to the right where Stewart Bissette's men were engaged on the far flank. He was closest to camp. His men would have to do. Thomas shook his head in resignation as yet another runner brought him news that his men were 'hard pressed and needed help'.

There was no help. For any of them.

-

"I don't believe it," Davies murmured as he watched the Imperial attack melt down.

"Order Graham to take his men over the wall and support the cavalry," Parno ordered a runner. "He is to keep his command tight and together, and just push. Let Allen and the cavalry keep dealing out the damage while Graham and his men simply keep them off the line." The runner sketched a salute and slid down the ladder, off to find Graham.

"Over the wall?" Enri asked softly. "Is that wise?"

"It won't be a problem today," Parno assured him. "The enemy is disorganized at the moment. Their left is still okay but it shouldn't last. Have Freeman concentrate all his archers against the attack on the far right and see if he can break them. Meanwhile," he turned to the young Captain from the artillery commander. "Tell Major Lars to target carefully and start lofting special rounds onto the enemy infantry. Aim for their center mass and avoid hitting our own men. Use spotters as needed to ensure that he's on target. The goal is to cause as many casualties as possible. They're bunched enough now that the special rounds should work fine. Might even break them if they're accurate enough."

"Yes sir," the man nodded, and moved to carry his message.

"It's a risk to land those rounds so close to our own men," Enri noted.

"Lars is pretty good at what he does," Parno replied. "And we need to break this bunch. Destroy them if we can. Completely."

-

"We're doing a number on them, but it's not without cost," Brigadier Sam Walters said as he rode to where Allen was surveying the scene. "I don't know what losses are across the whole command but we've lost at least ten percent of our force and a lot of horses."

"War costs," Allen sighed. "We can't do anything about that, Sam. We have to accept those losses in order to get anything done. We can't inflict this kind of damage on the enemy without getting hurt ourselves. Just how it is."

"I realize that," Walters sounded almost impatient. "I'm just pointing out that we're losing men and horses and our attack has slowed as the enemy begins to turn and face us. We're going to hit a point where we're no longer able to-,"

Whatever he was going to say was lost in the explosions of Soulan artillery fire walking its way through the Imperial formations. The effect was almost instantaneous as Imperial pressure began to lessen.

"Damn, there's infantry coming over the wall!" Walters pointed to their own lines. Allen looked and could see what was probably 1st Corps scrambling over the fortifications and forming up before them.

"We can keep pressing for now, I'd say," Allen sounded pleased. "Wouldn't you agree Mister Walters?"

"Looks like it," the Brigadier said reluctantly. "But this action is butchering our ranks."

"And we're decimating theirs," Allen reminded him. "Like I told you, Sam. You can't prevent casualties. All you can do is take steps to limit them and take care of them when it happens. The Prince does that. But this is a golden opportunity for us to get rid of this bunch and chase them all the way to the Ohi and beyond. We have to take advantage of it, regardless of what it costs."

"Now. Send a runner to Bellamy and Vaughan telling them what's happening and to pull back abreast with us rather than stay behind the mass. Disengage and return to the line, prepared to harass and interdict the Nor all the way down the line. I don't want them pinned and pressed by-,"

Allen ducked on instinct as another salvo of Roda Finn's 'gadgets' landed among the fleeing and near-panicking Imperial troops.

"See? Now get those runners away!"

"Yes sir!" Walters nodded and grabbed the nearest men who were waiting for orders. Soon four of them were galloping down the line, two for each general. Allen didn't see that as he was watching the battle intently. Surprise or not, panicked or not there was still a great big bunch of enemy soldiers on their doorstep. They couldn't give them any time to get organized.

-

"We have got to get some organization about this or we're gonna get cut to pieces!" Thomas declared. Before he could say anything else, Abe Springfield stumbled into Thomas' command group, his own staff following him closely.

"Abe, you okay?" Thomas asked.

"Hell no, I'm not okay!" the older man growled. "That damn Wilson may be the stupidest son-of-bitch I've ever served under. He walked us right into a classic ambush. We are boxed on three sides and got the river on the fourth. Worse, they've rolled us up where we can't focus all our strength on them at once. We have to face them on too limited a front. And now-," Springfield ducked as yet another string of explosions walked its way through both his own and Jurgen's troops.

"You seen Metz?" he asked Thomas as he straightened.

"No," Thomas shook his head. "He may have gotten caught in that initial cavalry charge. He was behind his men with nothing but his color guard. My far right division wasn't far enough over to catch any of it so..." He shrugged. It was likely that Eric Metz had met the same fate as many of his men.

"I sent three men to find Jurgen," Springfield grimaced. "None have succeeded so far. Doesn't mean he's dead but it ain't good. What did that dumb ass Wilson want you to do?"

"First I was supposed to form up here and 'interdict' the cavalry charge,"

Thomas replied. "Then, before I could just magically make that happen Sterling sent a runner saying that Soulan cavalry was rampaging through our camps so I was to detach one division to stop that. Since then, nothing."

"In the camps?" Springfield repeated. "How much of their cavalry are we facing here?"

"Pretty much all of it, I'd say," Thomas said. "And now I'm getting reports that their infantry is coming over the wall in pursuit."

"We have to get out of here," Springfield said grimly. "We've got to retreat now and save what we can. At this rate we're going to lose the entire army!"

"Alright," Thomas didn't hesitate. Doing this would probably see the both of them executed but both men were brave enough to face that if it meant their men weren't thrown away for no gain. With the decision made, neither wasted any time. Thomas turned to his waiting runners.

"Everyone to your division commander and tell him we are going to conduct a fighting withdrawal back to our own line! Don't break and run or the horsemen will just run us down. We will withdraw, fighting, and reform behind our own fortifications. Go!" As the men ran off, Thomas grabbed two more men.

"You two. Head for the left and find General Vanhoose, tell him we are withdrawing. We are executing a fighting withdrawal, got it? We are returning to our own lines and reforming there."

"Yes sir!" the two shouted and then headed off on their own mission. Thomas turned back to Springfield in time to see his runners moving off as well.

"I sent two men to find Vanhoose and let him know what we're doing," Thomas said. Springfield nodded.

"Five minutes, you think?" he asked, and Thomas surveyed the field before him.

"If they give us that much time," he finally answered.

-

"We can't give them too much time," Parno said to no own in particular. "We have to keep the pressure on. Their men are in a panic and their confidence is shot. We have to capitalize on that." He turned to a runner.

"Tell Lars to concentrate all his fire in the middle of that mob," he ordered. "And change one third of his shot to half-barrel pitch. Aim for the middle of the mob and we can avoid friendly fire. Watch for the red pennant to hold fire. Go on!"

The man slid down the ladder and was gone.

"What have you overlooked, young warlord?" Cho Feng spoke for the first time during the entire engagement. Parno almost panicked as he turned at the soft words.

"What? What did you say?" he felt his heart hammering in his ears now.

"What have you overlooked?" Cho asked again. "Things look promising. You have dealt your enemy a great blow, but they still out number your men and you have lost soldiers as well. Have you allowed yourself to lose sight of the battle?"

"No," Parno shook his head, running through everything in his head. "No, I haven't. Not that I know of anyway. Wilbanks has orders to evade to the north if necessary to escape, Allen has orders to prevent his men from being pinned against the Nor lines, Graham has orders to keep his men tight and avoid rushing into the enemy." He paused, running over everything in his head one more time before shaking his head again.

"I haven't overlooked anything, Cho," he said finally. "Unless I have," he added, looking at his teacher's face.

"No, I believe you have covered everything this time," Feng almost smiled as the corners of his mouth twitched slightly.

"You do that just to upset my stomach, don't you," Parno accused.

"I must keep you on your toes and focused," Feng didn't bother looking apologetic. "You are prone to tunnel vision. I must break you of that habit."

"Well, thanks for that," Parno's sarcasm was thick. "Meantime, we're doing well against their army."

"Do not forget the force that left," Cho reminded him.

"Got scouts watching them and a full battalion burning the town before they can get there," Parno replied at once. "They won't find anything but ashes when they get there."

"Very well," Cho nodded. "Now the deciding factor lies with your men."

"Yeah," Parno agreed, turning back to the battle. "So, it does."

-

Thomas was just getting his withdrawal organized when the Soulan artillery fire worsened. It seemed they had pulled all their available pieces from other duties and ordered them to concentrate on the packed mass of Imperial troops. Northern artillery had long since fallen silent as Soulan cavalry ran wild through the rear areas. And now the southerners had decided to add flaming pitch to their fire. He could hear the screaming even over the din of battle as hundreds of men were coated with the flaming substance. Uniforms melted to skin, swords became too hot to hold and shields burned in the hands of the soldiers who carried them. Thomas was sure there were worse ways to die than being covered in a flaming fire that you couldn't extinguish and couldn't remove.

He just couldn't think of any right off hand. That was all.

"Alright, that's it!" he yelled. "Start pulling back now! If we don't we're going to get overrun when that bunch breaks!" he pointed to the men in front of them, now caught under the withering fire of southern artillery. "FALL BACK!"

-

"They're falling back," Allen nodded in satisfaction. "Hit them on their flanks again and again," he whispered to himself. "Don't let them breathe even for a minute!"

The fire had panicked the northern soldiers even more than the explosions. No one wanted to be burned. There was no treatment for such a hellish injury and the pain had to be intense. He shivered just thinking about it, fear tingling down his spine.

He hoped they wouldn't have to endure it.

-

Preston Wilbanks looked at the damage his men had inflicted with grim approval. His extreme right flank battalion had fallen on the Imperial Artillery line with a vengeance, destroying every piece and setting fire to them and any pitch they had ready to hand. Afterward they had hunted down every Imperial artilleryman that had run and killed them where they found them.

There were supply dumps all through the camp that were now on fire, burning food, clothing, equipment, anything and everything that an army needed to live and fight in enemy territory. Personal tents were also burning anywhere that his men had passed them, as they just lowered their torches as they rode down the line, the dry canvas igniting with ease. Anyone they had found in the camp had been put to the sword regardless of who they were. He had felt a tinge of unease at that when they encountered a field hospital, but only a tinge. They were invaders of his homeland and they needed to know the cost for that invasion.

But now it was time to go. His lookouts had reported that the Imperial Army was breaking, returning this way even now. And while the Norland Army wasn't faring well against the Soulan Army, a lone cavalry division already weakened by detachments would not fare well against the remainder of such a large force.

"Sound Recall and Assembly," he ordered his buglers. Both nodded and lifted their horns.

All of the camp Soulan cavalrymen left whatever they were doing and rode to the sound of the horns, striking down anyone who got in their way but not going out of their way to attack anyone anymore. Time would not be on their side and they knew that.

Wilbanks started his horse northward at a slow walk, bearing slightly west out of the camp. As his men gathered to the horns, he would lead them a few miles north and then turn west as the Marshal had recommended, making a large loop to return to his own billets.

Behind him his men gathered, grabbing any injured comrades on their way out and pulling empty horses with them. Their work here was finished and they were leaving, but they would leave no one behind if they could help it.

-

"Don't leave anyone behind if we can help it!" Springfield was yelling to everyone around him. "Take the wounded with you if you can! There's a black flag flying on their wall and another with their cavalry. They won't accept any surrender and they won't offer one either!"

"Bloody savages," a man next to him muttered and Springfield snorted.

"What would you do if they were invading us instead?" he asked and the man looked startled, though whether it was the question or the fact that Springfield was asking no one could tell.

"I... I don't... I'd follow my orders, sir," the man fell back on the most dependable answer possible.

"And that's just what they're doing," Springfield nodded as if his point were made for him. "Don't think you can just walk into the lion's den and beard him without at least getting scratched. We walked into a lion's den today, boy. And we got mauled."

"Yes sir," the man nodded. Springfield snorted at the idea that the young man knew what he was being told but it wasn't worth the effort. Why was it that everyone accused the South of committing unspeakable acts when it was nothing the Empire hadn't done to them, both past and present? Springfield was many things but he wasn't a hypocrite. While he would carry out his orders to the best of his ability he didn't fool himself thinking that those orders were any more righteous because of who issued them or who carried them out.

How many wounded Soulanies had they put to the sword since the war started? How many civilians had they killed? Springfield had no idea of the numbers but he knew it had happened. It was standing orders. Why should the southerners be different? Why shouldn't they fight just as dirty as the north did?

He had a momentary twinge of panic at the thought that Soulan finally had someone commanding their army that didn't mind getting his hands a little bloody. Clearly, he had no problem issuing orders that Soulan hadn't issued in a very long time. He doubted Imperial historians could pinpoint the last time the 'gallant' men of Soulan had put a wounded soldier to death.

But they were damn sure doing it now. Springfield had a sudden vision of the Imperial Army trying to fight off an invasion against men like they had faced today and shivered again at the idea. What if Soulan had grown tired of being invaded and suddenly decided to return the favor, fighting the way they were fighting right now, this minute?

A vision of Lovil flames danced across his vision and was gone just as quick. He thought of the cities in the line of march toward the Imperial Capital and how much damage the Soulan Army could inflict if they took the notion.

Yes, if the Soulan Army was fighting the same way the Empire had always fought then the Empire might be in for a rude awakening.

-

"Order Graham to press them as they fall back," Parno ordered as he watched through a telescope. "Keep his men tight and in control, but keep pushing. And send someone to remind Lars to keep walking his fire back so it doesn't hit our men."

Enri turned and detailed runners to carry those orders and then turned back to see Parno was now looking westward to the cavalry line.

"That's it, Allen, that's it," the Prince said softly. "Don't let them rest. Don't let them get organized. Hit them again!"

"Sir, we are taking a big risk here," Enri mentioned carefully.

"How's that?" Parno didn't look away from the battle.

"We have a large portion of our army exposed here, sir," Enri mentioned. "Practically all of our cavalry and the best trained infantry corps we have at present as well as the freshest. All exposed to the enemy without benefit of any cover at all."

"Make your point Mister Willard," Parno's voice took an edge, though he still didn't turn around.

"That was my point, sir," Enri replied. "Our army is extended about as far as is safe to do so at present."

"Why?" Parno's one-word question caught the Brigadier by surprise.

"Sir?"

"Why is that 'as far as is safe to do so'?" Parno finally turned to look at Enri as well as Davies and the rest. "What would you recommend? Stopping? When we have them on the run and broken?"

"It would be the prudent thing to do, sir," Davies nodded. "Preserve our army for another day."

"This is our 'another day', gentlemen," Parno snorted. "Do you honestly think we'll get this opportunity again? The enemy out in the open where we can devastate them? Demoralize and smash them to pieces? I can't trick their commander into doing this again, gentlemen. As it is this was as much good fortune as it was good planning. You want me to abandon what might be the one opportunity we get to eliminate this threat? To possibly send them running back home and out of our Kingdom? Off of our bread basket!"

Neither man replied, and that seemed to agitate Parno further.

"Well?" he demanded. "Is that what you're recommending that we do? Just walk away and wait for another miraculous opportunity to beat them?"

"Sir, we are merely advising you what is prudent," Enri Willard tried placating his Marshal. "The survival of our army is of the utmost importance."

"No, the survival of our Kingdom is of the utmost importance, Mister Willard," Parno replied flatly. "That is the purpose of having an army at all! There isn't a man on this field I wouldn't sacrifice, myself included, if it means freeing Soulan of any occupation. This is an opportunity we won't get again! We have to kill every Imperial soldier we can and beat them so badly, so soundly that they're afraid to meet us in battle again! We have to break them and destroy their confidence! Send them running with their tails between their legs like the cur dogs they are and kill every one of them we can! Kill them all!" Parno was yelling now, his face red.

"My Prince," Cho Feng interceded calmly. "The battlefield needs your attention," he said gently. "You are in peril of losing sight of that which is most important," he almost whispered. "Victory."

"Right," Parno almost muttered as he turned his attention back to his telescope. "You two want out, then get out," he said over his shoulder. "No hard feelings and what not. But I'm going to kill every Nor I can right here and right now. Our army knows their business and what they're about. They also already have orders not to endanger their commands."

"I will withdraw the army, but I will not do so until we have killed the last possible Imperial soldier."

The was an uncomfortable silence on the tower as the two men in question exchanged looks. Neither could summon enough gumption to protest again, but neither man would leave the tower, either.

They were spectators now.

-

General Allen had ridden north along his line, speaking briefly with the Generals of the divisions under his command. Brief clashes with sword and what lances remained along with mounted archery were taking a harsh and deadly toll on the enemy, but Walters had been right; their own losses were mounting.

"I'd guess our losses at nearing twenty-five percent across the board," Milton Vaughan said when Allen had reached him. "Our losses are less than that I should think, but Fordyce and Coe's men have been in thicker combat than us. We're facing broken men right now, but there are a lot of them, still."

"I know, but this is a chance we'll not get again," Allen replied, eyes roaming the battlefield even as the two spoke. "We have to take advantage of it. We have to."

"I don't disagree," Vaughan voiced his support for the plan. "Just pointing out the issues involved. If we can keep the pressure on we may can run them all the way to the Ohi."

"I'd love that," Allen admitted. "Assuming we don't lose too much strength and the Marshal adds Wilbanks and O'Hare to our numbers, we might be able to keep them running."

"At least three divisions of mounted infantry over there, too," Vaughan reminded him. "They could help."

"True, they could," Allen nodded. "That will be up to the Marshal. For now, we just need to make sure and keep the pressure up. And stay out of the envelope that artillery is using!"

"No kidding."

-

"We're missing twenty-seven men at the moment," Wilbanks aide, a young Captain, reported. "We have one company doing sweeps behind us by squad looking for any men and horses left behind. Otherwise everyone is here."

"Good," Wilbanks nodded. "We're on our way out. Have the scouts take us north a couple miles and then start looking for good ground to the west. We'll head west for three or four miles and then loop around for our own camps."

"Yes sir." The man rode away, leaving Wilbanks to his thoughts. His losses were all but non-existent, which he hadn't expected. Apparently, the Imperial commander had committed his entire force to the attack, leaving the camp wide open. He and his men had done tremendous damage to the Imperial Army's supply caches and dumps. His men were still burning as they went, setting fire to anything that would burn. He nodded his approval without voicing it or even realizing he had done it.

"We spotted a large group headed into the thicket yonder, sir," a scout rode up to him and pointed back toward the interior of the camp. "Right smart of 'em, sir. Several hundred."

"Are they a threat to us?" Wilbanks asked.

"No sir," the scout shook his head. "No archers that I saw and just a few pikes. I think they're just trying to get away," he added.

"Let them," Wilbanks said easily. "We're on our way out, anyway. They aren't in our way and I have no desire to try and get into the brier patch with them."

"Me neither, sir, begging your pardon," the man grinned.

"Carry on," Wilbanks returned the smile and sent the man on his way.

"Excellent," he voiced his thoughts aloud this time. "Excellent."

-

"Why are we retreating?" Wilson asked. "Sterling! Why are we-, Sterling!" He turned to see the other staff officers looking anywhere else but at him. "Where is Brigadier Sterling!" Wilson demanded.

"You sent him away, sir," a young aide with more bravery than brains replied. "Ordered him off the tower."

"I did?" Wilson frowned. "I don't... well, no matter. Find out why we're retreating! Who gave that order!"

"Sir, I don't know if we're retreating so much as being beaten back," another staff officer said softly. "The enemy have infantry over their walls and advancing while their cavalry keeps our men rolled up and unable to deploy."

"Where is our artillery?" Wilson demanded. "Have them engage that cavalry and drive them off!"

"Sir, our artillery was overrun and destroyed over a half-hour ago," the brave young aide spoke up again. "All of our artillery is out of commission and many if not most of our artillerymen are dead or wounded."

Wilson looked at the young man dumbly, as if he was having trouble processing what he was hearing.

"Are you trying to tell me all of our artillery is gone?" he finally demanded.

"I'm afraid so, sir. So are the majority of our stores. Soulanie cavalry rode through the camp and did a huge amount of damage as they went, sir. The estimate right now is that at least sixty percent of our stores are burned or presently burning."

"How did they get into camp!" Wilson almost screeched.

"Sir, the camp was empty," the staff officer reminded him. "We sent every available man in the attack. There was nothing left here but a few men who were injured and the non-combat personnel like blacksmiths and Quartermaster troops. Most of whom are dead or missing at the moment."

"We've lost over seventy percent of our food stores, ninety percent of our medical supplies and all of the personnel who were caught anywhere in camp were slaughtered if they couldn't get away or hide. Many were burned alive in the fires I fear. And our medical personnel were not spared. We have very few medical staff remaining."

Wilson listened to this cascade of failure with dawning comprehension. He finally seemed to realize the magnitude of the defeat he was facing. He licked suddenly dry lips as he tried to find a way to salvage something, anything at all from this disaster.

"Who ordered the retreat?" he asked, turning back to the battlefield.

"As I said, sir, I don't think there was an order. It appears more that our men broke under the combined archery and artillery fire and are simply falling back on their own. Once it started it would be impossible to stop. General Metz's corps in particular have taken very heavy losses and are completely shattered. General Metz himself is missing and presumed dead along with his staff. General Jurgen is also missing at present and his corps are falling back in disrepair."

"Generals Thomas, Springfield and Vanhoose are slowly withdrawing, trying to maintain at least some order among the army, but General Springfield's men have also taken very heavy losses. They are close to breaking as well."

"Breaking?" Wilson snorted. "Our men shouldn't be breaking! They should be attacking! Order the three of them to halt their withdrawal and return to the attack! We're close to destroying the southern army! Just one more good hard push could do it!"

"Very well, sir," the staff officer turned and gave three runners their orders, telling them to stress that General Wilson had ordered it. He then called Springfield's runner aside and added that he should tell Springfield, as senior corps commander, that Wilson had likely suffered a breakdown of some kind. The man simply didn't know what else to do. The runner nodded gravely and took off after his brethren, hurrying to find General Springfield.

CHAPTER TWENTY-EIGHT

-

General Gerald Allen looked at the battlefield and considered his options. The enemy were packed tightly into the box the Marshal had made for them and we being pummeled by salvo after salvo of artillery. With 1st Corps now on the move, slowly but inexorably moving north and pushing the enemy back, it was time for Allen to change things about a bit. He rode to where General Fordyce was observing his division. The older general looked at Allen and smiled in spite of the situation.

"We've given them a shellacking today," he said triumphantly.

"And we're not done, either," Allen nodded in reply. "I want you to disengage here. Allow 1st Corps to keep the enemy in retreat. Reform your division and move north behind the line to link up with General Vaughan's left. We're going to leapfrog our men north and keep that bunch packed in as tight as we can for the artillery. Every Nor bastard they kill is one less we have to face, whether it's today or the next time. No bugles," he added. "Use runners and pennants and anything else, but no bugles. Let's not have the entire line falling back because of a miscommunication. Make sure your runners emphasize the no bugle order."

"I'll get on it immediately," Fordyce nodded. "Know that our losses are adding up, however," he pointed out. "We are not combat ineffective but I estimate we've lost about eighteen to twenty percent of our strength."

"I know, and I'm sorry," Allen grimaced, his eyes showing his sadness. "You shouldn't have as hot a time further down. No one there is fighting other than to get away."

"We'll be moving as soon as possible," Fordyce promised. Allen sketched a salute and moved to find Sam Walters. The brigadier was doing pretty much the same as Fordyce was, observing the division that he had nominal command of since Allen's ascension to 'corps' command.

"Sam," Allen said as he stopped next to his subordinate.

"General," Walters returned the gesture without looking. "Our losses are around fifteen to twenty percent in total so far. But we're still pushing and shoving."

"Fordyce is about to move north," Allen told him. "I'm sending him to flank Vaughan and extend the line. I want you to be prepared to do the same if the situation warrants it. Be prepared to have runners sent to issue the command to reform behind the line in preparation for movement north. Absolutely no bugle calls whatsoever. None. I don't want any possibility of a mistaken bugle call ending up ruining our chances of a great victory."

"We'll mind it," Walters promised. "How long before we need to move?"

"You may not move at all," Allen replied. "Just make your plans now. Once Fordyce is in place, we'll see what happens. For now, just start making preparations."

"Will do, sir."

-

General Abraham Springfield received the message from the runner with a stony-faced nod, accepting that he had to do something and do it right now. He turned to see General Thomas looking at him carefully.

"I'm assuming command of this army," Springfield told him formally. "Wilson has apparently had a stroke or a meltdown or something. He's standing on the tower talking to himself or to people that he sent away or... I don't know. Angels or something. Who knows. I'm taking an infantry company and going up there." He turned to the runners waiting on him.

"Find General Figg, tell him he is now in command of 5th Corps as I have been summoned to the tower. He is to continue a fighting withdrawal in cooperation with Generals Thomas and Vanhoose. Understand?"

"Yes sir!"

"Off with you," he motioned them on their way before turning back to Thomas.

"You have a solid company commander who has a company that's still mostly intact?"

"Yes," Thomas nodded. He turned and caught the attention of a young captain, motioning for the young man to join them. He trotted over, sword in hand.

"Sir?"

"This is Captain Charles Thomas," General Thomas told Springfield. "No relation," both he and the young Captain said at the same time and chuckled in unison at their old joke. "Captain, gather your men and accompany General Springfield. You will take orders from him and only from him until I tell you otherwise. Do you understand what I'm telling you?"

"I do, sir," the younger man nodded gravely.

"Then double quick about it," the general ordered. The younger Thomas hurried back, bellowing commands to his men.

"Is he really no relation?" Springfield asked without thinking.

"No, he's a distant cousin, but it's distant enough not to matter," Thomas smiled tiredly. "We've joked about it off and on since he joined my command. He's a bright young man with a good head. He will serve you well."

"Thanks."

-

"Fordyce is moving this way and will hook up with you on your left," Allen had to yell to be heard since Milton Vaughan firmly believed he couldn't command unless he was actually in the fight himself.

"Okay," Vaughan nodded. "How far are we going?"

"If we can keep them running, I'd like to chase their ass all the way across the Ohi!"

"Sounds like a plan to me!"

-

"Who is that?" Wilson demanded, seeing a group of men moving toward him. "Are they deserting? Running?"

"I think that is General Springfield, sir," an aide replied, silently adding *Lord, hear my prayer.*

"What in hell's creation is he doing back here?" Wilson demanded as Springfield reached the tower. "Springfield, what are you doing here?" Wilson shouted down before anyone could answer.

"Just a minute," Springfield replied, climbing. Captain Thomas and a full squad of his men were ahead of him. By the time Springfield reached the top of the ladder the platform was very crowded indeed.

"What's the meaning of all this?" Wilson demanded. "I don't have time for this foolishness! And why the hell aren't you up there, leading your corps in the attack I commanded just minutes ago?"

"General Wilson, our men are in retreat because they're getting the ever-loving shit beat out of them and there is no way to stop it short of hopefully containing it within our own lines. That is just a fact of nature, sir, and it will not change. Do you understand that?" Springfield asked carefully.

"I understand that I ordered them to attack and that is damn well what they had better do or I will hang the lot of them!" Wilson all but screamed, spittle flying from his mouth. "Now you get your ass back down there and-,"

"General Wilson, it pains me to do this, but you leave me no choice," Springfield cut in gently. "I hereby relieve you of your post as commander of this army pending a medical evaluation of your fitness to command. It is obvious to me that you have suffered a malady of some kind and are not in your right mind. Captain Thomas and his men will escort you to the nearest medical tent where you can receive care." He nodded to the Captain without waiting for Wilson to reply.

"Sir, if you'll come with me, we'll get you some assistance," Thomas said softly.

"Springfield, I'll see you hung!" Wilson screeched. "Captain, take this traitor to the stockade!" he demanded of Thomas.

"I'm sorry sir, but I can't do that," Thomas said firmly. "I need to get you to the medical tent as soon as possible sir. If we delay it could mean serious damage to your health." *Like being thrown off the tower for instance*, he didn't add.

"I gave you-," Wilson started but Springfield was looking at Thomas.

"Take him bodily to the ground and then to the doctor. Stay with him. Do not allow him to issue any more orders but don't let him come to harm."

"Sergeant," Thomas said simply and a burly sergeant stepped forward with two other men. One to each arm guided a still protesting Wilson to the ladder and then tied a rope under his arms. The now deposed general was still cursing as they began to lower him to the ground.

"Go," Springfield nodded to Thomas, who nodded back silently and descended out of sight. Springfield turned to look at the commands staff.

"Find me some runners."

-

Parno watched Fordyce's division fall back and reform, nodding in silent approval as they galloped north and began to extend the line as 1st Corps now covered the area the cavalry had been covering before.

"Good move," he murmured. He had grown nearly immune to the almost constant barrage of explosions walking their way through the enemy formation, more of a gaggle than anything at this point, killing scores of soldiers with each round.

"They're pack in so tight they can't get away," Parno laughed. "We're heaping the damage on them and there's nowhere for them to go!"

Davies and Enri Willard exchanged uneasy glances at the Marshal's glee over such wholesale slaughter. Cho Feng watched them both with care, for the first time not certain the two were worthy of his young warlord. Their hesitancy and squeamishness were uncommon. He hoped it was merely concern for being caught over extended that made them so.

"Looks like they're getting organized, dammit," Parno's voice drew everyone's attention back to the battlefield. "Their retreat is getting at least a little organization about it in their rear areas. Won't help those packed in so tight up here but it will prevent us from killing them all." His voice rang with regret at that.

"We are still inflicting heavy casualties on them milord," Davies replied. "They are paying a very heavy toll. Much higher than their last attack."

"That is true," Parno nodded thoughtfully, Davies' earlier offense apparently forgotten. "Still, I had hoped for more. I'm not ungrateful, just hoping for more. Our men have performed splendidly in this action and no more could be asked of them. It isn't anything they have done or left undone. Sometimes the enemy gets something right as well."

"They haven't escaped yet, milord," Enri Willard joined in. "They're only just getting themselves organized and even that only in the rear areas. We may yet damage them greater."

"Perhaps," Parno nodded agreement even as a thoughtful look crossed his face. "I hope Wilbanks is alert for this."

-

Preston Wilbanks sat by with his small escort as the last of his men moved past, with Wilbanks own aid and two squadrons of cavalry bringing up the rear.

"We have accounted for everyone, General," the young captain informed him. "We have retrieved our dead and all our horses as well, other than one horse that was killed in action along with his rider. We stripped the horse of its gear and the trooper is draped over another animal. We are the last to leave the engagement zone."

"Well done," Wilbanks declared. "We're moving north for two or perhaps three miles. Scouts are looking for a way west and when they locate it we will head that way for an hour and then strike back south to reach our own lines. I'm satisfied we have done a tremendous amount of damage to the Imperial war machine. You agree?" he looked around him.

"Yes sir," came the chorus and Wilbanks laughed.

"Then let's be gone from here, gentlemen," he ordered. "I'd say we might be able to get a good drink tonight, we play our cards right!"

-

Major Greg Tandy watched the last of the Soulan cavalry depart through his glass, sighing in relief that they hadn't decided to attack his men in their small thicket. He turned his attention back toward their camp and his sigh this time was one of defeat. Once again, the southern cavalry had ravaged the army's rear areas. Despite all the warnings of history repeating itself, here they were, everything lost. Most everything anyway. He turned to the men assembled behind him.

"Look boys. We have a few minutes to make sure we're supplied. You know as well as I do that when the infantry gets back they will strip this place bare. We got lucky that our camps weren't in their path, but every supply depot in this area is a smoking wreck. Captain," he looked at the second highest ranking officer in the group. "Organize men into parties and have them scour the camp, looking for wounded. While we're at it, we will also look for equipment and food supplies we can use. Bring anything you find to the General's mess tent in the Division commons and we'll stash it out of sight. Maybe we won't starve," he said bleakly. "Those of you who aren't mobile enough to help with that can start helping to clear away any damage to our areas. Some of you have your camp outside of our division area, so strike your tents and bring them here. We need to stay together or we may find ourselves in a world of hurt. Now get moving!" he clapped and men started moving.

Tandy turned to look at the damaged camp once more, shaking his head slowly. This morning a mighty army had been camped here. Hundreds of thousands of men. The best trained, best equipped army in the history of the Empire some had said.

How much of it remained? How much would survive what was to come?

-

"Better," Springfield nodded as he watched what remained of the Imperial Army beginning to organize their resistance. He turned to the senior staff member still present.

"You said Wilson sent a runner to Venable and Baxter with orders to return?" he asked.

"Yes sir," the man nodded. "But at best it will be-,"

"At least two days, I know," Springfield nodded. "I don't think the Soulanies will press this attack," he added, turning back to the battlefield. "They've hurt us and they know it. Why waste their men against us when there's no need?"

"Perhaps, sir," a new voice replied, "but they do want us out of their lands and this is an ideal time to press their attack. I doubt they shall ever have a better time and they will recognize it." Everyone turned to see Britton Sterling standing by the ladder.

"Sterling, where have you been?" Springfield demanded.

"Assisting our few wounded to the remaining medical tents, sir," the young brigadier replied. "I was ordered away pending court martial but thought I would see if you required my assistance."

"How did you let things get this bad?" the older man demanded. Sterling seemed to stand straighter at that, his face reddening with anger.

"General, with all due respect, you may be able to make decisions as you have, but I cannot. I lacked the power or the authority to do so. I have taken every opportunity to urge caution to General Wilson, to the point of being threatened with hanging. There was nothing else for me to do. If they are truthful then the others will bear witness to that."

Heads nodded all around as the staff officers agreed. Springfield looked at them in turn before nodding himself.

"Very well. Tell me then, what is the state of our camps?" he ordered.

"We have lost well over eighty percent of our stores, General," Sterling didn't try to soften the blow any as he didn't know how. "We have lost all of our artillery, though some pieces may be salvageable. However, our artillery crews have been all but eliminated by the southern cavalry raid."

"We have three remaining medical tents on the far left," he continued. "All others have been destroyed along with their supplies. All personnel in those tents are either confirmed dead or unaccounted for. Civilian and non-combatant personnel within the camp have also been killed save for a handful of smiths and the wranglers watching over the horses that are unfit for service. Ambulances kept ready to retrieve the wounded were destroyed, burned, and their horses taken. Tenting in most areas has been burned, all of it destroyed westward of roughly the center of the camp. We've also-,"

"I get it," Springfield held up a hand. "We're crippled."

"At best, sir," Sterling nodded.

"You say some artillery may be salvageable?" the older man asked.

"Possibly, but someone with more expertise than I have in that area would have to examine them to make sure. The pieces further west of here were all set fire after being coated with oil and pitch. I doubt they can be saved."

"I need you to go and reorganize what's left of the medical parties," Springfield said finally. "We're going to have a lot of wounded. Hopefully we'll be able to pull most of them out with us, but I don't know yet. Take whatever tenting remains as necessary to give the doctors a place to work. Take half the company below to help you and corral anyone else you can. Send a runner back if you discover anything else that I should know right away. Otherwise report back when you've had a chance to record everything so I can take a look. I need to know what we still have and what we're still capable of."

"Yes sir."

-

"Milord!" a runner breathed heavily as he got to the top of the tower. "Major Lars compliments milord. The enemy is moving beyond his range and 1st Corps is moving into dangerous territory within the pocket! He requests they stop or else requests permission to cease fire. We are at the edge of the range where accuracy can be guaranteed."

Parno sighed in defeat as he realized that what remained of the northern army was going to escape.

"Very well," he said at last. "Tell him to cease fire. General," he looked at Davies. "Sound recall. Recall and Reform. Enri, send runners to Allen for recall as well. Return to camp." He nodded to a lieutenant standing to the side.

"Raise the red pennant, lieutenant. This engagement is decided."

-

General Springfield watched in silent thanks as the southern cavalry began to pull back, away from what was left of his army. He could hear bugles blowing from across the field and realized that they were calling it a day. The sudden quiet as the southern artillery had ceased fire left him wondering what was wrong.

"Runners to all corps commands," Springfield addressed the men behind him. "Return to line of embarkation, bringing any wounded that can be retrieved. Men to sleep in line of battle behind our formations. Once that is accomplished all corps commanders or senior surviving division commanders are to report to headquarters." He paused as he watched the army struggling to return.

"We have to save what we can."

-

"Damn it!" Parno muttered under his breath as he watched the Imperial Army returning to their lines, out of his sight. "I was so close. I really thought we had them."

"We've still accomplished a good deal here, sir," Enri Willard offered. "The exchange was brutal but completely in our favor."

"But it may not have been decisive," Parno replied. "It may not have been enough to get rid of them."

"You can order your cavalry to pursue," Feng noted, his tone not endorsing or dismissing, merely taking note. Parno was shaking his head.

"No. They're exhausted and their horses are too. And they've taken losses. We may have come out better, but we got hurt, no doubt. No, get them back," he turned to Davies and Enri Willard. "Get them back behind our lines, fed and cared for. And I don't want a single Soulan trooper left on the field. Dead or wounded, I want them all back." He turned back to the field.

"And kill any Nor wounded still out there."

-

It was quiet in the carriage. They had stopped for lunch and a call of nature but then returned to the road in less than twenty minutes, allowing the horses a break as they walked for an hour rather than taking a faster pace.

Harrel had awakened, ate a bit and drank some water. With the assistance of two larger troopers had made a nature call and then returned to his quilts where he passed out from exhaustion. Now they were back at speed, moving briskly along once more.

Stephanie was looking out the window, thinking back on the two weeks and odd days she had just spent at the front, much of it with Parno. A faint smile came to her lips as she thought of how things had turned out.

"That's a very nice little smirk, dear," Edema broke the silence, looking across at her. Stephanie laughed softly, trying not to wake Harrel.

"I suppose it is," she admitted.

"I believe the words 'thank you' are in order," Edema arched an eyebrow, humor sparkling in her eyes despite the situation. Stephanie nodded, acknowledging her debt to the older woman.

"More than a mere thank you, Edema," she smiled again, wider this time. "More than anything."

"Did the two of you make any long-term plans?" Edema asked.

"We didn't actually do much planning of any kind," Stephanie admitted, a faint blush coloring her cheeks. Edema giggled slightly.

"No, I suppose not," she teased. "Well, at least things between you two are good again, yes?"

"Oh yes," Stephanie replied slowly. "Very good."

"Splendid!" Edema beamed, but her smile faded quickly. "I'm sure it will be alright, dear," she added in a softer tone.

"I imagine so," Stephanie nodded. "He had been expecting their move for several days and had been planning for it. I don't know what he knew or specifically what he had done, just that he thought he had managed to outmaneuver his enemy." She sighed as her hands fidgeted in her lap.

"It will be days before we learn anything of what happened," she said, looking once more out the window carriage.

"Yes," Edema nodded. "And longer for me," she added. "We will stay a night or two at the palace but it's far past time for me to be at home."

"Yes, I suppose it is," Stephanie agreed. "I'll miss having you around."

"I doubt that," Edema snorted. "Wasn't that long ago you didn't want to be near me."

"Well, anyone can be wrong," Stephanie shrugged, serious, but then her mischievous side took over. "Without your deceit and treachery and underhandedness and-,"

"Just a simple 'thank you' will suffice," Edema sighed, shaking her head in mock sadness as she returned to her novel. "After all I have done for you, too..."

Stephanie's laugh could be heard well outside the carriage as it continued to roll southward.

-

"How are we doing?" Winnie asked as she surveyed the work around the square in Carroll.

"Fine," the engineer nodded. "They have a handy few people and young Mister Garrett's men are a welcome help. Good strong lads. The palisade will be nearly finished by nightfall I should think. The townspeople can finish the front berm themselves without difficulty."

"Good news," she smiled. "Remember the platforms for the archers," she added.

"I was doing this work long before you graced the world with your presence, milady," the old engineer chuckled. "We shall not forget."

"Thanks," she smiled again and impulsively leaned in to kiss the old man's grizzled cheek.

"Wha-, stop that!" the old man spluttered in surprise. "What would my wife think!" he added with a twinkle in his eye.

"She'd just think you were the same old charmer that first caught her eye," Winnie laughed. "If you need anything just send someone after me. We'll be on the range most of the rest of the day," she returned to business.

"Will do, milady."

-

Everyone has reported back, milord," Davies reported.

"Pull Freeman and Herrick off the line and let Graham's men stand to for now," Parno ordered. "They aren't gonna hit us again for a while, if at all. Graham's men are in good shape. Let Freeman and Herrick rest and refit."

"Very good, milord," Davies nodded, scribbling hasty orders and handing them to runners.

"I want estimates on our losses as soon as possible, but don't interfere with anything else," Parno added. "I'd also like a ballpark estimate of Nor losses if we can guess at it."

"Yes sir," Enri Willard nodded.

"And make sure our screen and scouting elements are on the ball," he added finally. "I don't want that bunch to the west to come storming back and catch us off guard. Plus, I want to know the instant they decide whether they're returning or headed south."

"We'll see to it sir."

-

General Darrell Thomas placed his surviving men in the center of the Imperial fortifications, knowing that despite their fatigue they would be the best remaining force in the army to anchor the line in the event of an attack. Passing the burned-out skeletons of destroyed artillery pieces reminded him not to expect much to be left of their camp. He was moving to the eastern part of the area covered by his men when he ran into General Vanhoose.

"You're taking center?" Vanhoose asked without preamble.

"I thought it best," Thomas nodded. "My men are tired and I took losses but compared to Abe and Calisto, we're in better shape."

"I'll take from your left to the river then," Vanhoose nodded. "We'll have to stretch out of our old emplacements but we're like you; we got hurt, but nothing like those two. I heard that Eric-,"

"Probably gone," Thomas nodded. "And no one has seen Jurgen since early on, either. I'm hoping we can scrape together enough from them and Abe's men to handle the right side of the line. I know they got hammered pretty bad."

"I'd say that's an understatement," Vanhoose nodded. "And this camp looks like the landscape of hell," he added, looking around at the smoke from hundreds of small and large fires.

"Yeah, it's pretty bad," Thomas sighed. "From what I hear we'll be eating light for a while."

"You're assuming that the Soulanies don't come screaming across that field in the morning to finish the job," Vanhoose declared flatly.

"I think they'll wait and see if we leave on our own," Thomas speculated. "They know how bad they hurt us."

"True."

Preliminary reports from corps commanders, sir," Enri dropped several papers on Parno's desk. "Also, an estimate from General Wilbanks on the damage he was able to inflict on the Nor camps."

"I'm most interested to know that, too," Parno dug through until he found it.

"He did a number on them for sure," Enri nodded. "We may not have killed them all today, but I'd say they'll damn sure be hungry by this time tomorrow if not sooner. And their wounded won't be recovering any time soon, either."

"Men sleeping in the open, possessions destroyed, support personnel killed," Parno was nodding as he scanned the report. "Outstanding!"

"Yes sir."

"Losses?" Parno set the paper down and looked up at his Chief of Staff.

"Just estimates so far, milord," Enri replied.

"What are they?"

"4th Corps lost over five thousand killed and some eleven thousand wounded. Some are slight, some may not live to see the sunrise. 5th Corps lost similar numbers with just under six thousand killed and slightly over nine thousand wounded. 1st Corps reports an estimate of nine hundred dead and one thousand seven hundred wounded."

"General Allen reports total losses of four thousand two hundred killed and four thousand nine hundred wounded. He also reports they lost roughly two thousand horses dead and another thousand or so injured. Some maimed and others only slightly so." Willard paused.

"Sir, considering the nature of this engagement, those numbers aren't bad at all," he pointed out finally. "Any loss is bad in my book, but... there's no way to avoid losses in war. My father once called casualties the currency of combat. General Davies says that all a good soldier can ask is that his commander spend him well. I'd say we spent well today, all things considered."

"We did what we had to," Parno nodded. "Very well. If we're short of anything let me know at once. I don't think we'll see any action from the Imperials tomorrow or for a while after that either. We still have to be wary of that bunch to the west, but until we see how they jump, we'll use this time to get refit."

"We're already working on it, milord," Enri promised. "All smiths are in the cavalry camp even tonight, hammering out shoes. Wranglers and horse doctors have been working for hours already. And all of our wounded save maybe the last few from the cavalry engagement are in hospital already. Our training and organization are paying off in spades tonight, sir."

"Good," Parno nodded. "Good."

Enri paused again, seemingly searching for the words to say what was on his mind. Parno waited, having guessed at what was coming.

"I'm sorry about earlier today, milord," Enri finally said. "My job-,"

"You job is to caution me," Parno held up a hand, cutting the apology off. "You did. You and General Davies did exactly the right thing. As I told you on the tower, even if you had left there were no hard feelings and would have been no repercussions. I can't very well condemn someone for doing their job properly, now can I?" he smiled slightly and Willard let out a small laugh.

"Be bad for morale, I imagine," he admitted.

"Then let's say no more about this," Parno ordered. "You did nothing wrong. Neither of you. I saw an opportunity and I took it. It was risky, but I had planned for those risks as best I could. As you said, all we can do is spend well. I tried to make sure we did that today."

"I think you accomplished that just fine, milord."

"We'll see."

CHAPTER TWENTY-NINE

-

"Report, gentlemen," Abe Springfield ordered softly. They were sitting in the open, the small building Wilson had used as a headquarters now a smoking ruin.

"2nd Corps can muster around thirty-one thousand two hundred and twelve men fit for battle," Joel Vanhoose started. "More or less fit, anyway," he added with a sigh. "We lost at least nineteen thousand men, killed and wounded, and the count is still going. I should have a hard number later tonight or by first mess in the morning."

"3rd Corps has thirty-nine thousand, seven hundred and ninety-one men on line at present," Thomas was next. "Our loss estimates are also still being tabulated, but the estimates so far is three thousand eight hundred dead and seven thousand three hundred wounded."

"4th Corps has about eighteen thousand men fit for duty," General William Kelby reported softly. His head was sporting a bloody bandage as was his left hand. "We have over thirty thousand men either dead, wounded or missing. No way of separating them at the moment. I have staff officers looking through the hospital areas for our wounded. We brought out every man we could reach. General Jurgen is missing as is all of his staff, believed to have been caught in the cavalry envelopment during the Soulanie counter-attack. And when I say fit for duty, know that I mean able to stand to," he added finally. "I doubt they would actually hold in a determined attack. 4th Corps was shattered."

Springfield nodded silently.

"5th Corps," General Braidy Figg went next, "has twenty-two thousand and seven hundred men on the line at present. I won't say fit for duty because they're broken, most of them. Our losses will top twenty-five thousand dead, wounded or missing, but no way to break it down or give you a final number tonight. It's bad, though. Crippling," he told his former corps commander. Springfield nodded again, knowing it was going to be bad. They all turned to the last man at the fire, and also the most junior.

"6th Corps... has pretty much ceased to exist," Brigadier Stanley Moxie reported softly. "I'm the senior surviving officer that we can find at the moment. We have a little over six thousand survivors so far."

Survivors. The word hung in the air around the small fire. That was exactly what they were, too; survivors. The men of 6th Corps had survived the worst defeat in recent Imperial history.

"We have taken many wounded to the hospital tents," Moxie continued. "I don't know that all of them were ours, we were grabbing men from the ground from anywhere and tossing them over shoulders. The southerners were carrying a black flag," he looked at the general officers around the fire. "The men saw it, too. Hard to miss when you have thousands of men who scream like demons from hell riding you down. No one we left on the field will be alive in the morning." He stopped and shook his head slowly.

"I'll try and have a definite report for you tomorrow sir, but... don't expect it to improve much. There's no command staff remaining at all, and our support personnel were caught in the cavalry attack on the camp. There's... nothing left. Just a few of us who managed to get away."

"I understand, Brigadier," Springfield nodded. "Do what you can and we'll talk about what to do with your men in a couple days. Right now, the important thing is to take care of the men who survived."

"As you say sir," Moxie nodded slowly.

"Well gentlemen, things are bad," Springfield said to the group. "No sense trying to put a good face on it either. We're fucked. We've lost damn near half the army in this debacle and the half we got back we can't feed. Most of our equipment is gone, our artillery is destroyed, hell we don't even have tents for our men since we took what little was left to provide for the wounded."

"Wagons and ambulances burned, horses taken, support staff and personnel killed where they stood," he went on. "Seventy percent of our medical staff killed along with any wounded they were treating in hospital. And Wilson had to be relieved of command," he finished with a sigh. "I don't know how well known it is yet, but Wilson apparently had some kind of nervous breakdown when the Soulanie cavalry hit. He was more or less babbling by the time they sent for me. Threatened to hang his Chief, then to hang all of our men for 'retreating'. I tried to reason with him and found his mental faculties to be impaired and relieved him of command." He paused for a minute.

"I expect I'll be executed for it, but... better for me to be killed than to just continue throwing our men's lives away. I did what I thought was right and that's all anyone can do. Now," he looked around the fire.

"Here's another cold, hard truth. We can't stay here. We don't have enough supplies left to feed this army tomorrow, let alone for the time it would take for sufficient supplies to reach us from the north. We are screwed and there's no two ways about that. The nearest place for resupply is Louisville, and there won't be much there, either. We weren't scheduled to receive another supply run for a month yet, so I doubt there's even a train ready or supplies gathered to bring to us yet, and it would take nearly two weeks for a slow and ponderous train to get here. A train that would attract Soulanie Cavalry like melons attract a hornet. They'd swarm it just like hornets in fact and we wouldn't get a damn thing out of it."

"We've got a few horses, but most of them are in terrible shape. Some were put down already from what I understand. We're in a jam that I can't see a way out of that doesn't include abandoning our wounded to die and leaving General Venable's corps on their own in enemy territory. Wilson sent a runner to tell him to return here, but who knows if he made it through? I'm sending another tomorrow morning, but assuming Venable has already arrived in Unity it will take a day at least for the message to reach him and a minimum of three days for his units to return."

"He carried supplies for about five weeks in unsupported operations, and he has all of our remaining cavalry with him. With those supplies we can feed the army as we move north, using his baggage train to move our wounded. We can spend that three or four days on half rations and see if we can rebuild a few of our wagons, even if they're just buckboard style, to transport wounded north on. We'd have to depend on horses that are weak and not trained too well for traces, but it would be better than nothing which is what we have now."

"I am wide open to suggestions at the moment," he admitted. "I've tried to cover what I can, but I'm not going to fool myself that I know everything. So, if you have ideas, trot them out. Now is absolutely the time for it."

Silence reined for a moment as the others digested what he had said. Moxie was the first to speak, surprising himself as much as the others.

"We can't try to surrender," he said gently. "Soulanies aren't accepting any surrender. Whatever we do, that has to be off the table."

"Agreed," Springfield nodded. "They're ruthless bastards this time around, though I can't blame them. If they were invading us, I'd be the same way." Heads nodded at that.

"If we can salvage the wagon wheels and axles then we can just use logs to build platforms on them," Vanhoose said finally. "Pile blankets in there to soften the ride, maybe pine boughs beneath that, try to cushion the ride as much as possible. We don't have enough axles even if we save all of them to need all the horses, so plan to use eight or ten horses per wagon and that might take some strain off them. We could move more and move faster that way."

"Good idea," Springfield encouraged. "Whatever we can salvage will help."

"We may can get wheels and axles from some of the artillery, too," Thomas suggested. "Even if they aren't normal wagon wheels, it beats nothing."

"Also true," Springfield nodded. "Hadn't thought of that. Good idea."

"Nothing says we won't be attacked on the way home," Figg hated to bring it up. "It's a long and dangerous trip back to the Ohi. Moving like we're talking about might take two weeks or more. That's a long time for southern cavalry to be riding up our ass."

"Nothing we can do about that," Springfield shrugged. "It's a valid point but there's still nothing we can do. We will use Baxter to the front and Venable to the rear to try and protect us as much as possible, but that's really all we can do."

"We might send a man with a flag of truce to let the Soulanie Marshal know what we're doing," Kelby suggested. "Tell them we're leaving and ask for safe passage north."

"Never happen," Thomas said at once and both Vanhoose and Springfield nodded in agreement. "They won't pass up the chance to completely destroy us if they can. All that would do is set us up better for them to tear apart."

"I have to agree," Springfield said when Thomas fell silent. "They'll know in a few days anyway. If they're inclined to let us go, then they will without our asking. If not, there's no need to give them extra time to cut us off."

"Have the able-bodied men cut saplings to make stretchers from blankets and tent canvas," Moxie threw in. "We have thousands of men who aren't injured that can carry a man on a stretcher between them. It will be difficult, but it can be done. We can also rig travois behind individual horses to pull men behind, or what little supplies or equipment we can save. Tent canvas works but a strong wooden frame will help the canvas last. It only has to make it to the Ohi, after all."

"Damn good idea," Springfield enthused. "Another I hadn't thought of and it will work, too. Alright, we seem to have the start of a working plan here. Good ideas to follow up on and gives us plenty to keep the men busy. We start at daybreak trying to get out of here. Assuming we can get Venable and Baxter back here in five days, I want us ready to go no later than the day after, once they've had time to rest. Meanwhile, we need to try and feed our men. I'll work on that in the morning. Probably be horse meat," he admitted. "But we should still have some cattle somewhere back there, so that's a start. We can slaughter them and start smoking them over open fires. We'll jerk some of it in strips and give them to the men to carry on the road north. Get some sleep gentlemen," he stood, ending the meeting.

"We're still in a battle, and we better win this one."

-

"Will we stay another day, milady, or do you plan to leave in the morning?" Case asked as dark neared.

"What do you think?" she asked him. "What do all of you think? Are they far enough along that we can let them finish on their own?"

"I think so," the old engineer nodded. "They have some good hands and they know their business. We've set out a good plan and provided tools they didn't have enough of. They've too few able bodies, honestly, but Mister Garrett's men have cut trees for two days and we've hauled them all in close. They have the raw materials to finish what we've started."

"Many of them already were proficient with a bow, including a lot of the women," Winnie nodded. "We've provided them with extra bows as well as arrows, and they know how to make more. One woman told me cane is plentiful around here and that will make decent arrows. Not great perhaps, but not bad, either. Arrowheads might be scarce but we left a mold for the blacksmiths to use and they have raw materials."

"We've provided three dozen people who asked with swords and made sure they can use them," Conway offered. "They aren't good enough for militia, but they can at least defend themselves. But let's be honest here," he looked around the group. "A raid the size of the one that hit Nasil comes through here, none of this will last more than about ten minutes. The first eight of which will be the Nor bastards looking the place over, pardon my language," he nodded to Winnie.

"The best this will do is help protect them against small raiding parties and give them a fighting chance against any Tribals that come this far down. We've set them up pretty well. They either will or won't finish. They have to be willing to invest in their own safety at least as much as we do."

"True," Case agreed. "And we have started them on the right road. Are we all in agreement that they should be fine on their own?" Heads nodded around the circle. Case looked at Winnie.

"I would suggest we be on our way come morning then," he told her.

"I agree," she nodded. "Make it happen then. We'll make all preparations we can before bedtime and be ready to roll right after breakfast. Thank you all," she said, effectively dismissing the group.

"Three days to Jason?" she asked Case.

"Roughly," he nodded. "Depends on how good a time we make. But no more than four for certain, unless there's a problem with the bridges."

"No more ferry?" she asked.

"No more ferry."

"Good."

-

It was an exhausted bunch that stopped at the small inn along the road to Nasil, having ridden hard to escape whatever attack was happening. It was difficult for Stephanie and for Edema not to know what had happened, but they had to accept it. They would know as soon as word reached the palace. That was all they could hope for.

Harrel was exhausted just from travel and was placed in a room with a pair of young lieutenants who would look out for him. Stephanie checked his condition and helped him eat, then tucked him in for the evening.

There was very little discussion of the events of the day as the tired group ate, washed and then trooped to bed. With both escorts there was no shortage of manpower and the guard was strong during the night, just in case.

Despite her fatigue, sleep did not come to Stephanie Corsin-Freeman for a long time.

-

Parno read the remainder of the preliminary reports from his corps commanders while he ate supper, nodding on occasion and frowning upon others. Things had gone very well, but not as well as he had hoped for. Still, as Enri had said, they had done well.

It was strange to go to an empty tent that evening. He had come to expect Stephanie to be there when he arrived and had enjoyed talking with her about their day. He had never felt lonely in camp until now. Before his tent was just a place he came to sleep at night. For the last two weeks or so, it had almost been a home. It had felt right to come into the tent and find her reading or brushing her long hair or... just waiting for him to arrive.

Tonight, it felt wrong. He stripped out of his uniform and dropped across his bed, assuming he wouldn't sleep at all. Yet as he stretched out the fatigue and stress hit him and he was asleep in mere minutes.

He would dream of home tonight. Of the smell of food cooking, the sound of happiness in a home, something he had never known. He would dream of mundane days and romantic evenings and children running through the yard.

Tonight, he would dream of peace.

-

Memmnon wondered why he was edgy. He had no idea what was happening, anywhere. That wasn't unusual, but it was annoying. He missed Winifred. More than he had imagined he would, and he hadn't thought that possible. He had dined with her father the past two nights, the two talking pleasantly of anything other than the fact that she wasn't there. He absence ate at him, but there was no help for that.

He stood on his balcony overlooking the city and wondered where she was. What she was doing. Perhaps she was asleep already. He had no way to know any of that either.

It amazed him how as King, he knew so little of what was going on. He decided he would have to get used to that as well.

Just as he had to become accustomed to so many other things. His mind flitted briefly to Therron, and even more briefly to Sherron. Where was his wayward brother tonight? What lies was he telling to whoever would listen? What difference would it make? He shook his head slowly. It made no difference. Just something else he couldn't know.

Surrendering to that fact, he retired for the evening, telling himself as he did so, just as he did every evening, that tomorrow would be better.

Sometimes it even was.

-

Therron looked at the glowing lights of the Coastal Provincial Coalition governor's mansion with great delight. Finally, he was here! His carefully prepared presentation would be placed before the governor before the night was over, and he would finally be able to get the assistance he needed. Soon, very soon he would be on his way home to assume the throne.

The young captain leading his escort led them around to the side entrance of the mansion grounds, where the horses could be left and what baggage they had could be taken by the staff. Therron wasn't pleased to be taken to such a lowborn entrance but decided to hold his tongue for now. He could complain about that when he saw the governor. Just as he would complain about that Colonel. They would soon learn that even here the McLeod family wielded power. Great power indeed.

Therron left his horse with one of 'his' marines and marched toward the nearest door, walking into the mansion without even waiting to be announced. The entrance way was one for staff and residents, as evidenced by boots and cloaks left in the small foyer. Therron ignored that, tracking mud into the immaculate mansion without a care, walking steadily through the great house.

"You there!" he pointed to the first person he saw. "Take me to the governor! At once! Tell him that Prince Therron McLeod is here to see him at once!"

The man looked nonplussed for a moment and was clearly trying to formulate a reply. Therron didn't give him time.

"What is it man!" Therron demanded. "Speak, damn you!" Being spoken to so harshly seemed to remind the man of who and where he was, as he straightened himself to his full height, face reddening under such treatment.

"Good sir," the man's cultured voice was in contrast to Therron's bellowing. "The governor is not in the mansion at present. As you are a visiting dignitary I can provide you with a suite upstairs and the opportunity to..." he paused and looked Therron's disheveled appearance over with a jaundiced eye, "clean yourself and your clothing."

Therron almost goggled at the treatment this mere servant dared to show him. Striding forward in a determined manner, he stopped a mere hand's width from the man.

"How dare you! How dare you speak to me in such a manner! Now I demand you take me to the governor! At once do you hear!"

"Sir, as I said, the governor is not in," the man replied calmly. "He is-"

"When will he be 'in'?" Therron demanded.

"He and the government are scheduled to return in two months time, sir," the man took great relish in saying.

"Then I... did you say two months!" Therron's mouth caught up to his hearing.

"I did indeed, sir," the man nodded. "The governor and most of the government are presently at the summer mansion to the south. It tends to be cooler there are it is on the ocean front. They shall return here in the autumn. I should think two months, give or take two weeks or so. It depends on travel time."

Therron gaped at the response as he realized what he'd been told. He had to have been within a few days of this summer mansion when that bastard colonel had sent him here!

"I demand to be taken to this summer mansion at once!" Therron yelled.

"I'm afraid that won't be possible, sir," Therron heard and whirled to see his escort commander standing behind him in the doorway.

"I beg your pardon?"

"My orders were to deliver you here to the mansion, and keep you here until such time as the governor returns, or sends for you. We are here, and here we shall stay."

"And I say we're leaving in the morning and moving to this summer mansion!" Therron exploded. "You knew the governor wasn't here, damn you! Have the men ready to ride at daybreak!"

"No."

Therron had turned away from the captain when he heard that simple reply. He turned slowly back to face the younger man, his face purple with rage.

"What did you say?" he asked in what he assumed was a threatening manner.

"I said no," the captain seemed to take great relish in saying. "My orders stand, sir. Orders issued by a member of the Counsel itself and a member of the family of regents. His orders can only be over ridden by the governor himself. Those orders were to bring you here, at your request, and keep you here safely until the governor arrived. So, I suggest you make yourself comfortable and avail yourself of the amenities of the governor's home. Because you will be here for some time." He walked to the man Therron had been dressing down as Therron looked on the verge of apoplexy.

"My orders, sir," the young captain said respectfully.

"Good work," the man accepted the scrolls with a nod, eyeing the seals on them. "We will take things from here. You and your men should rest for a day or so and then return to your post."

"Yes sir," the captain snapped a salute off and whirled to leave.

"Before you speak again, let me introduce myself," the man before Therron said quietly. "I am Brigadier Norman Read Standish-Prescott, commander of the House Guard here at the mansion, and in charge of quarters until the governor's return. So, let me repeat my offer of a suite upstairs and a chance to freshen up. A meal can be sent up to your room, though it won't be anything fancy, I'm afraid, as most of the kitchen staff have gone home for the day. Still, we should have some leftovers remaining from dinner. Hunley!" he called out louder. In seconds a man in a dark suit appeared.

"Yes, Brigadier?"

"This is Therron McLeod, Prince of Soulan," Prescott's voice was amused rather than angry. "Set him up in the VIP suite on the second floor. He will be with us until the governor returns, at least. Then have Belinda prepare him a plate from the what remains of evening mess and take it up to his room. Extend him every courtesy of course," his voice reeked of sarcasm.

"At once, sir," the man bowed slightly. "If you will follow me, Prince McLeod?"

Therron fumed at such cavalier treatment.

"Do you have any idea who I am?" he asked softly.

"Of course, I do," Prescott scoffed. "You already told me who you were. Funny thing is, this is my cousin Nathan Standish's seal," he indicated the parchment in his hand. "His post is less than two days ride from the summer enclave. I have to wonder why he didn't tell you that."

Therron's mouth worked but no words would come. Standish had tried to talk to him but Therron had interrupted him with his demands.

"Nathan is the Governor's son, though I doubt you knew that," Prescott continued. "Standish is his mother's maiden name. My sister," Prescott's eyes darkened. "He uses it to avoid any hint of favoritism. I'm curious now to see what Nathan has included in this message. I'm sure it will explain why he thought it better to send you here rather than Directly to see Governor James."

"James?" Therron finally managed to speak. "What happened to-,"

"To Picon?" Prescott smiled. "Governor Picon had a fondness for the ladies, I'm afraid, and a habit of not taking 'no' for an answer. Unfortunately, he refused to take 'no' for an answer from the wrong young woman and her father killed him. Quite the scandal as you can imagine. Anyway, Nathan Hailey James is now the Governor of the CPC and head of the Governor's Council. One of the reasons he went early to the summer enclave was to organize his new government. I'm sure if he gets the details ironed out early he'll be back sooner. Meanwhile, Hunley will show you to your room. Do have a pleasant evening... Prince."

With that Prescott turned his back on Therron and departed, leaving him alone with the butler.

"If you will, sir?" Hunley prompted.

Therron followed the man without another word, stunned at the retinue of revelations he'd just been handed. Charleston gone. He had pissed off the new Governor's son, and now apparently his brother-in-law, too. And he was still almost three months from speaking to the governor.

With every step he climbed behind the butler, he felt his chances of becoming King of Soulan falling behind him. By the time he arrived in the suite assigned him, he knew that any hope of his getting assistance from the CPC was probably gone. And even if he did get it, in three months it would be far, far too late to matter.

All this way. All this bloody way, sleeping on rocks and trees, eaten alive by mosquitoes and other bugs. Eating horrible food while in the saddle... all for nothing.

All for nothing.

CHAPTER THIRTY

-

Parno was awake before breakfast and took the opportunity to walk through the camps. Once he would have done so alone or with just Harrel, but no more. Now he was surrounded by no less than twenty men, all looking as if another assassin was going to jump out from behind a tree any minute.

And maybe they would. After the last time, Parno didn't pretend to know what was happening any more.

The men were obviously tired, but even after the hard day they had endured, he could tell that morale was high. They had soundly beaten an army twice their size yesterday. They had every reason to feel good about that.

He finally made his way to his own command tent, his once again now that Harrel was on his way south, and found breakfast waiting for him there. He ate alone, in silence, reading through late reports that had arrived in the night. Scouting reports mostly from men trying to get in close to the Imperial lines.

It appeared that the Nor were in bad shape. Worse than he had first imagined, really. He would have to wait for Wilbanks' report to get a better guess at how badly the Nor camp had been damaged but so far things look promising.

He didn't kid himself, however. The knockout punch he had hoped for had evaded him. The losses to his own army might be less than the Nor, but they were no less painful for it. His army was now significantly weaker than it had been just two days prior. The Imperial Army was as well, but they still had numbers. Hopefully not enough, and more hopeful still they had too many to feed, but until they could verify any of that, all he had was supposition.

It would be a long day of waiting for reports and listening to reports and collecting information. Like a picture made from other pictures, he would have to assemble his overall impression from smaller impressions from all over the battlefield.

Such was his life.

-

"We're making good time," Winnie noted. They had been on the road for over an hour already.

"This is a good stretch of road," Case nodded in agreement. "Makes it easier to pull the wagons. We're moving at a good clip."

"Ever been to Jason before?" she asked.

"Once, about seven years ago or so," he nodded. "I was a new lieutenant at the time and made a sweep of the trade routes in the west. We stayed overnight in Jason, two nights really. It's a good-sized town. Largest in this area outside of Shelby."

"What's there?" she asked him, curious.

"It's mostly agrarian," he told her. "Livestock is a big thing there, but so are row crops, including silage. There are a lot of laborers that live on larger farms as full-time hands. Their pay isn't the best, but it includes room and board, which is a big deal."

"Sounds hard," she commented.

"It is," he nodded. "Back breaking labor at times, and not a little dangerous, especially cattle work. Trail work is even worse. But that pays better, too."

"We have too little area for large operations like that back home," she told him. "Like I said the other day, this is more flat land than I've ever seen before."

"Well, there's a lot of game here, too," Case pointed out. "You'd probably enjoy it, other than it being a good deal hotter here than where you come from."

"The air is heavier," she nodded. "I know that doesn't make sense, but it is."

"No, it is," he agreed. "And the humidity is almost always going to be worse. It's just one more difference in a long line of them."

"How long do you think we'll need to spend in Jason?" she changed the subject.

"No way to know until we get there and see what we see," he shook his head. "They may have a stockade already. Or at least a berm. May have an unorganized militia and be making patrols of their own. I know there is a small militia garrison there. Remember we asked for a squad of them to accompany the constable we sent for. But that garrison has a lot of ground to cover. I doubt more than twenty of them would be in town at any given time."

"It would be nice to find they're at least partially organized," she admitted. "That would give us more time working with the people who might have come from other areas, answering the runners."

"The more we can reach, the better," he nodded.

"I guess we'll just have to see what turns up."

-

"I think we can slow down today," Stephanie told Captain Winters as the carriage was being loaded and Harrel helped aboard. "I'd prefer we move more cautiously if possible, for Harrel's sake."

"We will," he promised. "Yesterday was just to get ahead of any possible threat. I would say that things went pretty well based on what little I heard before we left. The Prince had a sound plan and good contingencies. If the Nor weren't careful then he mouse-trapped them nicely as they tried to attack."

"I hope so," she sighed. "At any rate, thank you," she smiled.

"You're quite welcome, milady."

-

Abe Springfield had met the new day with trepidation and soon learned he was right to do so. By nine that morning he had learned the total of losses for the Imperial 1st Army from the previous day of battle. To call them 'ruinous' was too kind.

Ninety-four thousand, four hundred and twenty-eight confirmed dead. Thirty-eight thousand and twelve wounded, many of which were not expected to survive more than another day or two. More than half their original strength gone.

Worse, the supply situation was at least as grim as the one he had painted for them the previous evening, and the medical situation was much worse. The lack of medical professionals was going to increase the number of wounded that didn't survive and the lack of supplies to treat the wounded would just add to that number. The men who were still fit for duty, and that was stretching the definition of 'fit' beyond recognition, wouldn't be much better off either, with everyone already on half-rations of normal servings. That was made possible only because their cattle held for slaughter were well away from the areas visited by Soulan cavalry. He could smell beef roasting even now and was keenly away that he was just as hungry as any of his men were.

His messenger to Venable had left as soon as it was light enough to see, using one of the last fit horses in camp to ride for Unity and lay a message in Venable's hands as well as another for Baxter. There was some doubt in Springfield's mind that Venable would obey the command to return, denying Springfield's authority to issue such an order. Springfield didn't think Baxter would balk at taking orders from Springfield, but there was no real way to know until he saw what happened. Springfield suspected that once Venable had time to consider his position, cut off and beyond any hope of resupply, that he would see the sense in Springfield's orders and return as soon as possible.

That was all he could do at this point. He had too much on him to worry about it any further right now. He did know that his men would have to start north in no more than five days or risk them being too weak from hunger to make the trip and still carry the wounded. Men were out with axes this morning to cut small trees to make the frames for travois that would be strung behind the horses that were capable of pulling them. Wounded men would be placed there along with the few supplies they still had, pulled along the road by horses that were all but incapable of doing anything else. There was no guarantee they could pull the wounded for that matter, but it was all he had for now.

"Sir," a voice broke into his thinking and he turned to see the leader of his engineer unit waiting to report, hand raised in salute.

"Yes?" Springfield returned the salute.

"Sir, we can I believe salvage at least thirteen wagon frames from the wreckage. Using smaller logs, we can replace the burned wagon beds and use them to transport many of the worst wounded. But not all," he added sadly.

"Anything you can make work is better than what we have now, which is nothing," Springfield nodded in approval. "Go ahead and do what you can. Whatever it is, I'm sure the men will appreciate it."

"Yes sir," the man nodded and went about his business. Springfield watched him go and wished for a minute he could change places with the man. How nice would it be to hand all of this over to someone else and just take orders again?

"Sir," yet another voice, with yet another report, or problem. Suppressing a sigh, Springfield turned to see the next man.

"Yes?"

-

"Well, Preston, it looks as if you took my order seriously," Parno chuckled as he finished Wilbanks' report.

"Damn straight... er, milord," Wilbanks remember where he was.

"You and your men may well have just ended this war," Parno ignored Wilbanks discomfiture. "I don't know as yet what they will do, but my guess is they will go back north, assuming they have no large stockpiles of supplies nearby. Good work."

"Thank you, sir," Wilbanks nodded.

"According to this, you think you destroyed all of their artillery?" Parno asked.

"All they had deployed at any rate, milord," Wilbanks nodded. "Possible they have more that we didn't see, but anything they were using is gone. Burned and in some cases busted."

"Outstanding," Parno nodded firmly. "Are your men okay?"

"They are fit and ready for another go, sir," Wilbanks sounded enthused. "I think they saw the results of their training pay off and now they're ready to go at them again."

"I like that," Parno nodded. "But for now, rest your men and horses. If the Nor do take out for the north, we'll hound them all the way, and your men will be in the van of that operation. So, refit, rest and be ready for orders."

"Yes sir."

-

Parno read over his preliminary report once more, satisfied that he had left nothing of importance out in his dispatch to Memmnon. He included his own plans, contingent on what the Nor would do now, and how he expected things to progress if the enemy did as he expected.

Finished, he sealed the report with wax and his signet seal, the seal of the Crown Prince no less, and slid it inside a leather case that would be given to a Royal Courier. With a deep sigh he leaned back a bit, stretching his back.

"A weary sigh for someone who has won a great victory," Cho Feng's voice immediately robbed him of any relaxation as he jerked upright to see the oriental man standing before him.

"How the... you know what? I don't care," Parno waved his hand tiredly. "And yeah, I am tired. Stress more than anything, I guess. How are you?"

"I am quite well," Cho nodded. "What do you plan to do now?"

"I'm going to rest my army for two more days while I wait to see what my enemy does," Parno replied at once. "My men are tired and so are their horses. Their spirits are high, however, and I'm going to let them rest and enjoy it." He rose and walked over to the map.

"I expect the enemy to recall this group," he pointed to Unity, "which of course means I destroyed a town for nothing," he added bitterly. "They can't receive word of what happened here before this evening and more likely tomorrow before noon. I expect them to start back the next day, tomorrow assuming their rider makes it through by nightfall."

"Meanwhile, I expect the Nor still in camp to prepare to move north. Hopefully their plan is to leave Soulan altogether, but they should at least pull back to the Ohi, where resupply can be achieved easier. In the event they do withdraw, I'm going to hound and harass them all the way to the Ohi river, killing as many of their men as I can before they can cross over. After which I may burn the bridges there and at Shelby," he added softly. Feng raised an eyebrow at this news.

"I thought you wanted those bridges for what was to come next," he said quietly.

"And I may still," Parno nodded. "But... I'm not sure I still want to do that. I'm not sure I want to be responsible for the greatest war on this continent since... well, I don't know since when," he admitted. "And I'm not sure I want to put my army or my people through that again. Instead, I think I will concentrate on creating the most powerful army ever seen and hold them in preparation for when this could happen again."

"A strong standing army is costly," Cho warmed.

"So is an invasion," Parno rebutted. "No matter if it's them invading us or the reverse. I want to destroy them, don't get me wrong," he looked at his erstwhile teacher. "But the cost..." he shook his head slowly. "It has cost us so much so far.

The cost to invade, to conquer... it would be worse. So much worse."

"It would," Cho agreed. "It always is. You have but to look at your enemy to see it proven."

"Our navy has to rebuild and that will take time and money," Parno went on. "We still have internal issues that have to be dealt with. And we need to strength our interior. The Nor very nearly were able to defeat us in one fell swoop because we don't have much in the way of interior defenses. I'm going to change that. I'm going to change a lot of things, in fact," he added.

"You will still invade the north, won't you, Parno McLeod?" Cho said solemnly and Parno looked at him.

"You cannot hide it," the older man said calmly. "Every preparation you have mentioned merely strengthens your position once you decide to take your men across the River Ohi into enemy territory. You have not decided against such a move, only delayed it until you are confident of victory."

"Maybe," Parno said mulishly, refusing to admit that his teacher has seen right through him.

"There is nothing wrong with making proper plans, young Warlord," Cho chuckled at Parno's discomfiture. "Nor in making adequate and proper preparations. Your secret will be safe with me."

"Will you still be here to help me?" Parno asked him. "Or do you plan to return home if this is the end of our war?"

"For me, this land has become my home," Cho told him plainly. "I have no reason to return and every reason to stay. So yes, insofar as I am able, I will assist you. And should the gods allow it, then when you go north, I will ride at your side for so long as I am able to do so."

There was a comfortable silence between the two, broken only when Parno gave a quiet and heartfelt reply.

"Thank you."

-

"We'll make camp here tonight," Case said as he motioned for the wagons to circle on each other. "This is a good spot and there are two creeks, one to either side. We can get off the trail but still be right beside it. Easier to get moving come morning."

"Okay," Winnie nodded. "It's pretty here," she noted. "What are those buildings?" she asked, pointing to a collection of empty structures nearby.

"Part of an old community that once stood here," he told her, dismounting. "A very old community in fact. No idea how old that I've ever heard put into words. The buildings were strongly made and have stood the test of time. I daresay with a bit of work they could be made habitable again, should someone have the desire."

"Why come nobody does, then?" Winnie slipped back into her old way of speaking as she looked at the buildings.

"No need for it," Case shrugged. "There aren't a lot of people around here, really, and with the war on most of them are gone. This area is abandoned because there's no one around to live here."

"What's wrong with this place?" Winnie asked, correcting her way of speaking now.

"I didn't say anything was wrong with it," Case pointed out. "And as far as I know, nothing is wrong with it. There's just no one who wants to come this far out to live. It's a long way from anywhere out here."

"Okay, that is true," Winnie nodded, dismounting to join him on the ground. "Still, if someone established a trading post here, right along the route, then that make this place more attractive for settlement."

"Might well do it," Case nodded. "Be a good retirement project," he added thoughtfully.

"Hm," Winnie nodded slowly. "Might at that. Convince retired military men to settle somewhere like this. Maybe as constables to patrol the trade routes even?"

"Well... I hadn't thought of it in those terms," Case admitted. "I was talking about the trading post and maybe some farm or livestock operations in areas where there's just not anything else going on."

"That too," Winnie agreed. "Something to make note of, but we've got more than enough on our plate for now I recko... I should think," she corrected.

"That is true, but it's still a good idea," Case nodded.

"I think I'll have my secretary make a note of that," she said finally.

-

General Peter Venable looked at the smoldering ruin before him and wanted to curse. He didn't, mostly because it would not look appropriate or professional for someone of his stature and rank to be cursing in the midst of his command staff and whatever soldiers were close enough to hear him.

But he wanted to, nevertheless.

Unity, the village he and his men were to occupy, was leveled. Smoke was hanging over the area like a thin fog and there were still small flames flickering among the ruins, but the town was, for the most part, ashes. Not a single building was standing. The fire had spread from the town, igniting several small grass fires that had burned themselves out, but the heat from the ashes indicated the damage was recent, perhaps even overnight.

"What now?" Baxter asked him, eyeing the same ruins.

"What do you mean?" Venable asked, turning to look at the cavalryman. "Our orders aren't changed."

"True," Baxter nodded. "Still, we can't rightly occupy a village that doesn't exist anymore, can we now?"

"That is true," Venable nodded. "I suppose we make camp and send someone to tell Wilson what's happened. Meanwhile we... we secure this area and wait to see if we're attacked."

"I'll have a few patrols out to scout the area," Baxter nodded. "Make sure we're alone out here."

"Good," Venable nodded. "Four days to get here and this is what we-," he stopped as a rider came galloping up, almost sliding to a halt.

"General Venable, sir," the man saluted tiredly. "From General Springfield," he handed over a messenger bag.

"Springfield?" Venable's eyebrow rose at that.

"Yes sir," the man nodded. "He's taken command of the army, sir."

"What happened to Wilson?" Venable demanded.

"I don't know but for rumors, sir," the man admitted. "General Wilson had to be taken to medical, but I don't know for what. It happened while we were attacking."

"Attacking?" Venable hadn't liked anything he'd been told so far, and he especially didn't like this. "Why the hell were we-," he stopped himself short and opened the message. Baxter resisted the urge to look over his shoulder as Venable read through the message quickly and then again more slowly. His sharp inhalation of breath told Baxter that the news wasn't just limited to Wilson's health. Venable finished and handed the message to Baxter without comment.

Baxter read the terse message from Abe Springfield in silence just as Venable had. The losses to the army, the dire shape of the army and their camp, their supply problem, everything.

"This... this is a disaster," Baxter kept his voice low as he spoke, not wanting to stir trouble.

"And then some," Venable let out a breath he hadn't been aware he had been holding. "There's no point in starting back now, we'd not get far and the men are tired. We'll make minimal camp tonight and leave with the light tomorrow. We'll stay together. Either of our commands alone will invite attack so we'll stay together." He looked as if he expected Baxter to argue.

"Sounds like a good plan," Baxter nodded. "I'll still set out patrols to clear the area. This may be part of a larger scheme, and they know we're out here."

"Good point," Venable nodded. "I'll have camp established and we'll eat early. It's a three-day forced march back and that's without the heavy train we have. We'll be lucky to make it in four days. And we'll be in danger every step of it."

-

Parno looked at his map once more, preparing to turn in for the evening.

He was so tempted to send his cavalry after the group to the east. So much so that he had already written the orders out. Twice. Each time he had torn them to shreds, and that had lasted about thirty minutes before he had started thinking about it again.

Like right now.

It would be so easy. His cavalry, catching them by surprise, riding them down. Perhaps take a mounted infantry division to add to their numbers, add in Wilbanks, even the Black Sheep. An all-out effort to destroy this group before they could reunite with what was left with the main Imperial army.

But each time he held off. Each time he thought about the casualties he would be bringing on his own men and how many men and horses he might lose. Fifty thousand infantry and another twelve thousand cavalry would make for major battle. Even if they could catch them by surprise, which they wouldn't if the cavalry were even partly on the job.

But it was so tempting...

He abruptly stood, shaking his head. No, he wasn't going to give in. He had a good plan, he was in a good position and he was reasonably certain that his enemy was going to depart. They might wait for the group from Unity, or the spot where Unity once stood anyway, but he doubted they would wait for anything else.

No. He wasn't going to give in. He was going to bed. He would go to bed and he would get up tomorrow and see what the world looked like. With one last, long look at the map he turned off the lantern hanging in the center of the tent and left.

-

During the night a new line of thunderstorms developed over the western plains. While not nearly as strong as the line a few weeks prior, the one that had seen Parno return to the Hogshead Inn for more comfortable accommodations, this line was still strong and brought heavy rain with it. Rain that turned the ground to mud beneath soldiers who were camping in the open because of the minimal camp established near the empty, ash covered ground that had once been Unity.

Rain that fell none too gently on the circled wagons of the train that included Winnie Hubel and the people helping her with her mission. Winnie had lowered the small shutters on the windows of her carriage to keep the water out and lay listening to the rain drumming on the top. It was very similar to the sound of rain beating down on the roof of the small cabin she had grown up in. She found it to be a comfortable and calming sound, even with the slight wind rocking her carriage. The wind whistling through the narrow openings she had left in the shutters cooled the carriage and helped her fall into a deep and restful sleep.

In an inn now two days ride from the front, Stephanie someday-to-be McLeod heard the same sound and could not help but think about the last storm that seemed to blow her and Edema into the army camp. The same rain that had made them a day late arriving and had probably meant they had been there when Parno was almost assassinated, save only by the intervention of Harrel Sprigs, who was sleeping, she hoped, in the next room. Had it not been for the last storm she would have been gone when the assassins struck. While Parno would likely have survived thanks to Harrel, it was unlikely that the young secretary would have been so fortunate. As she drifted to sleep, she wondered idly if this rain would bring something useful with it.

Rain that made Parno McLeod, laying in his tent on the floor because there was a leak over his bed, think of a young woman he had known a mere few days but who had made a great difference in his life, giving her own in place of his.

Rain that soaked Abe Springfield to the bone because he refused to take one of the few remaining tents when so many men under his nominal command were laying in the open, staying dry any way they could. Rain that would make roads muddy and hard to travel on for at least two days, including the roads traveled by Venable and Baxter returning to the main camp, assuming they followed his orders at all.

Rain that washed the paint from Blue Dog's body as he lay under a stand of pine trees with some of his warriors, the others spread over several acres of thick woods, all the protection they required from the elements. He pictured the Imperial map Wilson had shown him in his mind, drawing a line from where they were to a large dot on that map that indicated a large population of people. People who would have no warriors to speak of and perhaps many women and much loot. He smiled faintly as random drops of rain fell on him through the leaves. The raiders moon would be soon indeed. And this storm would blow clouds from the sky. He would sleep well knowing that in a day or two he and his men would be headed for a rich target.

Rain fell, thunder crashed and lightning filled the sky. Not as violently as earlier but impressive no less. Memmnon McLeod watched that lightning and felt a keen sense of absence that Winnie Hubel left when she wasn't present. He wished she was here with him, but if wishes were granted then he would still be Crown Prince and there would be no war. He closed the balcony doors as the rain began to lash at the palace, leaning his head against the cool glass even as he reached to close the shutters to protect that same glass. He would sleep, eventually, but it would not be restful. He might be comfortable, but he would not be content.

Misery for some, comfort for others, and rain for them all. All night long.

CHAPTER THIRTY-ONE

-

"What a morning," Case sighed as he watched the train struggle to get moving. While the road was hard surfaced and resistant to rain, their campsite was not. Wagon crews struggle to get horses into their traces and then to get wagons moving in the mud. Eventually the men of Lieutenant Garrett's company used ropes with their horses to pull the wagons onto the road. Finally, two hours later than planned, the wagon train was once more on its way.

"It is indeed," Winnie nodded, riding beside him. "Not as bad as that last one, though. The one that kept us from leaving on time."

"No, I don't think so either," Case agreed. "The road is a good one, so while we're a little late getting started, it shouldn't hold us back any more."

"Another day to Jason then?" she asked him.

"Today and tomorrow," Case nodded. "We may make Jason by tomorrow evening, in fact, if we can make good time. If nothing else we should be close tomorrow night."

"Sounds good."

-

"Well, this is a fine morning indeed," Karls Willard said, sarcasm dripping from his voice.

"So, it is," Parno nodded absently, not taking note of the sarcasm.

"Rain is a necessary element for nature as well as man," Cho Feng pointed out serenely. "While it is often something to be endured, it is also beneficial."

"Always so cheerful," Karls sighed. "Why are you always so cheerful? Why is he always so cheerful?" he turned to Parno. "Why do we have to put up with that? All that... cheerfulness."

"One must look for the good in life, young warrior," Cho smiled brighter if that was possible. "To counter the dark times, one must have some light."

"Well, I need coffee before I can worry about light," Karls replied. "And maybe something to eat, too."

"Nourishment is a necessary component for a warrior, particularly in time of war."

Karls just shook his head as he accepted a bowl from a steward and sat down. Feng already had a bowl of mostly fruit. Parno had already had a bowl of raisin and apple mixed with oatmeal but found himself still hungry and asked for more. The steward nodded, hiding his surprise, and took the bowl to get more for the Marshal.

"You are preoccupied this morning," Cho mentioned, watching Parno from across the fire.

"I guess," he admitted with a nod. "I've been thinking about what to do next."

"What do you mean?" Karls asked. "We should definitely press our advantage, shouldn't we?"

"We're going to, but I'm trying to figure the best way to do that," Parno agreed. "There is still a sizable force to the west. Probably near Unity. The Nor should recall them now, may already have in fact, but I can't be sure of that until we see movement from them. And reports of them would take a day to reach us at best. Right now, they're over there," he pointed north to the Nor lines, "scratching for food and I hope trying to get ready to head home. That is the best-case scenario."

"My problem," Parno continued, "is trying to decide if I should make an attack on the returning column or let them team up with what's left of the Imperial Army over there. If I let them get back, then it will be harder to kill as many of them as we can before they can escape. But attacking them, even on the road, is sure to lead to many casualties. Would it be more costly to attack them alone, or wait until they are part of what's left of that lot over there?" he motioned to the north.

"I see your point," Karls nodded slowly. "Be nice if we could end the war, wouldn't it?" he asked out of nowhere.

"So, it would," Parno didn't look at him and Cho didn't miss that.

"The more you kill now the less you kill later, is that it?" Cho asked.

"Yes," Parno admitted. "I want to kill them all," he added with a ruthlessness that sounded strange but wasn't out of place. "I want it to look as if the land swallowed their army completely and left nothing. If they want to do this again they would need an entirely new army. Start from scratch."

"That would be awesome," Karls agreed, enthused by the idea. "Can we? Destroy them, I mean?"

"Maybe," Parno nodded slowly once more. "If we can get our artillery around them, maybe with mounted infantry in support, and catch them on their return home. We could at least force one last engagement, and a decisive one at that. Perhaps even more so than yesterday. For that matter," he plucked at his bottom lip, "Graham's men should be up to a hard forced march, and they're strong enough to protect the artillery... but, there's a problem," he sighed as he thought his plan through.

"And that would be?" Karls asked. "Cause I like the sound of that plan just fine, myself."

"It is ridiculously unsafe to transport Roda's gadgets," Parno reminded him. "Doing so quickly and over rough terrain is just asking for a calamity. A calamity of epic proportions, no less."

"Hadn't thought of that," Karls admitted, his early excitement now in abeyance. "And I don't relish facing those numbers without the special artillery," he added.

"Nor do I," Parno agreed. "We'd still have the Hubel arrows, but I honestly don't know how many are still in stock."

"What about the mines?" Karls asked. "They aren't so hard to carry. Place them on both sides of the road with crossbows waiting, detonate them as the Imps are even with them, and then let the cavalry sweep in to finish the job."

"I don't know how many mines we have, either," Parno had to admit. "We didn't use them in the attack so there are some still in the field, but I don't know what's left in storage. I do like the notion, though," he added, smiling ruefully at Karls. "Why not make a plan that uses that idea? I need it no later than tomorrow, though."

"Sure, I can do that," Karls agreed.

"Meanwhile, we need more information on what the enemy is doing," Parno accepted his bowl from the steward as he returned with more breakfast for the Marshal. "I'll have to see what we can come up with."

-

"We here," Blue Dog used a stick to make an X on the muddy ground. "Three days ride maybe to here," he made another X. "This," he indicated the second X, "is large Southmans city. Women, stock, much loot. We wait for raider moon and then we go. We rest here today, maybe tomorrow, too. We want ground to be hard enough to allow hard riding. Fast riding. We move and camp around here," he hit a spot near the second X, the one that represented the large city. "Then we hit city at daybreak. Have all day to raid, and then all night to ride. Be long gone before Southmans know we here. They all busy with Northmans right now. Good time for Lakonati to make war and take trophies. Agree?" He looked around at the faces circling him. All nodded.

"Rest men today," Blue Dog repeated. "Tomorrow too, maybe. We hunt, we prepare for long move. We take enough, we cross over and go home with what we catch, eh?" Smiles came to him at that.

"Send hunters to take game or Southman cows. We eat good while we dry meat for ride. Check horses, check weapons. Make sure we ready in two days. No more. Go."

They went, leaving Blue Dog to look at his rough sketch. He had lost a great deal of his reputation when the southern cavalry had intercepted their attack on the disorganized cavalry still on the field. He had lost many warriors and horses for no gain of any kind.

As a war chief, Blue Dog's power, his authority, was dependent on his ability to provide good targets for his men. Failing that, he needed to make his men rich through raiding. Hitting soft targets was an excellent way to do that.

His numbers had swelled again with recent additions from across the river and he now had over nine hundred warriors. Warriors who were well trained and experienced in the ways of war. They would follow him a little longer simply because he had always done well. One failure would not end him as a war leader. Continued failure would, however.

But with a soft target like this, there would be no failure.

-

Lieutenant Colonel Aubrey Jae Winburn shook his head in disgust as he shook the mud from his boots before mounting his horse. Last night's rain hadn't been too hard on them for the most part, taking shelter in abandoned barns and houses, but the mud was still there. As he settled himself into the saddle, Captain Cam Benn, the commander of the Pioneer company Winburn and his men were protecting, rode up beside him.

"Morning, Colonel," the engineer greeted. "Lovely weather we're having, what?"

Winburn had to smile at that. Benn just had a way about him that made you want to like him. It seemed he was always in a good mood, even when he had every reason not to be.

"It'll do until we get some good weather," Winburn replied with a chuckle. "Your boys ready to go?"

"We are," Benn nodded. "Don't see any need for it as yet, though. Tell me, Colonel, where are we supposed to wait for news of any movement south?" Winburn pulled a small but detailed map from his tunic and opened.

"Here," he pointed to a bridge over a small river. "About a half day ride from Jason. Word will reach us there if any southern movement is seen out of the Imps at Unity. Rider should reach us in a day, which gives us at least three days to do whatever damage we can."

"Should have been here," Benn said, examining the map and pointing a location much further north. "Good place to drop a bridge and prevent their movement. That's marsh country. Very difficult to maneuver in."

"It's also right on top of the Imps, and they have about a regiment of Tribals running around somewhere," Winburn informed him. "We can handle the Tribals, so long as we aren't caught unprepared. Handling sixty thousand Nor is a bit more than we can take on alone."

"Well, yes," Benn took the information in stride. "This is also a good place," he indicated the meeting place. "Not quite as good but completely doable. And we can certainly wreck it in less than a day."

"That's outstanding," Winburn nodded. "We should get there this afternoon late, maybe. We can make camp unless there are more abandoned areas nearby. Then, we wait to hear one way or the other." Winburn replaced the map in his tunic pocket.

"Sounds good," Benn nodded. "Well, let's get this circus moving, what do you say?" he grinned.

"I say yes," Winburn had to chuckle again. "Let's ride."

-

Abe Springfield listened to the chief medical officer as he rattled off a list of 'demands' that 'had to be met' in order for him to 'insure the wellbeing of the troops'. Finally, Springfield just held up a hand and silenced the man.

"Doctor, has it occurred to you that I have no way to provide those things right now?" he asked calmly. "That we are so badly in need of supplies due to enemy action that saw a great many of your own colleagues killed as well as seventy-five percent of our support staff and some ninety percent of our supplies?" The doctor hesitated before answering.

"I knew that many of the other doctors had perished," he admitted. "I was not aware of the meager supply issues. I thought we were simply not doing a good job distributing them."

"Can't distribute what you don't have," Springfield shrugged. "Right now, I'm trying to figure a way to move our wounded north when we go. We have almost no wagons, few horses that are serviceable, and no way to feed our men save for a small ration of beef. Beef that has to be stretched way to far because all of our meal, flour and beans were destroyed by the enemy. Had they seen the cattle I'm sure they would have taken them just like they did the trace horses from the wagons and artillery park." Springfield stood, hands at his side.

"The simple fact is that we'll be lucky to live out the week," he said flatly. "So, concentrate more on doing what you can with what you have, because it's all we do have. I've sent a runner on one of our last good mounts north, to the camps around Lovil. I don't expect them to have much, but maybe they can meet us half-way with what they do have. I'd settle for empty wagons to help haul our wounded in. At this point we're building travois to pull behind horses that may or may not be able to do the work. So, while I understand your problems, I can't do anything about them that isn't already being done."

"I see," the doctor nodded. "Perhaps... have we considered appealing to the southerners?" he asked hesitantly. "Perhaps even surrendering, or suing for peace in exchange for safe passage north and medical supplies for our wounded?"

"First of all, how do you think the Emperor would respond to that news?" Springfield asked and the doctor paled a good bit. "Secondly, the Soulanie are engaged in Black Flag warfare, doctor. That means they will not offer nor accept surrender. They intend to fight to the death and will kill every one of us if they get the chance. Including killing every wounded solider left on the battlefield and that were in the hospitals they destroyed. I seriously doubt they will be interested in any suggestion that they provide medical assistance to our men."

"Good God," the doctor almost whispered. "They're... barbarians!"

"Are they, Doctor?" Springfield asked. "If the situation were reversed and they were invading the Empire, do you not think we would follow the same practice? For that matter we have followed that practice in every war, including this one."

"We have?" the doctor blurted.

"Ever treated a wounded Soulanie soldier or civilian?" Springfield asked.

"Well... no."

"And that's why," Springfield nodded firmly. "So, no more talk of asking for mercy. The Soulanie are all out of mercy, doctor. They carry the Black Flag with them in every operation. A statement of their intent to kill us all. Now, return to your duties, do the best you can, and start preparing the wounded to move."

"Some of them won't survive such a move," the doctor noted.

"None of us will survive if we stay," Springfield shrugged. "We do what we can, with what we have."

-

"Well, this is a mess," Baxter muttered and Venable nodded. The two men were riding together for a while, discussing their problems as well as what awaited them.

"Nothing like a good rain to make things more difficult," Venable agreed. "That idiot Wilson," he shook his head. "This was my idea, you know," he admitted. "We lost two division along this road, or else in that town, for no apparent reason. Made Wilson think there was something here they didn't want us to see. I was tired of sitting still so I suggested we take the damn town in force, dig in and force them to take it back. 'Dare' was, I believe, the word I used. If it wasn't, I was certainly thinking it."

"Did you know about his plan to attack the southern lines?" Baxter asked.

"Hell no," Venable shook his head. "He said nothing of it to me, and I'd be willing to wager he said nothing of it to any of the other commanders. Always keeping secrets, that one. He tried to use us to lure their cavalry away I'd wager as well. They probably made it appear as if they were pursuing us and then looped around to take a position where they could wait and see what happened. You'd think he would learn that needlessly complicating operations just makes them more risky."

"Well, if he hasn't learned after this, he won't ever, I guess," Baxter shrugged.

"I doubt he'll live long enough to learn anything else," Venable said darkly. "This is his third major failure, and this one will likely end the war, at least for now. He had to be relieved because he was babbling on the command tower and trying to continue the attack with broken troops. He left our supply areas wide open to attack and the southerners took full advantage of it. I would imagine the Emperor will order his execution for this. I can't swear to it, of course, but... the Emperor abhors incompetence. He didn't replace Wilson before because the failures he made weren't from incompetence or negligence. It's a fact that the enemy sometimes does something right as well, and the Emperor recognizes this. But..." he paused and shook his head, "this is something else altogether. Wilson tried to be smart, and ended up walking into a trap that has cost the Empire a hundred thousand casualties and probably the war. That won't be forgiven so easily."

"I'd imagine that is true," Baxter replied carefully. "In any event, his return to command has to be doubtful at best."

"True," Venable nodded. "The one I pity the most is Springfield. He did what had to be done to preserve what remained of the army, but... I don't know that the Emperor will see it that way. Seizing control of the army, retreating in the face of the enemy, and now giving up territory we had already conquered and held in strength? I don't know," he shook his head slowly. "He did the right thing, but the right think sometimes doesn't look the same from a thousand miles away. He took a great risk, personal risk, to save the army from destruction. I hope the Emperor will recognize that. The man probably deserves a medal, but medals aren't often awarded from a debacle like this."

Baxter said nothing, taking in what Venable was saying. He had said nothing that wasn't true, certainly. But Baxter knew that Venable also didn't know of his relation to the Emperor. At least he was pretty sure he didn't. And perhaps Abe Springfield was in the wrong, Baxter didn't know, but he was automatically conditioned to accept Springfield's side over Wilson.

And he was certainly not above writing the Emperor and letting him know what had happened and what Springfield had managed, assuming Springfield was in the right. He would have to wait and see what transpired, assuming, of course, that he lived through all of this.

A rather large assumption at the moment.

-

Everyone on both sides had much to do and when busy, time seems to speed by. In fact, when you are racing against the clock, time seems to go by much too fast for comfort. Meanwhile, when you are eager to get something started, time can crawl.

Calm weather and easy conditions saw Winnie's wagon train rolling into Jason right as the sun was sinking behind the trees the next evening. Her train was welcomed and pulled into town to take advantage of accommodations available. For the first time in many days, the people on the wagon train slept in beds and ate food that hadn't been prepared over an open fire. While there were nowhere near enough stables for their horses, there was silage available and the horses seemed appreciative as they ate a combination of oats and corn.

Winnie called community leaders together that evening and explained over supper dishes why she was there and what she hoped to accomplish. Mention of Tribals operating in concert with the Nor were enough to convince everyone to help. It was decided that they would start with first light the next morning.

Meanwhile, Venable and Baxter camped their men now within a day or perhaps a day-and-a-half of the main Imperial camp. Heavy guards were set and the men camped in line of battle, just in case.

Parno looked at the plan Karls had come up with, nodding with approval and making preparations to put it into operation if the opportunity afforded itself. It would depend on what the enemy would do. If they departed and gave Parno the opportunity to lay such an ambush, then he would take it. Scouting efforts were increased and movement warnings went out to all cavalry and mounted infantry units.

Blue Dog was satisfied with his men's preparations over the two-day period. They had sufficient supplies to ensure a good hunt when they reached this town Blue Dog had told them of. Their horses were well rested, as were they. They would leave with the sun, headed south. They were confident that they would have a good hunt with most southern men away at war. But there was one thing he hadn't thought about and hadn't figured into his plans.

A single scout, a member of Parsons' command and one who had encountered the savage Tribal warriors before he ever heard of Doak Parsons, had stopped to rest his horse and take a look around him. Creole Perkins was his name. He was tasked with carrying word south to the pioneer company that the Nor had left Unity headed back toward their own camps. Creole knew there were supposed to be Tribal warriors in some strength around him, and while his main mission was not to look for them, only a foolish man didn't watch for such danger.

As he examined the area around him, he saw a hunting party taking an unattended cow, slaughtering it on the spot and taking large bloody hunks with them by horseback. His skin crawled as he realized that had he not stopped to rest his horse in a covered area, he would have rode right into this hunting party and paid for it with his life.

As he watched, they rode south, away from him. Perkins waited for some time before moving again, uncertain there weren't more of them somewhere. Once satisfied that he was alone, he mounted his horse and begin to head slightly southeast, away from where he thought the Tribals might be and toward where he was supposed to meet up with a pioneer company. While the Imperial Army might not be headed this way, the Tribals damn sure were.

The men waiting for him needed to know that. And so did anyone in their line of advance, assuming they were still headed south.

-

"I wish we knew what was going on," Stephanie mourned as they made their final stop. Tomorrow would see them back at the palace, where Edema would rest for a night or two and then head home.

"I know dear," Edema nodded. "I wish that myself. I've been watching for a courier to pass by on his way to the palace, but so far, I've not seen one. Perhaps tomorrow."

"Perhaps," Stephanie nodded. "I know he had a plan, and it was a good one, assuming he was right about the enemy intentions and movements. If all went well then... well, perhaps tomorrow," she ended with Edema's words. She didn't trust herself to guess at what might have happened.

"Parno is very good at what he does, Stephanie," Edema reminded her. "So are the men around him. I know it's useless to tell you not to worry but do try not to worry so much. He won't be in combat, after all."

"One assassination attempt already, and Harrel isn't there to protect him this time," Stephanie almost moaned.

"No, but his security will be much tighter from now on, too," Edema nodded. "Concentrate on what you can have an influence over and try to forget the things you can't."

"At this point I don't seem to have much influence over anything," Stephanie sighed. Edema gave her a secretive smile but didn't bother to add more.

Her young friend would figure it out soon enough.

THE END

A MESSAGE FROM AUTHOR
N.C. REED

And so, another installment in the life of Parno McLeod comes to an end. For a tale that was supposed to be a trilogy this story has morphed into something much greater than I had ever imagined. Over 600k words at the moment and still at least one more novel to go.

Then of course there is what happens next. Will Parno invade the north? Or will he choose to retire to his valley and raise fat cows and fat babies, hoping for peace in their future? Or will it be something else entirely? At this point who can say.

And finally, there is the tale of Tyree himself. Who was he? Where did he come from? And how was it that he became the first king of Soulan in the aftermath of the Great Dying? One day we may get to see how all that came about. See how we arrived at the life of Parno McLeod.

Until then, however, I hope you enjoy this installment of Parno's tale. Thank you for reading, and for those who recommend me to others, I sincerely appreciate that. A reader's recommendation or compliment is always worth its weight in gold to me. I mean, if I had any gold. Thank you all who have made Parno's tale so much greater than it sounded in my imagination.

N.C. Reed

THANK YOU FOR READING!

If you enjoyed this book, we would appreciate your customer review on your book seller's website or on Goodreads.

Also, we would like for you to know that you can find more great books like this one at www.CreativeTexts.com

www.ingramcontent.com/pod-product-compliance
Lightning Source LLC
Chambersburg PA
CBHW020658110726
47901CB00001B/234